Praise for Margot Hunt

"Psychological suspense fans will be satisfied."
—*Publishers Weekly* on *For Better and Worse*

"The action builds to a huge reveal that leaves the reader wondering which of the two women is more twisted."
—*Publishers Weekly* on *Best Friends Forever*

"Margot Hunt's debut psychological thriller opens with an attention-grabbing opening sentence and doesn't let go until the final secret has been revealed."
—*RT Book Reviews* on *Best Friends Forever*

"Margot Hunt's richly drawn women wrap their hands around your throat and don't let go. A suspenseful page-turner that kept me puzzling over who did it until the last few pages. Fantastic!"
—Cate Holahan, author of *The Widower's Wife*, on *Best Friends Forever*

"Friends or husbands? Who do women tell more truth? Give more allegiance? Margot Hunt shocks and astounds as she explores these tugs of loyalty in *Best Friends Forever*, a psychological thriller that kept me off balance even after turning the last page."
—Randy Susan Meyers, bestselling author of *The Widow of Wall Street*

Also by Margot Hunt

Best Friends Forever

FOR
BETTER
AND
WORSE

MARGOT HUNT

mira

mira

ISBN-13: 978-0-7783-0790-7

For Better and Worse

In loving memory of Valerie Jean Wright,
who was funny as hell, told the best stories
and had the most fabulous taste in shoes.

FOR
BETTER
AND
WORSE

PROLOGUE

Seventeen Years Earlier

On their first date, Will took Natalie to a cozy French bistro in uptown New Orleans. The restaurant was painted a dark, moody red and had gilt-framed mirrors on the walls that reflected the candles that flickered on every table. It was a popular eatery and every table was full, even on a Thursday night. It was also nearby the Tulane University campus, where Will and Nat were both law students. They'd each ordered the steak-frites—which had given them reason to exchange a brief smile. *We're so compatible we ordered the same thing!* And shared a bottle of the house red, which was better than expected. While they sipped their wine, and waited for their salads to arrive, they chatted about the Contracts class they had together.

"Word on the street is that Professor Harley met his wife when she was his student," Will said.

"Seriously? Isn't there a rule against professors dating students?"

"I'm sure there is. Maybe they kept it quiet until after she'd graduated," Will said, thinking that Natalie had especially nice eyebrows, and wondering if it was odd that he found them erotic. Was it weird to be attracted to a woman's eyebrows?

"Still, he was taking a pretty big risk."

Will shrugged. "They must have thought it was worth it. Maybe it was true love."

Nat felt her cheeks flush at his mention of love. She looked down at the wineglass in her hand and rotated the stem slowly. Nat had been surprised when Will asked her out, and she still wasn't entirely sure she was interested in him. Yes, he was funny and handsome, but he certainly wasn't her type. Most of her past boyfriends had been thin and pale, with esoteric taste in music and movies, and who went too long between haircuts. Whatever it was they were interested in—computers, postmodern literature, political activism—they were always *very* serious about it.

Will couldn't have been more different. As far as she could tell, he didn't take anything seriously. He was also blond and broad-shouldered and square-jawed. He even had dimples, for Christ's sake. She knew without asking that he was athletic. A former lacrosse player, she guessed, or maybe he'd rowed on his school's crew team. He had lightly tanned skin and blue-gray eyes, that changed a bit depending on what color he was wearing, and he was undeniably cocky—a trait Nat had *never* found attractive. And yet... Will made her laugh. They sat next to one another in Contracts class—Professor Harley had passed around a seating chart on the first day, so everyone was stuck in the seats they'd randomly chosen for the rest of the semester—and Will would pass her notes with funny comments or sketches he'd drawn on his notepad. Then Nat had bumped into Will at a mixer the law school had sponsored at a local bar. They'd spent the evening talking and laughing together, and at the end of the night, Will had asked her out. Natalie had to admit—to herself, at least—that she was intrigued.

Will lifted the bottle and poured more wine into Natalie's glass. "What are you planning to do after law school?"

"I'm going to move back to Florida and hopefully get a job with a public defender's office to learn the ropes," Nat said promptly. "Then, once I have some experience, I'm going to open my own criminal law practice."

"Are you always so indecisive?" Will grinned at her.

Natalie was slightly put off by Will's grin. Yes, it was sexy and charming, but she had the feeling that Will trotted it out whenever he wanted people to think he was sexy and charming. She had never liked players.

"You don't know what you want to do yet?"

Will shrugged. "I guess wherever I can get a job. If I can get a job. The market for new lawyers isn't exactly hopping at the moment."

The waitress appeared with two salads, lightly dressed, and set them down on the table.

"This looks very tasty," Will said once the waitress had left. "And by eating it, I'm taking care of my monthly vegetable serving."

"You're not a veggie person?"

"I like vegetables that look and taste like meat. Or tacos."

Natalie wrinkled her nose. "Ick."

"Just what every guy hopes he hears on his first date."

Will grinned at Nat again, and this time she couldn't help but return the smile.

"But you must have some idea of what kind of law you want to practice," she said, returning to their pre-salad conversation.

"I know I don't ever want to be inside a courtroom, if I can help it," Will said, spearing lettuce on his fork. "But beyond that, I have no idea."

"Really? I think being in court would be much more interesting than spending all day in an office. It's partly why I want to go into criminal law."

"What's the other part?"

"You know." Nat waved a hand. "Standing up for the wrongly accused. Truth, justice, the American way. All of that high-minded stuff."

"You might be missing a fairly big downside," Will suggested. He pushed his plate away and leaned forward, propping his elbows on the white tablecloth.

"Like what?"

"All of your clients will be criminals."

Natalie lifted one finger. "Accused criminals."

"Okay, but if you only defend the wrongly accused, you'll starve slowly. Or, maybe starve quickly. Odds are pretty good that you'll be spending a large portion of your time with some pretty despicable people." Will was enjoying the back-and-forth. He'd had a crush on Nat since they'd met on that first day of Contracts class. For one thing, she was hot, with her compact athletic body and long, wavy brown hair, and Will very much approved of her fondness for short skirts. But he also liked Nat's dry wit and the way her blue eyes lit up when she was engaged in a conversation. He kept finding himself wanting to impress her. "You might want to think your plan through."

"Not a chance. Besides, people who've been *accused* of committing a crime—" Nat began.

"You mean criminals?" Will interrupted.

"Innocent until proven guilty," Nat corrected him, although her smile softened the reprimand. "How different are they from you and me? They're just people, some of whom made bad choices, yes, but some of whom just ended up in bad situations, or had a run of bad luck. Couldn't that happen to anyone?"

The waiter appeared. He poured the rest of the wine into their glasses, then cleared the salad plates. "Your entrées will be right out."

"Thank you," Nat said, smiling at him.

Once the waiter left, Will said, "It might not be politically correct to say so, but for starters, most criminals—excuse me, people accused of committing a crime—aren't as smart as you and I are."

"That is arrogant!" Nat stared at him in disbelief. She should have known that anyone who had an endless supply of striped oxford shirts, and who wore loafers without socks, would not be her type.

"Why?"

"Because it's cocky. And superior. And smug."

"Cocky, superior and smug, huh? Don't hold back, let me know how you really feel."

"You can't go around saying that you're smarter than other people."

"Even if it's true?"

"Especially if it's true!"

"Have you heard those guys on the radio who do that weekly *Stupid Crimes* spot? Just yesterday they were talking about a man who chained an ATM to the bumper of his truck, tried to drive off with it and ended up leaving the bumper—complete with the attached license plate—at the scene of the crime." Will began to laugh. "And then when the police went to arrest him, he tried to claim that he hadn't been trying to steal the ATM, but that—get this—the bank had hired him to test how secure it was. I'm smarter than that guy, for sure."

"You have to give him credit for a really creative excuse."

"No, I don't. And if your crime is highlighted on a radio spot called *Stupid Crimes*, you're probably not a criminal mastermind."

"Okay, yes, some criminals do really dumb things," Nat agreed. "But not all of them. Some of them are dealing with drug or psychiatric issues, or have other extenuating reasons for why they're committing crimes."

"Maybe, but still—the smart ones don't get caught."

"Do you really think that's true?"

"I do." Will took a sip of his wine. "I bet if we wanted to, you and I could plan the perfect crime. Maybe even the perfect murder."

"But why would we want to?" Natalie could feel herself drawn toward him again. At least Will wasn't boring. Most of the law students she met were such grinders, and talked incessantly about their class notes and outlines and class standings.

"I don't know. Don't you have anyone you'd like to knock off?"

"I have to admit, I really can't stand Professor Carlson," Nat said. Carlson was their Civil Procedure professor, and he took great and obvious pleasure in using the Socratic method to humiliate his first-year law students. "In fact, I hate him with every fiber of my being. Everyone does. I'm pretty sure even his dog hates him."

"Perfect. Let's say we decided we want to kill Professor Carlson. I bet we could do it and never get caught. I mean, that guy has to have a lot of enemies, right? Several decades of law school graduates who he ritually humiliated."

"How would we go about doing that?" Nat asked.

"That's an excellent question. Obviously, nothing as tacky as buying a gun and shooting him."

"Of course not. We wouldn't want to be vulgar while committing a homicide."

"Exactly. Poison, maybe?" Will suggested. Outside, a boom of thunder sounded. Rain began to patter rhythmically against the tall glass windows of the restaurant. The hum of conversation around them, mixed with the clinks of cutlery on plateware, somehow made their conversation seem even more intimate. Will wondered if he should order another bottle of wine.

"Isn't poison supposed to be the favored murder weapon for women? Although, now that I think about it, I might have read that in an Agatha Christie novel."

"The only problem with poison is that someone, somewhere, has to buy the poison," Will mused. "That can be traced. And then you'd have to find a way to administer the poison without your victim noticing."

"You're not giving up already?"

"Of course not. I just want to make sure we get it right, and don't end up in jail for the rest of our lives. What about bludgeoning him to death, then finding a foolproof way to discard the murder weapon? Like a log that could be burned. Or, there's the garrote, always popular among assassins. All you need is a length of piano wire and nerves of steel."

"Yikes, that's even more brutal than a gun."

"If you're not willing to get your hands dirty, you may not make the best accomplice," Will pointed out.

"I would be an excellent accomplice." Nat tossed her hair back over her shoulders. "What about DNA or fingerprints or witnesses?"

"First of all, there wouldn't be any witnesses. We're too smart for that. And whatever our murder weapon of choice would be, obviously we'd take precautions not to leave behind any physical evidence. We'd be too careful to take any unnecessary risks," Will asserted. "And most important, we'd never confess. You'd be amazed how many people break down under police questioning. If you refuse to say anything, refuse even to be interviewed, it forces the police to build a case against you. And if they don't have any slam-dunk evidence, how are they going to do that?"

"You make it all sound so easy," Nat said.

"Easy, no. I doubt it would be easy to take a life. But I think if you had to—I mean, if *we* had to—" Will amended, "we could absolutely get away with it."

"I'm not sure if I should be flattered or frightened," Nat mused.

"Definitely flattered," Will said, flashing another cocky grin.

"Well, then." Nat raised her wineglass in a mock toast, as another boom of thunder sounded outside. "To our future as criminal masterminds."

Will clinked his glass against hers. "To getting away with it."

PART ONE

Natalie

CHAPTER 1

I hadn't known it at the time, but it was the last normal weekend of my life.

If I had known what was coming, I might have chosen to spend those days differently. I wouldn't have wasted time cleaning out the refrigerator, for example, or spent that hour running to nowhere on the treadmill at the gym. But no matter what was looming, I still wouldn't have missed our family's weekly trip to the beach on that beautiful Sunday in late February.

It was one of the best parts about living in our small seaside Florida town of Shoreham. Most of the rest of the country was digging out from under the most recent snowstorm and shivering through frigid temperatures. We, though, were enjoying perfect beach weather. Not too hot, not too cold.

"Come on, you guys," Charlie yelled over his shoulder as he thumped up the wooden boardwalk that led from the parking lot to the beach. He was leading our dog, Rocket, on a blue nylon leash, and the black dog trotted after him, his favorite ratty tennis ball clenched in his teeth. The boardwalk sloped crookedly over the dunes, winding through overgrown sea grape shrubs, and they were both soon out of my sight.

"I guess he's not waiting for us," I commented.

Will was pulling our beach chairs and assorted gear out from the back of our SUV.

"Do you want me to carry the beach bag?" he asked.

"No, I've got it." I heaved the bag up onto my shoulder.

"Are you sure? That thing weighs a ton."

"I said I've got it." I headed toward the boardwalk, Will trailing after me.

We'd started the tradition of going to the beach every Sunday morning that the weather allowed, no matter what my trial schedule looked like, or how busy Will was at the office, when Charlie was still a toddler. Back then, Charlie's favorite beach activity was to stand at the shoreline, and play tag with the water as it rolled in. He'd run from it, giggling and screeching when it reached his plump little feet. The memory always made me smile, especially now that Charlie was eleven and his baby years had disappeared, never to return.

"The water looks great," Will said as we reached the end of the boardwalk. The ocean was finally in sight, navy blue and churning with white-topped waves. "I hope it's warmer than it was last week. It took three days for my testicles to descend back to their normal resting place."

"Good to know. Thank you for sharing that."

"You know I like to keep you informed about the status of my testicles."

I shaded my eyes and looked for Charlie. He'd already dumped the boogie boards and was down by the shoreline, throwing Rocket's tennis ball for him where the sand was firm. Rocket was a small dog with ears too big for his head and an energy level that never fully abated. He raced after the ball, barking happily.

"There they are." I nodded in our son's direction.

Will and I wove our way down the beach to join them. When

we reached the spot Charlie had chosen, Will set up the chairs while I dropped the heavy canvas bag on the sand, relieved to be rid of the weight. I wasn't sure why I'd insisted on carrying it, when I knew Will wouldn't have minded.

My husband grabbed his boogie board. "Last one in is a boy band singer," he called out to Charlie, who laughed his deep, froggy laugh that always made me smile. Charlie ran to get his own board, and the two of them waded out into the ocean. Rocket raced behind them, although he ventured only a few inches into the water, and backtracked every time a wave rolled toward him.

I sat down, took in a deep breath of salt air and felt the tension in my shoulder muscles relax. It was good to be outside in the sunshine, after a week of sitting under the fluorescent lights at my office.

It had been a rough week in the life of Natalie Clarke, criminal attorney and defender of the downtrodden. One of my clients, a single mother named Melanie Bell, had been arrested a few months earlier for drug possession, after the police found a plastic sandwich bag full of pills in her car during a routine traffic stop. Unfortunately for Melanie, it was her third offense, and the best plea deal I could get out of the State's Attorney assigned to the case—a sour-faced woman named Christine Christof, who hated defense attorneys, as though our doing our jobs was a personal offense to her—was a ten-month sentence. It wasn't a great offer, and when I'd relayed it to Melanie, she'd burst into tears, insisting that she couldn't possibly be away from her three young children for that long.

Against my advice, Melanie decided to instead take an open plea. This meant that she would plead guilty to the drug possession and let the judge decide on her sentence. I tried to explain to her that this was a risky strategy. Yes, the judge might be sympathetic to her situation. If she went to jail, her children would end up in foster care, which was never ideal. Melanie had successfully completed a drug addiction program five years earlier, and remained clean until her recent relapse was brought on by a painful hernia surgery. Even though she was a good candidate for another rehab program, the judge could also just as easily give her an even longer sentence than the one being offered by the State's Attorney. But Melanie had insisted, and on the previous Thursday morning, had entered her open guilty plea.

The judge sentenced her to eighteen months.

Melanie lashed out physically and verbally, and eventually had to be restrained by the deputies assigned to the courtroom. I had to stand aside while they fastened handcuffs to her wrists.

"I'm so sorry, Melanie," I said, meaning it. I had told her the risks, warned her what could happen, but in the end, it had been her decision. Still, I felt badly for her. I couldn't imagine being separated from Charlie for that long.

When Melanie stopped fighting the deputies, she turned to look at me with an expression that was so malevolent, so hateful, I almost took a step back.

"You fucking bitch," she said. "This is all your fault."

And then Melanie spat in my face.

I'd felt a mixture of pity and revulsion, watching the deputies drag her away. But mostly, as I wiped her saliva off my face with a crumpled tissue I'd found in the bottom of my briefcase, I'd felt weary. I had been practicing criminal law for almost fifteen years, first as a public defender, then opening my own practice. And, yes, there had been moments during that time when I'd triumphed, times I'd helped good people out of bad situations. But then there were the days when my clients felt justified to spit in my face. Somewhere in between were all the other days when I mostly felt ineffectual, a small cog in a broken judicial system.

I knew a morning at the beach would chase away my ennui. I would burrow my feet into the sand, gaze out at the calming vista of the sky meeting the sea, and let the sun bake my skin until I couldn't stand it any longer and had to dive into the water to cool off. It was just what I needed.

"Do you have sunscreen on?" I called out to Charlie.

He feigned deafness and raced back out into the waves to join his dad. I rubbed SPF 50 onto my pale arms as I watched Will and Charlie ride their boogie boards through the surf. Rocket barked happily in the shallows, waiting for them to reach the shore.

"Mom, did you see that wave?" Charlie yelled. "It was three stories tall!"

The wave wasn't even close to being that big, but I grinned and gave him a thumbs-up.

"Are you coming in?" he called.

"In a minute," I said. "I want to sit for a bit and read my book."

Charlie bent down to pet Rocket, then turned and ran back in the surf after his father. My eyes drifted toward my husband, who was joking and laughing with Charlie about something. Will had started going to the gym regularly recently, and it was starting to pay off. His stomach was flat again, and I could see new definition in his arm and chest muscles. I was glad he was taking better care of himself.

At least, I told myself I *should* be happy about it. And yet… I couldn't help but wonder what had prompted this sudden change in lifestyle. Anxiety fluttered up inside me whenever I wondered if it wasn't a *what* that had prompted a change, but instead a *who*.

Was it possible Will was having an affair?

A decade earlier, I would have laughed at the idea. Back then, when Charlie was a baby, and we were both trying to figure out how to balance parenthood with demanding careers, Will had still been my best friend. We'd delighted together in Charlie's smiles and general adorableness, and even the lack of sleep seemed like something we'd one day look back on fondly. Every evening, once Charlie was asleep, we'd collapse on the couch together, usually with a glass of wine and something mindless on the television. And on the weeks when I was in trial, Will

would get Chinese takeout, and listen to me practice my closing arguments over cartons of fried rice and kung pao chicken.

I wasn't sure when that had changed. As the years had marched
on, first slowly, then faster and faster still, I could feel Will moving away, a distance growing steadily between us. These days,
he preferred to retreat to the home office after dinner, rather
than spend the evening alone with me. Romantic weekend trips
were a thing of the past, replaced by Saturdays spent at Charlie's
soccer games or ferrying him around to karate class and classmates' birthday parties. I couldn't even remember the last time
we'd gone out on our own, without clients or friends accom-
panying us. We hadn't had sex in months.

And now, suddenly, my forty-year-old husband had lost fifteen pounds and was looking like he had in his twenties.

I knew it didn't necessarily mean anything nefarious was going
on. It wasn't like weight loss was proof that Will was having
an affair. Except…there was also his recent obsession with his
phone. The device was practically glued to his hand, day and
night. Will never, ever left it behind, not even just to head into
the kitchen to rummage through the fridge. And whenever I
walked up behind him, he'd suddenly set the phone facedown,
so I couldn't see what he was doing. When I asked him why he
was hiding it from me, he said I was being paranoid.

Am I being paranoid? I wondered.

Will and Charlie rode in on a wave together. Charlie whooped
as he fell off his boogie board and the wave crested over him.
Will managed to stay on his board, but just barely. He stood up
to shake the water out of his hair. I was fairly sure he was sucking in his stomach, and wondered if it was for the benefit of the
gaggle of tanned, bikini-clad twentysomethings who were sitting a few yards away.

"Dad, come on," Charlie said, ready to plunge back into the
ocean.

"I'm going to take a break," Will told him. "Rocket is dying to chase his ball."

Rocket, hearing both his name and the word *ball*—his favorite of all the words he knew—started barking frantically. Will grabbed the damp and sandy tennis ball and pitched it down the beach. Rocket raced off after it. The bikini girls watched and laughed as the small dog leaped athletically in the air to catch the ball in his mouth. Rocket trotted triumphantly back to Will, his whiplike tail wagging happily.

"He's adorable," one of the girls said, rising up on her elbows, flaunting a taut core. And another, not to be outdone, chimed in. "What breed of dog is he?"

Will turned and grinned at them. "He's a terrier mix, but he thinks he's as fierce as a rottweiler and as fast as a greyhound."

The girls tittered with laughter. "That's so cute," one of them cooed.

I rolled my eyes behind my sunglasses.

"Mom," Charlie called. "Take a picture of me riding this wave!"

I obediently pulled out my digital camera and stood. Just as I was wondering if the sunlight was too bright, too harsh, a cloud passed over, softening the glare. I quickly snapped a bunch of photos as Charlie turned back to the ocean and paddled out with his boogie board.

That night Will grilled hamburgers for dinner while I baked sweet potato fries and tossed a salad. I tasked Charlie with bringing out the plates and silverware to the table on our back deck, and followed behind him with a tray of side dishes and condiments.

"What's your favorite dinosaur?" Charlie asked once we were all settled in at the table, burgers in hand.

"Triceratops," I said immediately.

I knew this game and the responses it required. What's your

favorite mammal? Elephant. Marine animal? Whale. Fictional animal? Phoenix.

"Triceratops?" Charlie repeated scornfully, although he knew this would be my answer. "They're so lame."

I dipped a sweet potato fry in barbecue sauce. "They're one of the only dinosaurs that could fend off an attack from a *T. rex*. That's not lame."

"Dad, what's your favorite dinosaur?"

"I don't have one."

"Just pick one," Charlie insisted.

"What's the one in the *Jurassic Park* movie that kills off all the humans and opens doors with its claws?"

"The *Velociraptor*," Charlie said. "But they weren't as big in real life as they were in the movie. And they had feathers, so they probably looked more like a bird."

"Pretty scary bird," Will commented.

Charlie took the tiniest of tiny bites of his hamburger. "Did you know they discovered a giant prehistoric snake called the *Titanoboa*? I saw a video of it online fighting a *T. rex*. Although that would never have happened, because they lived in different time periods."

"Then how did they manage to get a video of the fight?" Will teased him.

Charlie looked perplexed. "It was a reenactment. They didn't have video cameras then. Or people."

"I know. I was kidding. Eat your dinner."

After we finished, Charlie and I cleared the table, and Will loaded the plates into the dishwasher.

"Go take a shower," I told Charlie. "And don't forget to use soap."

"I always use soap. Except for that one time I forgot. Oh, and that other time."

"That's why I always remind you."

Charlie headed off toward his bathroom.

"Who forgets to soap up in the shower?" Will asked.

"Your son," I said. I opened the refrigerator door and began putting the condiments away. I looked up to see that Will was watching me. "Why are you staring at me?"

"Did you get your hair cut?"

I lifted a hand self-consciously to the nape of my neck, which still felt naked. "A few days ago. You just noticed?"

"You had it clipped back all weekend."

I actually hadn't been wearing it up. My new bob was too short to put in a ponytail, a fact that was already making me regret cutting it so short. I suddenly felt self-conscious. "Do you like it?"

"Sure."

Will kept looking at me with an odd expression on his face. "What?"

"Why did you ever cut your hair short? When we were in law school, it was really long."

"You know I cut most of it off when Charlie was a baby."

"Why?"

"Because he used to grab it and pull it all the time. Don't you remember? For such a tiny baby, he had a death grip. Besides, it took forever to dry, especially in the humidity. And it wasn't very professional."

"I liked it," Will said.

I started to have the odd, unpleasant feeling that we were talking about something other than my hair. It wasn't a conversation I wanted to have at the moment, so I turned back to putting away the condiments.

"Don't forget to update the calendar when you get a chance," I said.

We kept a large monthly whiteboard calendar in the kitchen, with everyone's schedule laid out in their own color—mine in red, Will's in green and Charlie's in blue. We were all so busy, with work and school and assorted extracurricular activities, it was the only way to stay on top of our plans. I made sure Charlie's and my schedules were marked in for the next week by Sunday, but I always had to remind Will to update his agenda.

"I love it when you talk sexy like that," Will said, as he added a detergent pellet to the little tray on the inside door of the dishwasher.

I smiled. "You think calendars are sexy?"

"No, I hate calendars. And I hate that calendar in particular."

I glanced at the calendar, which had an attractive wood frame. "What's wrong with it? I bought it at Pottery Barn."

"That doesn't make it better. I sometimes have nightmares about that calendar chasing me down and eating me alive."

"What's going on with you? Why are you being so hostile toward our calendar? It's an inanimate object."

"It's *your* calendar, not *our* calendar. And sometimes I just chafe against all the strict Natalie-imposed dictates over our lives."

I shut the refrigerator door and turned slowly toward him. I could feel my temper rising, pressing hotly in my chest. "What the hell is that supposed to mean?"

Will shrugged, which suddenly struck me as an annoyingly passive-aggressive gesture. "I just wonder sometimes what would happen if the calendar wasn't filled in. If Charlie's every activity wasn't planned out. Hell, if we didn't live or die by the weekly menu plan. What would happen if this Thursday, we had steaks on the grill, instead of—" Will walked over to read the calendar, where I'd also written in the dinner menu for the week "—baked pork chops. Would life end as we know it if we didn't eat pork chops on Thursday? I don't think it would. I think we'd be just fine."

I stared at him, wondering where this attack was coming from.

"You may not have noticed, but we both work full-time," I said tersely. "I plan out our menu, and the corresponding shopping list, so that we actually eat home-cooked meals instead of having takeout every night. If you have a problem with how I do that, you're perfectly free to take over the meal planning and grocery shopping."

Will sighed heavily. "Never mind."

He closed the dishwasher with more force than strictly necessary, then brushed by me to open the refrigerator. Will grabbed a bottle of beer—which, ironically, I had purchased the day before during the very weekly shopping trip he apparently found so oppressive in his life—and popped the top off.

"What's going on?" I asked.

"Nothing."

"It's clearly not nothing. My menu planning and shopping list somehow offend you. Please elaborate." I crossed my arms over my chest.

Will ran a hand over his head and looked tired. "No, you're right. I shouldn't have said anything."

But now I wasn't ready to let it go.

"Then why do you keep picking on me? First my hair, now the calendar. The menu planning and shopping list... Is there anything else you'd like to criticize?"

"I'm not criticizing you. I just wonder sometimes what would happen if something in your life went off plan. How you would handle it."

I let out a humorless bark of laughter. "What are you talking about? I'm a trial attorney. Things go off plan all the time. Every day. Just a few days ago, one of my clients spat at me."

"But that's just it—there are bright line rules that determine what happens in court. When your client spit on you, the deputies cuffed her and dragged her away, right? Which is exactly the response you'd expect. It's probably the reason you were drawn to this profession in the first place."

"Thank you for that psychoanalysis."

"I'm not criticizing you. I'm just making an observation. You like rules and order and calendars." Will waved a hand in the direction of the whiteboard. "It's your comfort zone. You wouldn't be happy as a soldier in Fallujah, wondering if you're about to be ambushed by insurgent forces."

"And that's what you think your job as an estate lawyer compares to? A soldier in a war zone?"

"No, of course not. I wasn't saying anything of the kind. But, yes, I do think that I'm more flexible and easygoing in general."

"How nice of you to share that sentiment with me," I said sarcastically.

Will took another swig of his beer, then looked around as if he'd lost something. I wondered why he was suddenly so antsy when I saw that his gaze fell on his phone, sitting facedown on the counter. He grabbed it and typed a pass code to unlock the screen. That was another thing—he never used to have a lock screen on his phone.

"Why do you keep your phone locked?"

"What?" he answered without lifting his head.

"You never used to lock it. You said it irritated you to have to punch in a pass code every time you wanted to listen to a voice mail."

"It's supposed to be safer to keep it locked. What if it was stolen? I have clients' information on here," he said. "Speaking of which, I need to go send out a few emails before I wind down for the night. I'll take Rocket for a walk when I'm done."

Will strode off. A few beats later, I heard the door to our home office close.

I spent a few minutes scrubbing the kitchen counters with more force than necessary, breathing heavily through my nose. So now I was a control freak? Yes, I liked to stay on top of our schedule, but why was that such a bad thing?

I finally gave up trying to get the coffee stain out of the granite countertop and threw the sponge in the sink. I stalked upstairs to our bedroom, where I changed into my favorite soft cotton pajamas. Our master bedroom decor was tranquil and serene, with soft gray walls and a low modern platform bed made up with simple white linens. I had kept clutter to a minimum, to keep it a calming, restful place. Although at the moment I was feeling anything but calm and restful.

I pulled out my laptop and sat down on the bed with it. I had downloaded the photos I'd taken at the beach earlier, but I hadn't had time to go through them. Photography was a relatively new hobby for me. Will had given me the camera as a Christmas present, which had been a nice surprise. At first. Right up until Will had commented—in an annoyingly condescending tone—that he thought I'd benefit from taking up a new pastime.

Anyway.

I still wasn't very good. Usually, I just shot a ton of photos and then deleted most of them, which is what I did now. There were a few cute pictures of Charlie riding the waves on his boogie board. One of Charlie and Will grinning at one another. I moved those over to a file to edit later. Then I saw one of just Charlie that stopped me dead. I enlarged it and leaned forward toward the screen.

In the picture, my son was facing away from the camera, looking out toward the ocean, his board tucked under one arm. His slim shoulders set back, the blades resolutely pushed together. His round hands gripping either side of the boogie board. His orange swim shirt, a size too big, pulling up and gathering at around the waist. In front of him, the ocean was swirling darkly. The water looked almost alive, churning angrily.

I had been there, of course. I had taken the picture. But I didn't remember the water looking so foreboding at the time. Now, blown up on my laptop screen, it looked like Charlie had stopped to consider whether he should take another step forward.

It looked like he was about to walk straight into danger.

And even though I knew my son was in his room, safe and alive, my stomach knotted with fear.

CHAPTER 2

There were two sheriff's cars parked in front of Franklin School the next morning—a cruiser and an SUV. I noticed them as soon as I pulled into the parking lot and joined the car drop-off line that snaked around the school.

"Are you having an assembly today?" I asked.

"I hope not," Charlie replied.

"Why? I used to love assemblies when I was in school. They get you out of class for a while. That always makes the day more interesting, right?"

"But they're *so* boring." Charlie's shoulders slumped and his head lolled forward as he acted out just how boring they were. "Last week, a policeman came to talk to us about cyberbullying, and it lasted *forever*."

"The police were just here for an assembly last week?" I glanced back at the sheriff's cars again. "I wonder why they'd be back so soon."

Charlie shrugged. "I just hope we don't have to listen to any more stories about kids committing suicide because they were bullied online."

"That's what they talked to you about? Kids committing suicide?" It sounded like a dark subject for fifth graders.

"Yep. We had to watch this movie where all the kids were ganging up on this one girl. They were sending her mean texts and posting stuff about her on Facebook. So she killed herself."

"How horrible. What did you think about that?"

"I don't know. It seemed kind of dumb. Why wouldn't she just block them so she couldn't see what they were writing?"

"I don't know, sweetie. Maybe she didn't know what to do."

"But it would be easy to block the people who were bullying her and not have to see what they were posting," Charlie argued. "And then she wouldn't have had to kill herself."

"Life isn't always that black-and-white," I replied.

"Well, it should be."

We reached the front of the car line, where a few of the teacher's aides stood ready to help the smaller kids out of the cars. I put my SUV in Park so Charlie could climb out. He turned back to grab his backpack and other belongings.

"Do you have everything?" I asked.

"I think so."

"Have a great day, honey. I love you."

"Love you, too." Charlie slammed the door shut and headed toward the group of students waiting to be ushered inside the school. I watched as he reached his best friend, Jack, who grinned at him, and they launched into a conversation that involved a lot of arms waving and wide-eyed excitement.

Someone in one of the cars behind me honked. I looked up in my rearview mirror.

"Seriously?" I said out loud. I shook my head, put my car in gear and pulled forward.

I was just turning out of the school when my phone rang. I

checked the caller ID. It was Mandy Breen, my best friend. I hit the accept button on my car interface.

"Someone just honked at me in the car line," I said by way of greeting.

"I know, I heard," she said. "I was three cars back from you."

Mandy's daughter, Beatrice, was in Charlie's fifth grade class. She also had another daughter, Amelia, who was a third grader at Franklin.

"Do you know who it was?"

"Someone driving a silver Mercedes sedan with one of those annoying Peace Love Happiness magnets on the back."

"That's Laura MacMurray's car. I would have thought she was too evolved to lower herself to honking. She must be late for a hot yoga class."

Mandy laughed. "Do you have time to go grab a coffee?"

"I wish. I have to be in court in thirty minutes. Rain check?"

"Of course. Hey, do you know why the police are at the school this morning?"

"No idea. I assumed they were doing some sort of safety presentation for the kids, but Charlie said they were just at the school last week."

"That's what the girls told me, too. You don't think it's anything we should worry about?"

"Like what? Do you think Mrs. Fischer is running a drug ring out of the school office?"

Mrs. Fischer was the school office administrator. She was in her late sixties, had a helmet of steel-gray curls and rarely smiled. She scared the hell out of all the kids and most of the parents.

"I wouldn't be surprised. I could totally picture her as the head of a drug cartel, cutting up the people who double-crossed her and feeding their body parts to alligators in the Everglades," Mandy joked.

"That's quite a vivid imagination you have."

"I know, it's a gift, really." Mandy laughed. "Let me know if you hear anything."

"Will do. Hey, wait, before you go, I have to ask you a question. But I want you to be honest."

"I'm always honest. Well, actually, that's not true. I'm often full of shit. But I'll do my best."

"Do you think I'm controlling?"

There was a pause. "Do you want me to tell what you want to hear or do you want me to tell you the truth?"

"Seriously? You really think I'm controlling?"

"Honey, you have an entire walk-in closet in your house dedicated to wrapping presents."

"That's not true."

"Yes, it is. You showed it to me."

"Okay, I do have a closet set aside to store gifts in that *also* has a pull-out wrapping station, but it's not a walk-in. It's just a regular-sized closet in the guest room, which, I might add, no one has stayed in since my mother-in-law died," I said. "How exactly does that make me controlling?"

"I don't even know what a pull-out wrapping station is, and, no, please don't tell me. But, yes, I would say that having a designated wrapping and gift storage area would put you squarely in the Type A column."

"Do you know how many birthday parties Charlie was invited to last year? Nineteen. That's a lot of presents to wrap, and that doesn't even include Christmas or family birthdays," I argued.

"Well, in that case, you're right, it makes perfect sense for you to have an entire area of your house dedicated to gifts and wrapping paper."

"Really?"

"No, of course not, I think you're insane. Totally bananas. But I love you, anyway. Talk to you later."

"Bye," I said, laughing as I hung up.

★ ★ ★

I had a couple of cases on the court docket that morning—
two separate drug possessions and one burglary of a commercial premises. None were overly complicated, but they took up
most of the morning, especially since I had to go over a prof-
fered plea deal with one of my clients. Happily, no one felt the
need to spit on me.

After court, I picked up some coffee to go and drove the short
distance to my office. It was an older building that had once
been a residential house, but had some time back been sectioned
off into four separate suites. I had one of the ground floor units,
which consisted of a reception area, my office and a small kitch-
enette. It was small and pokey, but it had a great view of the Intracoastal Waterway out of the rear windows, which I never tired of.

I balanced the paper coffee cups in one hand while I pushed
open the door.

"Hey, Nat," my receptionist, Stella, said. She was in her late
twenties and had lately been sporting a retro look—her dark
hair piled high and secured with a scarf, winged eyeliner, matte
red lipstick, knee-length floral dresses with big shoulder pads.

"I brought you a coffee," I said, setting down a latte on her
desk.

"Have I ever told you that you're my favorite boss?"

"I'm your only boss."

"I meant out of all the bosses I've ever had. You're also the
only boss I've had that hasn't sexually harassed me. How was
court?"

"Riveting as always," I said dryly. "Although I think Dex
Walker is going to take the plea deal."

"What are they offering?"

"Eight months. They were originally offering him thirteen,
but that would have meant state time. I talked them down to
eight so he can stay at the county jail."

"Which is just like staying at the Ritz," Stella joked.

"Compared to the state penitentiary, it practically is. Anything going on here?"

"Actually, you got a flurry of phone calls starting about a half an hour ago." Stella handed me a stack of messages on thin yellow paper. "It was weird. Three different women called you and all of them said they knew you through Charlie's school."

"From school?" I set down my coffee cup on the counter and flipped through the message. Ellie Jones. Keiko Bae. Sarah Forrester. I recognized the names—they were all moms of kids who went to Franklin School—but I didn't know any of them very well. Presumably that's why they were calling me at my office, since I doubted if any of the three had my cell phone number. "Did any of them say what they were calling about?"

"No. Maybe they're all dying to have you on the bake sale committee."

"Somehow I doubt that, considering I don't bake," I said. "Are you going to lunch?"

"Soon. I just want to finish getting these bills out first, if that's okay."

"Sure, go whenever you like," I said, picking my coffee back up.

Which was certainly not the response of someone who was a control freak, I thought, as I headed to my office. I closed the door behind me and settled behind my desk with my coffee. I considered returning the mysterious phone calls, but something stopped me. I didn't want to get sucked into some sort of school intrigue without knowing what was going on.

I pulled out my mobile phone and saw that I'd missed a text from Mandy:

OMG Where r u? Call me ASAP!!!

Something was definitely up. I wondered if it had anything to do with the police cars parked in front of the school. I called Mandy, who picked up immediately.

"Have you heard?"

"Heard what?"

"Robert Gibbons was arrested! Or, at least, I think he was," Mandy said, her voice high and her words tumbling out over one another.

"What?" I exclaimed. "Robert? No, that can't be right."

Robert Gibbons was the principal of Franklin School. I'd known him for years. Will and I had first met him and his then-wife Venetia when we moved to Shoreham fourteen years earlier. We rented an apartment in the same building where the Gibbonses lived. Most of the other tenants at the Harbor Bay complex were retired snowbirds, so as the only two couples under the age of sixty, we naturally gravitated toward one another. Will and I were newlyweds at the time, but Robert and Venetia had been married for a bit longer. We'd struck up a casual though convivial friendship, getting together for pizza and beers or going to see a movie on the weekend. We eventually bought houses in different parts of town, and as a result saw each other less frequently. Then Will and I had Charlie, while the Gibbonses remained childless. I was never sure if that was a choice or if they'd struggled with infertility. In any event, by the time they decided to divorce three years earlier, we hadn't all gotten together in a while.

Robert was a kind man who truly loved his job and was dedicated to Franklin School. A large part of the reason we'd decided to enroll Charlie at the school was that Robert had already been the principal there for a few years. He was an old soul who collected antique coins and read history books for fun. He certainly wasn't a criminal.

"I know, it *is* crazy. But I'm telling you, that's what I heard. Sarah Forrester saw the police leading him out of the school," Mandy exclaimed.

"Sarah called my office a little while ago. A few of the other school moms did, too."

"They all think you'll have the dirt on what's going on."

"I don't. This is the first I've heard anything about it. Are you sure he was arrested? Maybe he witnessed something, and they were just bringing him in to make a statement," I suggested. That seemed far more likely than Robert committing an actual crime.

"A witness to what? Has anything happened in the past few days?"

There was enough crime in Shoreham to keep me and a half-dozen other criminal lawyers relatively busy, but the town was hardly the crime wave capital of Florida. Almost all the crimes that did occur had to do with drugs or alcohol or, on the more serious side, assaults and child abuse. But I hadn't heard of anything noteworthy happening in the past forty-eight hours.

"Nothing," I said. "And I was in court all morning. If something big was going on, I probably would have heard about it."

"Maybe it has to do with something that happened at the school. Stolen tablets or something like that. And Robert had to go in and give a statement."

"That's probably the most likely explanation."

Actually, in my experience, when middle-aged people with no prior criminal records were arrested, there were usually only two likely possibilities—a DUI or a domestic assault charge. The DUI seemed the more likely option, as I didn't think Robert was seeing anyone. And I'd never gotten the impression that his and Venetia's relationship had been volatile. Then again, it was impossible to ever fully know what went on inside someone else's marriage.

Mandy ran down the wild speculations flying around the school mom gossip chain to explain why the police had been at the school. One theory was that an eighth grade boy had gotten in trouble for forwarding a naked selfie taken by a female classmate. Another was that the science teacher had been caught growing pot in her apartment. And yet another speculated that they finally discovered who had set the fire in the boys' locker room the previous year, causing quite a bit of damage to the gym. While she talked, I pulled up the Calusa County arrest report on my laptop and scanned through the names and booking photos. Robert wasn't included on the list, nor did any of the arrestees seem connected to the school.

"I'm pretty sure Mrs. Carson isn't growing pot in her spare time," I said dryly. "She's a CrossFit addict and competes in triathlons."

"I know, it's crazy what sort of stories the parents are coming up with, and it's only been a few hours. Wait, I just got an email from the school. Oh, *shit*."

"What?"

"They're holding an emergency meeting for the parents at seven o'clock tonight. And get this—they've asked us not to speak to the press."

I opened my Gmail account and found the same email in my inbox, marked urgent with a red exclamation point. It was from Naomi Rubin, who was a member of the school board.

To: Parent List
From: Naomi Rubin
Date: February 19
Subject: Police Investigation
Dear parents,
As some of you are already aware, the Calusa County Sheriff's Department has opened an investigation that might concern the Franklin School community. Please know that your children are safe, and there is no need to pick them up from school early today.

We will be holding a meeting for the parents tonight at 7:00 p.m. in McGrath Auditorium. We will update you on the situation and give you an opportunity to ask questions then. We would appreciate it if you would refrain from calling the school office with your questions in the meantime. We would also appreciate it if you would not speak to the press.

We hope to see you tonight.

"The press?" Mandy repeated. "What the hell is going on?"

"I guess we'll find out tonight," I said.

CHAPTER 3

Will and I walked into the school auditorium a few minutes early for the seven o'clock meeting, and both stopped suddenly, blinking at the scene in front of us. It was chaos. Franklin School had over two hundred students, ranging from kindergarten to eighth grade, and it looked as though nearly every parent of every child was already present. The auditorium had rows of chairs, but no one was sitting down. Instead, everyone was standing in loose groups, talking frantically at one another. The noise was overwhelming.

"What the hell is going on?" Will murmured in my ear, echoing Mandy's words from a few hours earlier.

"I have no idea." I took in the anxious expressions on the parents' faces, the sense of barely suppressed panic pulsating through the crowd. Everyone seemed to be bracing for the worst.

"Hey, Will." Zack Smith, a tall, lanky dad appeared, holding out his hand.

"Hey, man," Will said, shaking his hand.

"Are you playing hoops this weekend?" Zack asked.

He and Will launched into a discussion about the Sunday basketball league they were both in. I turned away, looking to see if Mandy had arrived yet. I spotted her across the auditorium—her long auburn corkscrew curls stood out among the sea of blonds—but before I could head over to her, I was intercepted.

"Natalie!" Keiko Bae rushed up to me. Keiko was a tiny woman, impossibly thin, with pale skin and straight blue-black hair. Even though I only knew her well enough to say hello to, she grabbed my hand and wrung it with both of her own. "Do you know what's happened? Everyone I've talked to says that you must know everything."

"I don't know anything more than you do," I said, extracting my hand from her surprisingly strong grip. "I saw the police cars in the parking lot at drop-off this morning, but that's all the information I have."

Keiko's face fell dramatically. "I thought you had contacts at the sheriff's office? Or with the district attorney?"

"I'm a defense attorney," I said gently. "They see me as the enemy, more or less. They don't keep me in the loop."

This wasn't entirely true. The State's Attorneys were certainly never very friendly to defense attorneys, but the sheriff's deputies probably viewed me as more of a coworker than an enemy. I saw them several times a week at court—going through the metal detector, hanging out in the courtroom while waiting for the judge to appear—and they were mostly genial and good-natured with me. They often passed on to me the local gossip in our small local legal world. But I hadn't heard anything about what was going on at the school. Which could mean that it was relatively minor. But it could also mean that it was *something*, and the deputies were under orders not to chat openly about it. That had happened a year earlier, when we had a rare first-degree murder case in our town. It wasn't a particularly complicated case—a drug deal had gone bad—but one of the men involved had been shot, and all the sheriff's deputies had remained tight-lipped about it until the trial was over.

Ellie Jones—curvy with short blond curls and the sort of ruddy skin that flushed easily and made her look perpetually agitated—spotted us and hurried over. Ellie's son, Max, was a friend of Charlie's. They were in the same class, and also went to the same karate school. Max was a sweet boy and I liked him, but I'd resisted Ellie's attempts to be closer friends. She was overbearing and something of a know-it-all.

Ellie looked from Keiko to me and back again, then leaned closer. "What did you tell her? And why didn't you call me back? Anyway, start again from the beginning. I want to hear *everything*."

Ellie hooked her fingers on my arm and pulled me toward her. I had to fight the urge to shake her off me. Why did these women keep touching me?

"I was just telling Keiko...wait, hold on," I said. I reached into my handbag and pulled out my phone, pretending to check my messages. It was really just an excuse to dislodge Ellie's grip on my arm. "Sorry. I have no idea what's going on, either. I'm hoping we'll find out tonight."

"Well, I heard that Robert Gibbons was caught extorting money from the school," Ellie said, not bothering to lower her voice. "That he transferred thousands of dollars from the business account into his personal bank account."

I frowned. "That doesn't seem likely."

"You never know. People are capable of all kinds of dark deeds," Keiko said, leaning forward and lowering her voice. "I once knew a man—well, I didn't know him personally, but I know someone who did—who emptied out his kids' college accounts. Can you believe that? I think he might have had a gambling problem, but still, that not's an excuse."

Ellie looked at her in irritation. "What does that have to do with anything?"

"All I'm saying is that people are capable of doing all sorts of bad things," Keiko said testily.

"Natalie's a criminal defense attorney and I'm a physical therapist. We're well aware that people are capable of doing bad things," Ellie snapped.

"God, excuse me for having an opinion." Keiko crossed her arms and glowered at Ellie.

I wondered what sort of bad people Ellie ran into as a physical therapist, but I knew better than to ask. She'd be more than happy to tell me, and I'd never get away from her.

"I just meant that transferring money from a school account to a personal account would be pretty easy to trace. No one with half a brain would do that," I said. "And anyway, I know Robert pretty well. He's not a thief."

"I wouldn't be so sure," Ellie retorted. "You never know what people are capable of."

"That's exactly what I said!" Keiko looked at me, incredulous. "Didn't I just say that?"

Thankfully, Will had finally finished his conversation with Zack Smith and turned back to me. It was my chance to escape.

"I think we're about to get started," he said, nodding toward the front of the auditorium.

Naomi Rubin—who was on the school board, and had sent out the email announcing the meeting earlier that day—was standing on the stage behind a microphone. The other members of the school board were also up on the stage, sitting in folding chairs behind her. This display of strength struck me as an ominous sign.

"Attention, everyone," Naomi said. The feedback on the microphone screeched, causing several parents to flinch. "Please take your seats so we can begin."

Everyone was eager to find out what was going on, so all the parents rushed to their seats more quickly and quietly than I would have imagined possible. Naomi waited patiently for everyone to settle in, although I thought she looked strained. She was a tall, striking woman with pale, freckled skin and wavy, dark hair, and she looked coolly professional in a cream sheath dress. She was a mother of four, all of whom had been students at Franklin at one time, although only her youngest—Candace, a seventh grader—was still at the school. The school board positions were all strictly volunteer, and I wondered if Naomi was sorry she'd ever agreed to serve on it.

"Thank you for coming tonight," Naomi began. "I know there are a thousand different rumors floating around about what's happening, so we—" she paused, and held out a hand toward the rest of the school board members "—thought it was probably best, in the spirit of transparency, to tell you what's going on. Or, at least, as much as we know." She paused to tuck a lock of hair behind one ear. "Today, the Calusa County Sheriff's Department notified the school that there has been a complaint filed against Franklin School principal, Robert Gibbons, of—" she paused to inhale deeply "—sexual indecency with a minor."

The impact of her words was explosive. After a few long beats of absolute silence, punctuated only by a few sharp intakes of breath, the room suddenly erupted in noise. All around me voices rose up, some angry, some fearful. I just sat there, trying to absorb the implication of her words. Robert, a man I had known for years, someone I considered a friend...had been accused of molesting a child. It was stunning, and the last thing I'd been expecting to hear.

I looked up at Will, and saw my bewilderment mirrored in his face.

"Is she serious?" he murmured. *"Robert?"*

"Please." Naomi raised a hand until the room had quieted. "I know this is shocking. But I have to stress that Principal Gibbons has not been arrested or even charged with a crime at this point in time. And I should also add, he strenuously denies these allegations. But the school board met and decided that it would be best for him to take a leave of absence from the school until this matter is resolved. We are very glad to inform you that Emily Randolph, who was the principal of Franklin for fifteen years, has agreed to come out of retirement, temporarily, to fill in as acting principal."

Naomi turned and gestured for an older woman sitting in one of the folding chairs behind her to stand. "Would you like to say a few words, Mrs. Randolph?" Naomi asked, before stepping aside. She looked relieved to hand over the microphone and duck out of the spotlight.

Emily Randolph stood and stepped forward. She had retired a few years before Charlie started at Franklin, although I recognized her from some of the photos in the display case at the front of the school. She had dark gray hair cut in a short, no-nonsense style and very straight posture, and was wearing a conservative skirt suit. She looked like a formidable woman.

"Thank you, Naomi, for that warm greeting. I do appreciate it." Emily Randolph adjusted the microphone downward and then leaned slightly toward it. "I know this is a difficult situation for everyone involved. I have faith that our justice system will work quickly to resolve these allegations. But for now, our priority is making sure our students are safe."

"Hold on a minute." Kyle Anderson stood up. I didn't know Kyle well, but I did know his wife, Penny, and their three giggling, sweet-natured daughters. Kyle was stocky and slightly overweight. He had an aggressive, red-faced manner. "You can't just leave it there. Who did Principal Gibbons abuse? Was it a student here?"

Mrs. Randolph held up a hand. "I do appreciate your concern. However, as I'm sure you can understand, we can't release any information about the victim. The *alleged* victim, I should say. He or she has a right to privacy."

"But that's the point, isn't it?" Kyle continued. "Was it a he or a she? We at least have the right to know if he was molesting boys or girls. And the age of the victim. Our kids go to school here. They could have been targeted."

"I agree," Ellie Jones said. She also stood. "You can't just drop this bombshell on us, and then not give us all the details. We have a right to know what happened. We have a right to know who the victim is, and what they're accusing Principal Gibbons of doing."

Judging from the nodding heads and murmurings from the crowd, quite a few of the parents agreed with her. I was still so shocked, I was finding it hard to breathe, let alone join in with the throngs demanding answers.

Emily Randolph again held up a hand, palm facing outward. "Please, ladies and gentlemen. *Please.* I know everyone is concerned, but you must understand that we cannot release any information about the alleged victim at this time."

I sat there, legs crossed, face impassive, heart pounding in my chest, and wondered how long it would take for everyone in this auditorium to know exactly who the victim was and what exactly he or she had accused Robert Gibbons of.

I gave it twenty-four hours.

As it turned out, I was wrong.

CHAPTER 4

"That was insane," Will said, steering my SUV out of the school parking lot and pointing it in the direction of our house.

"Yes, it was."

"Do you think he did it?"

I shrugged helplessly. "I don't know what to think. I've never gotten a creeper vibe off of Robert. Have you?"

"No, of course not." Will shook his head. "You don't think he's actually guilty, do you?"

"It seems so unlikely. I mean…it's *Robert*."

"There's really nothing worse to be suspected of. I'd rather be accused of committing a murder than molesting a child. Especially for a principal. Good God. This will ruin his life."

"Even if they never bring charges, or if it goes to trial and he's acquitted, I doubt he'll be able to come back to the school."

"Even if he's innocent?" Will asked.

"That won't matter. No one will ever be sure, and that will be enough to ruin his career." I sighed. "I've had clients who were falsely accused of molestation. It's pretty awful. It's one of those crimes where everyone assumes that you wouldn't be accused if you weren't guilty. It's like, you have to prove your innocence. How do you do that?"

"Did you believe any of them?"

"Some I did. I had one client, Paul Knowles, who was accused of molesting his stepdaughter. We were able to prove that Paul wasn't even in the state at the time she alleged the abuse happened. But that was after a bitter divorce. That unfortunately happens more often than you'd think. Ex-spouses use the kids to get revenge on one another."

"So, what? An angry parent manipulates their child to make a false accusation? That's sick."

I nodded. "But that can't be the case here. Robert doesn't have any children."

"Which means it might have been a student at the school who made the complaint."

"If it happened."

We stopped at a red light. Will turned to look at me. His worried face was illuminated by the lights of the cars passing by. "You don't think there's a possibility he could have hurt Charlie, do you?"

"Of course not," I said immediately.

"How do you know?"

"I just do." I would sense if something bad had happened to Charlie, I was sure of it. Besides, I had read up on the sort of behaviors that abused children often exhibit when I'd represented Paul Knowles. They frequently withdrew and often became depressed. Sometimes they'd regress and begin sucking their thumbs or wetting the bed. "Charlie's the same easygoing, happy-go-lucky kid he's always been. If something were wrong, I'd know it. Besides, he's never been alone with Robert."

"That we know of."

"He confesses every time he's gotten a check during class." The students at Franklin School received checks for committing classroom crimes, ranging from talking out of turn to leaving necessary supplies at home. "He would definitely have told me if he'd ever been sent to the principal's office. That would have been a huge deal for him. You know how much he hates getting in trouble. And he's incapable of keeping a secret."

Will didn't look convinced. "We should still ask him."

"Of course, although we'll have to figure out a way to ask that won't freak him out." My phone beeped, signaling a text had arrived. I looked at it. "It's Mandy. She said that some of the parents are meeting at B-Side to discuss what's going on."

"When?"

"Right now. Do you want to go?"

"Maybe we should, just to see if anyone has more information. Do you think Marissa will mind staying a little later with Charlie?"

Marissa was the teenage daughter of our next-door neighbor, and Charlie's favorite babysitter, even though I thought he was probably reaching the age where he was really too old to have a babysitter. When I had been eleven, I was already babysitting for other families. But I'd always been more protective of Charlie than my mother, Lindy, had ever been of me. I told myself that this was smart—after fourteen years of practicing law, I knew how dangerous the world was. But I always worried that I was coddling him.

"I'll message her and ask." I sent the text, which Marissa responded to almost instantly. "She says it's fine."

"Then I guess let's go. I could certainly use a drink right about now."

The B-Side Lounge was a hipster wine bar that often had a jazz band playing in the courtyard on weekends. But there wasn't any live music that night, a Monday, and only a light crowd grouped at the bar.

"Do you want something to drink?" Will asked.

"I'll have a glass of sauvignon blanc," I said.

Will went to order our drinks, and I headed outside, where a small group of school parents were already congregating on the patio. It was a relaxed, pleasant space, with iron tables set up around a burbling fountain and lit by strings of twinkle lights that hung from the brick walls and encircled potted palms. Mandy and her husband, Dan, were there sitting at one table with Grace and Ryan Carpenter, as well as Shannon Davis. Kyle Anderson was pulling another table over to make room for more people, helped by Jason Farraday. Jason's wife, Tish, looked intense as she talked to Ann Marie Delgado and—my heart sank—Ellie Jones. I should have known Ellie wouldn't miss an opportunity to insert herself further into the drama.

"I just felt like I had to stand up and say something," Ellie informed everyone loudly. "These are our kids who are at risk, after all. If we don't advocate for them, who will?"

"I agreed with every word you said," Ann Marie told her. "But I could never have spoken in front of everyone like you did. I would have been too nervous."

"I'm never afraid to speak up," Ellie told her. "I've always been very brave when it comes to standing up for what I believe in."

I managed not to roll my eyes and sat down next to Mandy.

"I'm glad you came," she said, patting my arm. "I'm so freaked out."

"I know. It's all a lot to take in."

Will appeared and handed me a glass of wine.

"Try not to chug it," he said.

"Don't tempt me." I took a sip of the wine, then turned back to Mandy. "So why are we meeting up? Is this just to rehash what Naomi told us at the school meeting?"

Mandy shook her head. My normally lighthearted best friend looked more serious than I'd ever seen her. "No, I think we're about to find out what's really going on." She turned to look at Grace. "I think this is everyone."

"Good, we should probably get started," Grace said. "I know some of us have babysitters waiting at home."

"Do you have information beyond what we were just told at the assembly?" Will asked.

"I heard that this isn't the first time Principal Gibbons has been accused of molesting a student," Ellie announced.

We all flinched at how loudly she spoke. The bar wasn't crowded, but there were some patrons there not affiliated with the school, and this didn't seem like a subject that should be discussed at full volume.

"It apparently happened at the last school he taught in. I don't know where, apparently somewhere out of state. That's why he moved here, and apparently may have changed his name," she continued.

"That's not true," I said quietly. "Robert has lived here for twenty years. Before he took the job at Franklin, he was the assistant principal at one of the local public elementary schools."

"And the school board does a thorough background search on everyone the school hires. If there had been even a whiff of something like this in his past, they would never have hired him," Mandy said.

Ellie flushed. "I'm just telling you what I heard."

"Grace has heard some information, too," Mandy said. She turned to Grace, who had sharp features and a long neck, like the subject of a Modigliani painting. "Why don't you tell them what you told me?"

"Okay, I will, but I want to say, I'm really not comfortable with this," Grace said. "I don't normally spread gossip, especially about something so awful. But I know everyone's worried about what did or didn't happen, and the source I heard it from is very reliable. She knows the whole story."

"Who told you?" Ellie asked eagerly.

"I'm not going to say," Grace replied. "But I will tell you this—the child who made the accusation was Tate Mason."

We were all quiet for a minute, absorbing this information. Tate was a few years older than Charlie, and he lived a few blocks away from our house. I occasionally saw him out on his bike, often with a fishing pole—some of the kids liked to fish off the old bridge in downtown Shoreham. I didn't know Tate well, but I had heard that he had the reputation of either being troubled...or being a troublemaker.

"I don't know who that is," Kyle said, breaking the silence. "What grade is he in?"

"Seventh," Grace said. "He lives with Jennifer and Peter Swain."

"Lives with?" Will asked, shooting me a quizzical look.

"He's a foster child," Mandy explained. "I know Jennifer and Peter want to officially adopt him. I think they're just waiting on the paperwork."

"Isn't Tate the kid who set the fire in the boys' locker room last year?" Dan Breen asked.

"They actually never proved that he was the one who started the fire," Mandy told her husband.

"But that's who everyone thought did it. Right?"

"Right." Mandy shrugged, and glanced around at the rest of us. "I'm sorry, but that's true, right? Everyone thought he was responsible."

"They did find a lighter in his locker," Ellie added eagerly. "And Mr. Patrick, the custodian, said he saw Tate going into the locker room earlier that day."

"Well, to be fair, every boy in the school who had PE that day would have gone into the locker room," Mandy said. "But apparently Tate had gotten detention earlier that week, and he made some threatening comments to Principal Gibbons. Something along the lines of, 'I'll get you back for this.'"

We were all quiet for a few moments, absorbing the ramifications this statement might have in light of the current controversy.

"Why wasn't he expelled after the fire?" Will asked.

"The school didn't have enough evidence to take action against him," Grace said. "And besides, I heard he's had a tough life, or at least he did until the Swains took him in. I think that everyone, ironically Principal Gibbons included, thought that it was better to let the whole thing go. To give Tate a second chance."

"Do you know what this kid is accusing Principal Gibbons of doing?" Kyle asked.

Grace nodded, her face grim. "He claims that it happened last month when the seventh graders were on their overnight class trip to St. Augustine. Principal Gibbons always chaperones the out-of-town trips. Tate told Jennifer, his foster mom, that Robert took him into his hotel room alone, and…well, touched him. Inappropriately. And apparently tried to get Tate to touch him back. Jennifer was the one who reported it to the police."

Dan exhaled loudly. *"Jesus."*

"But why would Robert do that?" Mandy asked. She shook her head. "The risk of getting caught would be enormous. What if one of the other chaperones or kids had seen him?"

"Robert denies it ever happened," Grace added. "He insists he was never alone with Tate."

"So basically it's the word of a troubled kid versus a man with a spotless record." Will shook his head. "I have to imagine that would be a tough case to prove."

Other parents nodded and began sharing what they knew about Tate. That he was frequently in trouble at school. That he had self-control issues and often had outbursts in class. That both of his biological parents were in prison.

I had the sense that opinion—so quick to assume the worst of Robert just moments earlier—was shifting rapidly. The victim wasn't a good kid. He was troubled. And an outsider.

Just a few minutes earlier, I was sure that the Robert Gibbons I knew couldn't be a child molester. But contrarily, everyone's willingness to assume the worst of this child turned my stomach. So what if Tate Mason had had a rough life? What if he had set that fire? Did that mean that he couldn't also be victimized by a predatory adult?

I glanced over at Will, hoping to catch his eye and signal that I wanted to go. He was looking down at his phone, tapping on it with one finger. I stared at him, wondering what could possibly be more important than the revelation that the principal of our son's school had been accused of molesting a child? Not to mention that Robert was a friend, and he was either guilty or falsely accused of a hideous crime. That either a child's life had been horribly impacted or a good and decent man would have his life ruined by a false accusation.

Mandy looked over at Will, too, and then she caught my eye. She knew his phone obsession drove me crazy. I had joked about it one day over lunch, comparing his phone habit to that of our teenage babysitter. I hadn't told her my suspicions about just whom he might be texting. It wasn't that I didn't trust Mandy—I did, and I knew she would keep my confidences to herself—but once I said anything, I wouldn't be able to take it back. Every time Mandy saw Will and me together, she'd wonder if he had cheated on me, and I would know exactly what she was thinking. I wasn't ready for that.

I drained my glass of wine and stood. "We have to go. Our sitter is waiting for us."

Will looked up in surprise, but he also got to his feet and pocketed his phone.

"I'll call you tomorrow morning," Mandy said.

I smiled at her and nodded. "Thank you for the information, Grace."

"I just hope I made the right decision telling you all. I would appreciate it if we could keep it between us," Grace said. Her eyes flickered toward Ellie, who was probably counting down the minutes until she could call everyone she knew and tell them about this latest piece of scandal.

"Of course," I said, although we all knew there was little chance of this group keeping what she'd told us confidential.

By tomorrow at the latest, every parent in the school would know that Tate Mason had accused Principal Robert Gibbons of molesting him.

CHAPTER 5

The next morning, I didn't go to the office straight after dropping Charlie off at school, as I usually did. Instead, I returned to the house, hooked on Rocket's leash and took him out for a walk.

Rocket was delighted at the unexpected treat. He pranced along at my side, his ears pricked up, watching for an errant squirrel or lizard he could pounce on. I wasn't nearly as energetic. I hadn't slept well, which wasn't surprising after the distressing news of the night before. My dreams had been chaotic and strange, and I woke up with my nightshirt drenched in sweat.

I hadn't talked to Charlie about Tate Mason's allegations yet. Will and I had returned home the night before to find him already asleep. That morning, he'd been distracted by the math homework he'd failed to complete the night before in the excitement of having Marissa babysit on a school night. I knew I'd have to talk to him about the subject soon, that afternoon if possible, before he started hearing stories from his classmates. But first, I needed to figure out what I was going to say. I had approximately seven hours to figure out how the hell I was going to broach such a difficult topic.

I shook my head and walked faster, trying to wake myself up. Our subdivision had a central park, complete with a man-made pond and a small playground, where I used to push Charlie on the swings when he was small. Rocket and I circled the perimeter of the park, then headed east on Palmetto Terrace under the shade of a row of oak trees. The cicadas were chirping above, their eerie rhythm seeming to grow louder with our every step.

Jennifer and Peter Swain lived on Palmetto Terrace, along with their foster son, Tate, and daughter, Zoë. I knew Jennifer from school events—we always chatted at the school auction and Mother's Day Breakfast, and both volunteered at track-and-field day—but I didn't know her well enough to ask how Tate had come to join their family. I was pretty sure Zoë was their biological child, since she looked just like Jennifer. Had they wanted more kids, and were unable to have them? Or had they been moved to take in a foster child out of a sense of social conscience?

I walked toward the Swain house, which was the last on the left of the dead-end street. I wasn't sure what exactly I was hoping to accomplish—I certainly wasn't going to ring their doorbell or otherwise impose on them, not when they were going through such a difficult time. I fully expected that Rocket and I would reach the end of the street, then turn right back around and head home.

I was wrong.

When I reached the Swains' house—a pretty, two-story yellow stucco home with a metal roof—Jennifer was outside. She was a tall, thin woman with a square jaw and masculine features. She wasn't conventionally pretty, but definitely striking. This morning, Jennifer was standing on her front lawn, dressed in a T-shirt, running shorts and suede gardening gloves. She was attacking a huge bougainvillea bush with a pair of long-handled shears, opening and closing the handles violently, while the pink-plumed branches rained down around her.

"Shit," she swore when one of the thorny branches caught against her arm.

"Hi, Jennifer," I said.

She started, turning around. Her face was red from the exertion and a trickle of sweat was running down her temple. She lifted a gloved hand to wipe it away, leaving a smudge of dirt in its place. "Nat. Hi."

"Sorry, I didn't mean to sneak up on you." I gestured to the piles of branches on the grass. "You were doing battle with your tree."

"Right." Jennifer turned to look at it, as if she was just now noticing she'd lopped off two-thirds of the tree. "If I don't cut it back, it takes over, but I think I might have gone overboard. I probably should have at least waited until it finished blooming."

"You're bleeding," I said.

Jennifer looked down at the scratches on her arm. "I look like I've gotten into a fight with a rabid cat."

"Maybe you should put some Neosporin on those."

"Probably." Jennifer signed heavily. "It's weird that you're here. I was actually going to call you this morning."

"You were?" I was surprised. Jennifer and I had always been friendly, but we weren't close. We'd never chatted on the phone.

"I'm assuming you've heard about…well. Everything. With Tate, I mean. Everyone else in town seems to know."

I nodded. "I'm so sorry. I can't imagine how difficult this must be for you and Peter. And Tate, of course."

"Yeah, it's pretty much been a living nightmare. Anyway, do you have a minute? I wanted to ask your advice on the legalities of all of this. Do you have the time to come inside for a minute? I just made a pitcher of iced tea."

"Sure, but I have Rocket with me." I gestured down toward my dog.

Jennifer looked at my small dog, and for the first time, a smile softened her face. "He's welcome to come in, too."

We ended up sitting out on her back patio, next to a kidney-shaped swimming pool. A pink flamingo raft floated aimlessly on the chlorinated water, occasionally bouncing off one of the rounded pool sides. I unhooked Rocket from his lead. He immediately raced away, ready to terrorize the lizards that had, until his arrival, been happily sunning themselves on the warm cement.

Jennifer brought out a pitcher of iced tea on a tray, along with glasses and a plate of banana-nut muffins. She offered one to me, then took one herself. Rocket instantly raced back to the table and shimmied to Jennifer's side, giving her a winsome look.

"Can I give him one?" she asked.

"Just a bite."

She tore her muffin in half and fed it to Rocket. He happily scarfed it down.

"You'll be his new best friend."

"I bake when I'm stressed out," Jennifer said. "But I don't have much of an appetite."

I took a bite of the muffin. "Yum, this is delicious."

"Thanks, they're Tate's favorite." Jennifer closed her eyes briefly and ran a hand over her face. "Not that muffins are going to fix anything."

"How is Tate doing?" I asked tentatively.

"Right now, he's happy because we let him stay home from school yesterday and today. Actually, whatever happens, we're not going to send him or Zoë back to that school. I need to figure out where they'll go now."

"Are they home?"

"No, Peter took them out in the boat. We couldn't think of what else to do, and all three of them love to fish. But as far as how Tate is going to be…that I honestly can't tell you." Jennifer shook her head helplessly. "He's always been the sort of kid who keeps things bottled up inside. I think it's because he had such a rough start in life. His biological mom was a drug addict who continued using right through her pregnancy. Then he was nearly two before Child Protective Services removed him from her custody, so God only knows what his baby years were like. After that, he was in and out of several foster homes before he came to live with us. Most foster parents are good people, kind people, but...well. Tate's made a few comments here and there that have led me to believe that it was not always easy for him. He was already seeing a child psychologist before any of this happened. Do you know Camilla Wilson?"

I shook my head.

"She's been fantastic with Tate. He actually talked to her first about...well, what happened to him. She was the one who encouraged him to tell Peter and me. These sort of traumatic events can have horrible long-term effects, but Camilla is hopeful that with enough help and support, Tate will pull through this," Jennifer said.

"I'm sure he will." At least, I hoped so. Tate had already been through more trauma than any child should ever have to deal with. "Have you taken in other foster kids?"

"No, Tate was the first. I had a high-risk pregnancy with Zoë, and after that, the doctors didn't think it was a good idea for us roll the dice again. But our family never felt complete. Peter and I thought about adopting a baby, and we were just about to start the process. But then I was at the library one day, and they had this whole display set up of kids who were in the foster system, looking for homes. I saw a picture of Tate, and I just... well, I just knew. He was the one. Peter thought I was crazy at first, but I talked him into it. We applied to be foster parents, jumped through all the hoops they make you go through. But it was worth it. Once Tate came to live with us, we all fell in love with him. He's ours. He's part of this family, and will be forever. But now…"

Jennifer breathed in a deep, ragged breath as tears filled her eyes. "All I can think is that if I hadn't insisted on bringing Tate into our family, this would never have happened to him. He would have lived somewhere else, with a different family, gone to a different school and probably would have gone on to have a happy life. But I had to be greedy and insist on having more children…"

She let out a raspy sob and rocked forward, her hands clenched into fists.

"Jennifer." I leaned toward her and put my hand on her arm. "You can't think about it that way. Terrible things happen for no reason. And just because they do, that doesn't mean that you're not a good parent or that Tate would be better off somewhere else. I'm sure he loves you just as much as you love him."

"Thank you for saying that." She looked up at me with sad, wet eyes. "But I feel like I've failed him."

"You haven't. Of *course* you haven't," I said.

Yesterday, I had been sure Robert wasn't capable of what he'd been accused of doing. That he could never, ever hurt a child. Today, talking to Jennifer, so distraught at the thought that her beloved child—and Tate *was* her child, whatever his legal status—had been hurt, I couldn't be sure of anything. Could Robert have exploited this child whose life had been so hard until recently? Had he? I badly wanted to believe it wasn't possible.

"Anyway." Jennifer dabbed at her eyes with a paper napkin, then drew in another deep breath, struggling to compose herself. "That's not what I wanted to talk to you about. I need to know…if the State's Attorney decides to prosecute…" she hesitated, as though she couldn't bear to speak Robert's name "…*him*. What will happen to Tate?"

"What do you mean, exactly? Are you worried they'll move

him to a different foster home? I don't practice family law, but I'm sure a good lawyer could stop that from happening. I can find a referral for you if you need one."

"Oh, no. That's not it. We have a *great* adoption attorney, and she told us not to worry about that part of it. The paperwork we needed to complete to adopt him is mostly done. Tate said that it's what he still wants, too. For us to adopt him, I mean. No, this is his home. Whatever else happens."

"Good." I nodded, glad to hear it. Whatever had happened to Tate, nothing would be gained by his losing these good people as parents.

"It's just...you're a criminal attorney, right?"

I nodded.

"I just need to know what we're facing. Tate would be the main witness. Maybe the only witness. Tate said that...well, that there was touching. *Jesus.* But, that's what we're dealing with. No penetration, no...fluids." She stopped to inhale raggedly. "Nothing that a doctor could testify to or that a lab could process. So, presumably, it would be Tate's word against...*his.*"

I was starting to realize, with an acidic churn of my stomach, why she was so eager to talk to me. She wanted me to assure her that Tate would make it through the criminal judicial process without being further traumatized. That the defense attorney would be gentle with him. That someone—someone exactly like me—wouldn't ask him difficult questions.

Or, worse—blame him outright.

"Here's the thing," I said, trying to keep my voice as gentle as possible. "Every case is different, of course. But the basic role of a defense attorney is always the same. It's to get the best possible result for your client. An acquittal, or at least, a favorable plea deal."

"What does that mean, exactly? I know what the words mean. But what would Tate be facing? What would he have to go through?"

It was my turn to draw in a deep breath. "It's entirely possible he'll be asked tough questions." That was the least of it, I thought. "They'll try to frame the case in a way that changes the narrative. Someone, other than the defendant, will be at fault. Someone has falsely accused him, for example. Or someone is trying to entrap him. It can be...difficult."

The truth was, it could be hideous, for everyone involved. I'd defended people accused of sexually battering a minor. It was a first degree felony in the state of Florida, with a maximum possible sentence of life in prison. If the accuser had other issues, or lacked veracity—or if there was the chance someone was manipulating them to make up the testimony—I'd want to cover that on my cross-examination. Any decent, capable defense attorney would do the same. No one wanted to go after the child who was claiming the abuse. But most of the time, you couldn't avoid it. Not if you were doing your job.

"You're saying they'll blame Tate. They'll claim he was asking for it, or he's making it up?" Jennifer began to literally wring her hands, pulling at her fingers and scratching at her skin. "They'll say that because he's a foster child and has been in vulnerable situations, that it's possible that...someone may have hurt him before...and that's confused him." Her voice broke and she was silent for a few beats. When she spoke again, her voice was a whisper. "They'll say he's lying."

"I don't know what the defense counsel's strategy will be," I said. "But it's certainly possible. You have to understand—their job isn't to protect Tate. It's to keep their client out of jail, or at least to get him the most favorable sentence possible."

I wondered if I sounded as guilty as I suddenly felt. It was my job, too. One that I believed in. Or usually did.

"Did you know what that man told Tate?" Jennifer asked abruptly. "He said that it was natural for older men to have sexual relationships with young boys. That it dated back to Greek times and was a normal part of every young man's development. But that he had to keep it a secret, because it was something moth-ers wouldn't understand. He's a sick, horrible, twisted pervert. Now you say my son is going to be the one put on trial. Not the monster who did this to him?"

She was crying again, the tears streaming down her drawn face.

I stared at her, suddenly unable to breathe, almost as though I'd been sucker punched in the stomach.

Robert was a history buff. And his particular area of inter-est was ancient cultures, like Greece and Rome. The last time we'd had dinner with Robert and Venetia before their divorce, he'd told us in great detail about a trip he'd taken to Washing-ton, DC, specifically to go to a special exhibit of ancient Greek artifacts at the National Geographic Museum.

Could Tate have known about Robert's fascination with an-cient history, and if so, had Tate made up the grooming story about sexual mores in ancient Greece in order to bolster his ac-cusation? It was possible, I supposed.

And yet it didn't seem very likely. In fact, it seemed highly unlikely.

Which meant…oh, dear God. Robert Gibbons really might have molested Tate. I hadn't truly believed it was possible until right that very moment.

"Are you okay? You look funny."

I glanced up at her. "What? Oh, no, I'm…fine. It's just a dif-ficult subject."

"Wait. You're not representing him, are you?" Jennifer's voice was sharp, and she suddenly sat erect in her chair. "He hasn't hired you?"

"No, of course not. I wouldn't be here talking to you if I was. That would be completely unethical."

"But you have represented people—*men*—who've done this to children." Jennifer stared at me, her eyes suddenly cold, her posture stiff.

I set down my empty iced tea glass on the table and got to my feet. Rocket ran over to me and waited while I hooked the leash on his collar, my hands shaking.

"Thank you for the iced tea," I said.

Jennifer didn't look up at me. Instead, she stared down at the table.

"How do you live with yourself?" she asked softly.

I didn't respond. Rocket and I saw ourselves out.

CHAPTER 6

I got to the office late that morning. I didn't have court, but I did have to churn out some paperwork—a motion to suppress, some discovery requests. I had a hard time focusing on any of it. I kept flashing back to my conversation with Jennifer and her disturbing revelation that Tate claimed Robert had told him sexual relationships between men and boys were common in ancient Greece. And then I remembered the disgusted way she had looked at me when she realized I had defended the sort of monsters who target children. As if by doing so, I was equally culpable for their crimes. That I was a monster, too.

Mandy called me just after lunch.

"Do you have time to grab a coffee before school pickup?" she asked. "I have news that I think you'll want to hear."

"What's going on now?"

"I'd rather tell you in person."

I felt a flutter of nerves. Just one day ago, my best friend asking to meet up for coffee wouldn't have this effect on me. Now I was bracing for the next terrible revelation.

"Sure, just give me twenty minutes to finish up what I'm working on. I'll meet you at Roasted."

"Sounds good. If you get there ahead of me, order me a latte."

Downtown Shoreham had a quaint, Old Florida feel to it, designed to attract tourist dollars. There were no chain restaurants or stores. Instead, all of the businesses were locally owned, from a seafood restaurant called the Salty Sailor, to cute nautical-themed boutiques, to an old-fashioned ice cream parlor. I beat Mandy to Roasted, our favorite coffee shop, so I ordered us each a latte at the counter, along with a giant chocolate chip cookie to share. Then I headed to the patio outside, which overlooked the Intracoastal Waterway.

The water looked calm, and there was a lot of boat traffic on the river for a Tuesday afternoon. Fishermen heading out to deeper waters, eager to take advantage of the nice weather, I guessed.

"Hey, you," Mandy said, arriving just as the waitress appeared with our coffees and cookie. She looked pretty and breezy in a plum tunic top, white jeans and leather sandals. Her curly hair was pulled back in a low ponytail, and she was wearing gold aviator sunglasses.

"Perfect timing," I said.

Mandy sat down across from me and smiled at the waitress, who handed her a white ceramic coffee mug. "Thank you. Is that cookie for you or for me?"

"I got it for us to share."

"You are my favorite person in the world." Mandy broke off a piece of the cookie and dunked it in her coffee before popping it in her mouth. "Yum."

I smiled. "Your affection is easily bought."

"Absolutely! Just ask my husband. So—" Mandy leaned in confidentially "—what have you heard?"

"Nothing new since last night." This wasn't true, of course.

There had been my illuminating conversation with Jennifer Swain. But I didn't feel comfortable repeating what she had told me, not even to Mandy. Which also meant that I couldn't tell her why my previous certainty that Robert Gibbons would never hurt a child had started to fade, replaced by a clanging alarm bell that was growing louder.

"It really surprises me that you haven't heard this. I thought you were more connected with what the police are investigating." Mandy broke off another piece of the cookie.

"I don't know why everyone thinks that I have some sort of inside knowledge about active police investigations."

"Don't you?"

"No. Although it would certainly make my job easier if the police detectives kept me up-to-date. Anyway, you said you had something to tell me?"

"Yes," Mandy said. "Do you know Gwen O'Brien? She's a Franklin mom, but I knew her from before we had kids. We worked together at the hospital."

Mandy was a nurse, and back before she married and had her children, she'd worked in the operating room at St. David's Hospital. She met her husband, Dan, an orthopedic surgeon, on the job, which they both tended to get the giggles about when they'd had too much wine. Mandy had confessed that in those heady, early days of their relationship, they'd made out all over the hospital, like a pair of teenagers.

"You know how it is," she'd said at the time, blushing and refilling her wineglass.

I had felt a pang of regret, not at all sure I did know how it was. *Had Will and I ever been like that?* I remembered wondering. *We must have been once, right?* Yet somehow, I couldn't quite recall it.

"Anyway, Gwen's a nurse, too, and back in our younger, wilder days, we were both always on the night shift, so I got to know her pretty well," Mandy now said. "Her son, Aiden, is in the seventh grade at Franklin."

"I remember you mentioning that you knew her," I said. "She's always seemed really nice."

"Oh, yeah, Gwen's a doll. Anyway, she called me today and told me that Aiden was on that same trip to St. Augustine, *and* that he shared a room with Tate Mason and two other boys. The police interviewed all three boys."

"Wow, already?"

That meant the police were working quickly on the case, which was unusual. Everyone thinks that the real-life police are just like their television counterparts—two hard-charging detectives, assigned to one important case at a time, working around the clock to solve it. This almost never happens in real life, where detectives juggle multiple cases, often working on their own and taking months to close out even simple investigations.

Mandy nodded. "And do you know what they all said? That they were all together—including Tate—the entire time. None of them would ever have had a chance to be alone with Robert Gibbons." She pulled off her aviator sunglasses to give me a meaningful look. "They said Tate must be lying."

"Are you sure about that?"

"That's what Gwen told me. So, if Tate was never alone with Principal Gibbons—"

"Then the State's Attorney won't be able to prove that it happened," I finished.

I knew I should have felt relief at this. If Tate had made the whole thing up, it meant my son hadn't been attending a school run by a sexual predator. But instead, as I sat there with the sun warm on my face, gazing out at the postcard-perfect view of the water, I felt chilled. I was a criminal defense attorney, after all. I knew all too well that the state not being able to prove its case didn't mean that a crime hadn't occurred.

"So what happens now? Will the police drop the investigation?" Mandy asked.

"Not necessarily. A lot depends on Tate and his parents. If they're resolute that the abuse happened, the state is more or less obligated to continue the investigation, and possibly to prosecute Robert."

"Are you serious?" Mandy stared at me. "Even if there are witnesses who say it couldn't have happened?"

"I don't know." I shook my head and shrugged. "It's hard to speculate. If the state thinks that the other boys' testimony is more credible than Tate's, they might drop it. Or they might offer Robert a plea deal."

"That's ridiculous. If Principal Gibbons is innocent, and Tate Mason just made up this whole thing because he has emotional issues, or he's had a rough life, or whatever the excuse is…well, they shouldn't let him ruin an innocent man's life!"

Mandy seemed almost angry with me, as though I were the appointed representative of the criminal judicial system, personally responsible for all its injustices.

"Why don't we wait and see what happens," I suggested.

"If they do drop the charges, Principal Gibbons will be allowed to come back to the school, won't he?"

"I don't know," I said again for what felt like the hundredth time in the past twenty-four hours. *I don't know what to think about the allegations. I don't know what will happen to Robert. No, I don't know who to believe.* "Did you talk to Beatrice and Amelia about any of this?"

Beatrice was eleven, the same age as Charlie, and her younger sister Amelia had just turned eight a few weeks earlier. We'd gone to her birthday party and given her a Lego kit that Charlie had picked out.

"I brought it up at breakfast this morning, but I didn't want to go into too much detail, obviously. I asked them if they'd ever been alone with Principal Gibbons, and they both said no.

Then I told them about how their bodies are private, that no one should touch them in a way that makes them uncomfortable." Mandy sighed. "I've told them that all of that before, of course, but it seemed like a good time for a refresher."

"How did they take it?"

"They were fine. And then Amelia fed her toast to the dog, and Bea tattled on her. Amelia complained that it wasn't fair that her toast had a cinnamon swirl in it, because she hates cinnamon more than anything in the world. Bea said that it wasn't fair that she had to put up with an annoying little sister. That she wished she was an only child like Charlie, which meant that of course Amelia had to burst into dramatic tears. You know, it was a typical morning at my house."

I smiled. Mandy's daughters were as high-spirited as she was.

"I haven't talked to Charlie yet," I admitted. "I'm going to bring it up with him after school. I'm not looking forward to it."

"Don't worry, it will be fine. I was dreading talking about it with the girls, but they were totally unfazed. Wait!" She looked down at the empty plate in dismay. "Did you have any of that cookie or did I just eat the entire thing myself? I did, didn't I? How could you have let me do that? I thought you were my best friend?"

"I'll buy you another cookie if you take over all of my mom duties for the rest of the day. Especially the part where I have to talk to my son about the fact that his principal might be a pedophile." I shook my head. "This is seriously screwed up."

"I know, and it's awful and scary, but at the same time..."

"At the same time, what?"

"It's like that old saying about when you hear hoofbeats, it's more likely to be a horse than a zebra."

"Who's the zebra supposed to be?"

"Look, I know this may make me sound like an asshole, but it's what everyone is thinking—it's more likely that a troubled kid would make a false report, than that a good man with no criminal history would suddenly turn into a pedophile in his late forties."

"I know."

"Then why do you look so freaked out?"

I shook my head and shrugged. "Honestly, I just have a bad feeling about this. A really bad feeling."

"It will be fine," Mandy said, putting her hand over mine. "As mothers, we worry all the time, and everything almost always works out."

"I know," I said, nodding. But I was silently thinking, *Except for those times when it doesn't.*

CHAPTER 7

As I reached the front of the car line, Charlie was talking to a cluster of friends. When he saw me, he waved and ran to grab his blue camouflage pattern backpack, which had been discarded by the brick school wall.

"Hi, Mom!" He climbed into the car. "Can Jack come over this weekend? 'Cause I just invited him to."

"Maybe. Let me check with Dad and see if we have any plans. Do you have a lot of homework?"

Charlie held his thumb and finger a half inch apart.

"What does that mean?" I asked.

"A teeny-weeny amount. I'll finish it in, like, ten minutes."

"Just don't put it off too late."

"I know, I know."

I turned left out of the school parking lot and headed back toward downtown.

"Where are we going?" Charlie asked. Our house was in the opposite direction.

"I thought we could go get some ice cream. How does that sound?"

"Really?" Charlie grinned. "Awesome."

I found a parking spot near Jinxy Cones. We headed inside to place our usual orders—a strawberry sundae with extra whipped cream and rainbow sprinkles for Charlie and a small scoop of mint chocolate chip for me. Ice cream in hand, we strolled down to the boardwalk, where we found an empty bench overlooking the water.

"Did anything interesting happen in school today?" I asked in between bites.

"We're having an egg drop contest in science," Charlie said.

"What's that?"

"It's an experiment where we drop eggs off the second story of the school."

"That sounds messy."

"Not if we do it right. We're supposed to wrap them in something that will keep them from breaking. Like bubble wrap, or those foam thingies that sometimes come in packages."

"Styrofoam peanuts," I said. "Is that what you're going to use?"

"I'm not sure yet. I was going to look up ideas on the internet. It has to be environmentally friendly, though."

"I wonder if Jell-O would work," I mused. "What if you made a huge vat of Jell-O, and suspended the egg in the middle of it? Then it would just bounce off the pavement."

Charlie shrugged, clearly unimpressed by this genius idea.

"Come on, it's a great idea," I insisted. "And how much fun would it be to create a giant Jell-O blob?"

"Is Jell-O environmentally friendly?"

"I have no idea. How flexible is your teacher on that point?"

"She said if our project isn't environmentally friendly, we'll be disqualified."

"So not flexible at all, then." I licked my minty ice cream

from my spoon and tried to decide how best to broach the topic I'd brought Charlie here to discuss. "I have something I need to talk to you about."

Charlie turned to look at me, his expression apprehensive. "Are you and Dad getting a divorce?"

"What?" I asked, startled.

"That's what parents always say when they're about to unload the divorce talk. First they buy you ice cream, then they say they have to talk to you about something."

"No, it's not. How do you know that, anyway?"

"I saw it on a YouTube video."

"Oh, well, then it must be true.

"So, you *are* getting a divorce?" Charlie's voice rose with anxiety.

Good work, Nat, I thought. *Great start to what already promises to be a hideously difficult conversation. Real Mother of the Year award potential.*

"No, honey, of course not," I said, reaching over to pat his arm. "I was being sarcastic. You know, because of how silly most of the YouTube videos you watch are. But, no, your dad and I are *not* getting a divorce."

Thoughts of Will and his obsession with his phone over the past few months, coupled with his recent pass code protection of it, immediately popped into my head, but I pushed them away. I had to focus on the issue at hand.

"Have you heard anything about why Principal Gibbons wasn't at school today?" I began.

"No. Why?"

"He's on a leave of absence, and I wasn't sure if your classmates had talked to you about it."

"What is that?"

"A leave of absence?" Charlie nodded. "It's when a person takes some time off work, but without quitting their job. And with the understanding that they may return at some point. It's like a time-out for grown-ups."

"Oh. Hey, is that a dolphin?"

"Huh?" I was momentarily confused by this non sequitur. "Where?"

"There." Charlie pointed toward the river. "Oh, never mind. It's just a stick or something. Or is that a grocery bag?"

"Anyway," I said, realizing his attention was flagging, and that I should probably get to the point, "the thing is, sweetheart, one of the kids at your school said that Mr. Gibbons touched him in a way that he shouldn't have. So I need to talk to you about that."

Charlie continued to silently spoon ice cream into his mouth while staring out at the water. I couldn't tell if he was listening to me or not. I set my half-empty paper cup down on the bench, then turned toward my son, and reached out to hold his hand. It felt solid and warm in mine.

"Do you know what I mean by that?" I continued. "There are places on our bodies that are private and that shouldn't be touched, unless it's by a doctor or, when you're grown up, by someone that you care about."

Will had gone over the basics of sex with Charlie when he was in the third grade and came home from school completely wigged out after one of his friends had told him that daddies inject babies into mommies. This had caused Charlie to conjure up a horrifying image of Will giving me a shot with a huge hypodermic needle, like the one his pediatrician used to give him vaccines, only big enough to hold a fully formed baby. It took Will the better part of an hour to convince him that sex had nothing to do with needles.

"I *know* that," Charlie now said, his voice dripping with condescension. He pulled his hand away from me.

"Good," I said. "That's good. But I still have to ask you. Have you ever been alone with Principal Gibbons? Just the two of you, with no one else in the room?"

Charlie didn't respond. Instead, he took another bite of his ice cream. I noticed that his narrow shoulders had begun hunching up toward his ears. I felt the first faint stirrings of alarm.

"Charlie?" I tried again. This time Charlie shrugged. I took a deep breath. *Stay calm, stay calm, stay calm,* I repeated to myself. "I really need to know, honey."

"I don't want to talk about it," Charlie said. He had stopped eating his ice cream, but he was still staring into the paper cup, where the vanilla ice cream was starting to melt, swirling with the bright red strawberry.

"I understand, but it's important that you tell me." I kept my voice as steady and reassuring as possible. "Were you ever alone with Mr. Gibbons?"

This time, Charlie nodded. A wave of emotion—terror, panic, anger—washed over me, leaving me breathless and almost dizzy. I wanted to ball my hands into fists and scream. *No. No! Not my son. Not my sweet, funny, innocent son. Not Charlie, please God, not Charlie.* And suddenly I found myself negotiating with a God I wasn't even sure I believed in:

Dear God, do anything to me, anything at all, and I will take it. But pleasepleasepleaseohGodplease, don't let it be possible that Charlie was hurt. Please, that's all I will ever ask of you, please just to keep him safe. If you do that, I'll even start believing in you. Do we have a deal? Do we?

I realized I was holding my breath and had to remind myself to inhale, exhale, inhale again.

"Charlie," I said, and I was stunned to hear how calm I sounded. "Did Mr. Gibbons ever touch you in an inappropriate way? In a place that he shouldn't have been touching you?"

Charlie bent his head forward so that I couldn't see his face. I knelt down in front of him on the boardwalk. I plucked the ice cream cup out of Charlie's hands, and set it on the weathered bench beside him. Charlie clasped his hands together, but I pried them gently apart and held them. He still wouldn't look at me.

"Honey, it's okay. You can tell me anything. I won't be angry at you, or upset…but I have to know." I wondered if Charlie could hear my heart beating, because of how hard it was thumping against my chest. So hard, it was physically painful.

Charlie still didn't speak, so I gave his hands a soft shake.

"Charlie?" I said again, and this time I couldn't keep the quaver out of my voice.

Charlie lifted his head and looked straight at me. There were tears streaming down his cheeks.

CHAPTER 8

Will didn't get home until nearly ten o'clock that night. I knew he was going to be late. The managing attorney at his law firm was wooing a potential candidate, and had asked Will to join them for dinner. At least, that's what Will had told me he was doing. I had no reason to think he was lying, but I actually didn't even care. If Will was having an affair, today's news had knocked that to the bottom of my list of concerns.

"Hello," Will called out, entering through the side door from the garage.

"I'm in the living room."

He came in, still wearing his tie, although he had his jacket off and slung over one arm. He looked at me curiously. "What are you doing?"

I was curled up on the couch, holding an enormous glass of red wine, wanting only to numb myself after the onslaught of emotions of the day. I'd brought Charlie straight home after our talk by the river. He'd showered and gotten into his pajamas early. I made him pasta for dinner just the way he liked it—

with butter and lots of grated parmesan cheese, no tomato sauce. We'd watched *Toy Story*, which was still his favorite movie, although he was probably getting a little too old for it. I wanted him to have a quiet night, filled with all the things that made him feel safe.

And the entire time, all I could think about how sure I'd been that I would know if something bad had happened to Charlie. How could I have been so foolish, so completely self-deluded? It kept washing over me, the pain so intense, it took all of my self-control not to curl up into a ball and weep. But I had to keep it together for Charlie's sake. I hadn't yet told Will about what had happened. It just wasn't the sort of news you conveyed over the phone, not if you could help it. It also gave me extra time to absorb the horror of what had happened before I had to talk it through with another adult.

"How was your dinner?" I asked, ignoring Will's question.

"Fine." He shrugged. "I wasn't blown away by the candidate, but most of the other partners like him. We'll probably extend an offer."

"Why didn't you?"

"I'm not sure. He was fine. A bit of a suck-up, although I guess that's standard for job interviews." Will sat down heavily at the other end of the couch and loosened his tie. "What's new here at Casa Clarke?"

"Quite a lot, actually." I drew in a shaky breath, and ran a hand through my hair. "I have news. It's not good."

Will's expression turned serious. "What's going on?"

I hesitated, dreading that this moment had arrived. Right now, Will was smiling, looking slightly buzzed from the cocktails he and his partners had undoubtedly ordered with dinner, happy—or happy enough—with his lot in life. He might resent me, dislike his job on occasion, fret about our finances... but once I told him what I knew, he'd long for the days when those were the worst of his problems.

"Nat, you're scaring me. What happened?"

I told him everything Charlie had told me. How Robert Gibbons had approached Charlie on the fifth grade camping trip at Jonathan Dickinson State Park in early December. How he'd asked Charlie to help him set up his tent, and then, once the task was completed, suggested Charlie come in to admire his deluxe tent. How once they'd been alone, he'd told Charlie his story about ancient Greek men having relationships with young boys, as a rite of passage.

"He didn't know what that meant," I said, my mouth dry, my throat scratchy. "He thought it had something to do with the *Lord of the Rings* movie, when Gandalf tells the fire demon he can't pass."

Robert had explained, it was something slightly different… and could he show Charlie what he meant? Charlie had agreed. That was the point that he kept coming back to, through his tears and his stuffy nose and the sobs that caught in his narrow chest. *He had agreed.*

I stopped then, unable to go on. I touched a hand to my cheek and found it was slick with tears. I hadn't even realized I'd been crying. I looked up at Will to see that his cheeks were wet, too. I reached a hand out to my husband, but he ignored it. Instead, he suddenly stood, turned and took a few stumbling steps toward the kitchen.

"Where are you going?" My voice was a croak.

Will didn't respond. Instead, he made a fist and punched the wall.

"Jesus!" I stood. "What the hell are you doing?"

Will stared down at the wall, which had a large, noticeable dent in it, then looked down at his hand.

"You're bleeding," I said. I stood and went to the kitchen. I dampened a paper towel and tried to hand it to Will. He ignored it and went straight for the cabinet where we kept the liquor, pulling out a bottle of Scotch and banging the door shut

Will retrieved a glass from the cupboard near the sink and filled it close to the brim with the Scotch. I tried again to offer him the paper towel, but he waved me away.

"Charlie." Will closed his eyes and I knew that he was reliving our son's life. The helpless red-faced newborn. The jolly baby who loved to giggle. The toddler who got into everything and anything, so that we had to secure the whole house with safety locks and bumpers just to keep him safe.

But we hadn't kept him safe, after all. And I would never forgive Will or myself for that.

"How is he? I mean, I know he must be traumatized and upset, but…is he okay?"

"I think so. For now. I'm going to make an appointment for him with a child psychologist tomorrow."

Will nodded. "That's a good idea. It will give him someone to talk to. Other than us, I mean."

"I just need to make sure I find someone who's had experience in…this. Someone who will be in a position to help Charlie get through it. To heal."

"Should we take him to a medical doctor? Have him examined?"

"Charlie told me that the abuse was all touching, that there wasn't any…" I stopped, swallowed. "Penetration."

"Jesus Christ."

"I was concerned that having a doctor examine him—" I began.

"It might feel like another violation," Will concluded. He shook his head. "We've known Robert for years. He's been in our house, eaten at our table! How could he do this to Charlie? To us?"

I longed to go to my husband, to put my arms around him, to press my face against his chest. But something stopped me. I couldn't even remember the last time we'd touched, much less held one another. The space between us had grown too wide. When had that happened?

"What are we going to do?" Will asked.

"Well," I began slowly. "I've been thinking about that."

I hadn't been able to think about anything else since Charlie had told me.

"Have you called the police?"

"No."

"I guess we'll have to do that first thing in the morning."

"No." I shook my head. "*No. We are absolutely not* calling the police."

Will squinted at me, as though we were in a dark, smoky room, instead of our well-lit kitchen. "What? Why not? Is there someone else we should contact first? Like, a guardian ad litem or something?"

"No, of course not." Will had limited experience with criminal law, I knew, but the course had been a requirement when we were in law school. I wondered just how drunk he was. "Those are for kids who need someone to represent them to the court. Kids with abusive parents or no parents or who have chaotic lives that require extra help."

"So who do we report it to? We have to tell someone!"

"Do you know what will happen if we report this?"

Will stared at me silently. I had never seen my hale, preppy husband look so bloodless, so sickly white.

"First of all, the police will question Charlie," I continued. "They'll do their best to be kind and gentle, but they'll ask him about it again and again and *again*, to make sure that his story holds up through the retellings. Then, they'll have him examined by a doctor, who will also hopefully be kind and gentle, but who will be required to check him over thoroughly and intimately. Next, they'll have him meet with a social worker, who will, again, probably be a very nice person, we would hope, but her job will be to get Charlie to go into as much detail as

possible about the abuse. How he was touched, what he himself touched, what he saw, what he was told…and, just like the
police, she will take him through it again and again and again.
And that's just the beginning of the nightmare.

"If this case goes to trial, the defense attorney will have the
right to depose Charlie, and then anything goes. The defense
lawyer can—and probably will—ask Charlie if you or I ever
touched him in a way that made him uncomfortable or if his
grandparents did or one of his teachers. He'll ask Charlie if he
ever lies, and if so, how often, about what does he lie and has
he ever gotten someone else in trouble. And then he'll ask him
if he has anything against Robert, a grudge, or if he ever felt
like he was treated unfairly at school, ever saw anyone treated
unfairly, if that made him angry. And, if the defense attorney
has done his job, by the end, Charlie will be questioning himself. Did the abuse happen exactly as he thought? Or is it possible that he imagined part of it, maybe even all of it? Or maybe
it didn't happen the way he thought, and how can he now be
sure what really happened?

"And that's before it even goes to trial. Because that's where
Charlie will have to get up on the stand, in front of the judge,
and all the lawyers and deputies and six strangers sitting in the
jury box. Let's not forget he'll also have to face his school principal, who he's accused of doing terrible things to him. All of
them will be staring at Charlie and judging him while he is
forced to yet again go into painfully explicit detail about what
Robert did to him.

"Then one of two things will happen. Behind door number
one—Robert is convicted, which could possible give Charlie
some sort of closure, whatever that means, and Robert will go
to jail for a really long time. But Charlie will always wonder if
he did the right thing, second-guessing himself, because don't
forget, it will already have been planted in his brain that he
might not have remembered exactly what happened, after all.

Or, behind door number two—Robert is acquitted, and possibly goes on to hurt other kids. Charlie will spend the rest of his life wondering if he could have prevented that by being a better witness. And either way, he'll *always* be known as that kid who was molested by the principal. Even though these sorts of cases are supposed to be confidential, it will get out that it was Charlie. It always does. Do you have any idea what the drug and abuse rates, not to mention suicide rates, are for kids who have were sexually abused? They're astronomical."

I stopped to take a breath. My heart was pounding again. I shook my head definitively. "No. We're not putting Charlie through that."

Will sat down heavily on one of the tall stools lined up by the island. "So, what then? You're hoping that the other kid… wait, what's his name again?"

"Tate Mason."

"Right. Are you hoping that his testimony will put that fucking monster in jail? That we can keep Charlie out of all of it?"

I poured some more merlot in my glass. I didn't normally drink this late—it kept me up—but I doubted I'd be sleeping much that night, anyway. I pulled a stool out and away from the island counter, and leaned back against it.

"I'll be very surprised if Tate's case goes anywhere," I said softly.

"Why? What's going on?"

"Tate shared a hotel room with three other boys on the seventh grade class trip to St. Augustine. All three of them have said that they were always together, with Tate, and that there was never a time when Tate could have been alone with Robert. It will be Tate's word against theirs. And Robert's."

"Tate lied about it?"

I shrugged. "I don't know. It's possible that he's not being truthful about when or where the abuse happened. But no, I definitely don't think he made the whole thing up."

"How do you know?"

I closed my eyes for a minute, took in a deep breath, then looked at my husband. "Because Tate told his mom that when the abuse happened, Robert told him it was a normal practice in ancient Greece for older men to teach younger boys about sex."

"That's exactly what he said to Charlie."

I nodded. "I know."

We were quiet as Will absorbed this grotesque bombshell. I sipped my wine, even though I didn't even want it anymore, even though it tasted like vinegar in my mouth. When I looked back up at Will, I saw that he was wiping at his eyes.

"I know you don't want to go to the police. But if both boys are saying the same thing—that Robert told them both the same thing—wouldn't that make the case against him stronger?" Will's voice was a plaintive bleat.

"Of course," I said. "If their cases were tried together, although any half-competent defense attorney won't let that happen without a fight. They'll move to sever the cases, and have them heard separately. And the boys wouldn't be allowed to testify in each other's case. That's considered bolstering. It's not allowed."

"The entire system is fucked? That's just great." Will stood to splash more Scotch in his glass.

"Actually, because we're in such a conservative county, juries here always skew pro-prosecution. But none of that matters, because we're not putting Charlie through any of it."

"We can't just do nothing," Will insisted. "Especially if the other kid's case isn't strong. We can't just let Robert get away with it. What if he goes on to hurt another kid? If we don't do anything to stop him, that will be on us."

"Oh, no, we're going to do something."

"What? If you don't want to go to the police, what can we do? What options do we have?"

I set my wineglass down on the granite counter. I suddenly

remembered back to when we were remodeling the kitchen. I had spent hours, days even, worrying about the countertops. Granite? Quartz? Butcher block? And what color—gray, white, the cool black swirly one that Will had rejected immediately but I thought would make a stylish choice? I had thought that if we had the perfect kitchen, it would create the backdrop for our perfect family life—eating meals together at the island, teaching Charlie how to make meatballs, rolling out pastry dough for summer peach pies. Looking back, it all seemed so naive. Who the hell cared about what your countertops looked like when there were children out in the world *right this minute* being hurt? When *my* child had been hurt?

I looked squarely at my husband. "We're going to kill Robert."

CHAPTER 9

Will stared back at me. "You can't be serious."

"I'm completely serious. It's all I've thought about since Charlie told me what Robert did to him. It's the only real choice we have."

Will stood and held up his hands, palms facing outward toward me, as though he was worried I was about to run at him. "Stop it. This is crazy talk."

"Why is it crazy? You just said yourself we have to do something. We can't just let Robert go on, molesting other kids, ruining more lives."

"Then we report it to the police. I know it will be tough on Charlie—"

I cut Will off. "You don't know *anything* about how tough it would be on him. I've worked on these cases. I've seen what happens. We're not putting Charlie through that."

"And his parents being convicted for murder wouldn't be tough on him?" Will asked. "Jesus, Nat. We'd both go to prison for the rest of our lives."

"Don't you remember our very first date? When you told me that you and I were smart enough to get away with murder?"

"I was trying to impress you! Hell, I was trying to get you into bed." Will ran a hand through his hair—the same one he'd just punched the wall with—and winced. "I wasn't proposing that we actually go out and start killing people, like a couple of sociopaths."

"Sociopaths lack empathy and don't have a conscience. We would be removing a bad person from the world. It's not the same thing at all."

"What happened to Charlie is awful and horrible. Don't you think I'm upset, too? But we aren't the first parents to go through something like this. Normal people go to the police. They don't become vigilante killers."

"And they're wrong to do so," I retorted. "No one should put their trust in the criminal justice system. It's broken beyond repair. Guilty people get off, innocent people go to jail and no one's life is ever improved in any way."

"I can't deal with this." Will turned away from me. "I'm going to bed."

"We can't do nothing," I said to my husband's back.

Will stopped, and pivoted back around. He looked terrible. His eyes were bloodshot, and the color was gone from his face, making him look pale and vulnerable.

"I know you're upset," Will said. "I am, too. We'll talk about it more tomorrow when we're both calmer."

I nodded, but I didn't follow Will upstairs. Instead, I sat there at the kitchen island for a long time, slowly turning my wine-glass in one hand.

I thought about keeping Charlie home from school the next day, but he insisted on going. "Why wouldn't I go?" he said. "We're going to start our egg drop experiment today."

Because the man who was in charge of that school up until Monday harmed you, I thought. *Because I never want to let you out of my sight, ever again.*

Instead, I said, "Have you decided how you're going to protect your egg?"

"No, but I don't have to yet. We just have to write out our hypotho-thingy today."

"Hypothesis?"

Charlie nodded and took a bite of the peanut butter toast with honey I'd made for him. I wanted to grab him, hug him tightly to me, but I also didn't want to frighten him. It was probably best to keep him on his routine, I thought, which meant that school might not be a bad idea.

I remembered back to the previous day, when Jennifer Swain told me she wouldn't ever let Tate and Zoë return to Franklin. I wondered if we should keep Charlie enrolled at the school he was used to, where he had friends and knew his teachers, even though it was where his abuser still officially worked. Or was it better to give him a fresh start, where Robert's specter wouldn't be omnipresent, but where he'd also have to make new friends and find his way in the middle of an already troubling time? I'd add that question to the list I'd already started for the child therapist I planned to call that morning. At least I knew Robert wouldn't be anywhere near Franklin School, at least not today.

Will walked into the kitchen, freshly shaved and dressed for work. When he saw Charlie sitting at the table in his pajamas, munching on his toast, he froze, staring at the back of his son's head. Will looked at me, his face stricken. I shook my head at him, silently beseeching him not to pick this moment to talk to Charlie about what he'd gone through. Will seemed to understand what I was trying to communicate, as he nodded and rubbed Charlie's back.

"Hey, kiddo," he said. "How'd you sleep?"

"Good," Charlie said through a mouthful of peanut butter toast. "What happened to the wall?"

"The wall?" Will repeated. I saw him glance at the back of his hand. The knuckles were bruised from where he'd punched the wall the night before.

"Yeah, in the other room. It looks like someone hit it with a hammer."

"Oh…I banged into it," Will said. "I guess I'll have to get that fixed at some point."

"Did Mom tell you about my egg drop project?"

"No, she didn't. Why don't you fill me in?" Will sat down at the table across from Charlie, who launched into a long, detailed discussion of the various ways you could protect an egg dropped from a second-story balcony. Will listened intently, nodding his thanks when I handed him a mug of coffee.

For just a minute, watching the two of them talking over Charlie's school project at the breakfast table, while the sharp morning sunlight streamed into our kitchen, I was almost able to fool myself into thinking that everything was normal with my small family.

But then, the memory of what Charlie had told me the day before came rushing back, knocking my breath out of my chest. I had failed to protect my son and there was nothing I could do to change that. However, I could—and would—stop him from being hurt again. I would do whatever I had to do to protect my family.

I rinsed out my coffee cup and set it in the sink.

"Charlie, you'd better go get dressed," I said. "Or else you're going to be late."

Charlie obediently hopped up from the table, leaving behind his empty plate and juice glass, then headed upstairs to his bedroom. I would normally have called him back to clean up after himself, but I let it go, just this once.

"Are you sure school is the best idea?" Will asked quietly.

"No," I admitted. "I'm not sure about anything. But he says

he wants to go, and I think that keeping him on his schedule can't be a bad thing."

"What if the kids in his class are talking about…you know…?" Will's voice trailed off and he glanced up at the ceiling, as though worried that Charlie would be able to overhear us a floor away.

"They won't know about Charlie."

"No, but I have to imagine they'll eventually hear about the other boy, right?"

"I don't know. Probably." I shrugged helplessly. "I don't think there are any easy answers. We both want to protect him, but we also don't want to focus on it too much, right? I have to imagine that it's important to give him a sense of normalcy right now."

"You're probably right," Will agreed. He shook his head, and I could tell from the dark shadows smudged under his eyes that he hadn't slept much, either. Instead, we'd lain side by side in bed, not touching, both wide-awake until the weak morning sunlight began streaming in through the linen drapes. "We should probably get some professional help on how to best deal with this."

"I'm going to call a child therapist this morning to make an appointment for Charlie. I'm hoping when we meet with her, she'll be able to answer these questions. What we do, how we best handle everything."

"Good idea. Let me know what you hear." Will finished his coffee and stood. "I have to get into the office early. Do you want me to drop Charlie off on my way?"

"No, thanks, I'll do it. I have some errands to run this morning."

"Look, about last night," Will began. "I think we should talk about it."

I waved him off. "Forget about it. I was upset. It was the wine."

"Are you sure? Because you seemed pretty set on—" Will stopped, turned to check that Charlie hadn't come back into the kitchen. He needn't have worried. When Charlie descended the stairs, it always sounded like a herd of eleven-year-olds clattering down, rather than one single boy. Still, Will lowered his voice to a whisper before he continued. "A vigilante approach."

"I was angry."

"I know. I'm just as angry as you are. There's a part of me that wants nothing more than to drive over to Robert Gibbons's house and punch him repeatedly in the face until it's a bloody pulp."

"And the other part of you?"

Will shrugged. "That's the part that went to law school. That doesn't want to jeopardize my family or my freedom, just for the sake of revenge."

"Revenge?" I looked at him, surprised. "Who said anything about revenge?"

"Wouldn't that be the main motive?"

"No. The only motive, or at least the only one that matters, would be to stop him from ever hurting another kid. Revenge wouldn't have anything to do with it. But, like I said, forget about it. I was upset and venting."

"Good." Will looked relieved. "Let's talk about it later. We'll figure out what to do together. Okay?"

"Of course," I said.

I dropped Charlie off and watched him walk into school. He immediately sought out his friend Jack, who was clearly thrilled to see him. Jack launched into a story that involved windmilling his arms around wildly. Charlie grinned at whatever Jack was saying, nodding along happily. He looked fine, I thought, normal, even. I wondered how this sort of trauma worked. Was it something he was always aware of, always feeling bad about… or did it come and go, like a panic attack that hits when your guard is down?

I realized that I was clenching the steering wheel so tightly, my knuckles were white. I loosened my grip and pulled away.

As I drove, I made two phone calls—one to Stella, to let her know that I wouldn't be at the office until later that morning, and one to Camilla Wilson, the child therapist Jennifer Swain had mentioned to me the day before. Neither answered their phone, so I left a detailed message for each.

I tossed my phone into my handbag. As I drove, I went over my mental to-do list for the day. I had a few errands to run. Then I'd have to do some extensive research.

If I was going to plan and execute a murder all on my own, I had a lot of work to do.

CHAPTER 10

My first errand was to the bank, where I withdrew eight hundred dollars. This was a bit of a risk. If the police ever investigated me as a suspect, they'd look for unusual withdrawals. I normally used my debit or credit cards to make purchases, and rarely made large cash withdrawals. But I figured that if it came down to it, I could explain it away—groceries, dinners out paid for in cash, perhaps a new handbag.

Next, I drove to Best Buy. I needed a computer I could do some research on and then easily destroy once this was all over. I didn't want to leave a digital trail of bread crumbs behind. I browsed through the selection of laptops for sale before finally settling on an inexpensive tablet. I checked out, paying cash for it.

I was probably being overly cautious, because although Best Buy had a selection of cell phones for sale, I instead left and headed to Walmart to buy one. I normally hated how many ugly big-box stores had sprung up along US 1, but I saw now they had their uses. I doubted that by the time Robert's death was

being investigated—if it was ever investigated as a homicide—
anyone would bother scouring the security tapes of local chain
stores to see if there were school parents there buying everyday
items like tablets and phones. Still, it seemed like a good idea to
use an abundance of caution when planning a crime that could
potentially land me in prison for the rest of my life.

I purchased a cheap prepaid flip phone at Walmart, again paying in cash, although I did have to ask the electronics clerk to
unlock it off the antitheft hook it was hanging from. He didn't
seem to take any note of me at all, even whistling softly as he
scanned the phone and a card to load it with minutes, and pro-
cessed my payment. The whole transaction took less than ten
minutes.

I wasn't entirely sure if I would need a phone, but I figured
it was safer to get one just in case. I wouldn't be able to take my
smartphone with me when I went to kill Robert. I'd defended
several cases where the police had been able to determine that
my client was near the scene of the crime by subpoenaing the
suspect's GPS records from his wireless service provider.

There was a Starbucks a mile away from the Walmart. I
stopped there next. I bought a latte and took it to a table located
next to a power outlet. I plugged the new tablet in, and logged
on to the internet. I knew that using a public Wi-Fi connection
was a risk, but I figured it was a small one. After all, I wasn't
going to run an internet search on "best way to kill someone
without getting caught."

I had already spent most of the previous night thinking about
how I wanted to kill Robert. It hadn't taken very long to whit-
tle down the possibilities.

First and foremost, I wanted Robert's death to look like a suicide. It wasn't that I shied away from violence and bloodshed
on moral grounds—this was the monster who had hurt my little boy, after all. He deserved a messy end. I had never been a
violent person, but ever since Charlie told me what Robert had

done to him, I had been consumed by a simmering fury I didn't know I was capable of. I would happily slit Robert Gibbons's throat without hesitation and watch his life bleed out of him.

But a straight-up homicide would guarantee a police investigation. Shoreham was not exactly a hotbed of criminal activity. A murder would get a lot of attention, especially with such a notorious victim. The focus would quickly shift to the parents of one of his victims. No one knew yet that Charlie was counted among those who'd been hurt, but I couldn't be sure that would always be the case. And besides, I didn't want Jennifer and Peter Swain, or anyone else for that matter, to be falsely accused.

No, if I was going to pull this off, I needed it to look like Robert Gibbons, outed as a pedophile and facing a lifetime in jail, had despaired at the ruins of his life, only to see death as the way out. The police had to believe he'd committed suicide, so that there wouldn't be an investigation into his death.

My next step was to narrow down how to go about killing him, and successfully make it look like a suicide. When I first decided that Robert needed to die, I had hoped that Will would help me. I had been going to the gym three or four times a week and was in decent shape, but there was no way that I—a one-hundred-forty-pound woman—would be able to move Robert's body around on my own. He was a tall, broad man, and easily weighed well over two hundred pounds. That meant setting his death up as a hanging was out of the question, as was somehow knocking him out and then wrangling his body to his car to make it look like he'd died by carbon monoxide poisoning.

I could shoot Robert, but making that look like a suicide would bring far too many problems—I'd have to get a gun, one that couldn't be traced, and shoot him in a way that would fool a ballistics expert into believing the wound was self-inflicted. Besides, I didn't have any experience with guns. It seemed like a highly risky option.

This brought me to the favorite weapon of female murderers

in the sort of old-fashioned detective stories that take place in English country homes—poison.

But what kind of poison would I use? And exactly how was I going to administer it without Robert detecting it before he'd ingested a lethal amount? That was what I needed to figure out.

I pulled open the search engine and typed "best drugs for committing suicide" into the search box. I took a sip of my latte, drew in a deep breath and prepared to jump down a particularly twisted cyberspace rabbit hole.

I suppose I shouldn't have been surprised by how many websites and message boards there were devoted to discussing methods of suicide. But the earnest and spirited discussions on favored methods were disturbing.

Post by KatyBird on the message board ThisIstheEnd.net:

I bought the razor blades yesterday. Last night, when I was taking a bath, I imagined what it would be like to cut into my skin. I felt so peaceful, so relieved. I think I'm almost ready. I just need to figure out when. My boyfriend will be disappointed if we miss prom. J

Other posters responded to her post:

BlingBling10: That's so exciting, KatyBird! Let us know when you settle on a date.

Nuggin: Blades, huh? I thought you were gonna go with rope.

KatyBird: Yeah, not totally sure. Still thinking about it.

Nuggin: That's cool.

PopTartlet: I've been trying to figure out the best date thing too. I don't want to miss anything important, kwim?

I blinked and read the entry again. I knew teenagers could be melodramatic and self-centered, but were they really social networking their suicides? Ready to die, but not wanting to miss out on opportunities for awesome Instagram photos? It was equal parts disturbing and sad. I checked the dates and saw that the posts had been written over a year earlier. I hoped to God it was a stage they'd all outgrown.

Another poster, Almost Time, wrote out a long post describing his plan to kill himself using a suicide hood, which was apparently basically a large plastic bag that you placed over your head and sealed with duct tape:

Then all you have to do is get a canister of helium and run a hose into the hood, which you use to cover your head. Once the gas is turned on, the oxygen inside the hood will eventually be replaced by the helium. Death is peaceful, and only takes about ten minutes.

He sounded more mature and steadfast than the teenage posters had been. I clicked on his name. From his history of posts it appeared he was in his late thirties and had been diagnosed with pancreatic cancer a few months before he began posting on the forum. His posts were melancholy but straightforward—he didn't want to die, but since it was going to happen anyway and soon, he wanted to make a less painful exit from the earth. After near daily posts over a three-week period of time, his activity on the page had stopped abruptly in January.

I breathed in sharply and felt tears sting my eyes. Then I shook my head, trying to shake off my sadness for this poor man. I needed to stay focused.

I contemplated the suicide bag before reluctantly setting the idea aside. I liked that it masked the cause of death, but there were too many downsides. It would be hard to subdue Robert long enough to get the bag on over his head. And I could hardly wheel a tank of helium into his house without Robert—or one of his neighbors—noticing.

Actually, maybe I didn't have to worry about being seen entering the Gibbonses' house. Robert and Venetia had opted to build a house to the west of town on several acres of land. At the time, they said they wanted to avoid having to deal with homeowners associations and zero lot lines, even if it meant a longer daily commute. Robert had kept the house after the divorce.

I returned my attention back to the search results. There were quite a few web pages devoted to discussions about which drugs were lethal in large enough doses and how easy to find those drugs were. The problem was how to disguise the drugs. I could grind them up and put them in something, but it would have to mask the bitter taste. I clicked and clicked again, and finally stumbled upon a page discussing the hazards of combining opiates with alcohol.

Robert was a bourbon aficionado. If I could find a way to get him to drink a glass of bourbon laced with some sort of opiate… that might do the trick. But the question was, how?

"Natalie?"

I started. My head snapped up. Heart pounding, I threw an arm over the tablet.

Laura MacMurray was looming over me, a paper cup in hand. She was short and squarely built, with cropped dark brown hair. Laura was wearing her usual uniform of a long tank-top—this one the color of a greenish bruise—over black yoga capris with flip-flops. I'd known Laura for years—our children had even attended a baby music class together—but I'd never warmed to her.

"Laura…you startled me. Hi." I quickly flipped the tablet over, so she wouldn't be able to see what I was reading. Laura was exactly the sort of person who would read over my shoulder.

"I meant to call you the other day. I accidentally hit my horn in the car line. You probably thought I was honking at you to get off your phone, or whatever it was that was distracting you, but it was just a mistake," Laura blathered.

"I didn't even notice," I lied. "But I wasn't on my phone."

"Well, you know how some people are today. They can't go five minutes without checking in on their social media feeds. I think it's actually a really sad statement on our society these days. Everyone's turned into a phone zombie, even the mothers."

"I wasn't on my phone," I repeated. "I was just making sure that Charlie was okay."

"Why? Does he have separation anxiety when he goes to school? He's a little old for that, isn't he? Although I suppose it does take some kids longer to mature. You can't rush them. Quinn's never had that problem, but she's always been ahead of the curve. I think she has an old soul. Are you working?"

Laura tilted her head and looked doubtfully at the tablet lying facedown on the table.

"No, I was just reading…something." *God*, I thought. *Could I sound any more guilty, like I'm absolutely up to no good?* Which might technically be true, but it certainly wasn't something I wanted Laura to clue into. "The news," I added lamely.

"Do you mind if I sit with you for a minute while I finish my green tea?" Laura didn't bother to wait for a response before she sat down across the table from me.

Actually, I did mind. I minded very much. The idea of making conversation with Laura, with her odd rictus smile and smug, self-satisfied opinions on today of all days was maddening. I wanted nothing more than to tell her to fuck off and leave me alone, so I could continue to plot the murder of the monster who had hurt my child.

But I couldn't do that, so I forced myself to smile. "Of course not."

"Were you at the meeting Monday night? Could you believe your ears?"

My pulse quickened, but I managed to keep my expression neutral. "I know. It was a lot to take in."

"Do you know anything about this Tate Mason? I heard he might have been the one who started the fire in the boys' locker room last year."

Laura leaned forward eagerly, her tongue darting out to wet her chapped lips, greedy for information. Another time, I might have found it amusing that even Laura, with her gluten-free diet, conscious parenting and yoga obsession wasn't above engaging in a little toxic gossip.

Right now, I just wanted to slap her across her smug face.

"No, I don't really know anything about him."

"Really? I thought you were neighbors with his parents. Or, foster parents."

"The Swains. They live in my subdivision, but I don't know them well. Just from school. And Tate's a few years older than Charlie."

"I keep hearing that he's a very troubled kid. Violent, even. Alison Rombould's daughter is in his grade and she said that he acts out in class all the time. Apparently, he even swore at Mrs. Loughlin once. And—" Laura lowered her voice to a stage whisper "—Alison called Principal Gibbons to complain about how disruptive Tate was being. So that might have given him a motive to lie about Robert...you know." Laura looked around back behind her. "Touching him."

My stomach twisted with anger and disgust. It was bad enough that Tate had been victimized by an opportunistic predator. The last thing he needed or deserved was for his character to be gleefully smeared by school mothers. God knew what else Tate had been through in his short life. The hardest thing Laura had to deal with every day was striking the proper pose in hot yoga class. Her ghoulish interest sickened me.

"I doubt that Tate was motivated by revenge," I said evenly.

"It's just a theory." Laura frowned. She'd always hated being contradicted. "That's the problem with letting kids like that into a school like Franklin."

My eyebrows arched. "You mean foster kids?"

"*No.* I mean children who need extra help. It's a small school. They just don't have the resources to handle troubled kids like Tate Mason."

"I should get back to the office." I began to gather my things.

"Did Will tell you that Hugh and I ran into him at The Reef?"

"What? Oh…no. He didn't mention it." I felt a twinge of unease. Will went to The Reef without me? It was an Asian-Floridian fusion restaurant, and had been one of our favorite places though we hadn't been there in a long while. "When was that?"

"Last week. We were sneaking in a midweek date night. I think Will was there with some work colleagues?"

"Oh, right. They've been interviewing candidates for an associate's position at the firm."

Work. Of course that's why he was at The Reef without me midweek. I was actually surprised at the relief that flooded through me. In the wake of Charlie's revelation, I hadn't wasted a single moment of time worrying about whether Will was having an affair. In fact, I'd give anything to return to my previous life—just yesterday—where any of that mattered. My husband's wandering attention, worries that we weren't putting aside enough money for Charlie's college fund, a client spitting in my face. An imperfect life, but one where my son had not been hurt.

"I was just surprised you weren't there with him."

"Why?" I regretted the word as soon as it left my mouth. The last thing I wanted was to give her an opening. "Work meetings are work, even when they're held at nice restaurants. I try to sit them out whenever I can."

"Well, I guess every marriage is different, but Hugh doesn't like to go out in the evenings without me. It's sort of sweet, actually."

Rage flared up, so hot and angry, it took me by surprise. What was wrong with this woman? Why was she so fucking smug about everything?

"Hugh's an exterminator, isn't he?"

Laura stiffened. "He *owns* a pest extermination business, yes."

I waved away this distinction, clearly so important to her. "Well, I don't imagine he has many business dinners to attend, does he?"

Anger was making me careless. There was no benefit to picking a fight with Laura, I knew, but I couldn't seem to help myself. Maybe it was the strain of the past twenty-four hours.

Laura had stopped smiling. "I just thought you might be interested to know that Will was sitting next to a *very* attractive woman that he seemed to be paying a lot of attention to. Is that one of his coworkers? Or maybe it was the wife of one of his partners. Someone who doesn't prefer to 'sit them out.'"

To punctuate her point, Laura lifted her hands and made air quotes around the phrase.

I stood abruptly. "I have to get back to work, Laura. Enjoy your tea."

I swept my new tablet into my bag and turned to stride out of the coffee shop.

Laura MacMurray, I thought. *Fuck her, and everyone like her.*

CHAPTER 11

I left Starbucks and headed to the local wine and liquor super-store to buy a bottle of Blanton's bourbon. I remembered Robert once mentioning that it was his favorite. After a long search, I finally found a bottle tucked up on the top shelf at the end of the whiskey and bourbon aisle. I brought it up to the front of the store to check out. The cashier was a hipster guy in his twenties with sleeve tattoos and an elaborately manicured goatee.

"Nice," he said, nodding his head approvingly. "You really know your bourbon."

"It's a gift."

"Impressive. We don't sell much of this. Only the true connoisseurs buy it."

My pulse sped up and my breath caught in my chest. Damn, the last thing I wanted was for the cashier to remember selling a particular brand of bourbon. But, no, it was probably fine, I told myself. What were the chances that the police would ever know to talk to this particular cashier, much less for him to remember one of the hundreds, or even thousands, of customers he'd checked out? It was one thing to be careful, but there was no need to be paranoid.

"It's for my husband." I forced myself to smile. "He's a big fan."

"Man's got good taste."

The cashier rang up the bourbon. I paid for it with another chunk of my cash.

"Have a great day," he said, handing me my change. "Enjoy."

"Thanks."

My errands finally completed, I drove straight to my office. As I headed over the bridge that arced over the Intracoastal Waterway and drove toward downtown Shoreham, I again considered the chances of getting caught. If the police would ever be able to build a case against me. I'd spent most of the night before running over the possibilities, trying to calculate the risk.

Most criminal cases weren't difficult for the police to solve. They usually had physical evidence and accomplice testimony, often even a confession to rely on. I was always shocked by how many of my clients consented to a police interview, confessed in the middle of it and only then called me. There were many, many people serving time in Florida's prisons who wouldn't be there if they had simply kept their mouths shut.

But the police were just like anyone else. Some of them were dedicated and worked hard at their jobs, some were lazy and ineffective. But either way, the majority of the cases they dealt with were drug-related. They were used to wrapping those up neatly, with a minimum of fuss and effort on their part.

Here's how it normally worked: the police would stop someone they thought looked sketchy, often through a routine traffic stop, and ask to search the car. The suspect, for some reason I could never figure out, almost always granted them permission. The police would find something illegal in the car—drugs, paraphernalia, illegal weapons—and an arrest would be made. The suspect would end up spending weeks, if not months, sitting in jail pretrial, because even if they were approved bail, they almost never had the financial resources to pay for a bond. Eventually, they'd be appointed a public defender. Again, there were good and bad public defenders. Which one you ended up with was a crapshoot. But all the public defenders were overextended and had more cases than they could possibly do justice by. Their usual course of action was to solicit a plea deal from the prosecutor, which often came with the following stipulation—if the suspect agreed to be a confidential informant, and got video of a few friends or associates buying drugs, thereby handing the police another easy-to-prove case, then the charges against them would eventually be dismissed. This system allowed the police and State Attorney's office to put out impressive conviction statistics, while doing a minimum of work.

The cases where the police didn't have a confidential informant or a confession or significant physical evidence were much, *much* harder for them to prove. And even when the police did build a shaky case, I'd seen State's Attorneys give up on them quickly, simply because proving the case beyond a reasonable doubt would be too difficult. No lawyer likes to lose, especially in front of a jury.

The police would certainly treat a murder investigation more seriously than a simple possession case. But the basics of any police investigation were the same. And they would first need evidence that a murder had even happened. If everything went according to plan, Robert's death would be ruled a suicide.

So, yes, I thought I did have a good chance of getting away with murder. The key would be to minimize risks and not make any mistakes. Will might figure out what I'd done, but he would never turn me in.

Or, at least, I didn't think he would.

I parked my SUV in the tiny parking lot outside my office and headed inside.

"Hey, Nat." Stella looked up from her computer when I walked in. "How are you?"

"Good. Anything interesting going on here?"

"Not much. You have a message from Rio Frey." She handed me the yellow message paper. "He wants to know if you can get his parole terminated early. He's paid all of the fines and restitution, and said his parole officer would write him a recommendation."

"I'll call him back," I said. "Anything else?"

"Nope, that's it. It's been pretty quiet around here. What have you been doing? You didn't have court today, did you?"

"No, I was just running errands." I would have to be careful not to disrupt my schedule over the next few days or weeks, however long it took me to put my plan into place. I knew Stella liked working for me, and that she was probably loyal to a point. Still, I wouldn't want her to be able to testify that I had periodically disappeared from the office without explanation or otherwise acted strange in the days leading up to Robert's death. "It looks like I picked a good morning for it."

Stella laughed. "Don't worry, another crime wave will come along. It always does."

I headed back to my office. I had just settled in at my desk when my phone rang. I checked the caller ID and saw that it was Camilla Wilson.

I hit the accept button, then lifted the phone to my ear. I suddenly felt unsteady. Ironically, when I had been figuring out the best way to murder Robert, it had been easier not to think about what Charlie had gone through. The planning allowed me to compartmentalize. Now I was yet again faced with the raw, heartbreaking truth of what my son had gone through. The only reason I knew I'd be able to bear it was that I had no other choice.

When I spoke, my voice sounded higher than normal. "This is Natalie."

"Hello, Natalie, this is Camilla Wilson returning your call. You said in your message that you're interested in making an appointment for your son?"

"Yes. My son, Charlie. He's eleven."

"Can you give me an idea of what's going on with Charlie?"

"Do you want me to tell you now? Over the phone?"

"Why don't you give me as much detail as you're comfortable sharing, so when I meet with Charlie, I'll have a good starting point."

"Okay. Yesterday, after school…" I stopped, suddenly unable to go on.

"Natalie?"

"Yes, I'm here."

"Oh, good, I thought we might have been cut off. What happened yesterday after Charlie got out of school?"

"He told me…he told me…" I flexed the hand not holding my phone, then straightened my hand. It was shaking. I didn't think Stella would be able to hear me, but even so, I lowered my voice to a husky-edged whisper. "He told me he was touched inappropriately. That he was…molested by someone. Not a member of our family. It happened a little over two months ago."

"Do you know who it was?"

"Yes." I hesitated. "But I'm an attorney, Ms. Wilson . . ."

"Please, call me Camilla."

"Okay. Camilla. I know if Charlie or I tell you who molested him, that you'll be obligated to report it to the police."

"And you don't want that," Camilla surmised.

"I'm a criminal defense attorney. I know what happens to kids who go through sexual battery trials."

"I see. Well, if I don't know who molested Charlie, I obviously can't report it. But if I treat Charlie, there may come a time when he wants, or even needs to tell me."

But by then, I thought, Robert would be dead.

"I understand. But I'd like to keep it confidential for now," I said.

"I'm so sorry Charlie and your family are going through this." Her voice was calm, soothing even. "Please don't take this the wrong way, because it is not meant to disparage Charlie, but did you find this allegation credible?"

"Yes." I took in a deep breath, and exhaled it slowly. "I have no doubt in my mind."

Camilla Wilson had a cancellation the following day, a Thursday, right after school. For a long time after we hung up, I stared out at the Intracoastal Waterway and thought of Charlie. The sweet, bright, inquisitive boy he'd always been. And he'd always been so funny, so delightfully silly. Would this change him, the core of who he was? I knew that children were resilient, but sexual abuse had insidious consequences. As I'd told Will the night before, kids who suffered this sort of abuse were at a higher risk to become drug-dependent or depressed or even suicidal. I hadn't told him the other terrible statistic, which was that they often grew up to become abusers themselves, the terrible pattern repeating over again. Pain lapped over me and I squeezed my eyes shut, trying to absorb.

If I had a time machine, I could go back and stop Charlie from joining that camping trip or go back even further in time and enroll him in a different school. But all I could do now was help him heal. I hoped to God Camilla Wilson was as good a therapist as Jennifer Swain had assured me she was.

I turned away from the water. The phone message Stella had written out, with Rio Frey's name and number in stark black print on a faded yellow paper slip, was sitting in the middle of my otherwise bare desk.

I suddenly had an idea. It was risky, for sure...but it might have been the best of the bad choices I had in front of me.

I picked up my phone and made the call.

CHAPTER 12

"You wanted to see me?"

I looked up to see Rio Frey hovering at the door to my office, after Stella had sent him back. He was wearing a T-shirt with a beer slogan, swimming trunks and ratty flip-flops.

"Rio, hi. Come on in."

Rio Frey was a thin, wiry man. He looked older than his thirty-one years, although I couldn't tell if that was due to long-term substance abuse or lack of proper nutrition. It most likely had a lot to do with the fact that he clearly spent most of his time baking in the harsh Florida sun. His hair and eyebrows had been bleached white-blond, and his skin weathered to a dark mahogany.

He ambled into my office and sat in one of the two cantilevered visitor chairs in front of my desk. "I'm hoping to get my parole terminated early. My PO said he'd sign off on it."

"The court usually won't consider it unless you've paid off all of your fines."

"Yes, ma'am. I completed that last week."

I nodded, not surprised. Rio was a repeat customer, usually on drug possession charges, and he knew how the system worked. Actually, I'd always found him to be an interesting character. Despite his rough appearance and checkered criminal history, he'd always struck me as being pretty bright.

I knew a little bit about his background, at least what he'd told me in one of our earlier interviews. His mother had been an alcoholic and neglectful enough that he'd ended up in foster care a few times. He'd never met his father, but he had an uncle who looked out for him, who also periodically employed him at his scrap metal business during those times Rio managed to stay sober.

"I can file a motion with the court," I said. "If your parole officer is on board, we definitely have a better chance."

"He said he'd write a letter."

"Good. The judge will put a lot of weight on that. Although it's always a crapshoot with these sorts of motions, since we're basically asking the court to do us a favor. A lot depends on who the judge is, and what kind of a mood he or she is in that day. But if you have all your paperwork lined up, I'd say we have a fairly good chance of succeeding."

Rio shifted in his seat. "How much do you need to do that? I'm good for it, but like I said, I just finished paying off my restitution last week."

I nodded. One of the realities of criminal defense work was that few clients were able to pay their entire fee up front. Most were on payment plans with the understanding that the entire balance would have to be paid off before their case was fully resolved.

I had a different arrangement in mind for Rio Frey. I just needed to be very careful in how I approached it.

"I thought you might be interested in a trade."

Rio looked at me appraisingly. "What sort of trade?"

"I'll represent you for free. In return, you'll do something for me."

"Something," Rio repeated. "Let me guess, you're not in the market for scrap metal."

"I need some drugs." I kept my tone neutral. "Oxycodone."

"That's not what I was expecting you to say." Rio's lips twitched up in a smile. "At least I know that you ain't a CI."

Rio's latest arrest came about when a buddy he got high with agreed to become a confidential informant for the police, and tried to set Rio up by recording him buying drugs. Luckily for Rio, the video the CI had taken, hidden in a gym bag, had been blurry and the audio too garbled to make out what was being said. The State's Attorney had offered up a plea deal of time served plus probation, which Rio had gladly taken. It was a risk asking Rio to buy the drugs for me. But if he did decide to rat me out at some point in the future, it would be his word against mine.

"I'm not. Although technically, attorney-client privilege doesn't apply to this conversation, because we're colluding to commit a crime," I told him.

Rio's laugh was a rough growl. "I won't tell, if you don't."

"Can you get it for me?"

Rio nodded. "It's not cheap. Eighty milligrams will run you anywhere between sixty-five and eighty bucks a pill. Heroin's a lot cheaper on the street these days."

"No, I definitely don't want heroin. I'll need five pills." Rio nodded, so I took out my wallet, counted out four hundred dollars from my quickly dwindling cash supply, and handed it to him across the desk. "Let me know if you need more than this."

Rio pocketed the money. "I didn't take you for a pill popper."

"I guess everyone needs to dull some pain now and again."

Rio looked at me appraisingly. I noticed for the first time that his eyes were different colors. The right was blue, the left hazel. It was a bit disconcerting.

"I hope you know what you're doing," he said. "That stuff can be real dangerous if you're not careful."

I smiled tightly. "I'm always careful."

"Hi," Will said when he arrived home that evening. He was holding his briefcase, and had his suit jacket slung over one arm. "Where's Charlie?"

"He's up in his room. Last I checked, he was playing a video game on my iPad."

I was in the kitchen preparing dinner. I lifted a mallet and brought it down firmly on the chicken breasts sandwiched between sheets of plastic wrap. When I hit it with a loud *thwack*, Will winced.

"How has he been?"

"Fine, I think." I brought the mallet down again on the chicken with another *thwack*. "He hasn't talked any more about what happened, and I didn't want to push him. I made an appointment for him with a child therapist tomorrow after school."

"Good. Should I plan on going with you? Oh, wait, I can't. I have a meeting with the Greenwald people tomorrow afternoon."

"That's okay. I'm pretty sure it's just a preliminary interview."

"Any idea what to expect?" Will opened the refrigerator door and took out a beer. He twisted the top off and took a long drink from the bottle.

"I'm not exactly sure how this works, but I'm assuming she'll want some background information, then put some time aside to talk to Charlie, and probably to me, too. Hopefully, she'll help us figure out a plan for how we can move forward and help him heal."

Will ran a hand over his face. I imagined my expression mirrored his—tired, stressed, worried. We were going to have to pull it together for Charlie's sake.

As if he could read my thoughts, Will asked, "Are you okay?"

"I'm fine. Why?"

"You're acting odd. You're under a lot of stress, for obvious reasons."

"You don't need to worry about me." *Thwack.* "My mom called earlier. She invited Charlie to stay with her for the weekend."

I remembered Charlie had made plans to have Jack over, and made a mental note to remind him to cancel them.

"Do you really think having him go to your mom's house is a good idea?" Will looked skeptical.

My relationship with my mother, who lived about an hour south of us in Delray Beach, was often difficult. Growing up, she had been an emotionally distant and often highly critical parent, and we hadn't gotten any closer now that I was an adult. It had always seemed to me that she'd considered her job as my mother done on the day I turned eighteen. Now her life was far too full with her golf foursomes, bridge club, and dancing every Friday night at the country club to have much time for either me or my older brother. Because of this, I had expected her to be an equally distant grandmother. But I was surprised by how great she was with Charlie, at least for short periods of time. And Charlie loved staying at her house, which had a huge heated pool and was on a canal, so you could often see manatees or dolphins swimming by her backyard.

I dropped the mallet in the sink, then peeled the plastic off the chicken breasts. I sprinkled them liberally with salt and pepper.

"I thought it might be nice for him to get away for a few days," I said.

"Are you going to tell her what happened to him?"

"God, no. I mean… I just can't imagine her being helpful in any way whatsoever."

"I suppose it's something we should discuss with the therapist—who we do tell, if we tell anyone, and what we say."

Will hesitated. "Have you thought any more about reporting this to the police?"

"I haven't changed my mind, if that's what you're asking. There's not a chance in hell I'm putting Charlie through a police investigation."

Will shook his head. I wasn't sure what he meant by it—that it wasn't what he was asking or that he still couldn't believe I didn't want to go to the police.

"What are we going to do? We can't just let this go on indefinitely. We can't allow Robert to hurt another child. Not now that we know what he is."

"Right now, I think we should wait and see what happens."

"You mean with Tate Mason's case?" Will exhaled loudly.

"Well, yes. From what I've heard, the case against him isn't strong, especially if those other boys will testify that Robert was never alone with Tate. But…"

"But?"

"Juries hate child molesters. The last time I defended a sexual battery on a minor case, the jury was only out for twenty minutes before they came back with a guilty verdict."

"Was your client guilty?"

"He said he wasn't, but who knows? It was his word against the word of his adorable twelve-year-old stepdaughter. The fact that her mother was an angry, manipulative witch, who'd vowed to get revenge on him for divorcing her, wasn't persuasive to the jury. There are lots of people who believe children aren't capable of lying about being abused."

"I can see that," Will said, taking another swig from his beer. "It's hard to imagine a kid making that up. So you think they'll have a good shot of convicting Robert just on Tate's testimony?"

"It's possible." I kept my voice neutral. "And other families might come forward. I'm sure there are other boys who have been affected. Other boys he targeted."

Will set his bottle of beer on the counter and gave me a

searching look. "And what about what you brought up last night? The plan you were proposing?"

I returned my husband's gaze. "I told you, I was just upset."

"Good." Will looked relieved. "I've been worrying about it all day."

"Don't," I said, turning away from him. I dropped the chicken breasts in the preheated frying pan, where they began sizzling violently in hot olive oil. "I would never do anything stupid."

CHAPTER 13

Thursday morning, Stella announced through our office intercom that Rio Frey was there to see me.

"He doesn't have an appointment." There was a hint of disapproval in Stella's voice. She preferred to keep firm control over my schedule.

"That's okay. You can send him back," I replied.

Today, Rio was wearing a pink T-shirt with a picture of a fish on a line on the front, camouflage cargo shorts and the same ratty flip-flops he'd worn to our last meeting. He closed my office door behind him, then hesitated for a moment.

"Come in, Rio. Have a seat."

Rio sat in one of the visitor's chairs, pulled a plastic sandwich bag out of one of his cargo pockets. He leaned forward and set it on my desk. I looked down at the clear plastic sandwich bag. There were five round light blue tablets inside.

"Oxycodone?"

"Eighty milligrams each. Just like you asked me to get for you."

I nodded, satisfied. I didn't think Rio would try to hustle
me, but I'd double-check the numbers stamped on the pills
against an online drug database on my burner tablet later. I had
to make sure he hadn't just sold me generic ibuprofen. I took
the bag and tucked it into my handbag. "Did I give you enough
to cover the cost?"

"More than enough. I even have change for you." Rio set a
crumpled twenty dollar bill and a couple of singles on my desk.

"That's okay, you keep it," I said.

"No, thank you, ma'am. That wouldn't be right."

On another day, under other circumstances, I might have been
amused by Rio's prim refusal to keep the change from an illegal
drug deal. I took the bills and shoved them in a desk drawer.

"Any update on my parole termination?" Rio asked.

"I filed the motion yesterday. It will take a few weeks before
we get a hearing date. I'm pretty sure there won't be a problem,
especially if your PO is on board."

Rio nodded. He was well used to how slowly the legal system moved. "You'll let me know?"

"Of course."

Rio stood, but didn't immediately leave. He raised his tan
arms and scratched his head with both hands.

"I don't want to tell you your business," he finally said, "but
you've always been straight with me. You should be careful with
those pills. They can fuck up your life right quickly."

"I'll be careful," I assured him.

Rio looked at me for a long moment with his odd, two-toned
eyes. Finally he nodded and turned to go. "I guess I'll wait to
hear from you."

"I'll call you when we get our court date," I promised.

That afternoon, after picking up Charlie from school, I parked
my car in front of a pretty aqua-blue bungalow. There was a
discreet black-lettered sign outside that read, Camilla Wilson

MS. Charlie and I both remained seated in the car, staring at the building.

"Why do I have to see a doctor?" Charlie asked.

I shook my head. "She isn't a medical doctor, sweetheart. She's a therapist. She's someone who you can talk to, who will help you sort out how you're feeling."

"What if I don't want to talk to her?"

I thought about this. I didn't want him to feel pressured, especially since I worried that after what he'd been through, he might be feeling a loss of control over his life.

"You don't have to do anything you don't want to. But I think you should wait and see how you feel about it until after you meet her."

Charlie considered this, then finally nodded.

"There's just one thing I need you to remember," I said. "It's important."

"What?"

"I want you to talk to her—to Camilla—about what happened. If you want to. But...you can't tell her who it was that hurt you. That it was Principal Gibbons." The words felt like a betrayal, wrong and unfair. Charlie shouldn't have to keep secrets, not for me. But this was a secret that would protect him, too.

"I don't want to talk about him, anyway." Charlie folded his arms over himself.

"I know. But...you may want to at some point. And if you do, you can. You should. Just...don't use his name. Okay?"

Charlie didn't say anything. I waited a few moments, and finally hit the button releasing my seat belt and got out of the car. A moment later, Charlie followed, and we walked up to the office together. I opened the door, setting off a bell, then held it open for Charlie. After a slight hesitation, he went inside.

There wasn't a receptionist, just a small, neat waiting room with a few chairs, a table covered in magazines and a palm tree in a terra-cotta pot. The inner door opened and a woman stepped out.

"Mrs. Clarke?" she asked.

"Please, call me Natalie." I extended a hand.

"Natalie, then." She shook my hand. "I'm Camilla. It's nice to meet you."

Camilla Wilson was almost absurdly beautiful. She had large almond-shaped eyes, high chiseled cheekbones, full lips and luminous dark skin. She was wearing a yellow sweater set and palazzo pants made out of a slinky black material that allowed her to easily crouch down in front of Charlie.

"And you must be Charlie?"

Charlie nodded shyly.

"I thought so. Hi, Charlie. Do you want to come with me? I have some really cool toys back in my office."

"I'm too old for toys," Charlie answered.

"What do you like to do?"

"Play computer games. And draw."

"Perfect! I have some paper and lots of pencils and crayons. Why don't you come draw a picture for me?"

Charlie shrugged. Camilla stood. "You can come back, too, Natalie."

Camilla's therapy room was large and colorful, with a purple couch, a brightly striped rug and beach-themed pictures on the wall. Charlie sat down at a table that had a roll of paper spread across it and immediately set to work on a drawing.

"Why don't you sit here. There's an intercom, so you'll be able to hear what we're saying," Camilla suggested, gesturing to a table and chairs in an outer room with a window that looked in on the therapy room. I understood at once—I would be able to see and hear them, but be removed enough so that they would be able to talk freely. My stomach unclenched. The idea of Charlie going off with a stranger, even one as lovely as Camilla Wilson, had made me uneasy.

Camilla sat with Charlie while he drew characters from his beloved video games, explaining each one to her in turn. I had given Camilla an outline of what had happened to him the day before when we spoke on the phone. She asked him a few questions about school, which he answered. But when she attempted to guide the conversation toward the molestation, Charlie shut down and refused to talk. Camilla didn't press the matter.

"It's okay, Charlie. Why don't you finish drawing that picture while I talk to your mom for a few minutes," Camilla suggested.

She joined me in the observation room, sitting across the table from me.

"He's reluctant to talk about the abuse, but that's normal," Camilla said. "He has to trust me first, which might take a few sessions."

I nodded. "He hasn't wanted to talk about it at all, not since he first told me."

"That's completely normal. He'll need to talk about it eventually, if he's going to work through his feelings. Kids who've suffered abuse tend to be fearful and anxious, but they also often feel a profound sense of shame. We'll need to make sure he understands that what happened to him wasn't his fault. And that bad things do sometimes happen, and have happened to him, but they don't have to define his life."

Camilla blurred in front me as my eyes filled with tears. I blinked and tried to wipe them away before Charlie saw me. The therapist gently pushed a box of tissues toward me.

"You also have to remember that your feelings are valid, too. It's normal for you to grieve for your son's innocence, and to have a deep and profound anger against the man who did this to him," she said. "You and your husband might want to consider talking to a therapist, either together or on your own. It's quite common for the stress surrounding an outcry statement to cause strain in a marriage or within the family."

I nodded. "I'll talk to my husband about it. We were hoping

you could give us some guidance on how to act with Charlie. Should we try to act as normal as possible? For example, my mom invited him to stay with her this weekend, which he normally would love to do. But my husband isn't sure if it's a good idea for Charlie to be apart from us right now."

"I think that your first goal should absolutely be to create a feeling of normalcy. The most important thing is to make sure Charlie feels safe and protected. If your mother is a safe person for him, I don't see any reason why he shouldn't stay with her, if he wants to. But if he expresses a reluctance to be apart from you, I certainly wouldn't push it."

"Good." I exhaled. "He always has fun when he stays with her. I think it might be good for him."

"Are you going to tell your mother what happened to Charlie?"

"I'd rather not. My mother is…" I stopped and tried to think of the right words. "A very self-centered person. She'll have a breakdown, then find a way to morph the situation around to make it all about her—how much this upsets *her*, how she can't believe *she* has to deal with this. I'll just get angry. I can't imagine any of that is good for Charlie."

"No, it doesn't sound like it would be. However, it's possible that Charlie might exhibit some behavioral issues that your mother will pick up on. For example, kids who have been abused can have mood swings, become angry or sad, seemingly without reason. It's not uncommon for them to regress."

"Okay, I'll watch for that. Should we correct him if we see him doing those things?"

"I'd play it by ear. The most important thing is to be patient and loving with him. Make sure that he feels secure." She hesitated. "I know you said you didn't want to file a police report."

I shook my head. "I've actually defended sexual battery on a minor cases. I know how tough it is on the kids involved."

"That's certainly true in many cases," Camilla agreed. "But

there are children who have gone through the experience of helping to prosecute their accuser who afterward say that they're glad they participated. For some, it gives them back a sense of control over their lives. And many say that it helps them to know that their abuser won't be able to hurt other kids. That can be powerful."

"I'll think about it," I lied.

"I know you're concerned about not wanting to put Charlie through the ordeal of a criminal trial. I totally get that. My priority is to help Charlie heal. And you don't have to make your decision about whether you want to file charges immediately. We can wait a few weeks and see how Charlie's doing then."

I exhaled, my relief profound. A few weeks from now, Robert would be dead. Even if Camilla found out that he was the one who had molested Charlie, her legal obligation to report the abuse would end with his death. In fact, at that point, she would be ethically prohibited from telling the police Charlie had been one of his victims.

"I'm just trying to do the right thing for my son," I said.

"I think you should trust your instincts," the therapist said with a warm smile. "They seem to be good ones."

CHAPTER 14

Mandy called while I was driving Charlie home after his appointment. I hit the call accept button and her voice piped on over the car speakers.

"Hey, where've you been?" she asked.

"What'd you mean?"

"I've called you a bunch of times. Has Laura MacMurray taken over my position as your best friend?"

"What? Why would you ask me that?"

"Dana was going through the drive-through at Starbucks a few days ago and saw you two inside sitting together. She told me about it when I ran into her at sunrise boot camp this morning."

"Oh, good God." I exhaled. "We live in such a small town."

I kept my tone light, but in truth, I was alarmed. I hadn't been able to drink a cup of coffee with an acquaintance I didn't particularly like without being spotted and having the news pass on along via the Shoreham Mom Network. "Why were you having coffee with Laura?" Mandy asked.

"First of all, I wasn't. She ambushed me. And second, I was

drinking coffee. Laura was drinking holistic, detoxifying green tea."

Mandy laughed. "I'm assuming she was trying to dig for dirt on the school scandal. Have you heard the latest?"

I grabbed for my phone, nearly driving off the road as I did so. "Hold on, I need to take you off speakerphone. Okay, there. Go ahead."

"Is Charlie in the car with you?"

"Yes."

"Sorry, I should have asked before I started talking. Me and my big mouth."

I glanced at Charlie, but he didn't seem to be paying attention. He was turned away from me, staring out the window. "It's okay. What's going on?"

"It's unconfirmed, so take it for what it's worth, *but*…I heard that Jennifer and Peter Swain might withdraw the charges against Robert."

"What? Are you sure?" My voice was sharper than I intended, and Charlie twisted around to look at me.

"Mom?" he asked anxiously. "What's wrong?"

I shook my head and tried to smile reassuringly at him. "It's nothing, sweetie."

"Are you okay?" Mandy said in my ear. "You sound upset."

"No, I'm fine. Sorry. I haven't slept well the past few nights."

"I don't think any of us have. It's been an upsetting week all around."

"Where did you hear that? About Jennifer and Peter, I mean."

"Dana told me this morning when I ran into her at boot camp. She said they're having second thoughts."

"Does she know Jennifer?"

"I don't think so, but they have some mutual friends, which is how Dana heard about it."

The Shoreham Mom Network again, I thought. *Nothing in a small town stays secret for long.*

"Which was what, exactly?"

"Apparently, after the other boys on the trip contradicted Tate Mason's story, the police detectives wanted to interview him again, and also have him evaluated by a social worker," Mandy said. Her voice was quiet and somber, so unlike her usual cheerful zaniness. "There's a rumor going around that he might have been abused at a previous foster home, and that could have caused him to act out...to make a false allegation. I don't know if all or any of it's true, but if it is, I can see why Jennifer and Peter might have second thoughts about going forward. Can't you?"

"Of course." My mouth was suddenly so dry, it was hard to speak. "I don't blame them at all."

"I guess there's still an issue about who gets to make the call, since the Swains haven't formally adopted Tate yet. Is that how foster care law works?"

"I'm not sure. I've never practiced family law." I glanced at Charlie again, but he'd returned to staring at the window. "I do know that most of the legislation is set up to protect the best interest of the child, whatever that means."

"If they do withdraw the complaint, do you think Robert will go back to being the principal? I mean, he wasn't officially fired, right?"

"Anything's possible," I said.

My heartbeat had started to accelerate again, pounding insistently in my chest. I realized a part of me had been hoping that Robert would be arrested, and prosecuted for molesting Tate. If he were convicted of that crime, he'd likely spend the rest of his life in in jail. He'd certainly never be able to hurt another child.

And I wouldn't have to kill him.

"I don't know how I feel about that. I know what I said the other day, about how it's not right for a man's life to be ruined by a false allegation. But at the same time, the whole idea of innocent until proven guilty doesn't really sit well when we're talking about a potential predator working at a school. Do you know what I mean?"

"I know exactly what you mean."

I took a deep breath, trying to quell my rising anxiety. If I was going to do this…if I was actually going to kill Robert, I'd have to act quickly. Before he was reinstated at Franklin School. Even if there were parents like Mandy who were ambivalent about his return, the story was already spinning in the direction that Tate was a troubled kid who made a false accusation. Robert would be seen as the victim. Once he was back at the school, even if he remained on good behavior for awhile, I knew that eventually he'd molest another child. He'd irretrievably alter another young innocent life. Another child just like Charlie.

I was not going to let that happen.

I remembered, then, that my mother had invited Charlie to stay with her for the weekend. Could I execute my plan that soon?

"Nat, are you there?" Mandy's voice said in my ear.

"I'm here," I said. "Sorry. I was focusing on the traffic."

"Hold on, the beasties are running wild," Mandy said. I could hear Beatrice's and Amelia's voices rise up in the background, high and indignant. Mandy sighed. "We have drama."

"Go ahead and go," I said. "I'll talk to you later."

"Bye."

I hit the call end button and glanced over at Charlie, almost like it was a compulsion. Check in, check in, check in. *Has anything changed? Is everything okay, or, at least, as okay as it could be considering the circumstances?* I didn't want to ask him over and over again if he was okay, because of *course* he wasn't okay.

"Was Mrs. Breen talking about what Principal Gibbons did to me?"

Charlie's voice surprised me.

"No, sweetie. She wasn't talking about that. Do you remember I told you that—" I stopped suddenly, struggling for the right words. I didn't want to upset Charlie, but I also didn't want to lie to him "—Principal Gibbons also targeted another student? That's who she was talking about. The other kid."

"How do you know?"

"Because no one knows what he did to you. No one but you and me and Dad, and now Camilla."

"Will anyone else find out?"

I hesitated. After a few beats, I realized I wasn't breathing, so I focused on that. Breath in, breath out.

"No," I said carefully.

Charlie nodded and turned to look out the window again. I wondered if he was done talking, the topic so painful, he needed to push it away. But then, still looking away from me, he said, "Principal Gibbons said it was a secret. That I couldn't tell anyone or I'd get in trouble."

I could feel the acid rising up from my stomach, burning up through my chest and into my throat. If Robert had suddenly appeared before me, crossing the street in front of my car, I would have happily pushed my foot down on the gas pedal and run him over, damn the consequences.

"He wanted you to keep it a secret because he knew what he was doing was wrong. But that's not why you shouldn't talk about it with other people."

"Then why?"

"Because what Principal Gibbons did to you isn't your fault and it shouldn't define you. But if other people find out, they'll want to talk about it a lot. I don't want them to ask you those sort of questions—more important, you shouldn't have to answer for his behavior. I think that over time, you'll be glad that other people don't know about it." I took in a deep breath and hoped that I wasn't making a terrible misstep. The last thing I wanted to do was cause more damage. "It's keeping it private for *your* sake, not for anyone else's. But you can always talk to me, and you can always talk to Dad." I took a deep breath to gather my spiraling emotions. "Did you like Camilla?"

Charlie nodded. "She was nice. She liked my drawings."

"I thought she was nice, too. If you want, we'll go back and see her again. You can talk to her, too. It's her job to help kids who've had bad things happen to them."

He thought about this. "What if I don't feel talking about it with her?"

"That's okay, too. You might feel like talking about it some days and not so much other days. I think that's totally normal."

Charlie turned to look out the window again. We drove on for a few minutes in silence. I stopped at the traffic light outside our subdivision and turned on my right turn signal. I was just wondering if I should leave Charlie alone for the moment or try to draw him out further when he finally spoke.

"Okay," he said.

"Okay, what, honey?"

"I'll go see Camilla again."

"Oh…okay. Good," I said. I tried to blink away the tears that were suddenly burning in my eyes before Charlie could see them. I reached over and gently squeezed his arm. "I think that would be a good thing."

Charlie had karate class at six o'clock that evening. I wasn't sure he would be up to it after his appointment with Camilla, but he insisted on going. And Camilla had said that keeping his schedule as normal as possible was important. We swung home so that Charlie could have a snack, and change into his karate uniform, and then headed out again. After I dropped him off at the karate school, I drove to our local home goods store, where I was hoping I'd be able to purchase a mortar and pestle. I wasn't sure if they carried them, but I'd already decided it was too risky to buy a set online. If I had to, I'd drive down to the restaurant supply store in West Palm Beach.

But I was in luck. The home goods store had several different mortar and pestle sets to choose from. I picked out the sturdiest-looking one, a light blue ceramic with a large bowl and a heavy pestle. Then I walked around the store and threw some other items in my cart—throw pillows, cocktail napkins, candles—so that the mortar and pestle wouldn't stand out. I needn't have worried. The cashier who checked me out was a college-aged girl who scanned the items with a bored detachment. I paid for the items with the last of the cash I'd withdrawn.

I loaded the bags into my car, and drove back to the karate school to pick up Charlie. He came running out to my car, flushed pink from the exertion, a huge smile on his face. He looked so much like his normal self that tears suddenly pricked at my eyes. I curled my fist tightly, the nails digging into the soft skin of my palm, to ward them off.

"How was class?" I asked once he climbed into the car.

"Great! We practiced our high kicks, and we did so well that Sensei Jacob let us play scramble ball at the end. I was the last one standing."

"What's scramble ball?"

Charlie's animated description of the game—which, as far as I could tell, was like old-school dodgeball, but with foam balls that didn't sting when they hit you—took up most of the ride home. Will's car was parked in the driveway.

"What's for dinner?" Charlie asked as I gathered up my shopping bags.

"Pork chops."

I suddenly remembered Will's sniping at me about my weekly dinner menu. It had only been, what…four days ago? It seemed like something out of the long-ago past. I remembered how, at the time, I had decided to scrap the plan for baked pork chops, and serve something in its place, just to make a cheap point. Now it was hard to imagine wasting a moment of emotional energy on such triviality.

"Can we have pizza instead?" Charlie asked.

I was about to say no—I'd defrosted the pork chops earlier—but suddenly, as we walked up the brick-paved walk to our front door, I was hit by an intense desire to not cook dinner.

"Pizza sounds great," I capitulated.

Rocket greeted us at the door, leaping gleefully, his large ears pricked high.

"Rocket, I just saw you like an hour ago," Charlie said, but he laughed as the small dog gamboled around his feet.

Will also came out to greet us, still dressed for work, although he'd loosened his tie and wasn't wearing his suit jacket. "Hey, buddy. How was karate?"

Will opened his arms, and Charlie jumped into them. I watched them hug, and saw Will's eyes close as he squeezed his son close to him, and I was overcome with a rush of love for my small family.

Charlie finally broke out of his father's embrace. "Hey, Dad, do you want to play that new video game I was telling you about? The one with the warrior elves that kill everyone?"

"No way. No video games," I said. "Go hop in the shower, then get started on your homework."

"Ugh, homework," Charlie grumbled, but he headed upstairs.

I went into the kitchen with my shopping bags. Will followed and sat at the kitchen table to look at his phone. There was a bottle of sweating beer on the table in front of him.

"Please use a coaster," I said automatically, as I had a thousand times before.

"You went shopping?" he asked, ignoring my request.

"We needed a few things." I set the bags down and Will watched as I unloaded them.

"What's that?"

"This? It's called a 'throw pillow.' Otherwise known as a small decorative pillow that Rocket will soon turn into a dog bed."

"No, I meant the bowl thing."

"It's a mortar and pestle." I set it aside on the counter. "You use it to grind herbs…other things."

"And that's something we need?"

"Yes. I've been looking for one for awhile," I lied. "I'm going to call in an order for a pizza. Will you pick it up when it's ready?"

"Sure, but…"

"What?"

"There's pork defrosting in the sink. I thought that's what we were having."

"Change of plans."

"Okay."

"Is that a problem?"

Will looked at me for a few moments, as though he wanted to say something. But finally he just shrugged and returned to his phone, blanking me out. For once, I didn't have the energy to care.

I had to focus. I finally had all the pieces in place.

Now I just had to go through with my plan.

I waited until Will left to get the pizza. Charlie was in his room, probably breaking the rule about staying off his video game.

Once I was alone in the kitchen—with the exception of Rocket, who settled in on his blue denim dog bed with a self-satisfied sigh—I retrieved the five oxycodone pills from my handbag. I dropped them in the mortar and began to grind them with the pestle. They were harder to pulverize than I'd antici-pated. They didn't crumble like aspirin would. Other than one or two splitting into jagged halves, most kept their solid shape. I stared down at the contents of the mortar, sweat beading on my forehead, wondering what to try next.

Maybe I should use a coffee grinder? I wondered. We had a small electric one, but I wasn't sure if that would be effective grinding pills, which were quite a bit smaller than coffee beans. I could pound them with a hammer, but that would risk spraying bits of the very expensive pills about the kitchen.

I redoubled my efforts, grinding down with as much force as I could exert. But finally, I began to make progress. The pills began to give way, first breaking into larger granules, from which point I was able to grind them into a pale blue and hopefully lethal dust. I worried a bit about the color, but I had to believe it would be masked by the dark amber of the bourbon.

The task finally completed, I carefully scraped the oxy powder back into the sandwich bag with a butter knife, then secured it in the zip pocket inside my handbag. I thoroughly washed the mortar and pestle in warm, soapy water before loading both into the dishwasher and setting it to run on the power scrub cycle.

Will returned with the pizza just as I was finishing up.

"Dinner is here," he announced.

I nodded. "In a minute. I just need to wipe down the counters."

At Will's entrance, Rocket had stood and stretched, giving himself a vigorous full-body shake. He trotted over to Will and looked up hopefully, staring meaningfully at the pizza box.

"Not for you, buddy," Will said. "This is human food."

"Will you call up to Charlie, and tell him the pizza's here?"

"In a minute. I just wanted to ask you first…" Will hesitated, rubbing his face with one hand. He looked weary. I supposed neither one of us had been sleeping well. "How do you think Charlie is doing? I mean, really doing. He just seems so…" His voice trailed off again.

"Normal?"

Will nodded. "It's not like I want him to be upset, obviously."

"No, I know what you mean." I spritzed some cleanser on the counter and wiped at it with a paper towel. "I keep watching for signs that he's stressed or unhappy, but so far he seems okay. He had fun in karate class and said he did well on his math test today. He's excited about going to see my mom this weekend."

"That's encouraging, right?"

"Sure. But he didn't want to talk about what happened with the therapist at all today."

"Oh, that's right. I forgot his appointment was today. What's the therapist's name again?"

"Camilla Wilson."

"Did you like her?"

"I did. She seemed smart and compassionate. And she was great with Charlie. He just wasn't ready to talk to her yet. Of course, he'd just met her, so that may change over time."

"He shut me down when I tried to ask him about it," Will admitted.

"How so?"

"I just told him that I loved him and I was here for him if he ever wanted to talk about what happened. He shrugged, said he didn't. So I didn't push it."

"That's probably the best strategy for now." I tossed the paper towel in the trash and set the bottle of cleanser down on the counter. "I just worry that if he keeps his feelings buried, it will cause problems in the long run. I'm hoping Camilla will be able to help him with that."

"Did you talk to her about what we should do legally? Does she think we should go to the police?"

"She agreed with me that forcing kids to testify against their abuser isn't always in their best interest. Although she did say that it can help sometimes."

"Really? How so?" Will's voice was suddenly eager.

"It depends on the circumstances. But for some kids, it may help to know that they're helping to keep their abuser from hurting other kids."

Will exhaled. "What if that's true for Charlie? If Tate Mason's case doesn't hold up and Robert isn't prosecuted? Is it possible he could go back to his job? Would the school board let that happen?"

I won't let that happen, I thought. But out loud, I said, "I just don't know. I don't think there's any rush to make a decision. Why don't we let Camilla work with Charlie for awhile so we can get a clearer picture of how he's doing?"

"That's true." Will nodded eagerly. "It might help to get her opinion on whether she thinks Charlie is up to being part of a criminal prosecution. I know that's what you're worried about. But if we both think that he seems to be handling all of this really well, and the therapist agrees, then maybe we should move forward with it."

I should have let it go. After all, I was lying to him when I said that we could wait to make any decisions until Camilla had a chance to evaluate Charlie. No matter what she said, I had no intention of ever letting him make a formal complaint.

But it irked me that Will still didn't get why I refused to toss Charlie into the jagged-toothed maw that was our modern criminal judicial system, a world I knew far better than he did. So I didn't let it go. Instead, I placed both hands flat down on the top of the counter and looked my husband in the eye.

"When I was in fourth grade, Barb Hemmings told me that her uncle molested her. I remember it like it was yesterday. We were at a sleepover birthday party, and we were the only two girls still awake. She didn't even know the name for what had happened to her. Instead, she whispered to me that he put his train into her tunnel."

Will paled. "Why are you telling me this?"

"Because Barb and I went on to go to the same high school and graduated together and now we're both on the same alumni Facebook page. And every single time I see her name, whether she's posting about her kids or their new puppy or photographs of her family's latest vacation, I think about what she told me that night."

"Nat."

"Every single time."

"It sounds like your friend turned out all right."

"Who knows? It's possible she has lingering issues related to the abuse and just doesn't want to post about it on Facebook. But even if she went on to have a great life, an amazing life— and I certainly hope she did—it's still how I'll always remember her. As a victim. As the girl who was molested and didn't even have the words to describe what had happened to her. And I'm not going to let that happen to Charlie. I will not let this define how he's seen for the rest of his life by every single person he grew up with."

"The identity of the victim is is supposed to be kept secret," Will said helplessly.

"Go ask Tate Mason's foster parents how that worked out for them."

Will was silent. He slipped his hands into his pants pockets and stared down at our cream tiled floor. "Every time I think about what he did to Charlie, I just… I want to throw up. And then I want to find Robert and I want to hurt him. Badly." He looked up at me, his eyes bright with anger and pain. "Do you know what I mean?"

"Yes," I said, turning away from my husband. "I know exactly what you mean."

CHAPTER 15

It was raining heavily when I pulled into my mother's driveway Friday afternoon. Thunder rumbled ominously in the distance. The squall was typical of Florida weather, where one moment you were blinded by the intense sunlight, and the next it was storming violently. I put my car into Park, but didn't turn it off. Instead, I sat motionless for a few moments while listening to the rhythmic *click-clack* of the windshield wipers.

"Why are we just sitting here?" Charlie asked from the passenger seat.

"Are you sure you want to stay at Gram's this weekend? I'll understand if you don't want to."

Charlie looked at me like I was nuts. "Of course I want to stay. We just drove all the way here. Besides, I want to swim in the pool."

I nodded and turned the car off. My mother, Lindy, had heard us arrive and stepped out on her front porch, shielded from the rain by the overhang.

"Gram!" Charlie hopped out of the car and rushed toward

her. My mother opened her arms and wrapped them around her grandson. I moved slower to get out, putting up an umbrella so I could retrieve Charlie's small suitcase from the back without getting drenched.

It had always surprised me that my mother had turned into such a doting grandmother. Lindy had always seemed irritated by motherhood. She wasn't neglectful—I was always fed and clothed and driven around to various activities. But she never took any noticeable pleasure in spending time with me or my older brother, Patrick. We were always something that had to be dealt with, often with a sigh and aggrieved comment, before Lindy could get away to the tennis club and luncheons that filled her days. Our father, Hal—who passed away shortly after Charlie was born—had been the affectionate one, the parent who had taken more delight in his children.

Patrick now lived in California with his sweet-natured wife, Anna, and their two daughters. Once, on one of the rare occasions when Patrick returned to Florida for a visit, he and I had sat out on my mother's poolside patio that overlooked a canal. Patrick had stared out over the water, the sky ribboned orange and pink, and said, "Do you know she never went to a single one of my basketball games? Dad went all the time, but Mom didn't go to a single one. And I didn't even think it was weird at the time. It's only now, when I spend every weekend running around to the girls' soccer games and softball games and cross-country races that it finally struck me how odd that was."

"It was a different time," I offered. "I don't think there was as much pressure on parents to be so involved back then."

"Maybe." Patrick shrugged and took a long sip from his bottle of beer. "But I remember the other mothers being there in the stands."

In stark contrast, Lindy really did seem to delight in spending time with Charlie. She invited him to stay with her once a month. She always had a list of activities planned whenever he came to visit her. They'd go to the putting green, play board games and bake cookies together.

"Hi, Mom." I wheeled Charlie's suitcase up to the house, sloshing through the puddles on her tile-paved driveway.

"Natalie." Lindy gave me a cool kiss on the cheek. My mother, as always, had her hair set in a lacquered blond bob impervious to the gusts of wind. Her face was immaculately made up complete with eye shadow, contouring blush and lipstick. "Isn't this weather terrible? Come in out of the rain."

I shook out my umbrella and left it beside the front door. Lindy's house smelled like cinnamon room freshener and Joy perfume, the scents of my childhood.

"I can't stay long. The traffic was terrible coming down. It took me over an hour to get here."

"I was wondering what was taking you so long. I expected you here ages ago," Lindy said. She turned to Charlie, and a smile softened her face. "Go look in your bedroom, sweetheart. I got you a present."

Charlie whooped and ran off to the guest room. Once he was out of earshot, I said, "Let me know if Charlie seems upset this weekend."

"Why would he be upset? He loves staying with me."

"I know, he's just…been going through a bit of a tough time right now. So let me know if you see anything that concerns you."

"Why?" Lindy looked at my sharply. "What happened?"

Charlie came running back in then, sparing me from having to dodge Lindy's questions.

"Look what Gram got me!" Charlie held up a rectangular box that contained an overpriced video game he'd been obsessed with ever since playing it at a friend's house.

"Wow." I admired the box. "What do you say?"

"Thanks, Gram!" Charlie hugged his grandmother again.

He looked so happy, so normal, I could feel tears filling my eyes again.

Damn it, I thought, turning away before either of them could see me. I had never been outwardly emotional, but over the past few days, I couldn't seem to stop weeping. It was a normal response to the horror of what had happened to Charlie, I supposed, but I had to keep it together for his sake.

"I'm going to get going," I said. "Come give me a hug."

Charlie was so distracted by the longed-for video game, he didn't seem to notice my reaction and hugged me perfunctorily. I tried to tell myself that this was a good thing. If he'd been uncharacteristically clingy, it would have worried me.

Still, I could feel my mother's sharp eyes on me. It was inconvenient that she would choose that moment to drop the narcissism she normally wrapped herself up in.

"Are you okay?"

"I'm fine," I answered over my shoulder.

"Do you have plans for the weekend?" Lindy asked as she trailed me to the front door.

"Just errands," I said. "I have a few things I need to take care of."

"Well, try to take some time off, too. You and Will should go out to dinner. It's important to spend time together as a couple."

I don't know what surprised me more—the marital advice or how unusually caring her voice was.

"I'll keep that in mind." I looked back into her house, to where Charlie was sitting in the middle of the floor, ripping open the box to get to the game inside. "Take care of my boy."

"I always do," Lindy said, her tone again tart.

When I arrived back home, Will's car wasn't there. I parked in our driveway and checked my phone. Will had sent a text thirty minutes earlier saying he was going out for drinks after work with a few of the lawyers in his firm. On any other eve-

ning, this would have irritated me. Tonight, I considered it a
stroke of good luck, as it meant I didn't have to make up an excuse for why I was going to be out of the house.

I went into the house and, after greeting Rocket and letting him outside, I began my preparations. I had thought I'd
be nervous, but once my organizational skills kicked in, I felt
only a sense of calm purpose. I took out everything I'd need
and set it on the kitchen table. The sandwich bag containing
the ground-up oxycodone. The bottle of Blanton's bourbon. A
pair of plastic gloves. A package of cleansing wipes. The burner
phone and tablet, which I planned on destroying and discarding
after it was all over. I put everything except for the bourbon in
my purse, then tucked the bag of oxycodone in my pocket. I
retrieved my smartphone from my bag and hid it in one of the
kitchen drawers with the ringer off, just in case Will beat me
home and wondered why I'd left it behind.

I was ready.

I let Rocket back in the house, fed him and checked the clock.
It was just after six thirty. It was time. I drew in a deep breath
to steady myself and headed for the front door. I glanced out the
window and saw Gloria D'Angelo walk by with her black Lab. I
waited for them to pass. I doubted any of my neighbors closely
monitored my comings and goings, but I thought it was safer not
to talk to anyone, to draw attention to my leaving. Once Gloria had passed by, I let myself out, locking the door behind me.

I got into the car, started it and was just turning to rummage
through my bag to check one final time that I had everything I
needed when a loud rap on my car window caused me to start
and let out a yelp.

I turned to see my next-door neighbor Janice Green standing
there, smiling widely at me. She was wearing a hot-pink velour
tracksuit and bright orange lipstick that had smeared onto her
front teeth. Janice waved. I rolled down my window.

"Sorry, I didn't mean to sneak up on you!" Janice trilled.

I laughed weakly. "No, it's okay. I must have been in my own little world."

"Where are you off to?"

I stared at her for what might have been a beat too long. "What? Oh, sorry. I'm just heading to the grocery store."

"Well, I just wanted to let you know that one of your side sprinklers is broken. It turned itself on after you'd all left this morning and ran forever. Don came over and switched it off on the main box, but you'll probably have to get Will to look at it. If you don't get it fixed, your water bill will be sky-high!"

"That was nice of him. Please thank Don, and thank you for letting me know," I said. I didn't add that I was more than capable of resetting our sprinklers and didn't need to ask Will to do it for me. Janice was twenty years older than me. In her world, men were the ones who took care of everything yard-related.

"Say hi to that handsome husband of yours for me!"

I smiled. "Will do. Thanks again."

She waved, turned and picked across the lawn back to her house. I sat there for a few minutes, wondering whether this was a serious wrinkle in my plan. If the police ever questioned her, Janice might remember seeing me leave this evening. But how likely was that, really? If everything went according to plan tonight, the police wouldn't even be investigating Robert's death as a murder. And even if Janice had seen me leave, so what? Why shouldn't I be going to the grocery store at six thirty in the evening?

No, I needed to take care of this tonight. There wouldn't be a better time. Charlie was safely away at my mother's; Will was out getting drunk with his coworkers. Most important, Robert wasn't yet under arrest...or released from suspicion. And I was fairly sure that he would be at home, not wanting to risk going out anywhere where he could run into a school parent.

I pulled out of my driveway and headed west. I hadn't been to Robert's house in years, not since the last time Will and I had been invited there to have dinner with Robert and Venetia, but I remembered the way clearly. I drove over a bridge, down a main thoroughfare and past a series of gated subdivisions until I was finally at the edge of town. Here, the houses were spaced apart, often by several acres. I passed by a nursery with palm trees for sale, a horse farm and a dog kennel that advertised spacious, air-conditioned runs.

I took a right on Hibiscus Street, which stretched forward for miles through undeveloped land. It was so remote that if it had been late and dark, and I were lost, it might have creeped me out. For my purposes the isolation was welcome, since there was no one to see as I pulled into the driveway in front of Robert's one-story home. It was a good thing the press hadn't found out about the allegations against Robert. If the story had broken, there might have been reporters staked out in front of the house. Yet another break in my favor.

I turned my car off and took a deep breath, trying to steady my nerves. My hands were shaking, so I squeezed them into fists, then flexed my fingers, trying to relax them. I had to get a handle on my emotions. The only way I would ever be able to pull this off would be by remaining calm and clearheaded.

But how was I supposed to stay cool when I was about to face the monster who had irrevocably and deeply hurt my son?

"Get it together, Nat," I whispered.

I took a few deep breaths until I felt my nerves steady, then reached back to grab my handbag and the bottle of bourbon.

It was time.

I was going to have to face Robert and convince him that I was his friend.

And once I did that, I was going to kill the bastard.

CHAPTER 16

Despite my vibrating nerves and the breath sticking painfully in my chest, my first thought when Robert opened the door was that he didn't look like a monster.

Robert Gibbons was tall with broad shoulders and the beginnings of a paunch. He had thinning sandy hair, blandly handsome features and brown eyes that I once would have described as kind. He looked like an average dad or soccer coach or dentist. It was terrifying to consider how many evil people were out there, walking around freely, wearing perfectly ordinary, benign faces.

"Nat." He stood at the door, looking cautiously out at me. "What are you doing here?"

My pulse had ticked up, my heart pounding so hard, I wouldn't have been surprised if Robert could hear it. And he was standing so close to me, just a few short steps away. Before all of this happened, before this man hurt my son, I had always thought of myself as a peaceful, nonviolent person. Now there was something dark lurking inside me that wanted to hit him, bite him, hurt him.

But if I was going to protect my son and who knew how many other children, I had to swallow my wrath and affect a mask of sympathy and friendship. I had to find a way to smile at this man right up until the moment he was dead.

"Hey, Robert. I thought you could use a friend." I held up the bottle of bourbon. "And a drink. Not necessarily in that order."

Robert hesitated. I watched as he weighed the likelihood of my knowing what he'd done to Charlie. Could Charlie have told me? But if so, why hadn't I gone to the police? And then his eyes drifted to the bourbon, and the ghost of a smile appeared. "Blanton's. That's my favorite."

"I remember."

He stepped aside, gestured for me to enter. I was glad I had sprung for the expensive stuff.

"It's good to see a friendly face," Robert said, closing the door behind me. "I've been a bit lonely out here on my own."

"I can imagine. Actually, that's not true. I can't imagine what you're going through." I set my handbag down on a glass-topped console table next to the front door. "But I think I have some idea. I've represented clients who've been indicted for similar offenses."

"About that." Robert began, then paused. "I was going to call you…to hire you to represent me…but I didn't think…" He stopped again, and shook his head.

He didn't think it would be a great idea to hire the mother of one of his victims to defend him, I finished silently.

"Don't worry. If you had called me, I would have referred you to another attorney, anyway," I assured him. "Who'd you hire?"

"Paul Gasparino. Do you know him?"

"Yes. He's pretty good. Not as good as me." I laughed. "I'm kidding. Paul's great."

"I just wasn't sure I should hire a friend," Robert said awkwardly.

"You haven't been charged yet, have you?"

I knew very well that he hadn't. If he had been charged, he would have been arrested immediately. His name would have appeared on the report the clerk's office put out every day. Besides, if that had already happened, there was almost no chance Robert would have qualified for bail. Accused child molesters never did. However, I didn't want Robert to know I was monitoring his arrest status. It would make him defensive.

He shook his head and looked like he was feeling nauseated. "Not yet. Hopefully, not ever."

"Anyway, it's important that you'd be frank with your attorney. That's hard when you're preexisting friends," I continued. This, too, was bullshit. I had occasionally represented acquaintances over the years and it had never been a problem. Usually they just appreciated the discount I'd give them on my services.

But Robert nodded and looked relieved that he hadn't caused offense by not hiring me. This from the man who had sexually abused my son. Fury flared up, pressing hotly in my chest.

"So come on in. Let's crack that bottle open."

"Point me toward your glasses. I'll pour."

I followed Robert into the large central room, which still bore the signs of Venetia's influence. She would have been the one who picked out the white slip-covered sofas and bright turquoise throw pillows, the sisal rugs, the beach-inspired paintings of palm trees and flamingos on the walls. The paintings reminded me of how much Venetia had loved going to the arts and crafts fairs that were held nearly every weekend during the winter tourist season. She'd talked me into going with her once. I had watched her browse happily through displays of dream catchers and beaded jewelry, while I feigned enthusiasm. I wondered how Venetia was doing so far away from the Floridian beach culture she had thrived in.

And then I wondered what had driven her away.

Robert veered left into the kitchen. I stopped short at the doorway and blinked at the tower of dirty dishes in the sink, pizza boxes piled on the oak kitchen table and open chip bags littering the counter.

"I probably should have cleaned up a little." He looked around helplessly. "I'm not normally such a slob, it's just…"

"It's been a hard week," I finished. "Don't worry, I won't tell anyone."

Robert smiled weakly. "I hope I have some clean glasses."

He rummaged through a cupboard and pulled out two crystal lowball glasses that I suspected might have been a long-ago wedding gift. He set the glasses on the counter while I broke the seal on the bottle of bourbon. Before I poured, I looked up at Robert. "Do you have any crackers? I haven't eaten much today, and this will go right to my head if I don't have something to nibble on."

"Oh, right." Robert looked momentarily confused. "I think I have something in the pantry. Hold on." He headed off to the small walk-in pantry just off the kitchen. As soon as he was out of sight, I yanked the baggie out of my pocket, dumped half the powder inside one rocks glass and then poured a large slug of bourbon in after it. I used my finger to quickly stir the powder into the deep brown liquid. The powder wasn't fully dissolving—and it suddenly occurred to me that I should have done a test run at home—but it also wasn't noticeable, unless you looked closely. I set the glass on the counter, poured another for myself and was tucking the baggie back into my pocket when Robert finally emerged from the pantry. He held up a bag of chips.

"I have some crackers, but I think they've been open for awhile, because they taste stale. Are tortilla chips okay?" Robert stopped and looked around as if his own kitchen confused him. "I might have some salsa somewhere."

"The refrigerator?" I suggested.

"Maybe." But he took my suggestion and rummaged through the fridge, emerging with a large jar of salsa. He poured the salsa and chips into respective bowls, then nodded toward the living room. "Shall we go sit down?"

"Sure." I picked up his drink for him and followed him into the living room. He put the chips and salsa on the glass top coffee table, next to an ugly blue glass dolphin figurine. Once his hands were free, I handed him his bourbon.

"Thanks, Nat." Robert sat on the long sofa and I picked a spot on the matching kitty-corner love seat. I noticed he'd put down his bourbon without taking a sip and wondered if this would turn out to be a problem. What if he wasn't in the mood to drink?

"Shall we make a toast?" I held up my glass. "To old friends."

"The best kind." Robert held up his glass and we pretended to clink them together over the space I had left between us. My breath caught in my chest as he put the crystal glass to his thin lips and took a sip. Would he notice a funny taste or the particles of drugs floating in the amber liquid? But Robert just sighed and shook his head. "What a treat. Blanton's is my favorite."

"How have you been coping with everything?" I was surprised at how warm and sympathetic I was managing to sound. I was a better actress than I'd realized.

"Okay." Robert shrugged helplessly. "As you said, it's been a tough week. You probably hear this all the time from your clients, but I really am innocent. I didn't do those disgusting, horrible things I'm being accused of."

"Actually, my clients don't always insist on their innocence. Most of them are guilty, and don't pretend otherwise. So your maintaining your innocence will carry a lot of weight, if your case does go to trial."

"Really?" Robert's expression was so full of naked hope, I almost laughed.

I was lying, of course. Many of my clients maintained their innocence, right up until they accepted a plea deal or were sentenced, even when there was no doubt in my mind of their guilt. I think they believed I'd fight harder for them if I thought they'd been wrongly accused. The truth was, it didn't make a difference to me. My job was to defend the innocent and guilty alike, and I'd always taken that responsibility seriously.

But it was okay for Robert to think I was naive enough to believe his insisting on his innocence meant anything. I wanted him to relax, stay calm and drink every last drop of the poisoned bourbon.

"Still, I just can't stop thinking—even if Tate Mason does retract these accusations...wait." Robert looked nervous. "You know it was Tate who made the accusations, right?"

"Yes, I had heard that. He's a troubled kid, though, right?"

"Yeah, that's an understatement. Although I never thought he was capable of something like this." Robert shook his head. "I always thought he and I had a good rapport. That he trusted me, even."

"Sometimes when kids lash out, they pick a safe person in their life as the target," I suggested.

Robert nodded eagerly. "That's probably it! I think he's acting out, and that he'll come to his senses eventually and tell the truth. But what happens then?"

"The police will close the investigation. They wouldn't pursue charges against you without a complainant." I answered as though he had been asking me my legal opinion, even though I was pretty sure he was speaking in a broader sense.

"I know. That's not what I meant." He took another sip of his drink. Each time he brought the glass to his lips, I tried not to watch too closely to see how much he'd consumed or if he'd noticed anything was off about it. "Will I be allowed to go back to my job, like nothing's happened? Can the school fire me for being accused of something I didn't do?"

This time, I thought he was looking for legal advice, but it wasn't in my area of expertise.

"I'm not sure. I know the law in Florida is that an employee can be fired at will, as long as the reason isn't discriminatory. But employment law is not my specialty."

"But how can they fire me for something I didn't do? That's not right!" Robert sounded so outraged, I might have believed him to be innocent, if I didn't know for a fact that he wasn't. He would have made a very convincing witness, I thought. It was a good thing he wouldn't get the chance.

"Hopefully they won't," I said soothingly. "But worrying about it won't help anything. I know it's easier said than done, but you need to wait and see what happens."

"I know, you're right." He took another sip of bourbon. It looked like he was close to emptying his glass. "It's just hard sitting here day after day, all alone, wondering if today is the day the police are going to show up to arrest me. I haven't even been able to talk to..." Robert's voice trailed off and he turned to look at me sharply.

My stomach lurched. Had he figured out his drink was spiked? My mind raced, wondering what I should do. I didn't think he'd ingested enough of the drugs to kill him.

But instead of setting down his glass and accusing me of attempting to kill him, Robert pointed a finger at me. "Your phone!"

"What?"

"Can I borrow it?"

"Why do you need it?" My iPhone was safely at home in one of the kitchen drawers. I had brought the burner phone with me just in case I needed to make a call, but I couldn't let him use it. It was a cheap throwaway phone, and the fact that I had it—and not my smartphone—might make him suspicious.

"I just need to talk to...someone." He was sitting with one

leg crossed over the other, balancing an ankle against his knee, which he began to bounce nervously.

"But why can't you call them from your phone?"

Robert sighed. "I've been seeing someone. And she hasn't been taking my phone calls since all of this started. She might answer a number she doesn't recognize."

I was so surprised, I set my own glass—which I had only been pretending to drink out of—down on the coffee table next to the ugly dolphin. Robert had a girlfriend? I hadn't calculated for that when I was making my plan. What if he hadn't been alone when I'd arrived? Or, even worse, what if she suddenly showed up before I'd finished killing him?

"I didn't know you were dating someone," I said. "Is it anyone I know?"

Robert looked at me warily and I instantly realized why he was being so cagey.

"Someone from school?" I guessed. When Robert didn't say anything, my eyebrows arched up. "A married someone?"

"No!" Robert looked shocked. "I would never do that!"

Robert's prudish response caused another wave of disgust to wash over me. I had to fight to keep my expression neutral. He'd molested my son and at least one other boy, but he drew the line at having an affair with a married woman?

"I've been seeing Michelle Cole," Robert admitted.

Michelle was a school mom. I'd been surprised when she and her then husband, Cooper, had decided to divorce. They'd always appeared well matched—they were both athletic and outdoorsy, and before their divorce, seemed to spend every weekend they could out on their boat with their three boys. Their oldest, Zachary, was in Charlie's class at school.

The enormity of this suddenly hit me. Robert was dating a single mother of three boys. Was he romancing her just to have access to her children? It was a nauseating thought. No wonder Michelle wasn't returning his phone calls. She had probably spent the past week going over every single moment of their relationship, trying to remember if her boys had ever been alone with Robert. I wouldn't have been surprised if she'd shown up that night with her own plastic baggie filled with ground-up oxycodone.

"We've been dating for a few months," Robert continued. "There's nothing in the school rules about relationships between school administrators and parents, but we knew it would be a focus of gossip and speculation. We decided to keep it quiet until we knew where the relationship was going."

Robert sighed and took another sip of bourbon. He looked at the glass, as though surprised that it was empty. I sprang to my feet, suddenly worried that there might be blue residue at the bottom of the glass.

"Let me get you a refill," I offered, grabbing the glass.

"I probably shouldn't. I'm starting to feel a little tipsy." Robert touched a finger to his temple, as though he was trying to will himself into sobriety.

Not if I can help it, I thought. "You're not driving. One more won't hurt, right?"

I took his glass back to the kitchen before he could argue further. I glanced back to make sure Robert hadn't followed me, but he was still on the couch. He reached for a tortilla chip, dipped it in salsa and popped it in his mouth.

I quickly dumped the rest of the blue powder in his glass and filled it with another generous pour of bourbon. It was a good thing he was drinking it quickly. I wondered how long it would take before the drugs kicked in.

"Here you go," I said, returning to the living room and handing him his glass.

"Thanks. And thanks for coming over tonight, Nat. You find out who your real friends are at a time like this."

Robert's speech was starting to sound a little slower, a bit slurred. That was a good sign, I thought.

"What were we talking about before you left?" he asked. "Oh, right—Michelle. That's what I mean about finding out who your real friends are. This is the woman I thought I could possibly build a life with, maybe even marry someday. Now she won't even take my phone calls."

Robert sounded piteous and sorry for himself.

"Maybe she wants to give you some space," I suggested.

He shrugged. "Or maybe she thinks I'm guilty and doesn't want to be associated with me."

"I'm sure that she doesn't think that," I lied. "Not if she knows you at all."

"That's why I have to talk to her!" Robert had been lolling back against the couch, his eyes glazed. I was surprised at how fast the drug-and-alcohol combination seemed to be affecting him. I just hoped he stayed awake long enough to imbibe the second dose. Suddenly he sat up straight, looking agitated. "I have to tell her I'm innocent! You believed me. She'll have to believe me, too."

"I'm sure she will." I tried to keep my tone soothing. I glanced at his drink. He'd already consumed almost half of the second glass. A few more sips should do it.

Robert stood, looking a little unsteady on his feet. "Where's your phone? Is it in your purse?"

He pointed at my bag, which I'd left on a table by the front door.

"Actually, I think I might have left it in my car," I began, but Robert was already heading toward the entryway.

A sober Robert would never have rummaged through a woman's handbag without permission. This drunk and possibly already stoned Robert had no such scruples. I watched in stunned silence as he lurched over to my handbag and picked it up. He fished around inside, pushing aside my wallet, keys and makeup bag. Finally, triumphantly, he pulled out the cheap flip phone.

"Here it is!" He held the phone up. "I'm going to call Michelle!"

His *Michelle* was even more slurred. I was surprised at how quickly the drugs seemed to be affecting him. I wondered if he'd been drinking before I arrived. Now that I thought about it, his eyes had seemed a bit bright, his movements a bit slow when I first walked in.

"I really don't think that's a good idea—" I began.

Robert ignored me as he tapped numbers into the phone. I assumed he was too drunk to remember her phone number—and who memorized phone numbers these days, anyway?—but a moment later, he was holding the phone to his ear.

"Damn, it's going to voice mail. Should I leave a message?"

"No!" I said, alarmed.

He ignored me. "Michelle? It's Robert. Please call me back, either on this phone or on my regular phone. I need to talk to you. *Please*. It's important." He hesitated, swaying gently on his feet. "I love you. I know we haven't said that to each other before, but it's true. I just wish I could tell it to you personally instead of your voice mail. So, that's it. I love you and please call me back and I love you. Again. Bye."

Robert squinted at the phone, and hit another button, presumably to end the call. I held my hand out for the phone, and Robert handed it to me. He sat down heavily on the couch. "I'm not sure I should have done that," he commented.

I checked the phone. It looked like the call was still live, the voice mail presumably still recording. I hit the end call button and stared down at it. This wasn't truly a problem, I tried to reassure myself. The phone was prepaid and unregistered, so no one could connect it to me. And that was in the unlikely event Michelle actually kept the message and eventually gave it to the police. What were the chances of that? If I were her, I'd delete it immediately. According to Robert, no one had known they were dating, so I had to assume she wouldn't want to bring attention to it now that Robert was a pariah.

"What do you think? Did I sound too needy?" Robert asked anxiously. "Should I call her back and try to explain?"

"No, that would be a *terrible* idea." And then, not sure that I had convinced him, I added, "Let it go for now. I'm sure once she listens to your message, she'll want to talk to you."

"You think so?" Robert's face registered relief. He picked up his glass, drained it and held it out to me. "Would you mind getting me some more?"

"Sure," I said, standing and sliding the phone into my pants pocket. I went into the kitchen and checked the bottom of his glass. There was some blue residue there, but not much. Should I rinse out his glass? I wondered, but decided against it. If Robert had been suicidal, which is what I wanted the police to believe, he wouldn't have bothered to rinse it out. I added some bourbon to the glass, although not too much. I didn't want him to drink to the point that he'd start vomiting up the drugs.

"Here you go," I said, returning to the living room.

Robert didn't respond. He was lying back on the white sofa, his eyes closed, mouth slackened and open, his arms folded over his chest. I froze, wondering if it was possible he was already dead, when he suddenly let out a snore so loud, I actually jumped, pressing a hand over my racing heart.

I set his glass on the coffee table in front of him, then returned to my seat, watching him.

And then I waited for Robert to die.

CHAPTER 17

The wait was terrible.

An hour passed. And another. I snapped on the rubber gloves I'd brought with me, and spent part of the time washing and putting away the glass I'd used, then wiping down all the surfaces I'd touched with the antibacterial wipes. Once I was done cleaning, I returned to my spot on the love seat to watch Robert's chest rise and fall rhythmically. How long would it take for him to die? I thought about leaving, but that seemed risky. What if Robert somehow survived, and eventually woke up? Was that even a possibility after the large amount of oxycodone and alcohol he'd consumed?

At just before ten o'clock, I went to the bathroom to use the toilet. I kept my gloves on and thoroughly wiped down the toilet seat and handle after I was done. I opened the drug cabinet to look inside. There were the typical male items—a razor, shaving cream, toothpaste, bottle of aspirin. There were also a few prescription bottles lined up neatly on the top shelf. I turned them toward me, reading the names of the drugs inside. The first two were innocuous—one was a course of antibiotics, which Robert had apparently not bothered to finish, the other I recognized as blood pressure medication.

The third didn't have a label on it.

I picked the bottle up, opened it and shook a few of the pills onto my hand and stared down at them, horror dawning.

They were blue oxycodone pills, stamped with the same letter and numbers of the pills I had ground up and put in Robert's bourbon. Why did Robert have a prescription for oxycodone in his bathroom cupboard? Although that wasn't right, either. If these had been prescribed by a doctor and dispensed at a pharmacy, the bottle would be labeled. The fact that it wasn't meant that Robert had most likely obtained them illegally. Which meant…was it possible Robert had an oxycodone addiction?

I blinked, trying to clear my thoughts. Robert had been in a nasty car accident years ago, back when he was still married to Venetia. A teenager had been texting a friend and rear-ended Robert's car at a stoplight. I'd dropped off dinner for the two of them—white chicken chili and corn bread—to this very house. I remembered Robert had been sleeping when I arrived with the food. Venetia had told me in a hushed voice that he'd been prescribed some heavy-duty painkillers for his lower back injury. That had been, what? Five, six years ago? Had he been taking oxycodone all this time?

Everything I had read about the drug came flooding back to me. How it was possible to build up a tolerance to oxycodone. That the amount that would cause an overdose varied greatly. That it would take more of the drug—and in some cases, a lot more—to kill someone who had built up a tolerance than it would to kill someone who had never taken it.

I had made a terrible mistake by not factoring in the possibility that Robert could have already been taking oxycodone. Hands shaking, I put the bottle back in the medicine cabinet and closed the door.

While researching oxycodone online, I'd come across a story about a woman in the late stages of Lou Gehrig's disease who had attempted to commit suicide by overdosing on the medication. She'd underestimated the amount she needed to take, and ended up going into coma that she woke up from a few days later. That meant that if I had underdosed Robert, it was possible, maybe even probable, that Robert would wake up at some point—tonight, tomorrow, the day after—and know that I had tried to kill him. And what would stop him from going straight to the police?

Think, I told myself. *There must be a solution.*

But the panic that had taken root once I realized what was in the pill jar began to bloom into full-blown terror. My breath shortened, my pulse picked up, thrumming through me with a terrible urgency.

Run, my instincts whispered. *Escape while you can. Drive straight to your mother's house, pick up Charlie and then get as far away from Florida as you can.*

I tried to shake the impulse to flee. It wasn't that it was out of the question—as far as I was concerned, I'd much rather be a fugitive on the run than allow myself to be arrested and prosecuted for an attempted murder I was absolutely guilty of. But it was an option that would require considerable planning. It was not the sort of thing I wanted to do half-cocked and terrified.

Right now I had to focus on how to best solve the situation I was in now. I had to figure out a way to kill Robert, and still make it look like a suicide.

For that, I was going to need help.

I needed Will.

I picked up the burner phone, looked at it. I knew it was a risk to call Will on it, especially after Robert's call to Michelle Cole. But I didn't have a choice. And, I reminded myself, there was only a slight chance that the police would know Robert used this phone. If I used his house or cell phone to call Will, they'd have that information the same day they discovered his body. The only other option I had was to leave, drive home, hope Will was there and then drive back. But what if Robert regained consciousness while I was gone? He might call someone or even try to escape. I didn't have a choice.

I dialed Will's number and waited for him to pick up. It went to voice mail.

"Shit," I said out loud.

I wondered if he was still out, and not looking at his phone or maybe even at home, already asleep. I sent him a text:

It's me, Nat, calling from a different phone. Please call me back ASAP. It's important.

I waited. It took Will five excruciatingly long minutes to return my call. Finally, the phone let out a metallic trill of notes. I double-checked to make sure it was Will's number on the caller ID before I answered.

"Hey, what's going on? Is everything okay?" Will's voice said into my ear.

I was so relieved to hear from him, tears pricked in my eyes. "No," I said. "I need your help. Are you alone?"

"I can be, hold on." There was a pause, then Will returned. "Is Charlie okay?"

"He's fine. But I'm in trouble. I need you to come help me."

"What's going on?" Will asked again.

"I'll tell you when you get here."

"Where's here?"

I hesitated. "I'm at Robert Gibbons's house."

There was a sickly pause, and when Will spoke again, his voice sounded hollow. "You're at his house? Why?"

"You have to listen to me. This is important. Okay? Are you listening?"

After a pause that lasted several long beats, Will said, "I'm listening."

"You need to go back inside wherever you are, tell the people you're with that I'm not feeling well and you need to go home. Then I want you to drive home and put your cell phone inside the house. And then drive here. Do you understand? It's very important you don't bring your phone with you here."

"Wait, why do I need to—"

I cut him off. "Will, we don't have time. Please just do it. It's important."

Will exhaled in a ragged rush. For a few long beats, I wondered if he was going to refuse. But then he said, "I'll be there as soon as I can."

The line went dead.

It took Will over an hour to get to Robert's house, which was about thirty minutes longer than I had thought it would take him. I spent that time wondering if he was going to show up and worrying about what I would do if he didn't.

I even, at my darkest, bleakest point, questioned if it was possible that my husband would call the police on me.

But then I finally heard a car pull into the driveway, the headlights shining in through the front windows of the house. I ran to the door and had it open before Will even had a chance to get out of his car. Although it took him an abnormally long time to open the door and climb out, once he finally did, he didn't look entirely steady on his feet. I wondered how much he'd had to drink.

"Are you okay?" I asked when he got closer. His eyes were bloodshot, and his skin looked chalky under the greenish glow of the outdoor house lights. He was still wearing his suit and a button-down shirt, but he'd taken his tie off at some point.

"No, I'm not okay." Will stared at me, his eyes wide. "I'm freaking out about what I'm about to find inside this house.

Why did I have to drop off my phone at the house? And are you wearing plastic gloves? Holy shit, Nat, what's going on?"

"Have you been drinking? Are you over the limit? Should you have been driving?"

"I don't know. Probably. Is that the worst thing we have to worry about tonight?"

I exhaled deeply and shook my head. "It's not."

I opened the door wider and stepped aside so Will could enter.

"Where's Robert?" he whispered. "Is he home?"

"He's in here." I waved him forward and we walked into the open-plan living room together.

Will stared at the sight before him—Robert passed out on the couch, his head tipped back, his arms splayed to his sides, snoring with every exhalation.

"What's wrong with him?" Will asked, whispering.

"He drank two glasses of bourbon that I spiked with oxycodone." I kept my voice lowered, too, although I was fairly sure Robert was out cold. "I thought I gave him enough to kill him. But then I looked in his medicine cabinet and found a bottle of oxycodone there. He must have been taking them for awhile. I think he built up a resistance to them."

"Which means what?"

"My best guess? He'll sleep for a time, and then he'll wake up with a bad hangover."

I sounded almost flippant, but the truth was, I was so frightened, my entire body was trembling. I looked down at my hands, which were also shaking. I balled them together, hoping it would help me get a grip on my emotions.

"How much did you give him?" Will asked.

"Four hundred milligrams. I thought it was enough, especially combined with the booze, but probably not if he was already addicted to them. Do you remember Robert was in a car accident a few years ago? That may have been when he started taking the drug." I shook my head and wrapped my arms around myself.

I suddenly felt very, very cold. "Hell, his drug use may be the reason why he and Venetia got divorced in the first place. Or maybe he started taking them after his divorce, to dull the pain."

"Jesus fucking Christ, Nat. What have you done?"

I was surprised by how quickly my fury spiked up at these words. But then, anger always lived on the edge of fear.

"I did what needed to be done," I said.

"What, put him in a coma?" Will shook his head. "Do you have any idea how much trouble you're going to be in when he wakes up?"

You're. The word spoke volumes. And fine, yes, I was the one who'd created this mess. But Will knew why I had done it. For Charlie. For Tate, even. For the sake of every other kid Robert could have harmed.

"This isn't the time for recriminations."

"Why not?" Will turned on me, looking angrier than I'd ever seen him. "This seems like the perfect time to me!"

"I need your help to finish this." I bit out each word. "I can't move him on my own."

"Move him?" Will looked around, perplexed. "Where were you thinking of moving him to?"

"His car."

"His car?"

"Stop repeating everything I say. This needs to look like a suicide. If we put him in his car, with the pills and the bourbon, then do that thing where you run a hose around and turn the car on so that the carbon dioxide kills the person inside, I think it will work. The police will assume that he was suicidal. That the booze and drugs in his system were there to dull the pain of the moment."

"The thing with the hose?" Will sounded distraught. "What thing with the hose?"

"You have heard of people committing suicide by sitting in their cars, haven't you?"

"Yes, but they don't exactly teach you how to do that in high school driver's ed class."

"I'm sure we can figure it out." I was trying to be patient. I knew this was a lot to spring on him all at once, but we didn't have that much time. "Basically we need to run a hose from the exhaust back into the car."

"Without killing ourselves in the process," Will added.

"That would definitely be ideal."

"Where's his car?"

"It's in the garage. I already checked. His keys are on the counter."

Will shook his head, his expression suddenly blank. "Are we really going to do this?"

"We don't have a choice. If we don't finish this, he'll wake up and he'll know that I tried to kill him. I'll go to jail for the rest of my life. You probably will, too, because no one will believe that you weren't in on it. Are you going to help me or not?"

Will rubbed his hands over his face and suddenly pulled them away and looked down at them. "Aren't we shedding DNA just being here? What about our fingerprints, and hair?"

I held up my hands, still in their plastic gloves. "I've been cleaning."

"Do you have gloves for me?"

"No, but just keep track of where you touched, and I'll wipe it down."

"I want gloves!"

"You have got to calm down." I pulled off the gloves and handed them to him. "Here, take these. If the police think this is a suicide, they're not going to waste their time fingerprinting the house, anyway. And even if they did, we've been here before."

"We haven't been here in years." Will snapped the green gloves on. "So, what do we do? I take his feet, you take his shoulders?"

"I was thinking the other way around. The head end is probably heavier and you're stronger than I am."

We walked over to the couch and stood looking down over Robert's prone body.

"He's put on weight," Will remarked. "This isn't going to be easy."

"Maybe we could get the comforter from the bedroom, lay him on that and drag him out to the garage," I suggested. "The floors are all tile from here to there. It would be easier to slide him than to carry him."

"You don't think he'll wake up when we move him?"

And then, as though Will's words magically came true, Robert suddenly stirred. He groaned and lifted his head, pressing his hands to his temples. He looked blearily from me to Will, then back again.

"Will," he said. "When did you get here?"

Will looked up at me, alarm registering on his face. "Um, just a few minutes ago."

"Oh." Robert looked confused. "I didn't hear you come in. Sorry."

"That's okay." Will glanced at me again. I didn't know if it was possible for him to look guiltier than he did, even though he hadn't done anything yet. "Nat said you were feeling a little..." He trailed off, clearly searching for a word other than *drugged*.

"Drunk." Robert closed his eyes. "I'll be okay. I just need to rest for a bit and I'll be..." His voice trailed off, and he shifted his body, turning onto his right side. He settled in with a deep sigh, and the snores recommenced.

"Has he been like that all night?" Will asked.

"No, that's the first time he's woken up."

"Shit, now he's seen me. Do you think he'll remember that later?"

"What are you talking about?" It was my turn to stare at Will. "There isn't going to be a later. We have to finish this now."

Will blinked. "Okay. We're going to have to turn him onto his back."

I held my breath, expecting Robert to waken again, while Will gently pressed on Robert's shoulder. But Robert's eyes remained shut, his breathing heavy, as he obediently rolled onto his back.

Will exhaled. "Okay. Let's see if we can lift him. You get his legs."

I nodded and stood poised over his feet.

"Let's do it on the count of three," Will said.

Will tucked his hands under Robert's shoulders, while I did the same with his legs. I remembered from my boot camp class at the gym to lift through my legs, so I squatted down, ready to carry the weight up through my glutes and quads.

Will began to count. "One, two, *three*."

As soon as he said three, we both began to lift. Robert's eyes flew open again.

"What are you doing?" he asked, his voice thick, the words slurring.

This time, Will didn't look at me. Instead, he grinned down at Robert, as though they were two buddies at a party that had gotten out of hand. "We were going to carry you up to bed, buddy. We didn't want to leave you here to sleep it off on the couch."

"Why not? I sleep out here all the time." Robert lifted his head and looked at me. "Wait, what's going on?"

"Nothing," I said quickly.

But Robert's brown eyes were suddenly disconcertingly clear. "You know, don't you?"

"Know what?" I really did try to keep my tone as light and casual as Will's had been.

Robert continued to look at me, his expression a mixture of fear and dawning realization. I dropped his feet and took a step back.

"You have to believe me, I didn't plan on... Anyway, I didn't hurt Charlie," Robert said. He was still looking at me, his expression now beseeching. He had managed to stop slurring his words. "I know it's not considered socially acceptable, but it's normal. Beautiful, even. It's just another way to teach young boys...well, how to learn about their bodies. How to become men. It shouldn't be so stigmatized—"

Robert's voice was silenced when Will picked up an aqua throw pillow off the couch and pressed it down over Robert's face. Robert's body flailed, his leg kicking out. He somehow missed me, but knocked the ugly dolphin sculpture off the coffee table and sent it flying to the floor, where it shattered on the hard tiles. Robert made a sound, deep in his chest, that was somewhere between a scream and a groan, muffled by the pillow. Will held on, pressing down with all of his body weight, his face red with the exertion. It went on for so long, far longer than I would have thought it would take.

And then, finally, Robert's body went still.

PART TWO

Will

CHAPTER 18

Robert stopped moving. I waited a few more moments, using as much body weight as I could to press the pillow down on his fucking face, my breath shallow and ragged from the exertion. Finally, I staggered back, pulling the pillow off him. Robert was staring up, his eyes blank and unseeing, his mouth slack, his body still on the white sofa.

I was pretty sure he was dead.

That I had, in fact, killed him.

Oh, my God.

My heart began to race, and I could hear a white whirring noise in my ears as tendrils of panic snaked through me. It was just like one of those horrible dreams, the one where you're running from the police, falsely accused of committing some sort of terrible crime and know if they catch you that you'll spend the rest of your life imprisoned for a crime you didn't commit. And then you wake up, sweating and terrified, and trying to remind yourself that none of it was true.

Except that this time, the committing a crime part was true. And it wasn't just a bad dream.

I had killed someone, and there was nothing I could do to take it back.

Fuck, fuck, fuck. What had I done?

"What the hell did you just do?" Natalie's voice—sharp, angry, disapproving—cut through my shock.

"What?" I turned toward her slowly, my voice higher than normal. "What did you just say to me?"

Nat stared at me. Her eyes were round, and her short, dark hair was ruffled up and damp with sweat. "You killed him!"

"I know! Isn't that what you wanted? Isn't that the whole point of why we're here?"

"*No.* The *point* was to make it look like a suicide, so that the police won't investigate it as a murder! Wait." Nat crouched down beside Robert's still body, and pressed two fingers against his neck, checking for a pulse. I stared at her, not comprehending how she could touch his lifeless body. Just looking at it nauseated me. "Jesus. I think he's really dead."

"Again, I thought that was the point." I bit out the words. "Come on, we have to get out of here. What if someone shows up? We can't be here!"

"Hold on, let me think." Nat stood up and ran her hands through her hair. She stared at Robert's body for a few moments, hands on her hips, surveying the room. "We need to clean up first. Maybe we can still set it up so it will look like a suicide." She shook her head. "Although the medical examiner will probably be able to tell that he was suffocated to death."

To death.

I couldn't stay in the room any longer with Robert's body. I turned and stumbled away. I wasn't sure where I was heading—just away from that room, that horrific scene—but I found myself in the kitchen. I blinked at the mess—piles of dirty dishes, food containers, and there was the unmistakable odor of something rotting in the garbage. I looked around wildly, then saw a bottle of bourbon on the counter. I grabbed it, and after finding a glass in the first cupboard I looked in, poured myself a large glass. I closed my eyes as I drank, grateful for the warmth spreading through my core and the dampening sensation it had on my panic. I poured another few fingers of bourbon in my glass and sat down on one of the bar stools lined up along one counter.

Nat came in and looked at me. "Are you sure that's a good idea? You still have to drive home."

"This," I raised my glass, "is the first good idea I've had all night."

"Fine, but if you're not going to help me clean up, please give me the gloves back."

I hesitated, not wanting to part with them. I didn't want to risk getting my fingerprints on anything. But Nat held out a hand, clearly not willing to cede on this point. I yanked them off and handed them to her. She snapped them on, and without another word, got to work. She rummaged around first under the sink, then in what looked like a walk-in pantry, until she'd assembled cleaning supplies—a broom and dustpan, garbage bags, a roll of paper towels—then disappeared back into the living room.

I grabbed a dish towel and used it to hold the glass as I sipped my drink, trying to slow myself from glugging it down. I wasn't going to admit it to her, but Nat was right—I did have to drive, and while it was hard to imagine tonight getting any worse, getting pulled over for a DUI on my way back home after committing a murder would definitely fall in the Worse category. But it was hard to resist the instant solace the bourbon offered, which was cushioning my shock, swaddling my horror in an alcoholic blanket.

"Come in here for a second. I need to ask you something," Natalie called out.

I reluctantly stood, and—after taking a moment to find my balance—I wandered back out to the living room.

Robert was still there, still dead. I tried not to look at his prone body.

"I swept up the dolphin, but I'm not sure what to do with it. Should we take it with us? But that would mean we'd have to take the broom and dustpan with us, too, since there might be microscopic flecks of glass on them. Or I could just put the pieces in the garbage, hoping the police think that Robert broke it and cleaned up after himself. Which do you think seems less suspicious?"

My wife looked at me earnestly, still clutching a broom in one hand. I had literally no idea what she was talking about.

"Dolphin?"

Nat's brow furrowed. "The glass dolphin? It was on the coffee table, and it broke when Robert kicked it off the table. It was really loud. You didn't hear it?"

"I guess I was a little distracted by the fact that I was in the middle of killing him!"

"I'm going to take it with us," Nat decided, all too rationally. "I don't want them to have any evidence that there might have been a struggle. Besides, I don't think the police will notice that there isn't a broom and dustpan in the house. Oh, and we'd better take that throw pillow, too." She picked up the aqua-blue pillow I'd used to smother Robert and put it with the garbage bag. I winced and looked away. "I just need to wipe everything down one last time and we'll be good to go. Oh, wait, I forgot something."

Nat headed out of the room, and returned a few minutes later with a pill bottle. "Will you bring in the bourbon?"

"Why?"

Nat waved a hand toward Robert's body. "I'm trying to make this look like a suicide."

"I thought you said the medical examiner will know that it wasn't?"

"If they're careful. But that's a big if. People are human. They may run a toxicology screen on him, see the level of drugs and alcohol in his system, and decide to check the suicide box, instead of the homicide one. Do you think Robert would write a suicide note?"

"What?" I'd officially had too much to drink. My brain felt like it was running half-speed through a sludge of mud. "How would I know that?"

"Are you okay?" Nat gave me another long, searching look. "Just get the bourbon, and then sit down and don't touch anything. I'll finish up in here."

I did as I was told. I watched Nat set up the scene. She poured some bourbon into Robert's glass, then carefully wiped the bottle down with an antibacterial wipe. Nat twisted open the cap on the pill bottle and then tipped it over so that the little blue pills scattered on the glass top coffee table. It looked exactly as though someone had been swallowing pills, one by one, before passing out. Or worse.

Robert's laptop was open on the blond wood dining table, across the room from the sofa where his body lay. Nat sat down in front of it.

"Oh, good, it's not password-protected." Nat began to type, her plastic gloved fingers flying over the keyboard. "How does this sound? 'I feel terrible for what I've done, and would do anything I could to take it back. This isn't the man I wanted to be. I'm so sorry.'"

It actually wasn't bad, especially considering the circumstances and pressure she was under, but I wasn't in the mood to dole out compliments.

"Would he say something religious? About going to a better place or something like that?"

"I don't think so." Natalie frowned down at the laptop. "Robert wasn't religious. Don't you remember he turned down that job offer from St. Andrews because he said he wouldn't be comfortable being the principal at a parochial school?"

"Why would I remember that?"

"Well, he did." Natalie stood. "This will have to do. We should get going. Are you okay to drive?"

"I'm not sure."

"Jesus, Will, how much have you had to drink? We really need to get out of here. What if someone shows up? And we can't leave your car here. It would be a pretty big clue to the police."

Sarcasm? Really? I thought. *After she just made me kill someone?*

"I'll be fine."

"Give me your glass," Nat said. "I need to wash it."

She disappeared into the kitchen. I heard the sound of water running, and the cupboard being closed. "Come on, let's go." Nat strode back into the living room, where she gathered up her handbag, the garbage bag full of used paper towels and broken glass dolphin pieces, the pillow and the broom and dustpan, while I watched. I didn't offer to help.

Nat stopped at the door, and looked back at the living room, at the tableau of Robert's body sprawled lifeless on the couch next to the pills and the booze.

"What do you think?" she asked. "Is there anything we need to fix? We're not going to have another chance."

"I think I want to get the hell out of here before I throw up."

Nat shot me an odd look, a mixture of concern and exasperation. I ignored it and trailed after her out of the house. She closed the door behind us and headed to her SUV. She opened the back hatch and set the evidence inside.

"Are you going to be okay?" She turned toward me. "Why don't I go first. You stay behind me and try not to veer in and out of your lane."

"I'm really not that drunk. I'm just...freaked out."

"Try to stay calm. We still have some work to do before we're home free. Or, at least, I do."

"Like what?"

"Getting rid of the evidence."

"What are you going to do with it?"

"I'm going to smash up the cell phone and tablet, submerge them in water and toss them in a Dumpster."

"Tablet?" I asked.

"I used it for research, but I have to get rid of it. I also need to ditch the pillow and broom, although I'll take those to that apartment complex on Orange Avenue. I've had clients who've lived there. They rent the rooms by the week. It has a huge turnover. A discarded pillow and broom in the garbage bins will blend right in."

"Are you doing all of that tonight?"

"Hmm. No, I guess I'd better do that part tomorrow. Throwing stuff into Dumpsters will look suspicious at nighttime, if anyone's bothering to look."

Natalie opened her car door and got in. "I'll see you at home," she said before closing the door.

Somehow I managed to drive home. At one point, the road blurred and then doubled. But I closed one eye and my vision cleared, the center line coming back into focus, and I managed to stay in my lane. I drove the rest of the way with a hand over one eye, guided by the rear lights of Nat's car.

Once she had pulled into our driveway and exited her car, Nat opened the back hatch of her SUV. She pulled out the garbage bag full of evidence and slung it over one shoulder.

"Do you think you should bring that inside?" I asked, eyeing the bag like it was radioactive.

"What else am I going to do with it?" She tilted her head to one side. "I suppose we could burn some of it in our fire pit, but that could leave behind trace evidence. I think we're better off ditching it altogether."

"Trace evidence? Oh, my God." The panic began pulsing through me again. What the hell had just happened? What had I done?

"Don't worry," Nat said. "No one will ever suspect us."

"What if they do?"

"They won't, trust me."

Trust you? I actually wanted to believe her, as the alternative was too awful to contemplate. But this was the woman who had just turned me into a murderer. Suddenly I was overwhelmed with fatigue, the stress of the night and the alcohol I'd consumed dragging me down.

"I have to go inside," I said, turning away from Nat and stumbling toward the door.

"I'll be right in," Nat said calmly.

CHAPTER 19

Despite my exhaustion and excessive alcohol consumption, I couldn't fall asleep. I just lay there, staring up into the darkness, listening to the soft whir of the white noise machine Nat kept on her bedside table, claiming the noise muted the sound of my snoring.

Before we'd retired for the evening, Nat had changed into her favorite nightshirt, which was pink and had cartoons of owls screen-printed on the front. She'd brushed her teeth vigorously, moisturized her face and got into bed without forgetting to turn on the white noise machine. She'd fallen asleep almost instantly.

I wondered if she was a sociopath.

Was that possible? Could you be married to someone for almost a decade and a half, and only then realize that they were detached from normal human emotions? Could she have hid it for that long? Or was it possible for sociopathy to lie dormant all that time, suddenly to wake, turning what was previously a perfectly normal woman into a killer? Or more accurately, attempted killer. I was the one who had actually killed Robert.

Meanwhile, Nat slept like the dead.

The *dead*. I couldn't get the word out of my brain. It stuck there, droning incessantly in my ears. Dead, dead, *dead*. Robert was dead. Permanently, irrevocably dead.

At six in the morning, as the room began to lighten, I finally gave up on sleep, slid out of bed and pulled on my running clothes. I slipped out of our bedroom without waking Nat and headed downstairs. I'd been sort-of-kind-of training for a half marathon for the past year, although as my work schedule and enthusiasm waned and waxed, I'd put off signing up for an actual race. Today I was ready for a long, grueling run that would hopefully make my body feel as terrible as my psyche did.

I headed east down our street, took a turn north, another east, so that I was running toward the bridges that arched onto the barrier islands. It felt like I was running through mud, my legs heavy with the effort. As I ran, my footsteps fell into a rhythm and the word playing on repeat in my thoughts suddenly changed from *dead* to *murder*. Murd-*er*, murd-*er*, with each footfall. And even then, it seemed half-assed, since really, what I should be hearing in my head was murd-er-*er*, murd-er-*er*. Robert was the victim of a murd-*er*. But I was the murd-er-*er*.

As I ran, my brain kept playing the terrible scene on a loop— my lifting the pillow…pushing it down on Robert's face…the terrible inhuman sound he made…his body writhing violently before going finally, terrifyingly still…

I hadn't meant to do it. Hell, I'd fantasized about beating Robert to a pulp when I found out what he'd done to Charlie. But I never thought I was capable of taking a life.

Except I had.

And now the only question was, would I get away with it?

Oh, and the follow-up—had killing Robert condemned me to a life everlasting in a hell I wasn't sure I'd even believed in yesterday? It was funny how that worked. When you're middle-aged and a basically decent person, you don't spend too much time thinking about the afterlife. If there is one, great! They'll definitely let in a nice guy who's always paid his taxes and volunteered his free time coaching his kid's basketball team. And if there isn't an afterlife, why waste time and emotional energy thinking about it?

But now I'd committed one of the worst sins possible. Hell, the Catholics believed that taking your own life would earn you a ban from heaven. And I had killed *another person*. There was probably no coming back from that.

A queasy, oily fear took root in my bowels.

Just then, a police car screamed by, lights flashing, siren blaring. I was midstride, just running by a bank as the cruiser passed me. I started at the noise and my toe dragged against the pavement, tripping me up. I spun my arms wildly, just managing to stay upright. The police cruiser headed toward the bridge ahead, where apparently there was a criminal—not *me*, a *real* criminal—needing their attention. I leaned forward, bracing my hands against my thighs, panting heavily. Was this what the rest of my life would look like? Terror whenever a police car passed by?

My stomach shifted.

"Oh, shit," I said out loud.

I managed to stagger behind an ornamental landscaping bush before I vomited. There was nothing in my system, as I hadn't consumed anything since the bourbon the night before, but my stomach didn't seem aware of that. I retched and I retched until foul-tasting bile filled my mouth and my abdomen cramped. I stood there for a few long moments, hunched over, hoping the bush shielded me from the view of passing cars.

Come on, Clarke, I thought. *You've got to get it together.*

I finally stood upright, arching my back and willing my stomach to cooperate. When I finally thought I could continue on, I started to run again. I knew I should turn around and head for home—lack of food and sleep combined with what I now knew was a throbbing hangover was not the stuff that elite athletes are made of. But something inside me pushed me on, told me that I had to run up the bridge, that the very act of doing so would be a victory of sorts.

Almost as soon as I started up the bridge, I could feel myself starting to falter. But then, something odd happened. I thought of that fucking monster Robert touching my son, and encouraging him, no, *grooming* him to touch him back. Suddenly I began to run harder, faster. The road in front of me grew steeper as I headed farther up the bridge. My quads burned, my lungs felt heavy in my chest. And instead of *murd-er, murd-er, murd-er* playing on repeat in my thoughts, I heard, *fuck him, fuck him, FUCK HIM.*

I reached the summit, my breath heaving, my lungs burning. I tore off my shirt and let out an inhuman roar.

"Argh," I yelled, and I actually beat my fists—one of them still gripping my sweaty shirt—against my chest, as I ran in place, my knees churning high.

"Hey, Will."

I looked up and saw Tyler Young jogging toward me. Tyler was a podiatrist, apparently an extremely successful one, judging from his three-thousand-square-foot home on the water.

"Hey, Tyler." I wondered if he'd heard me roar and hoped that if he had, he'd have the good manners to ignore it.

Tyler held up a limp hand in greeting as he shuffled past me, barely lifting his feet from the ground. "Can't stop," he huffed. "Trying to keep up my pace."

"Go get 'em." I held up a fist as though I was cheering him on.

Tyler's oldest daughter, Emma, had been on a T-ball team with Charlie a few years back. I'd gotten a kick out of what a fierce competitor she'd been, the bow holding back her long, dark brown curls at odds with the steely, cold gaze she always had at bat. Unlike mine, Tyler's entire life hadn't taken a drastic, horrific shift over the past twelve hours. He was still a successful suburban dad, probably a little stressed out about the size of his mortgage. Possibly a little resentful that his wife had insisted on the Carrara marble in the kitchen or the surround shower in the bathroom that she'd seen on a commercial. Even if the added stress of those expenses meant that Tyler would indulge in an extra bowl of ice cream now and again, then try to run it off on Saturday mornings.

I was suddenly so jealous of Tyler's life, I found myself at the breaking point. Tears pricked in my eyes and my sight went blurry. I braced my arms against the railing of the bridge and hung my head. I breathed in deeply, feeling the salt air expand my lungs before I exhaled it slowly.

I turned around and jogged back down the bridge toward home.

"I was starting to worry about you," Nat said when I walked into the kitchen, sweaty and disheveled.

"Why, were you afraid I might have gone off and killed someone else?" I grabbed a glass from the cupboard and filled it up at the sink. I gulped the water down in one go and filled the glass again.

Nat waited while I hydrated. "You can't make jokes like that," she said, once I'd set the empty glass on the counter.

"Why not?"

"Why do you think? Someone might hear you."

I looked from left to right with exaggerated care. "The only person who can hear me is the one who manipulated me into becoming a murderer."

Natalie folded her arms over her chest. "I know you're upset. But you need to be careful. And when you're up to it, we need to go over our story for last night in detail, just in case we're ever questioned about where we were."

"Wait, now you want to talk about it? Because just a few hours ago, you decided to put us in this situation, to turn me into a fucking murderer without giving me any input into any of it whatsoever."

Nat shook her head. "What about Charlie?"

I stopped and drew in a deep breath. Memories of my son flooded me—the baby with the ridiculously long eyelashes grinning up at me, the little boy who high-fived Buzz Lightyear at Disney World, the tween with his infectious froggy laugh. The stripped-down truth was that I would do anything for him.

Including, apparently, commit murder.

And as much as I hated to admit it, Nat was right. I could feel myself spinning out of control. I needed to calm the fuck down.

"I know. I'll get it together before he comes home. Which is when, by the way?"

"I'm picking him up tomorrow afternoon."

"Good. I'll come with you."

"I thought you had basketball?" Natalie picked up the pile of mail that had accumulated on the white lacquered tray she kept by the back door and began flipping through it. She called the tray a *landing strip* and I hated it almost as much as I hated the whiteboard calendar.

I stared at my wife, who calmly looked through the mail, and wondered if she had lost her mind. I did play in a basketball league, every Sunday at two. Most of the guys in it were my age, or close to it, and I'd always enjoyed the camaraderie and the stress relief. But that was before I'd *killed someone*. Did Nat really think that life would just roll on as it had before?

"I'm not going to basketball."

Nat glanced up from sorting the mail. "Why not?"

"Why not? Because we—well, technically, I—killed someone last night! I don't understand how you can just stand there and...look through the mail like nothing's happened!"

"What would you rather I do? Run around in circles, waving my hands in the air?"

"I don't know. Maybe." My knees suddenly felt shaky. I sat

down heavily in one of the kitchen chairs. "You seem way too calm about all of this."

Nat tossed the mail back on the tray and folded her arms again. "I'm just trying to stay focused on what we need to do to get through it. To *not* get caught."

"Maybe we should go away. What do you think? We could drive up to North Carolina, rent a cabin for a few weeks and just wait and see what happens here. Lie low until the police have found the…body." My stomach gave another queasy lurch. "And if they buy the suicide story."

"No, we definitely can't leave town."

"Why not?"

"Do you remember the Curtis Webber case I tried last year?"

I didn't remember. Her clients ran together in a jumble of drug addicts and thieves, and I'd long since stopped attempting to keep track of which case she was working on.

"Remind me."

"Curtis was charged with the unlawful discharge of a fire-arm. Basically, he fired his gun into the house of a rival gang member. And the next day, he took off for Orlando. The police monitored his cell phone and were able to pick him up a few days later. At the trial, the State's Attorney was allowed to use that trip to show that he was fleeing the area, which showed consciousness of guilt."

"I'm not saying we flee. We just…drive slowly away."

"Still. We can't be seen acting out of character, making radical changes to our schedule, just in case we do fall under suspicion. We have to behave as normally as possible. You have to go to basketball tomorrow. And maybe we should go out to dinner tonight." She looked at me, obviously assessing whether I could pull off going out to dinner without falling apart.

"Okay." I nodded, and tried—and failed—to suppress an eye roll. "Act as normal as possible. Got it. No problem."

"I'm serious, Will. You can't break down in public or suddenly appear super stressed out. People will notice. You have to act like your normal, happy-go-lucky self."

I could tell from the flatness of her tone that this was not meant as a compliment. My temper, momentarily muffled by shock and the horror of the past twenty-four hours, flared back up.

"Maybe you should have thought about that before you decided to make this huge, life-changing decision without talking to me first!"

"I tried talking to you about it. You wouldn't listen to me."

"Because it was insane. It is insane. He's dead…and we can't take that back."

"I don't want to take it back." Natalie's expression turned cold. "I'm glad he's dead. And if you think that makes me a monster—too bad, you'll just have to live with that."

Natalie turned away from me and stalked out of the kitchen.

CHAPTER 20

Mark Sefton dropped his shoulder and rammed it into me just as I was about to dribble the ball past him. The impact was surprisingly hard. I reeled back as my feet slipped out from underneath me. I fell backward onto the slick wooden gymnasium floor, landing with a heavy, painful thud. While I attempted to regain the ability to breathe, Mark dribbled the ball down the court, set up his shot and swished the ball through the net. He made a fist with one hand, his arm bent in a ninety-degree angle. Rage surged through me, hot and violent.

"What the fuck, Mark?" I said loudly.

"You okay, man?" Zack Smith stood over me, holding out a hand.

I grabbed it, and he pulled me to my feet.

"Let it go," Zack advised. "That guy's always been a dick."

I'd known Zack for years, although we'd always had one of those superficial relationships that revolved around the basketball league and chatting at Super Bowl parties. His two sons went to Charlie's school, although they were a few years younger.

Charlie. I closed my eyes for a moment and wondered if there would come a time when just the thought of my son's name wouldn't engulf me with this sticky swamp of grief, fear and anger. I ran a sweaty wrist band over my face.

"Are you okay, man?" Zack asked. He squinted at me.

Actually, I killed the Franklin School principal the night before last. Now I'm in the middle of having a nervous breakdown, I thought. *But other than that, everything is A-OK.*

"Yeah, sure. Just a little hungover."

"Oh." Zack nodded, looking relieved that I wasn't going to pick the middle of the basketball court to start unburdening myself about job or marital problems. "What did you do last night?"

"Nat and I went out to eat."

"Where'd you guys go?"

"Piatti's," I said, naming what was usually my favorite local Italian restaurant, but which I might forevermore associate with the horror of this weekend. I had ordered my usual veal Parmesan. But when the plate was placed in front of me—oil pooling up on the meat, the red sauce gloppy and unappealing—I didn't think I'd be able to choke it down. Nat, who was calmly twining spaghetti around her fork, gave me a sharp look. I managed to take a few bites, washing them down with three glasses of Montepulciano d'Abruzzo from the bottle Nat had ordered. She'd had to drive us home, where I promptly passed out on the couch and then woke up at three in the morning covered in sweat, my head pounding.

"Cool," Zack said. He hesitated, then shook his head. "Crazy week at the school, huh?"

"Pretty crazy," I agreed.

"Do you think he did it? I'm hearing a lot of conflicting stories."

Another wave of fear and revulsion swamped me, but this time I thought I managed to keep my expression neutral. At least Zack didn't look at me strangely again.

"I hope not, you know? I'd hate for any kid to have to go through that."

"Yeah." Zack shook his head again. "I know what you mean."

"Are we playing or talking?" Mark called out, running backward down the court. He threw the basketball at me, harder than necessary. "You have possession, Clarke. Let's see if you can keep it."

"He's such a dick," Zack muttered.

But this time, my temper didn't flash back up. I was instead filled by a queasy emptiness, and the unshakable fear that Nat and I were never going to get away with what we'd done.

I was showered and sitting on the couch with a beer, watching the Dolphins game on television, when Nat and Charlie returned home.

"Hey, Dad," Charlie said, dropping his blue camouflage pattern backpack on the ground on the floor next to the front door.

"Don't leave your bag there," Nat said automatically.

"Hey, kiddo." I put down my beer and held open my arms. Charlie—ignoring his mother's instructions—came over and gave me a quick hug. I had to force myself not to grab onto him and crush him against me. "Did you have fun at Gram's house?"

Charlie threw himself onto one of the club chairs, shoulders first, legs waving up in the air. "We saw a manatee and I beat Gram at Mario Kart. Did you know the Flash can run at near light speed? That's faster than Superman. Although that's only in the Earth's atmosphere. Superman can probably fly faster than that in outer space, but it would be impossible to set up a race."

I was used to the non sequiturs that came with having an eleven-year-old son.

"Maybe they could have the Flash race on earth and Superman race in space and clock them," I suggested.

Charlie shrugged. "I don't think that would really be possible. Unless maybe Superman started at the International Space

Station or something. But then it wouldn't really be a race. It would be more like they were each just going for their personal best record."

I noticed that Charlie's face was chalky. There were faint dark smudges under his eyes. Worry gripped at me. Was it just garden variety fatigue…or was this a symptom of what could be a long-lasting trauma?

"Charlie, your backpack," Nat said again. "Go put it in your room. I'll get dinner started."

"What are we having?" Charlie hopped out of the chair and retrieved his backpack from the floor.

"Tacos," Nat said.

"Awesome," Charlie turned and ran up the stairs, his footsteps thudding heavily.

Nat, still standing in the doorway to the living room, shook her head. "Can you picture my mother playing video games? I would never in a million years have thought that was even possible."

"How's he doing? He looks tired."

"That's because my mother let him stay up late to watch a movie. As far as I could figure out from his description, I think it involved alien robots."

"Why the fuck would she let him watch something that inappropriate?" I said, surprising myself with the biting anger in my voice.

Nat looked at me strangely. "Because he wanted to watch it? Why do you think? Besides, it was rated PG-13, so I don't think it was necessarily inappropriate. Just maybe a little too exciting for right before bed."

"We have to protect him. That has to be our first priority right now." I grabbed my bottle of beer and took a swig. It had grown warm.

Nat walked over and sat down next to me on the couch, tucking one leg under the other.

"Are you okay?" she asked quietly.

I could feel my shoulder muscles bunching up. I tried to roll them back down. A brittle silence stretched between us and I realized that what I wanted—more than anything, except maybe to go back in time and stop the events of Friday night from happening—was for my wife to get as far away from me as possible.

"I'm fine."

Nat glanced up toward the stairs, but the sound of water running through the pipes signaled that Charlie had gotten in the shower. Charlie took outrageously long showers, so we were safe for a bit.

"We need to talk about our timeline on Friday night."

"What do you mean?"

"We need to get it straight between us in case we're ever questioned. Our story has to be tight. I left the house at 6:35. Just as I was pulling out, Janice Green came over to tell us that our sprinkler was broken—"

"What's wrong with the sprinkler?"

"Will, focus. I chatted with her for a few minutes, then told her I was going to Publix to pick something up for dinner. If anyone asks, I'll say I purchased a rotisserie chicken and paid in cash. There won't be video of me buying it—maybe I should have stopped for the chicken. Oh, well, too late now. What about you?"

"What about me?"

"Where were you that night before we spoke?"

I closed my eyes as the images of that night swam back to me. What had come before…and what had come later.

"We went to Rockbar Oysters," I said. "With one of the applicants for the associate's position."

"You went all the way out there? That's a thirty-minute drive. No wonder it took you so long to get to Robert's house."

"Yeah, I know." I tried—and failed—to think of a good reason why my law partners and I would have to drive to an out-of-the-way restaurant. "I don't remember. It wasn't my idea to go there. I think someone was in the mood for oysters."

"Who was with you that night?" Nat pressed on. "And what did you say when you left?"

"You know, the usual suspects," I hedged. I realized with fresh horror that this could possibly be a serious problem. I'd been so freaked out from the moment I'd killed Robert, I'd completely forgotten about the earlier part of my night. The part Nat couldn't find out about.

"Did you tell them that I'd called you and said I wasn't feeling well?"

"Actually…I don't remember what I said when I left. I'd had a few drinks. But, wait. You didn't call me from your cell phone."

"I know. I had to leave my real phone at home. Modern smartphones are basically GPS tracking devices. The police can subpoena records from your cell phone company and trace your movements through where your phone was. I had to use my burner phone to call you."

"Why did you have a burner phone?"

"I got one just in case I needed to make a call that night. Which I did." Nat hesitated. "There might be a problem. Robert used the same phone to call Michelle Cole earlier that evening."

"Who's Michelle Cole?"

"She's a school mom. Pretty blonde?"

I shrugged. At least half of the school moms were pretty blondes.

"Anyway, Michelle and Robert were dating, but were keeping it a secret, I guess because she was a school mom. But she hadn't been taking his phone calls, so he wanted to borrow my phone to call her."

"Why would you let him do that?"

"I didn't let him do anything. He was drunk and stoned and went through my purse before I could stop him."

"But what if this Michelle tells the police that Robert called her on the night he died from a number she didn't recognize? And then they pull the records from that number and see the phone call to me?"

Nat hesitated. "That would be a problem."

"Jesus Christ, Nat!"

"Don't panic. First of all, it may be a while before his body is found."

"Why does that matter?"

"The longer it takes, the more his body will decompose. The harder it will be for them to pinpoint his time of death."

"That's revolting." I felt another wave of nausea surge through me.

"Anyway, I don't think Michelle will go the police, even if she does figure out that Robert called her on the night he died."

"Why not?"

"I wouldn't if I were her. I wouldn't want anyone to know I was romantically connected to the local pedophile. If no one else knew about their relationship, I'm sure she'll want to keep it that way."

"But…it's a risk."

"Yes." Nat nodded. "It is."

"Oh, my God." I could feel the panic rising up again, twisting around my chest and lungs.

"Look, I've thought this through. It's only an issue if Michelle tells the police about the phone call—which I'm pretty sure she won't do—or if the police pull your phone records for some reason. Which they would only do if you were a suspect. So, yes, it's potentially a loose end, but I don't think a fatal one."

Fatal. The word did nothing to calm my snowballing terror.

"What did you do with the stuff? The evidence?"

"I took a hammer and broke the screens on the tablet and the phone, then submerged them in water for an hour. Neither one would turn back on, so I'm pretty sure I fried the circuits. I put them in a plastic bag with some raw chicken, and tossed them in a Dumpster behind the gas station. They don't have a security camera back there."

"Wait, you wrapped them up with chicken? Why?"

"Just in case anyone was Dumpster diving," Nat explained. "The smell of the rotting meat would act as a repellent. And the rest of the stuff—the pillow, the broken dolphin, the broom and dustpan—I left at the Dumpster by that apartment complex. Either someone will take them or they'll be off to the landfill Tuesday morning, when the garbage truck picks them up. Either way, the police will never find any of it, even if they knew to look for it. Which they won't."

Nat seemed so calm, so self-assured, but it perversely made my anxiety spiral even further out of control. Who was this woman I was married to?

She looked at me suddenly, her blue eyes direct.

"Is there anything that happened that night, before you met me, that I should know about?" she asked. "You have to tell me if there is. We need to have a clear timeline for that night ready, just in case we're ever interviewed by the police."

"No, nothing else. I was just out at Rockbar Oysters, having a business dinner."

I hoped to hell that she would never find out just how big a lie that was.

CHAPTER 21

After another sleepless night, I went to the office early on Monday morning. Partly, I wanted to avoid having yet another conversation with Nat, but I was also craving the normalcy of work. Maybe if I was at my desk, taking calls from clients, pushing paper from one stack to another, I would start to feel like myself again. The person I'd been on Friday before this whole nightmare began. The self that wasn't a murderer.

I was already showered, dressed and just knotting my tie when Nat woke up.

"What time is it?" she asked groggily. She sat up, supporting herself on one elbow. "Why are you up so early?"

"I have a busy day. Clients, partner meeting. Usual drill." I grabbed my jacket off the wing chair in the corner of the room. "You don't mind taking Charlie to school?"

"Of course not."

"Good."

"Hey…are you going to be okay?"

I was overcome with an unexpected rush of gratitude. Nat had noticed how distraught I was and was worried about me. I turned to her, ready to spill out all the dark and terrifying thoughts that my mind had been playing on repeat, when I saw her expression. It was not one of warm concern. Instead, it was coolly appraising, as though she were trying to decide if I was going to be a liability. The impulse to confide in her drained away.

"I'll be fine." I left our bedroom and closed the door firmly behind me.

My appetite had still not returned, so I left the house without consuming anything other than a cup of coffee from the pot I brewed. It churned acidly in my stomach the entire way to my office. I drove to work by rote, glad that the traffic was light at the early hour.

The law offices of Romano, Krall, Ricci, Peters, Anderson, Clarke & Miller, LLC, were unsurprisingly empty at seven o'clock in the morning. I closed myself into my office, which was located at the end of a hallway—not the corner office, which still belonged to Gil Romano, but one office over. I turned on my computer, and once it hummed to life, I began going through my emails. The familiar routine soothed me. I'd recently been hired by Arthur Santos, who owned a chain of Cuban restaurants, to completely restructure his estate—trusts for the kids, philanthropic legacies, the whole works. He'd had his assistant send me a ton of documents to go over, and this was the perfect time to let myself sink into them. This was what I did. This was what I was good at. As I sorted through the papers, scanning and processing the information within, my mind calmed. I felt comfortably numb for the first time since Friday night.

"Will?"

I started and looked up. Jaime Anderson had cracked open my door and was looking in at me. Jaime had been at the firm for a few years longer and had made partner just ahead of me. She was a very attractive woman—long, dark hair, high cheekbones, full lips that smiled easily. I'd had a crush on her for years.

And then, five months earlier, we'd started sleeping together.

"Hey," I said, leaning back in my chair. I rubbed my hands nervously on my knees.

"You're in early." Jaime leaned a hip against the door frame, shifting her weight onto one leg. Jaime always wore heels, the higher the better, a detail I found exquisitely sexy. She cocked her other leg behind her at a forty-five-degree angle and lifted a hand to one hip. She had glorious hips and she knew it—they were soft, rounded, incredibly feminine.

The affair had taken me by surprise. I certainly hadn't been looking to cheat on Nat. I hadn't even fully admitted to myself how unhappy I was with my marriage. But then one night, Jaime and I were both working late at the office on separate projects. She asked if I wanted to order food in. We'd shared containers of moo shu pork and chicken fried rice, and washed them down with glasses of pinot noir from a bottle that one of Jaime's clients had gifted her. One minute she was sitting across from me, laughing, her cheeks flushed, and the next thing I knew we were making out like a couple of hormone-addled teenagers. It had escalated from there, at times to the point of recklessness. We'd checked into local hotels a few times together, but even more often, we ended up making love on the couch in one of our offices. I knew if we kept it up, we were going to eventually get caught. Lisa Sing, one of the paralegals, had given me a few pointed looks that made me wonder if she'd already figured out what was going on.

I kept thinking I should just end it. I knew it was the right thing to do, but before it began, I hadn't fully thought through the consequences of having an affair with someone I worked with. Were we supposed to just stop sleeping together one day? Just return to our previous roles as coworkers both married to other people who occasionally flirted too much at the firm holiday party? But I hadn't been ready to give Jaime up. She was a delicious, fizzing secret that had transformed my boring, color-less life into something exciting.

Anyway. I wasn't up to dealing with that particular thorny issue today. I had enough to cope with.

I gestured toward my laptop by way of explanation. "I have a seriously busy day. I wanted to get some work done before the office cranked up to crazy."

Jaime looked back over one shoulder, checking to see if any-one was around. She stepped into my office, closed the door be-hind her. Jaime folded herself into one of the visitor's chairs in front of my desk, crossing one leg over the other. "What hap-pened on Friday night? You took off so suddenly."

I nodded and tried to take a deep breath, but it caught in my chest. *Robert lying on the couch... The pillow in my hand... The moment when his body stopped twitching...* I had to force myself to push aside the horrible montage of images that kept flipping through my head.

"Natalie wasn't feeling well. She had a bad stomach bug and asked me to stop at the drugstore on my way home to get her some medicine. She was in pretty bad shape."

Jaime pursed her lips into a moue. My leaving her to rush to Nat's aid obviously irked her. But she said, with the practiced deceit of any seasoned lawyer, "I'm so sorry to hear that. I hope she's feeling better."

"She's fine now," I said, wondering if I should have gone off script by adding in the part about stopping at the store on my way back to the house. I had a feeling Nat wouldn't be a fan of my making alterations to the carefully gone-over timeline for Friday night. Then again, Nat wouldn't be happy to know I'd left out the not insignificant detail that I'd been out on a date with another woman when she called me from Robert's house.

"And then I didn't hear from you all weekend," Jaime con-tinued. She looked at me with dark, inscrutable eyes. "I thought you would have called me to explain. Or at least texted."

"I…had hoped I'd…be able to," I faltered. With everything that had happened on Friday night, I hadn't even thought about Jaime. "The weekend got away from me."

Jaime continued to hold my gaze. "Is that really all you have to say? After bailing on me like that Friday? Jesus, Will, I was mortified. The waiter thought I'd been ditched middate. He actually told me how sorry he was when he brought the check, which you stuck me with, by the way."

My shoulders, that had finally started to relax while I was in my work-induced fugue, tensed up again. I should have known this was coming. Yet I had failed to prepare a plausible response for the woman I was having an affair with about why I had run off and left her in a restaurant, on her own, on a night we'd planned to spend together. We'd purposely picked a restaurant in the next town over. One that was made up of a maze of small rooms, where we could eat tucked away in a corner. It had been a risk since someone we knew might still have seen us. But that had actually made it even more exciting.

The idea that a mere three days ago I had been looking to add excitement into my life made me feel faintly nauseous.

"I'm really sorry about leaving you like that."

"You know, if this," Jaime made a circular motion with her hand, "is getting to be too much for you, just tell me."

It sounded like she was offering a way out. Just say the word and the affair would be magically switched off. But nothing was ever that simple. Besides, Jaime said things like that only because she wanted me to insist that no, breaking up was the last thing I wanted. She loved the idea that I found her irresistible, perhaps even more than she liked me. It had surprised me that despite how gorgeous and sensual she was, Jaime required a lot of reassurance. In that way, she was the opposite of Nat, who was perhaps the most self-contained and self-reliant person I knew. Sometimes I wondered if I had purposely picked a mistress who was in many ways the polar opposite of my wife.

"Of course it's not." I lowered my voice. "You know how I feel about you."

Jaime smiled, dimples appearing in her cheeks. "I'm not sure I do, after Friday night."

I stood, walked around my desk and leaned down, bracing my arms against the Jaime's chair. She looked up at me, her hair falling back behind her. I smiled—or gave my best impression of a smile—then leaned forward to kiss her on the mouth. She resisted only for a minute, before giving in and returning the kiss. Jaime pulled back, and looked at me.

"I was worried something had happened," she murmured. "I thought maybe your wife had found out about us. I spent the whole weekend wondering if she was going to call Thomas to tell him we're having an affair."

A few short days ago, that would have been my worst-case scenario for the weekend, as well.

"No, I would have told you if something like that was happening."

"Would you?" Jaime shrugged. "How would I know that?"

"Because I would never let you get ambushed like that."

"Oh." Her shoulders dropped a bit, and her expression softened. "I didn't know what to think, honey. You just disappeared."

To kill a man, I thought, the words bubbling into my head, against my will. *To hold a pillow over his face...while he struggled for his life...making a keening noise that didn't even sound human...*

Fucking A, Clarke, get a grip, I told myself.

"Again, I'm really sorry about that." I kissed her again. This time, she kissed me back more passionately, winding her hands into my hair. I felt the familiar rush of arousal her touch always brought, and was shocked that my body was still capable of this sort of response after everything that had happened over the past few days.

Jaime broke away first and stood. Even with her heels, she

only came up to my midchest, so she had to look up at me, arching her neck back.

"Just don't ever do that to me again," she said. And even though she smiled when she said it, I wondered if there was a more menacing warning behind the words. My stomach dipped and swayed, as it occurred to me that this woman knew I'd rushed off in a panic on the night Robert died. She was one of the loose ends that Nat had worried about…and that I couldn't tell Nat about.

Jaime kissed me again, briefly but warmly, before turning to sashay out of my office. "I'll catch you later, handsome. I have a settlement conference this morning. I have to go get ready to do battle."

Once Jaime had left, closing the door again behind her with a soft click, I sat back down behind my desk. It wasn't until I picked up the glass on my desk and saw the water sloshing around inside that I realized my hands were shaking. I set the glass back down.

Had Jaime really just threatened me or was the epic stress I'd been under the past few days making me paranoid? Jaime had on more than one occasion mentioned the possibility of our both leaving our spouses in order to be together. These comments always came at intimate times, almost always postcoital, and they'd seemed like a harmless fantasy.

Now I wondered if she was more seriously invested in our relationship than I had realized.

I stared down at my hands, still shaking, and wondered when my life had turned so horrifically unrecognizable.

My phone beeped. I looked around, wondering where I'd put it—at home, I tended to carry it with me all the time, because it was often Jaime texting me—but once I was in the office, I didn't keep track of it as carefully. It beeped again, this time coming from the direction of my suit jacket, which I'd shed earlier and draped over my office chair. I pulled out my phone and saw that the incoming texts were from Nat.

The first one read,

Have you seen the news?

The second one:

The police found Robert's body.

CHAPTER 22

I quickly went online to search for news of what happened. The website for our local newspaper didn't have much in the way of detail. The story simply said that the body of Robert Gibbons, a private school principal in Shoreham, had been discovered on Sunday night...which was less than forty-eight hours after I'd killed him. Someone—not identified in the story—had gone to his house after being unable to get ahold of him by phone.

I wondered who'd discovered his body and desperately hoped it wasn't the school mom Robert had been secretly dating. Michelle Cole, Nat had said. I remembered the name, although still not the face. If it was her, it meant that she was already in contact with the police...which meant it would be only a matter of time before they knew Robert had called Michelle on the night he died from the same phone Nat had used to call me.

I forced myself to read on. Whoever it was who found Robert had peered through the window, saw his motionless body and called the police. Robert's body had been taken to the coroner's office for an autopsy. Results were expected within the week.

I spent the rest of the day in a blind panic. Robert's body had been found too quickly. The police would almost certainly know the date of his death and probably even the time frame on that day. Anything that narrowed their investigation was bad news for us. And again, there was the phone linking Robert to me.

I went through the motions of what I had to do that day— talking to clients, giving Lisa Sing detailed instructions for a document she was drafting for me, attending a partners' meeting—without remembering any of it. The entire time, my heart was thumping painfully in my chest, and there was a weird rushing sound in my ears. I was pretty sure I wasn't hiding it well, either, from the concerned glances Jaime kept shooting me during the partner's meeting. It was too hot in the conference room, with the afternoon sun streaming in through the double-glazed windows, and I started to perspire, to feel my face flush. I wanted to take off my jacket, but didn't want anyone to see that I had sweat through my button-down shirt.

When it was just nearly five, I bolted from my office, not able to sit there for one moment longer. That morning, I couldn't wait to get away from Nat. Now all I wanted to do was get home to her, so we could hash out the implications of Robert's body being discovered.

Nat was in the kitchen when I got home, standing at the island and chopping vegetables for the salad we were having with dinner. I poured myself a large bourbon and sat on a stool, watching her work. The knife flashed up and down as she sliced carrots and quartered cucumbers.

"Where's Charlie?"

"Around here somewhere, so be careful what you say." She glanced up at me. "You look completely freaked-out."

"I am completely freaked-out." *Why aren't you more freaked-out?* I wanted to ask. "All I've been able to think about all day is what if it was Michelle Cole who fo—?"

She cut me off. "It wasn't."

"What?"

"Dottie Fischer found him," she hissed.

"Who?"

"You know, the school secretary. Mrs. Fischer."

"Her name's Dottie?"

"Yes. Did you think her first name was 'missus'?"

"I never thought of her as having a first name. How do you know she was the one who found him?"

"Mandy told me. She was in the school office, picking up her girls for a dentist appointment, and heard then. Apparently, Mrs. Fischer was so shaken up, she took the day off, which is practically unheard of for her."

I could feel my panic, which had been spiraling all day, let up a bit. "Why didn't you tell me? I've been freaking out that it was Michelle Cole who found him. Which would mean that she was in touch with the police. That she'd tell them about the phone call."

"I told you not to worry about that," Nat said.

"Of course I'm worried! I can barely eat or sleep or even see straight! And won't the fact that they found his body mean—" I lowered my voice then to a whisper "—that the police will know when Robert died?"

"Probably. But it is what it is," Nat answered.

"What is that supposed to mean?"

"Of course it would have been better if they hadn't found him so quickly," she said quietly. Her head was bent over her work, her short, dark hair curving alongside her face. "But we can't engage in magical thinking. We have to deal with the facts as they are."

The "magical thinking" comment stung. It wasn't the first time she'd accused me of engaging in it. Once, when we were in law school, I'd decided to go out drinking the night before our torts exam. I explained to Nat that it made more sense to relax and unwind the night before a big test, rather than cram.

Nat replied that this was magical thinking, also absolute bullshit. Being prepared was far more important than being relaxed, and besides, it was never a good idea to go into a test hungover. Nat got an A in the class, while I squeaked by with a C+. Also, I knew Nat liked to think of herself as the cool, logical, rational one in our relationship, and me as the shallow former frat boy who'd never fully grown up. It was irritating as hell.

"I still think it's terrible news." I glanced around to make sure Charlie hadn't appeared. "You said that the more decomposed the body is, the harder it would be to determine the exact time of death. And maybe even the cause of death, too. If a few weeks had gone by, they might have bought that it was a suicide."

Nat glanced up at me. "Yes, I do know that. But it wasn't realistic to think it would take weeks to find the body. Robert does—did—have a lot of connections. Eventually someone was going to get worried when they couldn't reach him. The most we could have hoped for was a few additional days."

"And you don't think their finding him early is an issue?"

"It's not an issue until it's an issue."

My temper flared. "That's easy for you to say. You're not the one who—" I stopped and looked around again, then lowered my voice to an angry growl "—is guilty of murder."

"Stop being dramatic. And, just so you know, in the state of Florida, attempted murder is a first-degree felony. I have just as much at risk as you do." Nat swept the diced vegetables into the large wooden salad bowl and began slicing a red onion.

"Well…if it ever comes down to it, I'll take the fall," I said, regretting the words almost as soon as I'd spoken them. I would? Why would I do that when this was all her fault? But it seemed like the right thing to do. "If we get caught, I'll tell the police that you were home that night. That I was the only one there."

If I'd expected Nat to swoon at this chivalrous statement, I would have been disappointed. Instead, she pointed her chef's knife at me and said, "You need to get your shit together. Jesus,

Will. Never tell the police anything. Do you hear me? *Nothing*. They'll never figure out it was us, as long as we keep it together and don't start behaving like every two-bit drug dealer I've represented, ready to spill their guts for the best deal possible. That's how we get through this. Acting normal and keeping our mouths shut."

I took a slug of my bourbon, appreciating the warmth as it slid down my throat.

"What about Charlie?" I asked. "Should we tell him about Robert's death? Talk to him about it together?"

"I already did," Nat said.

"Oh." I tried not to feel slighted by this. "What did he say?"

"He handled it really well. He got quiet, but then he finally said, 'Well, I guess that means he won't be able to hurt other kids.' And he seemed relieved that he wouldn't have to see him at school again, although he couldn't really put that into words. He has an appointment with Camilla, the child therapist, this week. I'll let her know what happened, so she can talk to him about it."

"You're going to tell her what happened?" I asked, my head snapping up. "All of it?"

"Of course not. What's wrong with you?"

I tried to give her a withering look, but either it wasn't particularly effective or Nat was impervious to it. Then something occurred to me.

"You know, Charlie still hasn't talked to me about what happened to him. I should probably try again, shouldn't I?"

Nat lifted one shoulder. "I suppose so. But at our first appointment, Camilla told me not to bring it up too often... I think it's like salting the wound. We're supposed to be open to Charlie talking to us and create a calm and safe environment where he feels he can do that...but we also want to make sure his life doesn't narrow to only being about the abuse."

"So you're saying I shouldn't talk to him?"

I stared at my wife, suddenly flooded with misgivings. I had killed a man because she told me he'd hurt our son. But could I even trust her now? What if she'd had another motive for wanting Robert dead? Yet almost as quickly as these suspicions flared up, they died away. Of course Natalie wouldn't make up a story about Charlie being abused. I was just exhausted, worn down by the stress of the past few days.

"You should definitely talk to him," Natalie said calmly. "Maybe just let him know that you're sorry this happened. You're there for him if he ever wants to talk about it or if he has any questions. He may find it easier to talk to you than to me or Camilla if he has any anatomical questions."

"Jesus," I said, and took another long sip of bourbon.

"We just have to be there for him. That's the most important thing right— Oh, hi, sweetie!"

"Hi," Charlie said, wandering into the kitchen. "What's for dinner?"

"Baked chicken, roast potatoes and salad."

"What am I having?" Charlie asked.

"Ha ha, very funny."

"Can I have a grilled cheese instead?"

"Nope, but good try," Nat said.

I watched my wife joke around with our son, as if everything were normal. As if our lives hadn't been turned upside down and shaken around like a snow globe. And then I drained my glass.

By Thursday, the only other news I'd been able to find online—and I obsessively searched the internet several times a day—was from a person on a crime enthusiast message board who went by the handle @flnewzie. On Wednesday, he posted,

Post by @flnewzie on the message board NewsieNews.com: February 28th, 10:42 a.m.
My newziesenses are tingling about the report that a Shore-

ham private school principal was found dead in his house a
few days ago. I did a little digging, and found out that a few
days before this guy died, there was an announcement on the
school's website that they'd brought in some chick to be the
acting principal...which means that this guy was either fired or
quit or placed on probation just a few days before he died. So
now I'm thinking, what if this guy was a kiddy diddler. There's
no other reason why it would all be so hush-hush. Amirite? I
wonder if he offed himself...or if he was offed by an angry parent? Either way, I bet there's a lot more to the story.

I stared at this post, aghast. It had taken all of a few days for
someone who didn't have any actual knowledge of the facts—
a random message board poster—to figure out what had really
happened. How long would it take a police detective to work
it out? I picked up the phone to call Nat.

"Hey, I only have a minute," she said by way of greeting. "I
have a client out in reception."

"This is important. I have to read you something."

"What?"

"I was researching Robert's death up online, and—"

"Wait, where are you?"

"My office."

"You're looking that up on your office computer?" Natalie
sounded incredulous.

"It's fine," I said, wondering if it was, in fact, fine. I had no
idea what Barry, our IT guy, tracked or was able to track. Probably every key stroke in the office. But still, it couldn't be that
big a deal. Every school parent had probably run an internet
search on Robert's death.

Although maybe not every hour.

"This is a conversation we should have in person," Nat said
evenly. "I'll talk to you about it tonight."

She hung up without another word.

★ ★ ★

That night, after Charlie was asleep, Nat and I huddled in the living room. We'd started doing this nearly every night since *it* happened. I worried out loud about everything that could go wrong, while Nat dismissed most of my concerns, and insisted that we go over the timeline of that night again and again. It was more time than we'd spent alone together in years. I was drinking a very large glass of bourbon—my second of the evening—and Nat had a glass of wine she was mostly ignoring.

"We really can't talk about any of this on the phone," Nat said. "In fact, I've been thinking about something. It's not a problem exactly…but a potential problem."

Even though she looked and sounded calm, terror coursed through me. Nat and I had very different ideas about what constituted a problem.

"Oh, my God, what?"

"Don't panic. But you do know they track phone calls now, right?"

"Who?" I asked.

She gave me an exasperated look, which was now becoming unpleasantly familiar. It was as though she had suddenly realized she was married to a complete moron. Like she was going to have to slowly walk me through information that should be obvious to anyone of normal intelligence.

"All phone calls are captured and stored digitally. At least, all cell phone calls are. It's been going on for awhile. It started as an antiterrorism program."

"How is that even possible? And who's doing this?"

"Who knows? The FBI, Homeland Security, the NSA, the CIA. Maybe all of them. It's not like they're open about their spying techniques."

"That's not legal, is it?"

Natalie shrugged. "It doesn't matter. The fact is, they're doing it. And here's the thing—if they ever focused their investigation on us, it's not inconceivable that they could attempt to subpoena transcripts of our cell phone calls."

"Including the one I made to you on Friday night?" I tried to remember, through my rising alarm, exactly what Nat had said to me that night. I had been sitting at a corner table with Jaime at Rockbar Oysters, having cocktails, when Nat had called. I'd ignored the call—it was an unknown number—but she texted me a moment later. I'd been a little buzzed and had felt a thrill of alarm when I saw it. I'd immediately assumed it had something to do with my affair, that she had somehow found out about Jaime...although I was less clear on why that would involve her texting me from an unknown number. I'd been so alarmed, so sure we'd been caught, that I jumped up from the table, signaling to Jaime that I'd be right back before hurrying outside. I stood in the parking lot in a pool of blue light shining down from a streetlamp and called Nat back, my heart hammering in my chest.

But what had she said during that conversation? Between the cocktails and my anxiety over being caught, I wasn't entirely sure. Had she said something about being in trouble? Yes, that was it. She had definitely used the word *trouble*.

"So if the police can access our conversations...they'll know that I called you and you said you were in trouble...and Jesus Christ, on the night when Robert died!" More of the conversation came back to me then. I groaned. "And then you told me to go home and leave my cell phone there, so I couldn't be traced."

Nat nodded calmly, as though she'd already thought through all of this. "Yes, I mean it's possible. But they would have to specify phone numbers in the subpoena. There's no way to tie that number to me."

"But it's tied to me! I got a text then called it back," I said, staring at my wife.

"If they pursue it. But why would they? If the police did pull the GPS tracking for our phones, they'll see that I was at home that night, and you were at a restaurant, before returning home. And then we didn't leave for the rest of the night. I'm assuming your colleagues will be able to provide an alibi that you were with them. There's no reason to think they'd suspect us."

At the word *alibi*, I'd felt a cold rush of dread. Of course my work colleagues wouldn't be able to alibi me. Except for Jaime. It occurred to me with dizzying horror that this could all go so wrong, so quickly.

"Unless they find out about Charlie," I pointed out. "That would give us a motive. It would make us suspects."

"They're not going to find out about that." Nat lowered her shoulders, bending her neck to one side and then the other, as if working out a kink. "Oh, and you really need to stop researching Robert's death online, especially at your office. That can be tracked, too. For all you know, your IT guy is a total creeper, monitoring what you all do."

I took another large swallow of bourbon, soothed by the heat of it against my throat. I'd never really understood before why people turn to alcohol. Staying comfortably anesthetized had its benefits, sure, but lurching drunkenness just looked bad. Now that I was in the middle of this horrific crisis, I was quickly starting to appreciate the impulse. I had taken to gulping my liquor, craving the numbness to come faster, last longer. It didn't work, of course. The numbness was hard to hold on to. Already my thoughts were starting to become slippery, fuzzy on the edges.

"This is a fucking nightmare," I said, shaking my head.

"Really?" Natalie gave up trying to stretch out her kink and began massaging her shoulder with one hand. "I think it's actually going okay. I mean, obviously it would have been better if we'd stuck to the original plan. But we couldn't, and for having to improvise as much as we have, it's going great."

"Great?" I repeated, dumbfounded. "How is any of this great?"

As Natalie frowned, three vertical lines appeared between

her eyebrows. When we were dating, I used to find this adorable. "So far, we've totally gotten away with it. No one's come
forward to say that they saw us near his house on the night of
his death. No one suspects us of anything."

"How do you know that?"

"Trust me, we would know. The police would have already
shown up at our door."

"So, we just sit and wait to see if they come for us? How long
will that go on for?"

Natalie shrugged. "It depends. I'm still hoping they'll get the
toxicology screen results back and determine his death a suicide."

"How likely is that?"

"It depends on how incompetent the medical examiner is. I
think when someone dies from suffocation, they can usually de-
tect signs of asphyxia. But I think it really depends on how hard
they look. If they find the drugs in his system and the drugs on
the coffee table...that might be enough."

"And then we're home free." I took another long drink of my
bourbon. "Hopefully."

"We may find out more tomorrow."

"Why, what's tomorrow?"

"We're going to Mandy and Dan's house for dinner. Mandy's
always a good source for what's going on in town. She hears everything. You didn't forget, did you?"

I tried to make sense of her words in my bourbon-steeped
haze. "Dinner?"

"Yes, I told you about it yesterday. Charlie's coming, too. He
and Beatrice have plans for a movie marathon. Something in-
volving superheroes, I think. He's very excited."

"We're going to a dinner party, like nothing's happened?" I
asked.

"Yes, that's the general idea. We're going to act normal. Avoid
suspicion."

"I don't know if I can do that."

"Okay." Natalie nodded thoughtfully. "Well, you have two choices. You can either stick with my plan, which is the one designed to keep us both out of jail. Or you can run around, melting down, basically behaving as if there's a large neon arrow pointing at you with the word *guilty* emblazoned on it. Which option do you want to pick?"

I tried to think of a withering comeback and realized I didn't have one.

"I'm going to bed," I said, standing. I was swayed a little and hoped Nat didn't notice.

"Good idea. Oh, and Will?"

"Yeah?"

"Stop drinking so much. It's going to make you sloppy."

CHAPTER 23

"This is delicious, Mandy," Nat said, eating another bite of her coq au vin. We were sitting in the Breens' dining room, eating at their formal cherrywood table. We'd also rated the good china and lots of candles, which was unusual. Normally, dinner at the Breens' meant barbecue and sitting out by the pool.

"I'd love to take credit, but Dan made it," Mandy said. "His cooking skills are the main reason I keep him around."

"True story," Dan said.

"I can see why. This—" Nat pointed at the coq au vin with her fork "—is insanely good."

"Don't overdo it," Mandy chided. "Compliments go straight to his head."

"You two are *so* cute," Lauren David exclaimed.

Lauren and her husband, Bret, who lived across the street, were the third couple at the Breens' dinner party. Their presence was possibly the reason why Mandy had gone to so much trouble with the place settings that night. I hadn't met the Davids before. Lauren was blonde with a very white toothy smile and whose favorite adjective was *cute*. She was wearing a strap-less turquoise top and a necklace made out of giant beads of the same color. Bret had a head shaped like a potato, which their twin nine-year-old boys had unfortunately inherited. The twins, along with Charlie and the Breens' two daughters, were all out-side, eating dinner on the patio. I could see Charlie through the glass doors. He was sitting next to Beatrice, and they had their heads bent toward one another as they laughed about some-thing. It was good to see him smiling. The previous night had been rough. Charlie had woken up after having a bad dream that upset him so much, he was up for hours.

"How are you, Will?" Mandy asked. "You're awfully quiet tonight."

I looked up at my hostess and hesitated for a few beats too long. I glanced over at Nat, who raised her eyebrows. I realized the silence was stretching out awkwardly.

"Sorry, I don't mean to be. It's just been a long week at work," I said.

"What do you do?" Lauren asked.

"I'm an attorney," I said. "Trusts and estates."

"Oh, I thought you were the attorney in the family," Lauren said, looking over at Natalie.

"We both are," Nat replied. "We actually met in law school."

"Cute!" Lauren exclaimed.

I didn't know exactly how to respond to that, so I took a bite of my potatoes. They had been sliced thin and cooked in cream and cheese. They were pretty good, or would have been if I'd had any appetite at all. I couldn't understand how Nat could sit there, eating and chatting, as if one week earlier, we hadn't killed a man. She seemed completely at ease, asking Lauren about whether she liked the Catholic school they sent their twins to, if Bret enjoyed his work as a financial planner, whether Mandy had heard that Franklin School was going to hold a fund-raiser at the local build-your-own-burrito joint next week.

I stared at my wife, listening to her talk about how much she loved school fund-raisers that got her out of cooking dinner for a night, and I wondered for the hundredth time since we'd killed Robert Gibbons—since I'd killed Robert—if it was possible that the woman I'd been married to for fourteen years was normal. I was a wreck. How could this not be affecting her in some way?

"We almost sent the twins to Franklin, but I'm so glad now that we went with St. Mary's instead," Lauren said. "Bret wasn't sure at first. Right, sweetie?"

Bret had just taken a bite of food, so all he could do was nod and make an indistinct grunting sound. He actually hadn't said much of anything that evening, mostly staying quiet while his wife filled every silence with her burbling chatter. I wasn't sure if he was naturally quiet or if he was actually as dim-witted I suspected he was. Then again, I wasn't being very talkative myself.

I could feel my phone vibrate in my pocket, alerting me to a text. I surreptitiously pulled it out, and—keeping the phone under the table—checked the text.

It was from Jaime:

Can you talk?

I quickly texted back:

No.

Her response pinged back a second later:

I need to talk to you soon.

I glanced up and saw that Nat was looking at me. I slid the phone back in my pocket.

Lauren was still talking. "Bret isn't at all religious, so he wasn't sure about sending the boys to a Catholic school. But I went to

Catholic school. I just think that kids who have religious up-
bringings end up having better characters." Then, as if just realizing that there were four parents sitting at the table who had
chosen a nonparochial education for their children, she quickly
added, "Not that Franklin isn't a great school. Although I still
can't believe what happened with your principal." She lowered
her voice to a dramatic whisper. "What's everyone at the school
saying about that? It's crazy, isn't it?"

I noticed Nat look at Mandy and Mandy's eyes widen in response. I wondered what that was about.

"No one knows what to think," Mandy said. "We don't even
know how he died or if the police are investigating it."

"You seriously don't?" Lauren exclaimed. She leaned forward, clasping her hands together, looking absolutely delighted.

"We've heard almost nothing," Nat said.

"You are totally going to totally freak out when I tell you
this." Lauren put up her hands, her fingers spread wide. "Daddy
told me that there is absolutely an active investigation into his
death. And they've uncovered all sorts of stuff already!"

I looked at Lauren, back at Nat and Mandy, who had both
leaned forward, paying rapt attention to the vapid blonde. I had
a feeling I'd missed something important.

"Your father?" I asked.

"Lauren's father is Garland Nolan," Mandy said. "The sheriff."

"That's right! My daddy's the sheriff," Lauren confirmed.
"He's gearing up for his reelection campaign. The twins are
going to be in one of the commercials. Isn't that cute?"

I caught Nat glancing outside at the twins and knew that she
was thinking. *Cute?*

"Anyway," Lauren continued, blithely unaware, "Daddy told
me that he thinks this investigation is going to totally heat up."

"Why, what happened?" Mandy asked.

"I can't believe y'all really haven't heard about this," Lauren
trilled. She looked over at her lumpen husband, who was still

silently eating, showing no sign that he was even listening to the conversation. "Can you believe they haven't heard about this, honey?" This time, Bret didn't even bother to respond. "Anyway, Daddy told me that the principal...wait, what was his name again?"

"Robert Gibbons," Nat and Mandy said in unison.

"Oh, right. I'm terrible with names. They think he was a—" Lauren lowered her voice to a whisper, as if the kids might be able to hear her from outside *"—drug addict."*

"What?" Mandy exclaimed. "That can't be right! I cannot picture Robert Gibbons doing drugs of any kind!"

"Actually, it would explain quite a lot," Dan said. "Forty-six-year-old men don't usually just keel over dead. Does anyone want more wine?"

"They're also looking into reports that his drug dealer was at his house the night he died," Lauren said.

"Robert had a drug dealer?" Mandy shook her head. "This is just getting crazier and crazier."

"I'll have some more wine," I said, holding out my glass to Dan, who tipped some pinot noir into it. I took a gulp of the wine, then another, before glancing at Nat. She was looking back at me, a slight frown on her face. I took another large sip.

"If his drug dealer was at his house, is it possible that he was... well." Mandy stopped, and looked sheepish. "I don't mean to sound dramatic, but...is it possible that he was murdered? I mean, do the police know what the cause of death was yet?"

"I'm not sure about that, *but...*" Lauren paused for dramatic effect "...I do know that they got the results back from his tox screen."

"Do you really think you should be talking about this?" Bret asked mildly. It was practically the first thing he'd said all evening, but then, he had finally finished his dinner. He stacked his fork and knife onto his empty plate. "Since they haven't officially released the results."

"Oh, it's fine." Lauren waved an airy hand. "It's not like anyone here was involved." She frowned at her husband. "Anyway, I can tell you, he had a lot of drugs in his system. I mean, a *lot* of drugs. So it was probably an overdose, intentional or otherwise. But y'all knew him. Would it surprise you if he were suicidal?"

This was how the gossip game worked, I thought. Lauren was more than happy to divulge information she really probably shouldn't be sharing, just as long as we made it worth her while. She wanted to add more facts to her story, like this was all a really interesting miniseries on Netflix, rather than a hideous real-life nightmare.

"No," Nat said firmly. "It wouldn't surprise me at all."

Mandy gave Nat a curious look but then shrugged. "I guess I can see Nat's point. Robert had been accused of doing a terrible thing." She turned to Lauren. "I'm assuming you know about that part."

"That he'd been accused of molesting a student at the school?" Lauren said this with such breathless excitement that I began to actively hate her. "Yes, everyone in town knows that. It's all anyone could talk about, or at least it was right up until his body was found!"

"There were some issues with the student's claims, and I know a lot of people weren't inclined to believe him," Mandy added. "Not without a further investigation. Which, I guess, probably won't happen now." She looked at Nat. "Is that right?"

"Not a criminal investigation," Nat confirmed. "But there could always be a civil case against the school."

"Oh, my God, *really*?" Lauren leaned forward. "The student's parents are suing the school?"

"No, I didn't say that," Nat said quickly. "I have no idea if they plan to take any legal action."

"So, go back to what you were saying before about his drug dealer being in the neighborhood on the night of his death?" I asked. I wondered if my voice sounded oddly high-pitched as I thought it might. I cleared my throat. "How do the police know that?"

"Oh, well, one of his neighbors reported seeing a black sedan drive by on Friday night. She said she didn't recognize the car, but that she saw it drive down the street, then drive by again a little later," Lauren said. "She said she'd seen the car around before, that the driver looked like a thug. Lots of tattoos, mean face. That sort of thing."

A black sedan. Nat drove a silver Honda Pilot. I had a blue Jeep. That meant it wasn't either of us the neighbor had seen.

"How did she know the car was going to Robert's house?" Nat asked. "His neighborhood is pretty secluded."

"You've been to his house?" Lauren exclaimed.

"Will and I knew Robert for years. We used to occasionally have dinner with him and his wife, back when they were still married," Nat said casually. "I don't think he even has any neighbors within sight of his driveway."

Her ability to remain unruffled during this topic of conversation amazed me. It was as though she had completely detached herself from the fact that she had drugged Robert with enough oxycodone to kill him. If he hadn't been an oxycodone addict… and, really, wasn't that something she should have thought about ahead of time? In fact, why *hadn't* Nat, the smartest, most organized woman in the world, considered that as a possibility? *It's just fucking careless*, I thought. I realized I was getting drunk.

Lauren lifted one bare tanned shoulder, let it fall. "I have no idea. Maybe she's the neighborhood busybody and followed his car or something. Some of the retirees on this street think that they're the neighborhood watch. Mandy, do you remember when they tried to organize a neighborhood watch here, and no one with, you know, jobs and children and lives, wanted to spend their nights patrolling with flashlights. They got so annoyed and said they'd do it themselves? Which was hilarious, because they all go to bed at, like, eight o'clock at night. When do they think crimes happen?"

"I do remember that," Mandy said, smiling.

"Daddy told me that the whole thing was supersilly. He said if anyone saw anything suspicious, we should just call him and he'd send a deputy out right away to take care of it," Lauren continued. "What was the ex-wife like?"

"Venetia? I liked her," Nat said. "She was funny, nice. And she loved the beach. I was surprised when she moved away from Florida."

"Where did she move to?" Mandy asked.

"Oregon, I think. We lost touch after she left."

"She probably knows something," Lauren said confidently. "The wife always knows."

"Uh-oh," Dan said. He reached out and squeezed Mandy's hand. "I hope I never get on Mandy's bad side. She knows all my darkest secrets."

"It's true." Mandy laughed. "I could burn you so badly."

"It's probably why Robert's ex moved so far away," Lauren exclaimed. "I'm sure Daddy's investigators will want to talk to her."

The woman never seemed to tire of talking, I thought, lifting my wineglass again. I was surprised to find out that it was empty.

"More, Will?" Dan asked, picking up the bottle of wine.

I could feel Nat's eyes on me, flinty blue. I resolutely ignored her gaze and held out my glass for another refill.

Nat ended up having to drive us home. Charlie was in the back seat, chatting away about the movie he and Beatrice had gotten halfway through before we had to leave.

"There was this great chase scene where the good guys were riding motorcycles and the bad guys were driving monster trucks. Then there was a huge explosion. It was awesome," Charlie enthused happily. "When can I go back to Bea's house to finish the movie?"

"I don't know, honey," Nat said. "I'll talk to Mrs. Breen, and we'll find a time when they're free."

"The bad guys kidnapped a kid," Charlie said.

"What bad guys?" I asked. In my wine-fogged state, I was having a hard time following his chatter.

"In the movie," Charlie said. "They kidnapped the president's son. And Bea said she heard that's what Principal Gibbons did. That's why he was fired."

"Who told her that?"

"Some kids at school have been saying it," Charlie said. The excitement had suddenly disappeared from his voice, leaving it heartbreakingly flat. "I wanted to tell her that's not what happened. But I didn't."

"Why not?" I asked.

"Because Mom told me not to."

I looked over at Nat. "You told him he couldn't talk to his friends?" I wasn't sure what about this made me so indignant— the pain in Charlie's voice, my latent anger with my wife. Or the five large glasses of red wine I'd consumed that night. But almost immediately, I realized that Nat had probably made the right call. But still. She should have talked about it with me first.

"I told him that what happened is private. That it would be best keeping it that way." Nat's voice was calm, but I could tell by the clip of her words that she wasn't pleased with me. "If he needs to talk to someone, he can always talk to one of us. Or Camilla."

Charlie kicked the back of my seat. "But no one knows the truth, so they're just making stuff up." I'd never heard him like this—fretful, angry, resentful. He'd always been such a good-natured, sunny child.

"I know that's frustrating," Nat said.

"I think it's okay for you to say that you don't think that's what happened. But maybe just not go into detail."

"Never mind," Charlie muttered.

"Why don't you talk about it with Camilla when you see her next time."

"I said, *never mind*."

"Okay," Nat said. She nodded to herself. "Okay."

We drove the rest of the way home in silence.

The next day, the police showed up at our house.

CHAPTER 24

I woke up the next morning feeling like death and wondered why red wine hangovers were always so much more brutal than run-of-the-mill hangovers. I stood in the kitchen, one hand braced against the island countertop, not entirely sure the water and painkillers I was bravely trying to swallow were going to stay down. My phone beeped at me. I pulled it out of my pocket and saw that Jaime had sent me yet another text.

Can you get away sometime today? Need to talk.

I wondered what the hell was going on with her. She knew that my weekends were normally off-limits. Between Charlie's soccer games, our regular family beach outing, my basketball league and the never-ending march of errands and chores that went along with typical suburban life, I didn't have the time. There were always trips to the hardware store, an oil change, or Charlie yet again needing a new pair of sneakers, having already outgrown the ones we'd bought him two months earlier. Jaime and I had agreed early on in the affair that we should be careful about how much we talked or even texted when we were with our families. Although she and her husband, Thomas—whose interests included Thai food and hot yoga—didn't have children together, Jaime had a college-age daughter from a previous marriage. Her weekends were never quite as jam-packed as mine. Maybe because of that, we'd never stuck too closely to the no-contact rule—we often texted back and forth on the weekends, in the evenings, even when we weren't alone and it was risky to do so. But insisting I meet her on a Saturday was unprecedented.

I'm not sure I can, I typed. I'll let you know if I can get away.

Her response pinged back almost immediately.

It's important.

The doorbell rang before I could respond.

"Nat?" I called out. "Can you get the door?"

Nat didn't answer. I wondered where she was. I'd been too hungover to do more than grunt good morning when I finally staggered out of bed. The doorbell rang again.

I sighed, pocketed my phone and headed toward the front door, wondering who could possibly be on our doorstep at eight thirty in the morning on a Saturday. I opened the door, squinting into the painfully bright sunlight, which seemed intent on drilling its way into my hangover.

"Mr. Clarke?"

I blinked a few times, trying to clear the sunspots from my vision. There were two men standing there, both wearing suits, which seemed odd for a Saturday morning. One of the men was older, probably in his late forties, with a thick build and a truly impressive head of dark hair that he wore swept back from his ruddy face. The other man was a lot younger, around thirty, with an angular face and a slight, wiry frame.

"Yes," I said. "I'm Will Clarke."

"I'm Detective Mike Monroe," the older man said. "And this is my partner, Gavin Reddick. We're from the Calusa County Sheriff's Office Criminal Investigative Division. We'd like to talk to you for a minute."

I stared at them mutely, unable to speak. I knew the silence was stretching on for far longer than reasonable, but I couldn't seem to remember how to talk. My stomach shifted queasily, the acidic hangover suddenly replaced by a feeling of cold liquid terror in my bowels.

"Mr. Clarke?" Detective Monroe looked concerned. "Are you okay?"

Shit, I thought. No, I did not want the police to be concerned about my well-being.

"Yes. Sorry. I just…had a late night." I had apparently regained the ability to speak, but just not coherently. "Um. What's this, um, about?"

"We'd like to come inside and talk to you," Monroe said. I noticed that he didn't ask questions, he made statements. It wasn't *may we come in*, it was *we'd like to come inside*. So far his partner, Detective Reddick, was silent, but I could feel his eyes—which were dark and a little on the squinty side—studying me.

"I don't know if this is a great time," I said. "Like I said, I had a late night…."

"Hi, I'm Natalie Clarke." Nat had appeared beside me in the doorway. Her hair was damp, which meant she'd probably just gotten out of the shower. She looked crisp in a polo shirt and khaki shorts. She held out her hand the police officers.

The detectives introduced themselves, each shaking Nat's hand in turn. If she was at all concerned that the police were at our house, it didn't show. I was stunned by how utterly self-possessed she seemed.

"We have some questions in connection with an investigation we're pursuing," Monroe said. "We were just telling your husband we'd like to come in and talk to you."

"Of course, please do," Nat said, opening the door.

I was flabbergasted. Nat had always told me to never, ever talk to the police. Did she think that just because she was a criminal defense attorney, she'd be able to sidestep every trap?

Nat led the detectives into the living room, while I trailed behind.

"Can I get you anything to drink? Coffee, or maybe a soda?" she asked.

"No, thank you," Monroe said.

"I'm good," Reddick said. "Thanks."

Nat and I took seats on the couch. The detectives sat on a pair of gray velvet club chairs, which were more attractive than they were comfortable. Nat and the policemen both seemed perfectly at ease. I was scared shitless and had to press my hands down flat on my thighs to keep them from shaking. The police were *here*. In our *house*. I had killed a man and now the police had arrived. It was taking all of my willpower not to keel forward and vomit on our living room carpet.

"We're investigating the death of Robert Gibbons," Monroe said, confirming what I'd already suspected. "I understand you knew him."

"Of course," Nat said. "Our son, Charlie, is a student at Franklin School, but Robert was also a personal friend of ours."

"What can you tell us about Mr. Gibbons? How well did you know him?"

"When we first moved to Shoreham, we lived in the same apartment complex as Robert and Venetia. Robert's ex-wife," Nat explained. "We'd get together with them for dinner or the movies. That sort of thing."

"Was it a close friendship?"

"Close? No, I wouldn't say close, necessarily. I mean, we were certainly fond of the Gibbonses, but we didn't spend the holidays with them or go on trips together," Nat said. She looked over at me.

"Right," I agreed. My voice caught in my throat and I cleared it. "They were the sort of friends you'd grab a pizza with on a Friday night."

"Exactly," Nat said. "And that happened a lot less frequently after we both moved out of the apartment complex."

"What about after the Gibbonses divorced?" Monroe asked.

I was surprised that neither detective was recording our conversation or even taking notes on a spiral-bound notepad, like the policemen did on television crime dramas. Was that, I wondered with yet another thud of fear, because they already knew everything we were telling them? Were they not looking for facts, but instead for inconsistencies?

"Things changed then," Nat admitted. "Venetia moved out of state and we didn't really see Robert as much socially anymore. Or at all, really. We did see him at school all the time, of course."

"How did Mr. Gibbons seem to you after the divorce?" Reddick asked, chiming in for the first time since the interview had begun.

"Seem?" Nat asked. "In what way exactly?"

"Did you notice any changes in his personality? Did he seem angry or depressed? Anything like that?"

"Well, yes." Nat bit her lip, and looked thoughtful for a moment. "I would say he certainly seemed downcast in the months after his divorce. Although that would be normal, wouldn't it?"

Neither detective answered her. I had a feeling that was another police tactic. Never answer a question in order to keep the target off balance.

"Robert didn't want the divorce," I said.

Both of the detective's heads swiveled toward me.

"Why do you say that?" Monroe asked.

I had no idea why I'd said it. Some combination of terror that the police were in our living room and a desperate wish to turn their focus away from Natalie's and my relationship with Robert. If the police thought Robert's death was somehow connected to his divorce, rather than to the fact that he was a pedophile, that would be a good thing for us.

"We went out one time for a beer after work. Just Robert and me," I said. "It was while back. Three years ago?"

I'd actually forgotten about it until just that moment. I'd run into Robert at school one day, while I was there dropping off Charlie's lunchbox, which he'd forgotten at home. I'd handed the lunch box to Mrs. Fischer, the terrifying school receptionist who'd taken it from me unsmilingly. I was just turning to leave when Robert wandered out of his office looking downcast, his hands in his pockets. He'd seemed so lost and unhappy that I'd felt sorry for him. I asked him if he wanted to grab a beer after work and had been surprised when he'd accepted. Robert wasn't really a beer-after-work kind of a guy. I figured at the time he was probably lonely.

Now, thinking about my gesture of kindness—and how Robert had repaid that by targeting my son a few years later—caused a bubble of rage to swell up inside me. Fuck Robert. Fuck him. I was glad he was dead.

"It was after he and Venetia had separated, but before their divorce was final," I continued, hoping I was successfully concealing my simmering rage. If Nat could keep her feelings contained, I could do the same. "He was still hoping at that point that she would change her mind."

"Did he say why she wanted the divorce?" Monroe asked.

I shook my head slowly. "No, he seemed genuinely confused as to why she left." I tried to remember my conversation with Robert that night, but it came back only in scraps. "We'd gone to Winston's, a local pub, and had each ordered a draft beer. Robert told me he'd tried to talk Venetia into giving their marriage another chance, maybe going to marriage therapy, but she'd refused. He said that once she'd made her decision, it was like she had just turned off her feelings. She was just done."

"And he never knew why?" Monroe asked.

"I have no idea." I shrugged. "That was the only time we talked about it."

"You said your son's name is Charlie?" Detective Reddick asked.

"Yes," Nat said.

Reddick nodded. "What grade is he in?"

"Fifth grade," Nat said. "He's eleven."

"Is it okay if we talk to him?"

"No," Nat said evenly. "It's not okay."

Reddick exchanged a look with his partner. "It's not like we want to bring him down to the station and put him in an interview room."

"That's right." Monroe grinned. "We don't break out the rubber hoses to use on kids. At least, not usually."

"We'll just ask him a few questions here. You can even be there with him."

Natalie raised her eyebrows and looked coolly back at the detective.

"I know I would have the right to be there," she said. "I'm a criminal defense attorney. I also know you don't have the right to question my son without my express permission, which I'm not granting. Unless you have probable cause that he was a witness to a crime." She looked from one detective to the other. "Do you have probable cause?"

The detectives exchanged another look. They obviously did not.

"I thought you looked familiar," Monroe said. "I've seen you in court. You represent the bad guys, right?"

"I protect the rights of my clients. For example, making sure the police don't cross the line in the course of doing their duties."

"We've spoken to a bunch of school families already," Reddick said mildly. "You're the first that's refused to let us talk to your kid."

My insides instantly dissolved into an icy liquid, or at least that's what it felt like. Was Nat making the right call refusing to let them talk to Charlie? And yet, I knew why she'd refused. We had no idea how Charlie would hold up under questioning, no matter how mild. If he admitted that Robert had touched him...Nat and I would instantly become prime suspects in Robert's death.

"That's fine," Natalie said. "But it certainly doesn't persuade me to change my mind."

"Do you mind telling us why?" Reddick persisted.

"I do mind, actually. I don't have to explain why I don't want the police questioning my eleven-year-old son about an alleged pedophile, which might be a little upsetting for him," Nat said. "And I'm sure the other parents didn't know they could refuse. It's not like you told them that, right?"

"*Alleged,*" Reddick repeated. He looked over at Monroe. "Lawyers know all the fancy words, don't they?"

Detective Monroe held up a hand, like a parent trying to silence squabbling offspring.

"Mr. and Mrs. Clarke," he said in a soothing voice. "Over the course of our investigation, it's come to our attention that Robert Gibbons might have been alone with Charlie at one point during a school field trip."

I froze so completely, I actually stopped breathing. I turned to look at Nat and saw that although she still looked composed, her color had paled.

"Who said that?" she asked.

"One of the chaperones."

"Which one?" Nat's voice had an icy edge to it.

"I'm not saying that anything happened," Monroe continued. "But Charlie might have some information that would help us with our investigation. That's why we'd like to speak with him."

"First of all, I would imagine all of the children at the school were in contact with Robert at one time or another," Nat said. "He was the principal. But second, Robert is dead. You're not investigating what he may or may not have done to any children. You're investigating his death."

Monroe tipped his head to one side. "The two might be related."

"I certainly hope not," Natalie said. "As I'm sure you know, there's a rumor going around that Robert was a drug addict."

The detectives exchanged a glance. Monroe nodded. "Yes, that's an angle we are investigating."

"Good. In my experience, when addicts get in trouble, it usually involves drugs," Nat said.

I was just grudgingly admiring my wife's cool response— which was pretty much the perfect retort—when Detective Monroe abruptly said, "Where were you on Friday night?"

And just like that, I was again flooded with terror. They wanted an *alibi*. The police were in our house, asking us for alibis. This was all moving too quickly.

"Friday night?" Nat repeated. She tipped her head to one side and looked thoughtful. "I think I was home that night. Wait, no, I did go to the grocery store in the early evening, but after that I was in for the night."

"And, you, sir?" Monroe looked at me.

"I was…out," I stammered. "With work colleagues. At Rockbar Oysters."

"Heard the food's good there," Monroe remarked. "But that's a long way to go for oysters."

"It was pretty good," I said. "Worth the drive."

"Will you give us the names of your colleagues?" Reddick asked. He finally pulled a notebook and pen out of his pocket and looked up at me, the pen poised over the paper.

"Sure," I said, desperately trying to think of which of my law partners would cover for me. "Um… Ben Miller was there. And

Alex Peters. Oh, and Jaime Anderson. And the kid we were in-terviewing, although I can't remember his name."

"Ben Miller. Alex Peters. Jaime Anderson," Reddick re-peated, scribbling in his notebook. I watched him write, feel-ing my blood pressure spike, my heart pounding in my chest. I wondered distantly if I could count on Ben and Alex, who I'd known for years, to cover for me. Either one would probably be fine providing an alibi to my wife—it was an open secret in the firm that Ben had an affair with one of the paralegals a few years back and Alex was on his third marriage. But I had to imagine they would not be comfortable backing a false alibi to the police. Hell, I wasn't even sure Jaime would do that for me.

"If that's everything, I'll walk you gentlemen out," Natalie said, standing.

The policemen got to their feet. Reddick took out a business card, handed it to Nat. She took the card, but didn't look at it. "If you change your mind about letting us interview Charlie, call me."

Nat nodded and walked to the front door, which she opened. The detectives filed out and Nat closed the door behind them. Before I could say anything, she raised a finger to her lips.

"Wait a minute," she mouthed.

"I was just going to ask where Charlie is."

"He's in his room. I told him he could watch a movie on my tablet, as long as he wore his headphones."

"Good thinking."

Nat glanced out the window. "Okay, we're clear. They're in their car, pulling out now."

"Thank God," I breathed. I ran a hand over my face and re-alized that I was damp with sweat. "I feel like shit."

"I can't imagine why," Nat said dryly. "Maybe because you drank a bucket of wine last night?"

My stomach shifted queasily. "I don't want to talk about it."

Nat snorted. "I bet."

"It was a Friday night."

"Jesus, Will. You have to get it together. The police are now involved. We have to be careful."

"I am." I realized this was a complete lie, so I drew in a shaky breath. "I will. Do you think they know anything?"

"No," Nat said. "That was a fishing expedition. They don't know anything about us. If they did, they would have brought us in for a formal interview. But that younger detective…what was his name?" She pulled his business card out of her pocket. "Gavin Reddick. I could tell his antennae were up. But that doesn't necessarily mean anything. Detectives are inherently suspicious."

"They're investigating Robert's death as a murder, then." The word murder was like a stale cracker in my mouth, crumbling on my dry tongue.

"I'm not sure."

"Let me put it this way—would detectives be interviewing us, or any of the other school parents, if they didn't already suspect that Robert was murdered?"

"Probably not," Nat admitted.

The icy liquid terror returned, pitching through me violently.

"When will we know if we're in the clear?" I asked.

Nat shrugged, shook her head. "I don't know. At this point, we're going to have to wait and see. I'm sure we'll hear something soon."

CHAPTER 25

The news broke on Monday morning while I was at work.

I had followed Nat's orders and stopped running internet searches on Robert's death. I knew she was right, it was too risky, too easy to track, although I wasn't about to admit that to her. But midmorning, while I was wading through a stack of business holdings for one of my trust clients, Nat sent me a text:

Sheriff Nolan is about to hold a press conference about Robert's death.

I turned to my computer and pulled up the website for one of the West Palm Beach news stations. The press conference wasn't among the top headlines—the shooting of a police officer the night before in Riviera Beach was dominating the news cycle, along with a story about a city commissioner who'd been indicted for fraud. I had to scroll down the page a bit. I found the story—"Calusa County Sheriff Garland Nolan to Hold Conference on Investigation into Death of Shoreham School Principal Robert Gibbons at 10 am." It was just after ten, so I tapped on the link and waited impatiently for the video feed to load on the website.

The news conference was underway. Sheriff Nolan was standing at a podium, with a cluster of microphones set up in front of him. He had a long face with an exaggerated chin, serious brown eyes and close-cropped gray hair. Now that I knew he and Lauren David were related, I could see the resemblance. She'd inherited his bone structure, along with his narrow lips, but certainly not his personality. Whereas Lauren was frivolous and chatty, her father looked like a man who rarely grinned. He was wearing what I assumed was his official uniform—a dark shirt, open at the collar, with patches on the arms and a gold star pinned over his heart.

"The body of Robert Gibbons was found last Sunday, February 25, after a visitor to his house spotted him through a window. Our medical examiner, Dr. Sarah Goldstein, has completed the autopsy. Her conclusion is that Robert Gibbons died of asphyxiation. We are now officially investigating this death as a homicide. Because the investigation is ongoing, I'm not going to comment further on any of our findings to date."

I watched in stunned horror as the gaggle of reporters immediately began shouting out questions, ignoring the sheriff's statement that he wasn't going to comment.

"How was the victim asphyxiated?"

"Can you confirm that there were drugs present at the scene?"

"Do you have any suspects?"

Oh, Jesus, I thought.

The sheriff looked irritated. "As I just said, I'm not going to comment further on what is an ongoing investigation."

I stared at my computer screen, trying to absorb the horror of what was happening. The police were officially investigating Robert's death as a homicide…and they'd already been at our house asking questions…and I'd given them a false alibi.

"Shit," I said out loud.

"What?" Jaime said from the doorway.

I startled and banged my knees on my desk. I fumbled to hit the volume button on my computer keyboard, silencing the sheriff.

"What are you watching?" Jaime asked, frowning.

"Nothing. I was just…a video started autoplaying." I gestured toward the screen. "I hate that."

"What happened to you this weekend?" She looked back over her shoulder to make sure no one was listening, then stepped into my office and closed the door behind her. I quickly closed the news website. "You never got back to me."

Jaime looked stunning, as usual. Today she was wearing a tight-fitting green sweater over a knee-length black skirt and high-heeled boots. Her dark curls were loose around her shoulders. Normally, seeing her like this, looking like a sexy librarian, would make me want to stand up and pull her into my arms. But not now. Not after hearing the sheriff utter the word *asphyxiation* in his deep, clipped voice.

"Sorry," I said. "I had a lot going on."

"I really need to talk to you."

"Oh…okay. What about?" I wondered if it was possible that the sheriff's detectives had already been to see her about my alibi, but then remembered that she'd started texting me before the police had interviewed Nat and me. "Is everything okay?"

"Yes, but I want to catch you up on what's going on. Are you free for lunch today?"

I wanted to say no. I wanted to explain, kindly but firmly, that my life had turned into a shit show over the past ten days. That continuing to juggle our affair while also dealing with the aftermath of killing the man who molested my son was inconceivable. That our affair would have burned out eventually anyway, so wasn't it better that we part now, as friends?

But one look at Jaime—her eyebrows arched up, her arms crossed—and I knew that wouldn't go over at all.

"Sure," I said. "Lunch sounds good."

Jaime and I arrived at the Lime Tree Café at a little after one. It was a small restaurant with white tablecloths, distressed wood floors and abstract modern paintings in primary colors hanging on the exposed brick walls. The lunch crowd had already thinned out, so we were able to grab a table in the corner, which offered some privacy. Jaime ordered a glass of chardonnay.

"I'll have one, too," I said to our very earnest waiter, who looked like he should still be in high school. "Actually, wait, no. I'll have a gin and tonic. Tanqueray, if you have it."

"Of course, sir." The waiter nodded and hurried off to get our drinks.

"You never drink at lunch," Jaime commented.

"I thought now was a good time to start."

"What's going on? You haven't seemed like yourself for the past week or so."

"Actually..." I began, but then stopped. If I was going to end this, it probably didn't make any sense to do it at the beginning of lunch. And before I'd consumed at least one alcoholic drink. Maybe two. *I'll wait until we got the bill and are nearly ready to leave,* I thought. *That will minimize the awkwardness.* So instead, I said, "The principal at my son's school died. The police are investigating it."

"Oh, right, I heard about that."

"Two detectives came to interview Nat and me about it on Saturday."

"Why?"

"They're interviewing quite a few of the parents from the school. Pretty much anyone whose kid might have been alone with Robert at any point."

"Charlie's okay, right?"

I couldn't tell Jaime about Robert molesting Charlie. Not now. Actually, not before, either. I had been in a moral free fall lately—adultery and murder were just a few of the sins I'd racked up. But violating Charlie's privacy was a line I could not, and would not, cross.

"He's fine. That's not the problem. The police asked Nat and me to give them alibis for where we were on Friday night."

"Oh!" Jaime said. She frowned, suddenly realizing what this meant. "*Oh*. And I suppose you couldn't tell them you were with me."

"No, I did tell them you were there. But I said Ben and Alex were with us. Nat was there when they asked me. I told her we took out a candidate interviewing with the firm."

"Do Ben and Alex know you used their names?"

"No. I should talk to them, I guess, but Jesus...what am I supposed to say? 'Jaime and I are having an affair, so if you could cover for me with the *police*, that would be *great*.'"

"I see your point."

The waiter arrived with our drinks. Jaime paused as he set them down in front of us.

"Would you like to hear the specials?" the waiter asked.

"Not really," I said.

To make up for my rudeness, Jaime bestowed on the waiter her most charming smile. "I think we'll need a few more minutes before we're ready to order."

"Of course, take your time," the waiter said, giving me a nervous glance before hurrying away.

"What's gotten into you?" Jaime asked.

"Nothing. But I'm going to get a club sandwich, and you always get the kale salad. Did you really need to hear the specials?"

"No, but you're not usually such a bear to waiters. Give the poor kid a break."

Jesus fucking Christ, I thought. "I'll try to be nicer."

"Anyway. I can't believe you lied to the police. That's seriously not good."

Oily terror twisted in my stomach. "I know."

"How are you going to fix it?"

"I don't know. Right now I'm hoping that the police aren't going to check my alibi."

"They may not." Jaime lifted one shoulder. "But if they do ask me, I'll just tell them the truth."

"Which is?"

"That you were with me. I'm your alibi, or at least I am until whatever time you ran out on me that night."

"Sorry. Again."

"It's fine. Actually, we should order. I have a client coming in at two thirty."

Jaime waved down our cherubic-faced waiter. He hustled over. Jaime ordered her salad the way she always did, requesting multiple substitutions. I tersely ordered my club sandwich. "Yes, everything on it. Fries on the side."

"So." Once the waiter had left, Jaime nudged my calf with the toe of her shoe. "Where were we?"

"My alibi."

"Oh, right." Jaime took a sip of her wine. "Jesus. I can talk to the police, if you want."

I considered this. "What would you tell them?"

"That we're having an affair." Jaime said in a matter-of-fact tone. "And that you only said Ben and Alex were with us because you didn't want your wife to find out what you were really doing. It's a pretty easy explanation, actually."

"But what if this gets out? You and me, I mean?" I rattled the ice cubes in my gin and tonic and considered this. Nat always told me that the police were gossips. Using my affair with Jaime as an alibi would certainly be a juicy story in our small town. Then again, if I was going to get caught for something, an affair was better than murder. "You'd be okay with that?"

"Actually, that's why I wanted to have lunch with you today. I have some news of my own. I told Thomas over the weekend that I want a divorce."

"You did?" I asked blankly. I knew from the slight tightening of Jaime's lips that this was not the response she'd been hoping for. "Wow, that's big news. Huge. How did he take it?"

"He wasn't as upset as I thought he'd be. Maybe it's something he's been thinking about, too." Jaime's lips curved up into a smile. "Maybe I'm not the only one who's met someone else."

"Oh." I another took a long drink from my gin and tonic, surprised when the ice cubes collided with my teeth. It was gone already? I looked for our waiter. Once I caught his eye, rotated my finger in the air to signal I wanted another round.

"So, what do you think?" Jaime pressed.

"If it's what you want, then I think it's great."

Jaime's eyes narrowed slightly. I knew immediately that I'd made a misstep. She wanted me to be thrilled that she was finally free, as if that were the only obstacle to our being together. I again wondered what mattered to her more—being with me or being able to think of herself as irresistible.

"That's it? That's all you have to say?"

"No, I do think it's great. It's a positive step for you. I know you've been unhappy with Thomas for awhile now."

"I thought you might think it's a positive step for *us*."

Our waiter stopped by with my drink. "Your entrées will be out shortly."

"Great, thanks," I said. The waiter nodded, and hurried away.

"But obviously you don't." Jaime's tone had become petulant. "Which is a little surprising. It's not like we haven't talked about this. At length."

That just wasn't true. Jaime had brought up the two of us having a future together a few times, but it was always when we were in the middle of having sex. I'd been a little distracted when she did this and mostly thought it was just a fun fantasy.

"Jaime." I reached over and rested my hand briefly on hers. "You know I care about you. A lot. But it's different for me. I have Charlie to think about."

"Kids are more resilient than you think," she retorted. "Look at Kirsten. Her father and I divorced when she was three and she's fabulous. Couldn't be better. Besides, you wouldn't be leaving Charlie, you'd be leaving Natalie. Florida is a fifty-fifty custody state. You'll still have a lot of time with Charlie."

I took another long drink, soothed by the numbness of the gin. I didn't know what would happen with my marriage, especially if Nat found out about my affair with Jaime. But I couldn't leave Charlie. Not now. The last thing that kid needed on top of everything else that had happened to him was for his parents to split up.

"It's just not a good time right now," I said cautiously. "Charlie's going through some stuff."

Jaime's eyebrows arched up again. I could tell she thought I was bullshitting her. "What kind of stuff?"

"You know. Typical for his age. Hormones and all of that," I fudged. "Look, I don't really want to get into the details. But trust me…this isn't a good time to drop a bomb into his life."

"Trust you?" Jaime gave me a long, level look. "It sounds like you're making excuses."

"I'm just trying to be honest with you."

"Oh, is that what this is?" Jaime twirled a pointed finger down at the table. "Honesty?"

I stared at her, taking in her wounded anger, and tried to think of something to say.

"Jaime, I can't leave my family right now," I said quietly.

The waiter arrived with our food. He set down Jaime's salad and my club sandwich and then looked eagerly at us.

"Can I get you anything else right now?" the waiter asked.

"We're fine," Jaime said flatly.

I looked at my already empty second glass, but decided that

a third gin and tonic would be pushing it. I really had to get some work done that afternoon.

Jaime waited for the waiter to scurry away before leaning forward, her voice lowered. "Is there a point in the future when you do plan to leave your wife? Because I was under the impression that whatever this is between us was more than a casual fling."

"It was. I mean, it is. Of *course* it is."

"Okay. Good. But…are you ever going to end your marriage?"

My marriage. I thought about Nat and how far we'd drifted from one another. How we'd slowly lost our passion, then even our friendship. And that was just the normal, humdrum bad stuff. That was before I'd made the chilling discovery that the woman I'd married fourteen years earlier, with the long wavy hair and naive idealism, had turned into a woman who could plan and execute a murder. Except that she hadn't completed the job…she'd gotten me to do it. Moreover, Nat had witnessed me killing Robert.

Leaving her right now, under those circumstances, did not seem like a wise decision. Even for me, who excelled at bad decision making.

"I can't leave Nat right now. I don't know…maybe in six months or a year. Things may change."

Jaime's expression turned cold and she nodded briskly. She picked up her fork to spear lettuce on it.

"So, what do you want me to tell the police?" she asked.

I hesitated, startled by this non sequitur. "Tell them the truth. You and I were together that night. Alone."

Jaime looked up at me, her brown eyes challenging mine. "Should I mention the part where your wife called you and you hightailed it out of the restaurant with barely a word to me?"

I stared back at her. Was that a threat? Had she possibly guessed what Nat and I had done? No, no way. No one would ever make the leap that either one of us would have anything to do with Robert's death.

Not unless they knew what Robert had done to Charlie.

But Jaime didn't know. She was just angry that I hadn't reacted to the news that she'd left Thomas with more joy, with declarations that I'd do anything to be with her. She didn't suspect anything more…did she?

No, I told myself. *Stop it. Between the stress and the alcohol, you're becoming irrational.*

"You can tell the police that if you want to," I said carefully. "But under the circumstances, I think maybe it would be better if you didn't mention it. It might make the police suspicious."

"Huh," Jaime said. "Interesting."

I picked up my sandwich, then put it back down. My appetite had disappeared.

"Is everything still okay?" Our eager waiter had appeared tableside again, ever hopeful to provide good service.

"I'll have another one of these," I said, holding up my glass.

I was already regretting the third gin and tonic when I pulled into our driveway after work. The buzz had worn off and morphed into an early-evening hangover. I wondered blearily what was for dinner. Hopefully something that involved carbohydrates that would absorb any alcohol still in my system. I hadn't been able to choke down more than a quarter of my club sandwich at lunch, not while Jaime was silently sitting there, chewing resentfully on her salad.

"I'm home," I said walking in the front door.

"I'm in the kitchen," Nat called out.

"You would not believe the day I had," I said as I set my briefcase down by the front door, then instantly regretted speaking. Where was I going with that? Was I going to tell Nat about how stressful it had been dealing with my mistress who was pressuring me to get a divorce? I shook my head, peeled off my jacket and threw it over the back of a club chair.

"We have company." Nat's voice was measured, contained. I stopped and looked up, my heart suddenly pounding as if I'd just gotten a shot of adrenaline. Were the police back? Was this the beginning of the end?

I walked back to the kitchen, bracing myself for what I'd find there. But it wasn't the police.

Venetia Gibbons was sitting with Nat at our kitchen table.

CHAPTER 26

There were an open bottle of white wine and two half-empty glasses on the table. I was surprised that Nat hadn't put a coaster beneath the bottle, which was sweating onto the bleached oak tabletop. She was normally fastidious about such things.

"Hey, you," Venetia said, standing. She was short, with blond hair that feathered back from her face. She had gained weight since I'd last seen her, although she was trying to disguise it underneath a voluminous hot-pink tunic and black stretchy pants. Her face was full and fleshier than it used to be, and her eyes were puffy.

"Venetia. Hi." I walked over to the table. Venetia gave me a quick hug. I caught a scent of her perfume mixed with cigarette smoke. I kissed her on the cheek. "How are you?"

"It's been a difficult week." Venetia gave a wan smile. "It was hard hearing about Robert. Even though we were divorced, he was a big part of my life for a very long time."

I glanced at Nat, who smiled enigmatically at me. A smile

that could have meant anything from, *Be nice to Vee, she's been through a lot* to *She's fucking onto us, give nothing away.*

I wondered when I had stopped being able to interpret my wife's pointed looks.

"I'm so sorry for your loss, Vee."

"Thank you." Venetia smiled at the old nickname. "I couldn't believe it when the police called me."

I went to the fridge, pulled out a bottle of beer and twisted the top off. "You live in Oregon now, right?"

"Yes, Portland. I own a pottery studio."

"Oh, like an art gallery?" I asked, sitting down at the table with them.

"No, the kind where people bring their kids in to paint mugs and bowls and things."

"There's one here in town," Nat said. "Charlie used to love going there when he was little."

"Isn't he still little?" Venetia asked.

"No, he's almost as tall as I am." Nat laughed. "It happens fast. One day they're sweet little babies, and the next thing you know they're preteens asking for new tablets for Christmas."

"Where is Charlie?" I asked.

"He went to Jack's house after school," Nat said. "They invited him to stay for dinner."

I nodded and felt my shoulders relax a little. I was pretty sure Charlie wouldn't remember Venetia—it had been years since he'd last seen her—but I didn't want him to draw the connection between her and Robert.

"What did the police say when they called you?" Nat leaned forward, resting her elbows on the table. "Did they ask you to fly in?"

Venetia shook her head. "No, I came on my own. Robert's parents are dead. He doesn't have any other family." She shrugged. "There's only me. I thought I should come and deal with...well, the funeral and everything else that needs to be dealt with."

"You're having a funeral?" I asked, my tone sharper than I'd intended.

"Of course." Venetia looked at me quizzically. "Why wouldn't there be one?"

Because he was a fucking monster, I wanted to say. Because no one should waste a second grieving for that man.

"Do the police have any leads?" Nat smoothly directed the conversation back on course.

"Well." Venetia hesitated. "Not that they told me about."

"Believe it or not, considering how fast the word usually spreads in Shoreham, we haven't heard much," Nat said. "It's all been kept really hush-hush."

Venetia looked nervously down at her wineglass, her fingers tapping against the stem.

"Well...there is something. I probably shouldn't say anything, but... I may need your help with something, Nat. It's why I came over to see you."

"Of course," Nat said. "I'll help however I can."

"I think I may need legal advice," Venetia clarified. She looked up from her wineglass and met Nat's gaze. "I may be in trouble. I'm not entirely sure what to do."

I'd been off my game lately. The day-drinking certainly wasn't helping. But I realized that I had failed to notice a rather significant fact. Venetia was terrified. Her eyes were large and too wide open, and underscored by dark smudges. When she lifted her wineglass to her lips, I could see that her hands were shaking slightly.

"What sort of trouble?" Nat asked.

Venetia didn't speak for a minute. She put down her wineglass and began nervously pulling at her fingers, cracking each knuckle in turn.

Nat glanced at me, her eyes flickering toward the door.

"Why don't I give you two some privacy?" I started to stand. "I'll go to the study."

"No, no, don't go." Venetia flapped a hand at me. "Sit down. I'm sure Nat will tell you, anyway."

I sat. We waited for another several moments while Venetia continued to fidget with her fingers.

"I knew something about Robert," she finally said. "Something...terrible. I haven't told the police about it because I'm worried I might get in trouble. Is that possible? Can I be in trouble for knowing someone did something...bad...and not telling anyone?"

"You'll have to give me more details." Nat's voice was surprisingly neutral. "Generally speaking, failure to report a crime isn't itself a crime, but there are exceptions. For example, you can be considered an accessory after the fact to a crime if you helped destroy evidence."

"Oh, good." Venetia looked relieved. "I definitely didn't do that."

"It's also a crime if you fail to report the abuse or neglect of a child. In fact, Florida has one of the broadest mandatory reporting statutes in the country. If you know of a child being hurt, and don't report it, you can be charged."

Venetia clenched her hands into fists and pressed them down on her lap. "No, it wasn't anything like that."

I saw Nat exhale and relax slightly. "Good. So what happened?"

"I've never told anyone this, but...it's bad. It's actually why Robert and I divorced."

"It did seem like your divorce was sudden," Nat commented.

Venetia nodded. "I was cleaning out the bedroom closet one day. Robert was out of town, at an educator's conference, and I decided to tackle it. It's one of those big projects you never get around to, you know? I wanted to pull everything out so I could wipe down the shelves, sweep the floors.

"There was a bunch of stuff on the top shelf, so I had to get the stepladder out to reach everything. It was mostly just junk— old tennis racquets, boxes of books, that sort of thing. But…there was also a briefcase. One of those old-fashioned ones, do you know what I mean? The kind with hard sides and the latches that snap down." Venetia mimed the snapping motion. "My dad had one like it when I was a kid. But I'd never seen this one before. So I took it down, and set it on the bed. At first I thought it was locked, because I couldn't get the latches to budge, but then suddenly they popped open and—"

Venetia stopped, her mouth sagging open, her eyes unfocused.

"What was inside the briefcase?" Nat asked. Her tone was professional, as though this were just another client interview.

"Pornography," Venetia said, looking up at her. "But not normal photography. Not men with women or even men with men. It was all…children. Well, children with adults. Picture after picture." She shook her head. "There were hundreds of images. Hundreds…"

"What did you do?" Natalie asked. She sounded calm, but there was an edge to her voice. I looked at her sharply, but she was still completely focused on Venetia.

"I ran into the bathroom and threw up." Venetia looked dazed as she shook her head. "And then I put the briefcase on the coffee table so Robert would see it when he got home. I was sitting on the couch waiting for him. He walked into the house, called out a hello, then saw the briefcase…and just stopped dead. He went pale." Venetia swiped a hand in front of her face. "All the color just drained out of him. And I knew.

"He tried to claim that it wasn't his, that it must have belonged to the people we bought the house from. But I knew from the way he'd looked at that briefcase when he walked in that it was his. And eventually, he broke down and admitted it. Said he had a problem. Promised he'd get help."

"And you just left," Natalie said.

"I had to." Venetia craned her neck to look at Nat. "Can't you see that? I couldn't stay married to him after I knew he was a—" She stopped, and when she finally spoke the word, it came out in a whisper. "Pedophile."

"But you also didn't tell anyone."

"I couldn't! How could I? It was just all so awful and humiliating, and— I just couldn't bear for anyone to know. You have to understand that."

"No," Nat said, and now her voice was like a shard of glass. "I don't understand how any decent person could allow a man she knew to be a pedophile to continue working in a school."

Venetia reared back as if she'd been slapped. "He told me he would never hurt a child. He told me that he used the porn to control his urges. I believed him."

"Then you're an idiot." Nat stood abruptly and walked to the sink with her wineglass, dumping out the wine inside.

"What?"

"You need to leave. Now. Please go."

"Nat—"

"Did it ever occur to you that those children in the pictures *were* being hurt? They were hurt when they were preyed upon. Hurt when their pictures were spread out into the world. Hurt every time someone like Robert looked at them. Did that ever occur to you, Venetia?"

Venetia looked at me helplessly, as if I could somehow protect her from Nat's wrath.

"Why don't I walk you out," I offered.

Venetia nodded and stood clutching her handbag to her side. But she hesitated.

"I should have told someone. I know that. They're saying that Robert might have molested a student at the school. It may be connected to why he was killed. But…they can't bring charges against me, right? I mean, it's not like I committed a crime. It's not like I'm the guilty one, right?"

Nat stepped toward her. Her face had flushed a dark, mottled red, and her eyes were blazing. She raised one accusatory finger. "That is exactly what you are. Guilty. Because you could have stopped him. You could have told someone what he was. If you did he would never have been allowed to spend one additional single second in that school, around those children. But you didn't, because you're a fucking coward. Now get out of my house."

Venetia didn't wait to be told again. She hurried toward the front door, while I trailed behind her. I glanced back over my shoulder at my wife, who was standing with her hands balled into fists, her face still a mask of fury.

"I didn't know he'd ever actually hurt a child," Venetia said, hesitating at the front door. "Please believe me."

I nodded, not sure of what else I could say. She wrenched open the front door and rushed out of it. I stood for a moment, watching her walk to her car in a disjointed, herky-jerky fashion, almost like a marionette on strings, before I finally closed the door. I turned and retraced my steps to the kitchen.

"That fucking cunt," Nat said. Her voice was shaking with rage. I'd never seen her like this before, not even when she first told me what Robert had done. "She knew. She could have stopped it."

"She was afraid." I wasn't sure why I was moved to defend Venetia. "Maybe she thought if it got out, it would taint her, too."

"So what? She left him here, working in a school, knowing what he was. That basically makes her an accomplice."

Accomplice. The word caused a chill to pass over me. If Nat thought Venetia was at fault, even in part…what would she do?

"Not if she thought it was just the pictures. She said she didn't know he'd act on the impulses."

"That's like letting an aggressive dog run loose in your neighborhood and then feigning surprise when it bites someone. She knew what he was. That's why she left him."

Natalie strode around the kitchen, picking up Venetia's wineglass, emptying it into the sink, putting the wine bottle away, loading the glasses into the dishwasher. The fury radiated off her. I watched her, my alarm growing with every cupboard door and drawer banged shut.

"You know there are more children out there, right?" Natalie's voice was bitter. "It wasn't just Tate and Charlie. I can practically guarantee you that there are more, kids who are too frightened to come forward, or whose parents know but decided not to come forward, like us."

"Not like us."

"What?" Natalie stopped her busy, angry work to look at me. "What did you just say?"

"*We* didn't decide not to go to the police. You decided that all on your own. Then you decided to deal with Robert all on your own, except that you couldn't, so you dragged me into it at the last minute to finish what you started. So don't say *like us*. And I'm telling you right now..." Even though we were alone, I lowered my voice. "I will *not* hurt anyone else. So whatever it is you're planning—"

"Planning?" Natalie looked blank. "Hurting someone? What the hell are you talking about?"

"You just said she was Robert's accomplice. That she's culpable for Charlie being hurt."

"She is culpable. Probably not legally—although I could make a case for that—but she certainly is morally guilty. But I'm not going to hurt her. Jesus, Will."

"I thought..."

"What? That I've suddenly turned into some sort of vigilante, running around striking down all the bad people in the world? I'm a criminal defense attorney, for Christ's sake. I represent the bad people."

I stared at my wife as it occurred to me yet again how little I knew her. Even after all the years we'd spent and distances we'd traversed together. Two weeks ago, I would have said she wasn't capable of attempted murder.

But, then, two weeks ago, I would have said I wasn't capable of putting a pillow over a man's face and smothering him to death.

"Just…promise me you won't do anything." I could feel the sweat beading up on my forehead and upper lip. "That Robert was the end."

"Are you fucking kidding me?" Nat closed the dishwasher door with more force than necessary. "I'm not a sociopath."

"You just seem a little…"

"What?"

"Upset."

"You think?" Nat smacked her open hands on the counter hard enough to make me wince, then turned toward me, her face again alight with anger. I realized how rarely I had seen my wife truly angry. Annoyed, sure, certainly aggravated. But I couldn't ever remember seeing her this furious, so enraged that it twisted her face into something ugly. "That monster touched our son and changed him to an extent that we probably won't even know until he's an adult. Maybe not even then. And that woman—" Nat pointed toward the front door that Venetia had departed through "—could have stopped it from ever happening. But she chose to just walk away. So yeah, I'm a little fucking pissed off at the moment."

We stared at each other for a long time.

"Can I get you anything?" I finally said. "Do you want some water or another glass of wine?"

"No. You don't have to worry about me. I'll be fine."

My wife turned and strode out of the kitchen. I sat back down at the table, feeling a little shaky. My phone beeped at me. I pulled it out. It was a text from Jaime:

The police were just at my house. Asked about where you
were Friday night.

    The kitchen felt like it had tilted and spun.
    What did you tell them? I typed back.
    She didn't respond right away. I stared down at the phone,
willing her to give me something, anything, a small detail that
would make this less horrifying.
    Finally, her response arrived with another piercing electronic
beep:

I told them the truth.

CHAPTER 27

The police showed up at my law firm the next day.

Before they arrived, I was holed up in my office with the door closed, trying to focus on the trust document I was drafting. Not surprisingly, I was having a hard time concentrating. My thoughts kept drifting back to the day before. I was still reeling from the news that the police were following up on my alibi, which meant I hadn't been ruled out as a suspect. After I'd gotten Jaime's text, I'd poured myself a double bourbon and drank it standing in the kitchen. The rest of the night was a blur, although I did remember that Charlie woke in the middle of the night. Nat had gotten up to console him and help him settle back down. I lay in our bed pretending to sleep while really not wanting to get up and risk either of them realizing just how drunk I was.

Then there was Venetia's confession and Nat's resulting fury, which would have unsettled me even aside from the terrifying news about the police. I felt like I was now constantly on a hill of shifting sand, unable to get my footing. Add in a roaring hangover and the fact that I hadn't been able to choke down anything to eat in over twenty-four hours. I was not operating at peak performance.

I was just thinking that I should probably take an extended break from alcohol, when there was a knock on my door.

"Come in," I called.

My door swung open and Ben Miller stuck his head in. "Do you have a minute?"

"Sure, come on in."

Ben stepped inside my office and closed the door behind him. He was an affable guy in his late forties, with the sort of annoyingly boyish good looks that women always went for. My main impression of him, after being law partners for a number of years, was that while he led a charmed life, he was about as deep as a puddle. He had a pretty, vapid wife and a couple of good-looking, vapid children who all excelled at sports. A few years earlier, he'd had an affair with Samantha Grey, a paralegal at the firm. They were caught when one of the executive assistants walked in on them making out in the supply room. The news had spread quickly. Samantha left shortly after, moving to another firm in town. The partnership spent a few uneasy months waiting to be served with a sexual harassment lawsuit that never came. Of course it didn't. Bad things didn't happen to Ben Miller.

"So, the police stopped by my house last night," Ben said.

My stomach shifted nervously. "Oh. Right. I was going to talk to you about that."

"You told them you were out with me a few Fridays ago?"

"I did." I hesitated. "I was out that night with someone. But not, obviously...you."

Ben nodded, understanding immediately as a fellow adulterer. "The thing is, I was out of town that weekend. Beth and I took the kids up to Disney World. Beth basically live-blogged the whole trip on social media. I couldn't back up your story."

"No, I shouldn't have used your name. That was a dumb thing to do."

"Was Nat there when you spoke to them?"

"Yep."

"Well, that's why you did it. Damn, it's not like you knew you were going to need an alibi for that night. That's some seriously shitty luck, man."

I felt an almost irresistible urge to punch Ben. "Tell me about it."

"Can I give you some unsolicited advice?"

"Sure."

"Next time, have your story planned out ahead of time."

"Good tip," I said.

There was another knock on my office door.

Ben raised an eyebrow. "You're popular today. Want me to get that?"

Actually, I didn't want him to get it, assuming that there was a better than average chance that Jaime was on the other side of the door, wanting to have yet another discussion about our relationship. I shrugged and said, "Sure."

Ben swung the door open. It wasn't Jaime. It was much worse—Detectives Monroe and Reddick were standing there.

"Mr. Clarke," Monroe said. "We'd like to ask you a few questions."

The detectives wanted me to go the Calusa County Sheriff's Office with them. I knew I didn't have to, that doing so might be stupid, but I figured that if I didn't at least attempt to answer their questions, they would just focus that much more intently on me. If they looked hard enough, who knew what they'd eventually find? If I could convince them that my false alibi had everything to do with my affair, and nothing to do with an actual crime, maybe they'd even cross me off their list of suspects.

I thought about calling Nat, but I knew she'd tell me not to talk to the police, or even worse, would insist on being there when they interviewed me. I could hear her voice in my head saying, *You never, ever talk to the police. They are trained interrogators, and what's more, they're allowed to lie to you. To tell you they know things as facts when they don't, or they have evidence against you that doesn't exist. Everyone seems to think that they can talk their way out of trouble, but it never works out. Instead, you risk handing them gift-wrapped evidence that can be used against you at trial.*

But this was different, I thought. I actually might be able to talk them out of suspecting me. And I was smart. I stood and put on my suit jacket.

"We'll give you a ride," Monroe said casually as we walked out of my office building.

"I'd rather drive myself," I said.

"We'll run you back here after," Monroe said. He was back to his declarative statements, trying to make me think I didn't have a choice. "I insist."

I might not have been a criminal defense attorney, but I was married to one. I knew I didn't have to go with them.

"I'd rather drive myself. I'll meet you there."

I turned and walked to my car without waiting for their response. As I did, I felt an unexpected surge of triumph...which lasted just long enough for me to get into my car and start it. Then it suddenly hit me that I was about to be questioned by the very people who, if they were doing their job correctly, would like to see me in jail for the rest of my life. That was enough for any sense of victory I had to drain away, replaced with a bowel-deep dread. I drove the entire way to the police station with a death grip on the steering wheel, barely seeing the road in front of me.

I managed to reach the Calusa County Sheriff's Office without crashing into anything at roughly the same moment as the detectives. I didn't have time to take in much about the inside of the building, other than that it looked a lot like every other government building I'd ever been in. It could have been the Department of Motor Vehicles, except for the fact that the receptionist was a uniformed police officer sitting behind what I assumed was bulletproof glass.

"We'll take you right back," Monroe said. He and Reddick flanked me on either side, as though they were worried I might make a run for it.

Should I run for it? I wondered. *Why the hell did I agree to do this?*

Reddick nodded at the police officer sitting at the front desk and he buzzed us through. The two detectives walked me back to an interview room, which had a table, chairs and camera equipment.

"You don't mind if we record this interview," Monroe said. He'd affected a chummy demeanor that did not fool me.

I tried—and failed—to remember from the one and only criminal law class I took at Tulane if they had the right to insist on recording the interview.

"I guess not." I shrugged.

"Good, good," Monroe said.

"Although I'm not sure what I can possibly tell you that will help your investigation."

"Hold on. Let's just get everything situated. Go ahead and sit right there and we'll get the tape rolling."

"It's not a tape, old man," Reddick said as he fiddled with the camera. "It's all digital these days."

"What can I tell you? I'm set in my ways," Monroe said. He grinned at me. "Hear him? 'Old man.' These kids, with their digital this and smartphone that."

I tried to smile back, but it felt forced.

"Hey, you need anything? Coffee, soda?" Monroe asked.

"No, thanks. We should get started," I said. "This is the middle of the workday for me."

"Right, and you guys bill by the hour," Monroe joked. "What do you pull in? Three, four hundred dollars?"

"Is that what you wanted to talk to me about?" I asked. "My hourly billing rate?"

"Nah, but it's not a bad life, huh? Certainly better than being a cop. Pays for the nice house, the pretty wife."

"My wife is an attorney, too."

"Right, right. She didn't want us to interview your son," Monroe said.

"I didn't, either."

"Okay," Reddick said. "We're live."

Both of the detectives sat down across the table from me. The interview had officially begun. I could feel the sweat begin to seep from my forehead, armpits, back.

"Do you know," Monroe said, back to his chummy, conversational voice, "that of all the parents we interviewed...and we talked to, what?" He looked at Reddick. "It must have been close to a hundred parents, right?"

"At least," Reddick said.

"There were only two families that wouldn't let us talk to the kids," Monroe continued. "Yours, and the Swain family. Do you know the Swains?"

The Swains were Tate Mason's foster family. I knew *that*.

"Sure," I said. "Their kids go to Franklin. It's a small enough school that everyone knows everyone, at least enough to say hello."

"The Swains had a beef with Robert Gibbons. Do you know anything about that?"

I nodded and shrugged at the same time. "Not firsthand, obviously. But yes, of course I heard about it. Tate's accusation. Like I said, it's a small school. News travels quickly. Hell, it's a small town."

"No fucking kidding," Monroe said. He chuckled. "I take my kid out for dinner the other night, and my ex-wife and her new husband were in the next booth over. That kind of shit only happens in small towns, right?"

"Right," I said. My mouth felt weirdly dry. I wished I'd accepted their offer of soda. I thought about asking for one, but that might tip them off to how scared I was.

"Anyway, Tate Mason already gave a statement when they first came in to press charges against Robert Gibbons, and his parents—his foster parents—didn't want him to go through that again. Which I can kind of see." Monroe spread his hands in front of him. "What's less clear is why you'd stop us from talking to your kid."

"My wife is a criminal defense attorney. She doesn't believe in talking to the police."

Monroe laughed at this. "And yet here you are."

"I don't have anything to hide," I said.

"Well," Monroe glanced at Reddick. "That's not strictly true."

"We checked your alibi," Reddick said. "Two of the three people you said you were with the night Gibbons died told us they didn't know what you were talking about. That they hadn't been with you."

"Yes." I hesitated. "I was at Rockbar Oysters, but... I was there alone with Jaime Anderson that night."

"So we gathered," Monroe said. He chuckled again. "I can't say I blame you. She's a good-looking woman."

"I didn't want to talk about it front of my wife for obvious reasons," I said. "Jaime and I were having an affair. It's over now, but still. I didn't want Nat to find out. She wouldn't take that well."

"What wife would?" Monroe gave a wry smile. "I've been married three times, so I have a bit of experience with marital relationships. I've yet to meet a woman who'd be okay with her husband dating someone else."

"Exactly," I said. "That's exactly it."

"So you were out having a romantic dinner with your girlfriend on the night Robert Gibbons died," Monroe said.

I shrugged, hoping I looked more relaxed than I felt. Sweat

was trickling down my back. "I don't know anything about when Robert died, but yes, I was out with Jaime on that Friday night."

"Except that Jaime Anderson said you left early that night," Reddick said. "You left before dinner was even served."

Why had she told them that? I wondered. Was this her revenge for my cooling things off with her? I'd worried about it, sure, but I still couldn't believe she'd go through with it.

"I thought I saw someone Nat and I know in the restaurant," I said. "I panicked. I wanted to get out of there before they saw me."

"Who did you see?" Reddick asked.

Shit, I thought. This was exactly why you don't talk to the police. If I lied about who I supposedly saw, I'd just be digging a deeper hole.

"I thought I saw Dan and Mandy Breen. Mandy is Nat's best friend, so obviously it would be huge problem if she saw me out with Jaime. But as I was walking out, I looked again, and realized it wasn't Mandy, after all. It was just a woman with similar hair."

"But you didn't return to your dinner date?"

"I didn't want Jaime to know that I was panicking. She wouldn't have liked that. Actually," I said, warming to this story, "that night is what made me realize that I had to end the affair. I have too much to lose. I couldn't keep risking everything."

"Ms. Anderson was under the impression that your wife called you and asked you to come home," Monroe said.

Natalie had called me. From her disposable phone. And then texted me…and then I'd called her back. None of this would be an issue, except that Robert had used that same phone to call Michelle Cole and left her a message. If the police had that piece of information, they could directly link me, and possibly Natalie, to Robert on the night he died. Nat had been convinced that Michelle Cole wouldn't go to the police, that she wouldn't want anyone to know she'd been involved with Robert.

I hoped she was right. Our future freedom now depended on it.

"I did tell Jaime that, but it was a lie," I said. "Nat didn't call me that night."

"You lie a lot to the women in your life," Reddick commented.

"Who can blame him," Monroe said, with another chuckle. "He has a lot on his plate."

"I made a mistake. I cheated on my wife, and...that was a huge mistake. I know that now."

"Uh-huh." Reddick tilted his head to one side. The way he looked at me made me feel like he could see straight into my thoughts if he wanted to. It scared the shit out of me. "Wanna know what I think?"

I looked at him, waiting.

"I'm pretty good at reading people," he said. "I can tell when they're bullshitting me. It comes in handy with the job, as you might imagine. And I'm pretty sure that right now, you're bullshitting us."

"Why would I make up that I am—or was—having an affair?"

"I don't think you're lying about that part," Reddick said. "But I do think you know more than you're telling us. You want to start over? Tell us what really happened? We'll even give you a few minutes to think about it. To come up with a better story."

I stood up abruptly, only realizing as I did that my knees were shaking. "I'm leaving."

"Hey, wait, don't do that," Monroe said affably. "We just have a few more questions to ask you. It won't take long."

But I did remember this part from criminal law class. "Unless I'm under arrest, you can't keep me here. I'm going now."

★ ★ ★

I sat in the living room on one of the uncomfortable velvet club chairs, waiting for Nat and Charlie to get home after Charlie's karate class. My tie was loosened, and I had poured myself a glass of bourbon. I knew I was going to have to cut back on booze eventually...but today was not the day. My trip to the sheriff's office had deeply rattled me. I still had an unpleasant task ahead of me. At this point, the bourbon was medicinal.

I was going to have to tell Nat about my affair. I didn't want to, but I didn't see any way around it at this point. I fervently hoped the police would assume I'd lied about my alibi because of the affair, and would lose interest in pursuing me as a suspect. But now they knew I'd left my dinner with Jaime early that night...that Jaime had told them I'd left after getting a call from Nat...and Nat had refused to let them question Charlie. Taken apart, none of those facts were particularly damning. But Detective Reddick had all but told me he knew I was lying about something. It was entirely possible, maybe even probable, that the police would continue to focus on me as a suspect. It was finally time, past time really, that Nat knew everything.

I didn't know how she would take the news that I'd had an affair. I'd justified it—both to myself and to Jaime—by how distant Nat and I had become. The space between us had stretched until I didn't know how to reach back over it to her. But maybe that was bullshit. Maybe I'd had the affair because my life had become so routine, so monotonous, drab, I needed something to give it color, life again. I had no idea if Nat had ever experienced that feeling, much less acted on it. Even if she had, I doubted she'd be sympathetic.

No, Nat was going to be angry. Angry at me for straying. Angrier that it was coming out now, of all times. Especially since it was possible that my affair was going to be the trip wire that brought us down, that kept us from getting away with murder.

The truth was, I didn't even know who Nat was anymore. I

didn't know what she was capable of. Was it possible that once she found out I'd been unfaithful, she would turn on me? Tell the police I had killed Robert—which, of course, I had—but leave out her own participation? Was it possible she still had the pillow I used to smother him or some other piece of evidence they could use to convict me?

No, I thought. She would never do that to me.

At least, I didn't think she would.

I drank some more bourbon, comforted by the warmth as it slid down my throat.

The front door swung open just after six o'clock. Rocket had been lying on the floor by my feet, and he gave out a sharp bark, running over to greet Charlie and Nat. They were in the middle of a tense-sounding conversation.

"I just want you to think about it for a few days," Nat said. "We don't have to make a decision right now."

"I'm not going to change my mind." Charlie's tone was churlish. "I'm not going back, and you can't make me."

"I'm not making you do anything. I'm just asking you to think about it. That's all," Nat said soothingly.

"I don't need to think about it! And I'm not going back there!" Charlie shouted. He ran up the stairs, his feet thudding on each step.

Nat walked into view, moving down the hall, one hand pressed over her face. I was struck by how distraught she looked. All this time, I'd thought she was the one who was holding it together, while I was slowly falling apart.

"Hi," I said.

She started. "Jesus. I didn't see you sitting there."

"What's going on with Charlie?"

"I don't know. He got in the car after karate, said he hated it and never wanted to go back. But he won't tell me what happened."

"He loves karate."

"I know, but there's no reasoning with him at the moment. I asked him if one of the other kids was mean to him or if something happened that upset him, but he absolutely refuses to discuss it."

"Do you want me to talk to him?"

"Be my guest. Maybe you'll have better luck than I did."

"Okay. But I need to talk to you about something first."

Natalie looked at me sharply. "What happened?"

"You'd better sit down."

Nat walked into the living room and sat on the couch across from me. She was composed again, but her expression was grim. She sat very still, her back erect, and folded her hands together. "What's going on?"

"The police questioned me today. They showed up at my office, asked me to go to the sheriff's office for an interview."

"What? Why didn't you call me? You didn't speak to them without a lawyer present, did you? Because I know you'd never do anything that stupid, especially after all the times I warned you about it."

"Apparently I am that stupid."

"Jesus, Will!" Nat exploded. Then she glanced up the stairs, aware of Charlie's close proximity. She lowered her voice to a hiss. "What's happened? What did they ask you? What did you tell them?"

"I think it went as well as could be expected."

"Did they question you about Robert's death?"

"Not exactly."

"What does that mean?"

"My alibi didn't check out," I said.

"Your alibi? Wait... For where you were earlier that evening? You said you were out with a few of the other partners."

"I did say that. It wasn't true."

I couldn't read Nat's expression as she stared at me. Maybe

it was the early-evening light, but her eyes looked darker than usual, almost a navy blue.

"Who were you with that night?" she asked in a deadly calm tone.

I hesitated. The moment that I'd been dreading was finally here. And now that it was, I was surprised to realize just how much I didn't want to destroy my marriage.

"There's something I have to tell you," I said.

PART THREE

Natalie

CHAPTER 28

I watched Will as he talked and talked and talked, droning on like he always did when he was nervous, and thought about how much I'd like to punch him right in his smug, aging frat boy face. The words he spoke flowed over me—*I didn't mean for it to happen... I was unhappy... Jaime was just there*—without penetrating my wall of rage.

Our son had been sexually abused.

While Will was out fucking a coworker.

They might seem like unrelated events, but were they really? Maybe if Will had put more energy into being present when he was with his family, none of this would have happened. In fact—and this just occurred to me at that moment—if he'd gone on that camping trip as a parent chaperone, Robert wouldn't have gone near Charlie. It was clearly a crime of opportunity. But no, Will was too busying flirty-texting with Jaime fucking Anderson to bother going camping with his son and protect him from the pedophile who targeted him.

In that moment, I hated my husband more than I'd thought possible.

"Would it help if I said I'm sorry?" Will finally asked.

"Are you seriously asking if I'll accept your apology before you've even bothered to make it?"

"No, of course not." Will stared down at the floor in front of him, momentarily contrite. "But we really need to talk about what happened today." He looked up. "I'm worried the police wanted to interview me again. The younger one seemed particularly suspicious. But maybe he's always like that? What do you think?"

"I think you're a fucking idiot for talking to them without having a lawyer present."

Will reared back as if I'd slapped him. "I didn't have a choice. They knew my alibi was bogus."

"You always have a choice. And it's always better not to tell the police a goddamned thing, than give them one false nugget of information that they can use against you."

The sight of Will's face, his expression shifting from boy-like guilt to indignation at my angry tone, made me feel physically ill. I stood abruptly and stalked into the kitchen. I opened the refrigerator and stared inside, not even sure what I wanted. Then I saw an open bottle of chardonnay. I grabbed it and poured a hefty amount into a wineglass.

Will, clearly not grasping the degree to which I didn't want to be near him, followed me into the kitchen.

"I think I did the right thing," he insisted.

"You'll have to be more specific. Are you referring to the part when you put your penis inside Jaime Anderson or when you lied to the police in the middle of a murder investigation?"

"Okay, maybe I deserve that."

"Maybe?"

"But we need to figure out what we're going to do. We need a plan."

"What sort of plan are you talking about?"

"What do you think? A plan for getting away with this. For what we did."

"My plan was to never come under police suspicion. You blew that when you decided to give the police a false alibi." I gulped my wine, barely tasting it.

"I don't think it's necessarily as bad as you seem to think. Won't the police assume I gave them the false alibi to cover up the...?" Will trailed off.

"Your affair? You were able to do it. You should be able to say the word."

"Fine. My affair. But if they thought I seemed guilty, they'll assume it was about that and not about Robert."

I shrugged. He actually had a valid point, but I was too angry to agree with him. "I don't know what the police think. I wasn't there."

"Do you think they'll subpoena my phone records?"

"They'd need probable cause to get the subpoena. I don't think they have it, at least not from what you've told me. But again, I wasn't there. I don't know what you said, or how it came across."

"I know you think I shouldn't have talked to them," Will said. "But they already suspected me of being guilty of something. I had to give them a reason for that, other than the murder."

"What murder?" Charlie appeared in the doorway to the kitchen. He was wearing plaid pajamas, his hair was still wet from the shower, which made him look even younger and more vulnerable than usual.

Will and I exchanged a startled, concerned look. How much had Charlie heard? My anger was making me careless.

"Nothing," Will said, putting his hand on Charlie's damp head.

"We were talking about a story on the news," I added.

"A murder," Charlie said.

"Yes," I said, exchanging another quick glance with Will.

"Who was killed?"

"No one you know," Will said. "No one we know, either."

"You were yelling," Charlie said, looking at me reproachfully.

"No, I wasn't."

"Well, not yelling exactly, but you were using your angry voice. Are you mad at Dad?"

I looked at my son, who was wide-eyed with concern. I remembered being his age, remembered my own parents fighting—my mother acid-toned, my father grim—and how even though they were never violent, it was like the very air in the house became unsettled. As though the conflict was something tangible that could seep into every corner of every room. Charlie had been through enough lately. He didn't need to deal with hearing Will and me argue, no matter how angry I was at Will.

"No," I said, softening my tone. "Dad and I are fine. I was just upset about what I heard on the news, that's all."

"Oh." Charlie looked relieved. "So what are we having for dinner?"

"Pasta. I was just about to start cooking."

"Can I play on the tablet until it's ready?"

"Fine," I said, smiling at him. "But only until dinner, then no more screen time for the rest of night."

"Yes!" Charlie held up a triumphant fist and hurried off before I could change my mind.

Will lingered, looking awkward. "Do you want help with dinner?"

"No," I said, opening the refrigerator and pulling out the ingredients for pasta carbonara. "I don't. And we should probably be careful not to argue in front of Charlie."

"I don't want to argue at all."

"I'm sure you don't." I pulled out a chopping board and began to mince shallots. "The person in the wrong never does."

Will put his hands in his pockets and walked over to the window, which looked out on our back deck and the yard beyond.

"I know I'm in the wrong," he said quietly. "I shouldn't have done it. And I'm not going to make excuses for my behavior. But I will make an observation... We haven't been happy for a long time."

"You think I don't know that?"

"No, I know you do. I'm just trying to say...this didn't happen in a vacuum."

"See, that's what pisses me off," I said, struggling to keep my voice low and calm so that Charlie wouldn't hear. "It didn't 'just happen,' in a vacuum or otherwise. You made a choice. The wrong choice. Marriage is hard. Everyone knows that. It's hard to stay connected when you're dealing with parenting and work and all the crap that life throws at you. But there were things we could have done to improve it. Marriage therapy or trying to spend more time together, getting away for a romantic weekend occasionally. You didn't even try."

"And you did?"

"I don't know." I shrugged helplessly, staring down at the cutting board. "Maybe not as much as I should have. Probably not at all." I looked up then, pointing the knife in his direction. "But at least I didn't start sleeping with someone else."

"I'm not defending that."

"Because it's indefensible."

"Yes. And because I'm sorry." Will hesitated. "Do you think this is something we can move past? Will you be able to forgive me at some point?"

I looked at my husband's tired, careworn face. The stress from the past few weeks had aged him. He'd dropped the glib manner I'd found so charming when we first met—and so grating as the years piled up. I almost felt sorry for him.

Almost.

★ ★ ★

After dinner, I took Rocket for a walk. It was already dark out, but my way was lit by the green glow of the streetlights. Nighttime dog walking was normally Will's job, but I needed to get out of the house. I'd managed to keep up the happy family pretense for Charlie's sake during dinner. Charlie had calmed down from his postkarate outburst. The conversation bounced around from favorite superhero movies, to an argument between two of Charlie's friends over whether some internet celebrity I'd never heard of was lame or not, to which vegetable everyone hated the most. I did my best to keep up, to smile and stay focused, all while ignoring Will's wounded puppy-dog looks. It was so typical that he was the one who'd had the affair, and yet suddenly I was the bad guy because I wouldn't—couldn't— immediately forgive him.

Rocket and I headed down our street at a fast clip. As I walked, I thought about all the times Will had been late coming home from work, claiming he was at a business dinner, and realized that he'd probably been with Jaime those nights. Then I remembered Laura MacMurray telling me that she'd seen Will paying attention to an attractive woman at dinner, and of course, of *course* Laura—whom I now despised—was the one who witnessed it, because the whole thing wouldn't be humiliating enough otherwise.

And then I thought about Will fucking Jaime, and wondered what they had been like together. Had it been hot and adventurous or tender and gentle? And which was worse? Our intimate life had deteriorated to the point that on those rare occasions when we did have sex, it was always the same stale, workmanlike routine. We never even kissed anymore. When was the last time my husband had truly desired me?

Then I wondered where they did it. At hotels? Or were they so bold, so fucking audacious, that they did it right there at the office on a couch behind closed doors? If so, the support staff probably knew all about it, because nothing got past those women. How mortifying it would be the next time I ran into any of them. What did it say about me, that the most galling part of finding out about the fact that my husband had been fucking another woman was how embarrassing it was?

I was angry-walking now, powering forward, my hands fisted as I swung my arms. I thought about leaving Will. Actually, no, I wouldn't be the one leaving. I'd return home and tell him with righteous anger to pack a bag and get out. That, I thought, would be a triumphant moment. It would feel good to see the hurt flash in his eyes, to watch as he finally realized just what his selfishness had cost him. He'd have to go live in one of those soulless corporate apartment complexes designed for divorced men, with utilitarian furniture and a small pool in the courtyard for when the kids stopped by for a Saturday visit.

"Nat?"

I'd been so caught up in my fury, I hadn't noticed Jennifer Swain up ahead of me on the sidewalk. She was walking, too, but slowly while she smoked a cigarette.

"Jennifer. Hi." I stopped, and tried to shore up my emotions, so that she wouldn't see how upset I was. "How are you?"

"A little stressed out." She gave a sad smile and held up the cigarette. "I haven't smoked in years, but here I am. Smoking again."

"Hey, I don't judge." I held a hand up in the air.

"Actually, speaking of judging… I think I owe you an apology."

"No, you really don't."

"Yes," Jennifer said, "I do. I was rude to you because you've defended sexual offenders."

"It's totally understandable why that would be upsetting for you."

"But it's your job. Someone has to do it, right? Why shouldn't it be you? I'm sorry I was so unpleasant."

"Well...thank you for that. How have you been?"

I'd been so wrapped up in first planning to kill Robert, and then dealing with the fallout, that I hadn't stopped to wonder how the Swains would cope with the news of Robert's death.

"Relieved. And, truth be told, I'm glad he's dead. I don't care if that sounds harsh. But...well." She shrugged. "Tate's having a hard time."

"I'm so sorry to hear that. What's going on?"

"How much time do you have?" Jennifer let out a humorless bark of laughter. "He's acting out. A few days ago, he set a fire in the trash can in his room. Let's just say it wasn't the first time he's started a fire, but it was one of the closer calls. The curtains caught on fire."

"Oh, no." I remembered the gossip that Tate had been the one who'd set fire to the school gym the previous year. "Was everyone okay?"

"Yeah, but it could have been bad. Luckily, Peter was home at the time. He was able to run upstairs with the extinguisher and put the fire out before it got out of hand."

"Tate's been through a lot," I said. An image of Charlie flashed in my thoughts and I inhaled sharply as the now-familiar pain hit me. Charlie had been through a lot, too. And who knew how many other children Robert had hurt? "You think he's acting out because of Robert's death?"

"I don't know. I thought it would make things easier. Tate won't have to testify against him in court, after all." Jennifer took a last drag off her cigarette and tossed the butt on the ground, grinding it under her foot.

"But?"

"His anxiety has been spiking ever since we heard the news. I don't know why. Maybe he was looking forward to confronting that asshole in court. Or maybe it was just too abrupt an ending. I mean... I can't think of anything better. Ding-dong, the monster's dead. That's a happy ending, as far as I'm concerned. But I'm not a thirteen-year-old kid. He's processing it differently."

"Right," I said, feeling the faint stirrings of guilt. It hadn't occurred to me that one of Robert's victims might have wanted an opportunity to confront him. I'd been thinking only of Charlie and how much I didn't want him to undergo the ordeal of testifying in court. How I needed to stop Robert from hurting any more children.

"Anyway, we've put our house on the market," Jennifer said.

"You have? Why?"

"We've decided we need a fresh start. Tate's adoption will hopefully go through next month. Once it does, we're moving."

"Where to?"

Jennifer lifted one shoulder in a shrug. "Away from here. We're thinking about Chicago. Peter's company has an office there. He's already put in for a transfer."

"Wow, Chicago. That will be a big change."

"It will. But I think it's what we need. A fresh start. Somewhere where no one will know Tate's history or have preconceived notions about who he is."

I hoped Tate got over his predilection for setting fires by the time they moved. As long as he kept that up, no one would ever see him as a good kid. A normal kid.

"Good luck with everything. Tate, your house, Chicago."

"Thanks, Nat. You, too."

Jennifer turned away and walked back toward her house. I watched her light up another cigarette, the scent of the smoke carrying on the wind toward me. Rocket pulled on his leash, anxious to get moving, so we walked on, moving slower now. My righteous anger had faded into a bleaker sadness.

Could I really ask Will to move out now, when Charlie was already in crisis? True, he wasn't lighting fires. Yet. But there was no point in pretending that his parents divorcing wouldn't be a huge blow. And who knew how he'd react to our separating? He was already having uncharacteristic outbursts of anger. Would things get worse? Would Charlie's anxiety escalate, or would he become destructive? It was hard to imagine my sweet-natured son setting a fire in his room. And yet…who knew how this would all play out? Charlie still had a lot of healing to do.

I did know one thing—as much as I wanted to return home and tell Will to pack his bag and get out, to go check into a hotel, I couldn't. Not now, anyway. Not while our son was in such a fragile state.

Rocket and I walked the long way around the neighborhood before finally returning home. When he heard the front door close, Will came out of the study, for once not hiding away with his phone. I ignored my husband as I fed the dog and filled his water bowl. When I finished I turned to head upstairs. Will was wise enough not to follow me.

I showered and put on my favorite pajamas and got into bed with my laptop. After all the evening's drama, I hadn't checked in with work since leaving the office. There were a few emails I needed to respond to, and then I checked the court's schedule for the next day. Finally, I pulled up the website that listed all the recent arrests in Calusa County. It was a habit I'd picked up from my early days of practice, when I worked as a public defender. Back then, I'd checked the list to see if there were any good cases coming up that I could request to handle. Now, I mostly checked to see if any of my previous or current clients had been arrested, which happened frequently.

I scrolled down the list, then stopped abruptly.

One of my clients was on the list. Rio Frey had been arrested the day before for revocation of his parole. No bond had been issued.

In the past Rio had always called me as soon as he was arrested.

The question was…why hadn't Rio called me this time?

CHAPTER 29

I walked down the long hall toward Pod Three in the Calusa County jail where Rio Frey was being held. With each step, the clack of my low heels echoed off the cement floor and concrete walls.

The Calusa County jail was not a pleasant place. Visiting clients in jail was a necessary part of my job, but it was never a task I relished.

That was particularly true today.

I reached Pod Three and hit the buzzer. A disembodied voice sounded over the intercom. "Name?"

"Natalie Clarke."

I had already checked in at the front, but it took the sheriff's deputy a minute to check my name against the list that been had sent back before the heavy metal door to Pod Three slowly and loudly slid open.

I stepped into the Pod Three interview room. The room had cinder block walls that had been painted a high-gloss lime green. The space was large enough to house three cafeteria-style tables with rounded edges—presumably so no one could bang anyone else's head against a sharp corner—surrounded by faded yellow plastic chairs that were bolted to the floor. At one of the tables, a priest was sitting with an older Hispanic man, his eyes closed as he prayed. The guard booth's observation room was at the near end of the space, although the deputies were concealed behind a one-way mirror. A deputy I hadn't seen before—young, twenty-something, doughy-faced—opened the door and leaned out.

"Who are you here to see?"

"Rio Frey."

"Got it. He'll be out in a minute."

I checked to make sure the intercom in the room was off, so the deputies wouldn't be able to listen in on our conversation, then took a seat at the farthest table from the priest and his now weeping parishioner. A few long minutes passed before another officer brought Rio in.

Rio was wearing royal blue scrubs and plastic shower shoes, and like most of the prisoners, unless they were labeled as high-risk, he wasn't wearing restraints. He looked like he hadn't shaved in a few days. I knew from his arrest sheet that he'd officially been arrested for violating his parole, but after a quick call to his parole officer, I'd learned that Rio had been picked up under the bridge, where a lot of addicts liked to hang out. He'd had a rock of crack and a pipe in his possession at the time of his arrest.

"Counselor," Rio said. "I was wondering if you'd stop by."

I was startled by how cheerful Rio seemed, especially considering how serious his situation was. His arrest for possession violated the terms of his parole, which meant that he would automatically have to serve out the remainder of his sentence. Plus he was facing the new possession charges on top of that. Worse, Rio had an extensive criminal history. The State of Florida assessed points for each prior conviction. The more points you had, the harsher each consecutive sentence would be. Rio was looking at seven years in prison, possibly more.

The sheriff's deputy nodded at me. I nodded back, signaling I was fine to be left alone with my client. The deputy disappeared into the guard station while Rio sat down across the table from me. He lifted the corners of his mouth up in a sly smile. He suddenly, vividly reminded me of the crocodile exhibit at the Palm Beach Zoo.

"You should have called me when you were arrested," I commented. "I would have represented you at your bond hearing. Although, obviously, it's hard to get bonds for parole violations."

He shrugged. "That might have been somewhat of a conflict of interest."

I looked at him sharply, but he just continued smiling his crocodile smile. A tremor of fear ran through me. I glanced over at the priest and prisoner sitting at the other table, but they were deep in conversation and not paying attention to us.

"Unfortunately, our motion for early termination of your parole is now pretty much dead in the water."

I was aiming for a tone of brisk efficiency, even though I was unnerved by Rio's self-possession. People reacted differently to being in jail. Most were upset, some were frightened, some were despondent, a few were just incredibly bored. But I didn't often see the sort of amusement flickering in Rio's startling different-colored eyes.

"I'm not too worried about that," Rio supplied.

Rio leaned back in his plastic chair, his legs sprawled in front of him, and lazily scratched his stomach. I was unnerved by this sudden change in his demeanor. Whenever I'd seen him in the past, he'd been polite and deferential. He'd even called me *ma'am*.

"I can talk to the State's Attorney assigned to your case," I offered. "I'll try to convince her that this was a onetime slipup in your recovery. We do have that recommendation letter from your parole officer. That will count for something."

This was all a complete lie. The State's Attorney handling the case was Felicia Dibble. She had been pissed off when the original case against Rio—the one with the poor recording of the drug deal—had gone sideways. She'd told me at the time that she believed justice had been thwarted—*thwarted* was the exact word she used, as though we were in a superhero movie where she was playing the role of the adorable yet plucky district attorney love interest. That she looked forward to the day she'd put Rio behind bars for a substantial period of time. A parole violation was the closest to a sure thing as it got for a prosecutor. Felicia probably wouldn't even take my phone call, unless it was to gloat over her imminent victory.

"I guess it's a good thing I have a backup plan."

I straightened in my seat, looked at Rio levelly. "And what, exactly, is that?"

"You know how they're always offering up those confidential informant deals? I think they've offered me one every time I've been arrested." Rio shook his head, looking amused. "I get to skate, just as long as I hook a few other fish for them first."

"You've never agreed to take a confidential informant deal. You've always said that CIs are the lowest of the low."

"That's true, I did say that." Rio nodded. "But I got to thinking, what's the point of having high-minded ideals like that, if I'm the only one who does? Do you know how many times so-called friends have burned me? Taken me down or tried to just so they could avoid a little time?"

"Maybe you need better friends."

Rio threw back his head and laughed so loudly, the priest at the next table glanced in his direction. "Maybe I do, at that."

I leaned forward. "You did me a favor a few weeks ago. I owe you one. I'll represent you on this VOP and the new possession charges for free."

"Thanks, but I think I'll pass."

"You'd rather go with the public defender? You know they

won't come by here to see you for weeks. And then they'll lean on you to take a shit offer, just to get your case off their desk."

"Nah, I think my case will interest them. A lot, actually."

"Why would you think that?" I asked, unable to keep the edge out of my voice.

Rio leaned forward and tapped on the table with the three middle fingers of his hand. "I have some information that the police would very much like to have. I happen to know a woman, a respectable attorney at that, who hired me to buy her some drugs. See, I think the police will be interested in hearing about that. They go to all that trouble setting up the tweakers and lowlifes with CIs. What do you think they'd do to score a bigger prize? Especially a criminal defense attorney who is always fucking up their cases." Rio let out a whistle.

I thought about all the times over the years that I'd cross-examined police officers at various trials. Often, the best defense strategy was to poke holes in the prosecutor's case. To challenge how the evidence was obtained, to point out shoddy police work. I'd frequently argued that police officers were careless or even incompetent. It was just part of the job. All defense attorneys did it. I'd never really stopped to think about how the officers I'd picked apart would feel about that. But Rio was right…they probably would enjoy taking down a criminal defense attorney.

Rio grinned. "I bet they'll be happy to cut me a really sweet deal if I agree to testify in that case."

"They won't believe you. You think you're the first career criminal to make up a lie in the hope that it will get you a better deal?"

"Lie, huh?"

"It's a pretty wild story. And hard to prove."

"Good thing I thought ahead then, isn't it? I took a page out of the CI handbook."

Another tremor of fear shot through me. "Which is what?"

"I made a recording."

My breath suddenly felt heavy in my chest. I could feel my pulse begin to skitter around. I forced myself to stay still, my hands folded on the table, and tried to breathe slowly and deeply to calm myself.

"Why would you do something like that?"

Rio chuckled. "Because I thought it was information that might come in handy at some point. Looks like I was right. And don't go thinking that you'll be able to find the recording," he added. "You won't."

"What do you want, Rio?"

"I want a deal. I want to get out of here."

"Then let me see what I can do to help you." I tried to keep my voice as calm and measured as possible. "I'll talk to the State's Attorney. See if I can call in a favor with her."

"Thanks, but I think I'll try it my way."

"Rio." I hated how desperate I sounded. "I have a family. I have a son who needs me."

"That's one thing you learn in jail." Rio winked at me. "Everyone has a sad story." He stood suddenly. The door to the guard station swung open, and the sheriff's deputy who had escorted Rio stepped out. "Everything okay out here?"

"I'm ready to return to my pod, officer," Rio said. He smiled down at me. "Thanks for stopping by, Counselor."

I watched numbly as the deputy led Rio out of the conference room, then turned and stumbled toward the locked metal door that led out of the pod. I glanced over at the priest, and saw that he was smiling at me. He tipped his head down in a silent greeting or maybe even bestowing a blessing. I blinked back at him. A response was probably required, but I couldn't begin to imagine what it was. I looked up at the guard station and raised a hand. A moment later, the doors opened with their dreadfully loud metallic clank. I stepped through into the hallway and the doors slid closed behind me.

I was suddenly struck by how truly awful the jail was. The

air felt heavy with damp humidity and the stink seemed to seep into me, clinging to my clothes, my hair, my nostrils. It was hot in the summer and freezing cold in the winter. The prisoners complained of bug infestations and thin foam mattresses. Contagious infections that weren't curbed with basic medical care. Starchy meals and intense boredom. Loneliness. Fear.

I began to walk down the hallway toward the exit, focusing on putting one foot in front of another, forcing myself not to run.

I tried not to think about just how terrible it would be if I weren't ever allowed to leave.

CHAPTER 30

"So that's it, then," Will said woodenly. "They'll know it was us. It's over."

He was standing at the kitchen door that led to our back deck, staring out at the darkness. It was late, after ten. I'd waited until Charlie had gone to bed, and made sure he was asleep, before I told Will about my meeting with Rio Frey.

"The police would have to agree to listen to his story first, which won't be as easy as Rio thinks. The sheriff's office isn't in the habit of taking meetings with inmates. And then the police would have to believe Rio, which also isn't likely."

"But you just said he recorded your meeting."

"He said he did, and I don't know why'd he'd lie about it. Although he is a drug addict and desperate."

"Do you have any idea where the recording is? Did he say if it was on his phone or on his computer?"

I shook my head. I had spent the better part of the afternoon thinking about the possibility of finding and destroying the recording. "He said I wouldn't be able to find it, and he's probably right about that. I don't even know where Rio was living before his arrest. At one point, he was staying one of those low-end hotels on the west side that rent rooms by the week, but I wouldn't know which hotel, much less which room. And that's assuming that he had the recording in his possession. He might have given it to someone else for safekeeping. How could we possibly track it down?"

"If the police hear it, they'll know Rio bought oxycodone for you," Will said.

"Yes. And that was the drug found in Robert's system at the time of his death." I bit at one of my nails, peeling away a jagged edge. It was a terrible habit that always worsened in times of stress. When I was in law school, by the end of finals, I would have bitten my nails so far down, they'd sometimes bleed. "It's still probably not enough to build a murder case against us. Maybe I have a drug problem and wanted to buy oxycodone for personal consumption. And, don't forget, Robert had the exact same drug in his house, so then there's no way to prove that the drugs in his system were the ones I bought from Rio. But there's also the fact that we refused to let the detectives talk to Charlie. And that you lied about your alibi." I lifted one shoulder in a helpless shrug. "It will give them a reason to narrow their focus to us. If they dig enough, they may be able to find more."

"Like the fact that you called my cell phone from the same phone Robert used to call Michelle."

"Right. If they believe Rio, it may be enough for them to get a subpoena for our phone records." Which were, by far, the most damning evidence against us. "And once they know what they're looking for...who they're looking for...they'll start pulling any video along the route from our house to Robert's. Traffic cameras, ATMs, that sort of thing. They'll build a case against us. It will be a circumstantial case, but I've lost enough of those to know that the state doesn't always need a murder weapon or blood splatter evidence to convict."

"Convict. Jesus." Will raised a hand to his face, pressing his fingers against his brow. He stood there for a few long moments, then turned toward me. "I meant what I said. If they do come after us, I'm going to take the blame."

"No way."

"Yes."

"Why would you do that?"

"Because if someone's going to jail, it should be me."

"Trust me, the women's prison is an easier place to do time than the men's."

Will went pale. "Jesus Christ." He shook his head before he straightened his shoulders. "No. Charlie needs you."

"And he doesn't need you?"

"Not as much as he needs you. And maybe *need* isn't the right word. He counts on you. You create—" Will waved his hand in the air "—all of this. You provide the structure in his life. The house, taking him where he needs to be and your goddamn meal calendar."

I laughed weakly and rubbed at my eyes. "I don't know why you're so hostile toward the meal calendar."

"I'll probably miss it when I'm in prison." Will tried to smile, but couldn't quite pull it off.

"Actually, it could be a novel defense. Two defendants, tried separately, and each comes forward at the other's trial to take the blame for the crime. How could the jury convict either one?"

"That sounds like the kind of hypothetical they used to ask us in law school."

"Right." I smiled weakly. "I wish we were back in school. Life was easier when the problems were hypothetical."

"Do you really think that could be a successful defense?" Will asked.

"No, of course not. They would assume that we were two married people who love one another and would say anything to get each other out of trouble. Then they'd convict us both."

We stared at one another as we started to absorb the reality of the situation we found ourselves in.

Rio Frey said he had a recording of my asking him to procure drugs for me. If he could get that recording in the right hands—and I still maintained that was not definite—this could be the beginning of the end. Will and I would be arrested, put on trial and possibly imprisoned for the rest of our lives. Away from one another, and worse, away from Charlie.

Dear God, I thought as a tremor of fear passed over me. *What's going to happen to Charlie?*

"I'm sorry about…well, everything," Will said quietly. "Jaime, the affair, all of it. If I could take it back, I would."

"Is that why you're offering to take the blame? Because you're feeling guilty about your affair?"

"No, of course not. I just wanted to say it while I still had the chance," Will said.

"Oh. Well…thank you," I said somewhat stiffly. I wasn't ready to forgive him, not even close, but on our current list of problems, Will's infidelity was nowhere near the top. "But look, nothing will happen too quickly."

"What do you mean?"

"Even if the police do listen to Rio, and even if they hear the recording, it could still take a while. It's not like they're going to show up tomorrow and arrest one or both of us." Everyone was always shocked by just how slowly the criminal justice system worked. In movies and on television, everything was always exciting and fast-moving. That wasn't how the real world was. The police would take their time, slowly building a case they could make stick.

"So when will they show up?"

I shook my head. "I don't know. I guess now we just wait and see."

I called my mother, Lindy, from my office the next day.

"I've had the most trying day," she said once she answered

the phone. "My house cleaner didn't show up. She didn't even bother to call and let me know she wasn't coming. Who does that? I came home from tennis to find my house a complete wreck, and I'm having people over for drinks tonight."

I blinked, trying to square what my mother considered a crisis with the mess that was currently my life.

"Maybe she's sick?" I suggested. "Or something happened that kept her from being able to call?"

"How hard is it to call? I wonder if this is her way of quitting. That's happened before, you know. My last house cleaner just stopped showing up altogether, I think because she was unhappy with the Christmas bonus I gave her. Can you believe that? And I always give out a key to my house. If someone disappears, it means I have to get the locks changed so that no one breaks in and murders me in the middle of the night."

"Why are you hiring people to clean your house who you think are capable of murdering you?"

"I don't, but it's not like I know the intimate details of their personal lives. I don't know what sort of degenerates they might interact with, who they might give my key to."

"Mom," I said. "I need to talk to you about something. It's important."

"What's wrong?" she asked sharply. "Did you get a bad mammogram? That's happened to me before. They get false positives all the time."

"What? No, it has nothing to do with a mammogram. Please just listen for a minute. There may be a time when I need you to come and get Charlie."

"Come and get him for what?"

"To stay with you. Look… I know that sounds cryptic, but I can't go into more detail right now." I turned my chair around so that I could look out at the river. It was a gray day and there wasn't much boat traffic. A lone pelican soared over the water, fishing for an early dinner. "I just need you to promise me that if something happens to Will and me, you'll be there for Charlie. You'll take him to live with you."

"What's going on?" Lindy's voice was sharp in my ear. "What are you talking about?"

"Like I said, I can't get into specifics. But I need you to promise me."

"Of course I will. But if you're looking for a guardian for Charlie in the event of your deaths, wouldn't you be better off asking your brother? I'm sure he and Anna would be happy to take Charlie. I know Patrick always wanted a son. He just never says anything about it because he doesn't want to hurt Anna's feelings."

I could feel a familiar flash of irritation. My mother had always had this effect on me. Even now when I was facing possible criminal prosecution and the end of my life as I currently knew it.

"That's not how biology works, Mom. It's the sperm that determines the sex of the offspring."

"What on earth are you talking about? Why are you bringing up sperm? It's eleven in the morning."

I took my phone away from my ear and stared down at it for a moment. Then I remembered Charlie, the purpose of the call, and put the phone back to my ear.

My mother was still talking. "You know, I've never fully understood what your brother ever saw in Anna. She's nice enough, I suppose, but she's just such a hippy, the way she's always going on and on about lunar cycles and soy products, which I really don't think are even that good for you."

"Mom. Listen to me. This isn't about picking a guardian for Charlie. It's about driving up here and getting him in the case of an emergency, which Patrick and Anna obviously can't do, since they live in California. Can you please just agree that you'll do that for me? If not, I'll ask Mandy, but that might be more problematic."

I was concerned that if Will and I were arrested at the same time, they'd immediately place Charlie in foster care, unless a family member was prepared to step in. I knew Mandy would take Charlie for as long as I needed her to, but I wasn't sure if Child Protective Services would release him to a nonfamily member, especially if she and Dan hadn't already been cleared to be foster parents. I remembered Jennifer Swain once telling me, when we were chatting at a school fund-raiser, about the hoops she and Peter had to jump through before they were allowed to foster Tate. I needed to make sure Charlie had a safe and immediate place to go.

"Of course I'd come get Charlie in an emergency. You don't have to ask. I'm his grandmother."

"Good." I let out the breath I hadn't realized I'd been holding. "Thank you."

"Nat, what's going on? And don't say that it's nothing. Obviously it's something or you wouldn't have called asking for vague future favors."

For one wild moment, I thought about telling her. It would be such a relief to let someone in on our horrible secret, to be able to share this burden. Every morning, as soon as I woke up, I would remember what Robert did to Charlie, and again hear my son's small, breaking voice as he told me about it. Then I would think about Robert's body slumped back on the couch, his eyes staring lifelessly up at me. I would wonder if today was the day the detectives would show up to arrest me. If it was the last day of freedom I'd have for the rest of my life.

My mother wouldn't be the worst person to tell. She wasn't a gossip by nature, and she had a cold-blooded realism that might even appreciate the efficiency of our killing Robert. It solved a problem, removed a blight from the world. Or if not appreciate it, she'd at least understand it. What parent wouldn't?

But in the end, I couldn't tell her. For all I knew, the police had already heard Rio's recording, were already listening in on my calls to build a case against me. It had been a risk to call and ask her for this favor, but I had decided that, as always, Charlie's well-being outweighed my own.

"I really can't get into it," I said, watching as the pelican suddenly dived sharply toward the water and scooped up a fish in its oversize beak. "But thank you. I really appreciate knowing you'll be there for Charlie."

"You'd tell me if something was really wrong, right?" Lindy asked. "If there was something I should be worried about?"

"Of course," I lied.

CHAPTER 31

I waited in the observation room at Camilla Wilson's office, watching Charlie through the window. He was sitting at the low table, drawing on a roll of paper with colored pencils. His appointments with Camilla had taken on a familiar routine. He'd draw, and she'd sit next to him and ask him questions about his pictures. He'd happily discuss the subjects of his drawings, which were almost always of characters from video games. But as soon as she tried to direct the conversation to the abuse he'd suffered, Charlie would shut down. He usually stopped talking. Once he told her flat-out that he didn't want to discuss it.

Camilla was good with him. She always wore soft, comfortable clothing that made it easy for her to sit or kneel nearby. She maintained the perfect balance between showing sincere interest without too much intensity. Still, I was starting to feel like we were running out of time. If Will and I were arrested, I knew my mother wouldn't relocate to Shoreham, but would instead bring Charlie to live at her house. It would be better for him in a way—new surroundings to distract him. Lindy lived far enough away that hopefully he might escape media attention. But it would mean a new room, new school, new routine…and no more Camilla. I'd ask my mother to continue to bring him to see a child therapist, of course, but it would be yet another new person thrust into his life. Who knew if he'd ever become comfortable enough to open up?

"That's new," Camilla said, looking at Charlie's picture. "No Nintendo today, huh?"

Charlie shrugged. "I like whales, too."

"Those are great colors you're using. The blues and grays. What's your whale's name?"

Charlie hesitated. "Fin," he finally said.

"He looks like a Fin."

Charlie lifted one corner of his mouth in a half smile. "He does, doesn't he?"

"What's Fin doing?"

"He's swimming away," Charlie said with such definitiveness, I felt a stab of pain in my chest. Eleven-year-olds should feel safe and secure in their lives. They shouldn't need to swim away.

"Where's he swimming to?"

Charlie didn't answer her for long time. He just kept scratching the blue pencil against the paper, his attention focused on his drawing. Finally he said, "Just away. Away from here."

"He doesn't like it here?"

"No, he does. It's just…sometimes I think it would be nice to go away, too. Somewhere where nobody knows you."

"A fresh start," Camilla suggested.

It was only when my vision started to blur that I realized tears were leaking out of my eyes. I grabbed a tissue from the ever-present box on the table in front of me and dabbed at them.

Charlie was quiet again. "I just wish everything was like it was before."

"Before what?" Camilla asked.

"Before I told my mom about what happened."

"I think your mom is glad you told her," Camilla said.

"I don't know. She's been sad ever since."

My tears were now steaming freely and unchecked. I leaned forward on the table, my hands clenched into fists. I wanted more than anything to run in there, pull Charlie into my arms, tell him that everything would be fine…and yet, I couldn't. I had to let Camilla work with him. He needed her more than he needed me right now, in this moment, even if he didn't realize it yet.

"I understand," Camilla said. "But it's okay for her to be sad. Just like it's okay for you to be sad or angry or happy. It's the way you feel and there isn't a right or wrong way to feel about things."

"I know," Charlie said, with heartbreaking maturity I didn't think he was capable of. "I just don't want her to be sad because of me."

"That's completely understandable," Camilla said. "Of course you always want the people you love to be happy. But that's the thing about feelings. You can't control how your mom feels, just like she can't control how you feel."

"Oh," Charlie said. "I guess."

"Do you want to talk about how you feel?"

There was another long pause, while Charlie set down the blue pencil and began coloring with a dark gray one. I was just thinking Camilla had pushed him as far as he was willing to go, when he quietly said, "I feel angry sometimes."

Camilla nodded. "I feel angry sometimes, too."

"You do?" Charlie looked surprised.

"Of course." Camilla smiled. "Everyone feels angry sometimes."

"What do you get angry about?"

Camilla thought for a moment. "The other day, I was waiting in line at the grocery store, and the woman behind me bumped me with her cart. Right in my bum."

Charlie laughed delightedly at hearing a grown-up say the word *bum*. I smiled, despite the tears still streaming down my cheeks.

"It's true," Camilla exclaimed. "And she didn't even apologize! It made me so mad, I'm surprised there wasn't steam coming out of my head."

"Did you tell her?"

"Actually, no, I didn't," Camilla admitted. "But I wish I had."

"Why?"

"Because I think it would have been better to say something. It was probably just an accident, after all. She might not have realized she bumped into me. And I was mad about it for like an hour after it happened. If I'd said something, and given her the chance to apologize, we both might have felt better."

Charlie nodded and chewed on the end of his colored pencil. If I'd been there, I would have told him to stop that, but Camilla—being wiser and more experienced than me—didn't say a word.

"The thing is," Charlie said, "Principal—wait I'm not supposed to say his name."

I tensed. I was pretty sure that Camilla's obligation to report that Robert had abused Charlie had ended with his death, but still. It was yet another risk.

"You can just say he," Camilla suggested.

"Okay. He knew what he was doing was wrong."

I stopped breathing. It was the first time Charlie had spoken about the molestation with Camilla. In fact, it was the first time he'd been willing to discuss it at all since the day he told me what Robert had done to him, when we were sitting beside the river eating ice cream.

"I'm sure he did." Camilla nodded. "How does that make you feel?"

"Angry," Charlie said shortly. He shrugged one shoulder up. "Like you were about the grocery cart."

"Yes. It's not okay when someone invades our personal space or when they touch us where they shouldn't."

"And he told me not to tell anyone or I'd get in trouble."

"But you did tell," Camilla reminded him. "And you didn't get in trouble."

Charlie considered this. "No. But…my mom was upset."

"But that's okay. People get to feel the way they feel. It's what we were just talking about. We can't control how we feel or how the people we love feel. All we can control is our own behavior. So if you're feeling sad or angry you can't just turn that off…but you can do things to cheer yourself up. Find things that make you happy that you can focus on instead. We can brainstorm some ideas together. Like going for a bike ride, or talking to a friend, or watching a movie you like."

"Okay." Charlie nodded. "I'm not sad all the time, you know."

"I know." Camilla smiled at him. "I'm so glad, Charlie."

Camilla met with me privately in the observation room while Charlie stayed in the therapy room, finishing his drawing.

"It seemed like it went well today," I said.

"Yes, I think we're making progress. He just needed some time to know he can trust me. To know that it's safe for him to open up to me."

I exhaled. "Thank God."

"We have a lot more work to do," Camilla said. "But if we can get him to start processing his feelings about what happened to him, that's definitely a good thing. How's he doing at home?"

"He's been having nightmares, and he wet the bed once. He was mortified."

"That's pretty normal for kids who've suffered abuse. It's a regression to a younger age, to a time when Charlie felt safer."

My stomach lurched. *How safe is he going to feel when his father and I are in jail, and not around to protect him?* I wondered.

"He started to tell me that it was the principal of his school who molested him," Camilla commented. "But you heard that."

"I did." I looked levelly at her. "But he's since died. Are you still obligated to report the abuse to the police?"

"It's a judgment call," Camilla said. She exhaled in a long, soft sigh. "Probably not. I'm more concerned with how Charlie's dealing with his death."

"He hasn't said much about it," I admitted. "Just that he's glad he'll never have to see him again."

Camilla nodded. "I'll try to get him to open up about it during our next few sessions. I wouldn't be surprised if he's conflicted about that. It would be natural for him to have hoped that the man who abused him would die or go away in some permanent way and then feel guilt when he actually did."

"God, I hope not. Charlie doesn't have anything to feel guilty about."

"That's the way kids' minds often work. If they don't understand something, they'll often process it in a way that blames themselves. It's their way of making sense out of a world that's often senseless." Camilla looked at me carefully. "It is interesting that the man who hurt Charlie died so soon after the allegations of his abuse started to come to light."

I looked at Camilla again, meeting her direct gaze.

She knows, I thought. *Or, at least, she suspects.*

"I certainly didn't shed any tears over his death," I said.

"No," Camilla said quietly. "I don't imagine you would."

"I think she knows we did it," I told Will that evening.

"Why do you think that?" he asked. "Did you say anything that would give her reason to suspect you?"

"No, of course not. But I could tell by the way she looked at me," I countered. "She knows. She wasn't even judgmental about it. It was more like she was...intrigued."

We were sitting on our back deck after Will had gotten home from work. Where, I reminded myself, he had spent the entire day sitting just down the hall from Jaime Anderson. Had they spent time together? Had they shared a secret whispered conversation or a passionate kiss behind a closed office door? Will said it was over between the two of them, but why should I believe him about anything. I shivered. The day had been unexpectedly chilly for early March and had grown colder as the sun began to set. I wrapped my arms around myself, trying to warm up.

Will noticed and said "Do you want me to get you a sweater?"

"I'm fine."

I didn't want to give him the opportunity to do something for me. Ever since he'd told me about his affair, Will had been overly solicitous. As though if he could stack up enough nice gestures, it would overshadow his infidelity. Unfortunately for him, it didn't work that way.

Will stood up anyway, went inside and returned a few minutes later with my favorite black cardigan. He held it out to me.

"Thanks," I said stiffly, putting it on.

"Of course." Will smiled briefly, but his expression quickly turned serious. "The therapist can't say anything to the police, right? That would violate doctor-patient confidentiality."

"Right. But I don't think she would, anyway."

"You don't think she approves of what we did?"

"I don't know. She didn't seem horrified, but maybe she has a good poker face. Her job is to treat kids who are victims of predators like Robert, so I can't imagine she's overly sympathetic to him."

Will shook his head. "That's screwed up. Are you sure she's the right therapist for Charlie?"

"She's great with him. He opened up to her today for the first time."

"Good." Will gazed out at the sky. The sun was setting, turning the sky to a luminous orange-red, swirled with puffs of cotton candy clouds. "Did you hear anything more about the investigation? Any news floating around the courthouse?"

"Nothing," I said.

"So it's possible that the police still don't know about the recording," Will said.

"Anything is possible at this point."

"Part of me hopes that nothing ever happens. Obviously." Will waved a hand. "But...another part of me feels like waiting for the ax to fall is almost worse in a way. That it would be better to know something, even if it's bad news, than constantly worry about what's about to happen."

"It's not," I said flatly. "Nothing happening is always better than something bad happening. Trust me on that."

What I thought but didn't say was, *Better to be worried and home with Charlie. Better to spend every day of the rest of our lives looking over our shoulders than be in jail.*

My phone rang from the wicker couch cushion beside me. I picked it up and checked the caller ID. It was the Calusa County Sheriff's Office. Which could mean nothing—it could be about a client or a case—or it could mean everything. I stared at it for a long moment before I hit the receive call button.

"This is Natalie Clarke," I said.

I listened to the voice on the other end of the phone.

"Okay," I said. "I'll be there."

I hung up and set the phone down next to me with shaking hands.

"What's wrong?" Will asked.

"That was the Calusa County Sheriff's Office. Sheriff Nolan has requested a meeting with me tomorrow morning."

Will stared at me. I could see the color draining from his face, the pink hue in his cheeks fading. "Has the sheriff ever asked to meet with you before?"

"No, never."

"So this isn't in connection with one of your cases?"

I shook my head slowly. "It's possible, but I don't think so."

"So tomorrow," Will said. He stared at me, the terror in his eyes reflecting back my own worst suspicions. "Tomorrow we might know something more."

"Tomorrow," I agreed.

CHAPTER 32

I got up early the next morning to make Charlie pancakes before school. I took my time with the preparations—browning bacon until it was crisp, making the buttermilk batter from scratch, adding a handful of plump blueberries to each pancake as it cooked.

I tried very hard not to think about the fact that this might be the last time I would ever cook breakfast for my son.

Charlie came into the kitchen just after seven, still in his pajamas, wide-eyed at the sight of the pancakes on the griddle, the already cooked bacon piled on a plate lined with paper towels to absorb the excess grease.

"Why are you making my birthday breakfast?" he asked. "It's not my birthday."

"I just felt like it." I smiled at him, then pulled him into my arms for a hug. I breathed in his sleepy smell and smiled even as I could feel tears pricking at my eyes. Charlie relaxed against me for a minute, but then began to wriggle out of my arms, eager to enjoy this rare breakfast treat.

Charlie climbed up onto one of the island stools. I stacked pancakes up on a plate, added some bacon to it and set in front of him, along with a glass of orange juice, the butter dish and a bottle of maple syrup.

"Dig in," I said.

"What's all this?" Will asked, walking into the kitchen. He had dressed, but not for the office. Instead, he was wearing jogging shorts and a sport shirt. "Pancakes? On a Wednesday?"

I shrugged. "I felt like cooking."

"Is there enough for me?" Will asked.

"Sure," I said, even though I would have liked a few more minutes alone with Charlie. Not to say anything particular or even to say goodbye. I was just greedy for more time. Mothers are watchers, carefully accumulating and storing the moments that make up their child's lives. The baby who sleeps with pale eyelids and feathery eyelashes. The toddler who delights in exploring his new world, chortling with each new discovery. The child racing the waves as they lap onto shore. I'd had so many moments over the years, but even so…it wasn't enough. It wasn't even close to enough.

I handed Will a plate of pancakes and bacon and he sat next to Charlie at the island.

"I bet I can eat more pancakes than you," Will said.

"No way," Charlie retorted. "I am the king of pancake eating."

"Challenge accepted."

I smiled as the two of them joked around, and poured myself another cup of coffee. I was glad Charlie didn't notice the dark smudges under Will's eyes or the gaunt hollows of his face. Will, for his part, was putting up a good show, playacting the fun-time dad he'd always excelled at being. It had always annoyed me—I was the one who nagged about homework and timely thank-you notes, while Will was the one who got to goof around and be silly. It suddenly occurred to me that those roles hadn't been forced upon us. We'd chosen them, neither of us quite hitting the mark.

If I somehow got out of this, I was going to change up that dynamic. I would relax, be more spontaneous, have more fun. Maybe we could take Charlie on a surprise weekend trip to Orlando, and binge on theme parks and chain restaurants.

Charlie hopped off his stool to deposit his plate into the sink. "I have to get ready for school."

"Don't forget to pack your gym clothes," I called after him, as Charlie ran out of the kitchen like it was a state of emergency. "And don't forget to put on deodorant!"

Will smiled wryly. "He always forgets that."

"Well, at some point, he'll have to remember." Then, remembering my errand that morning, I lifted a hand to my forehead. Charlie might have to learn to be more responsible, more self-reliant, sooner than we would have hoped for him. Much sooner. "Shit."

"I'm going with you," Will said.

"No, you're not."

"If they have anything on us, I need to tell them it was me acting alone," Will said. He glanced over his shoulder, to check if Charlie had come back into the room. "I have to. I want to."

"No, you really don't," I said, turning away to put the mixing bowl in the sink. I filled it with water to rinse out the batter, then opened the dishwasher and began loading it.

"No, I don't," Will admitted. "But I'm going to do it, anyway."

I closed the dishwasher and turned to look at him.

"Let me do this. Let me protect you. You and Charlie," he said. "You two are my whole life."

I looked at this man, my husband. His face was careworn, the lines at the edges of his eyes more deeply etched than they'd been a few short weeks ago. There was a time, not all that long ago, when I had been closer to him than anyone else in the world. I was still angry with him and hurt, too. But I also knew what he was offering here—freedom for me, a secure future for his son. It was not a small thing, nor would it come with an insignificant price.

"Don't do anything yet," I finally said, shifting my gaze. "Let me see what the sheriff has to say. Let's wait on making life-changing decisions until we have all of the information."

Will hesitated, but he finally nodded.

"I'd better go get ready." I drew in a deep breath, hoping it would calm my nerves. It did not. "I've got a big day ahead of me."

Sheriff Garland Nolan was sitting behind his desk, talking on the phone, when I was shown into his office by a young sheriff's deputy. He wasn't in his uniform today. Instead he was wearing a button-down shirt, the sleeves rolled up to the elbow, and an ugly yellow-patterned tie. I hesitated at the door, not wanting to intrude, but Nolan held up a hand gesturing for me to come in. I stepped inside his office, hoping I didn't look as nervous as I felt. The deputy closed the door behind him as he left. I instantly felt trapped and had to force myself not to panic, to stay calm, to remain focused.

"Hold on one minute," the sheriff said into the phone. He cupped his hand over the mouthpiece and looked up at me. "Please come in and have a seat, Ms. Clarke." I nodded and sat in one of the two visitor's chairs set up in front of his desk while he returned to his phone call. "No, I don't need to see the paperwork on that, but I am going to want to meet with you and Jim to go over your notes. It doesn't have to be today. Let's shoot for tomorrow instead."

While he wrapped up his phone call, I glanced around his office. It was largely utilitarian space—the sizable desk, the filing cabinets, a bookshelf along one wall, an American flag on a stand in the corner. There was a credenza behind his desk under the windows where several framed photographs were displayed. One was of the sheriff dressed in his official uniform, standing with his arm around an attractive older blonde. His wife, I assumed. She looked like an older and more sensible version of his daughter, Lauren. There was also a photo of Lauren and her twin boys taken at the beach. In the picture, Lauren was wearing a floral print dress and had an arm around each boy, identically dressed in white polo shirts and khaki shorts. It had clearly been professionally taken, and looked like a picture for a toothpaste advertisement, which was probably just what Lauren had hoped for.

"All right, that's fine. Yes. Goodbye." The sheriff hung up the phone and looked up at me. "Ms. Clarke, thank you for coming in."

"Of course." I smiled politely. "Although your assistant didn't tell me why you wanted to meet, so I'm a bit in the dark."

The sheriff looked at me for a beat too long. He had a narrow face, heavily lined, and gray hair clipped short. He didn't smile back at me, but then, he didn't look like the sort of man who smiled often. The deep lines around his mouth were set in a downward direction.

"A few issues have been brought to my attention," he finally said. "Matters I need to discuss with you."

I could feel my heartbeat quicken. *Matters?* "Like what, exactly?"

"Rio Frey is a client of yours, correct?"

Oh no, I thought. I had been holding out hope that the sheriff's request for this meeting was completely unrelated to Rio's threats, to Robert's death. Clearly, that was not the case. I forced myself to sit as still as possible, even though fear was pricking at every inch of my skin. I wanted nothing more than to run far, far away.

Stay calm, I reminded myself. *Don't give anything away.*

"Yes, I've represented him on a number of different charges. Most recently, I filed a motion for early termination of his parole. His parole officer was on board, so it was really just a formality."

"But then he got arrested again."

I nodded. "The judge actually hasn't ruled on my motion, but I'm assuming it will be denied now. It's hard to make the case that an early termination is warranted when the defendant is back in jail."

"But Frey didn't hire you to represent him on his most recent drug charges and parole violation," the sheriff commented. "Why do you think that is?"

"Maybe he wasn't happy with my services," I suggested. "I visited him in jail after his arrest. He said he was going with the public defender. He probably can't afford a private attorney."

The sheriff gave me another long, searching look that caused my entire body to go cold. He knew something, obviously. Why else would he have brought up Rio Frey? But the question was, how much did he know? Was he hoping to throw out tidbits of information and wait for me to fall apart and confess to everything? That wasn't going to happen. I knew better than to say anything that could be used against me.

It suddenly occurred to me that I was breaking my own rule. I was talking to the police. I was assuming that I was smart enough to navigate my way out of trouble.

Sheriff Nolan sighed suddenly and tapped his fingers against the top of his desk in quick succession, pinkie finger to index finger. *Rat-a-tat-tat.* "Rio Frey met with Detectives Monroe and Reddick from our Criminal Investigative Division. I believe you've met them?"

I had to force myself to keep breathing. "I have, yes."

"Frey told the detectives he had evidence that a prominent criminal defense attorney in town asked him to purchase oxycodone for her. He was looking to secure a plea deal before he handed over the name and evidence. Do you know anything about that?"

"Why would I?" I said.

"Because outside of the public defender's office there are

only three female criminal defense attorneys working in Calusa County. And you're the only one with a known link to Rio Frey. You went to visit him in jail recently even though he hadn't contacted you."

I looked sharply at the sheriff. The police weren't supposed to monitor communications between an attorney and her client. He looked steadily back at me.

"We keep track of who the inmates call. Frey hadn't called you."

"How do you know a family member didn't call me?"

"He hasn't made a single phone call since he was arrested. And you're the only visitor he's had during his most recent stay with us. So, the easy assumption would be that the criminal defense attorney he was talking about was you. Did you buy drugs from Rio Frey?"

I looked steadily back at the sheriff, making sure to meet his dark brown eyes. "Of course not. And no one who knows him would consider Rio to be a credible source or a reliable witness."

"No, I agree. Drug addicts rarely make good witnesses." The sheriff tapped his fingers on the desk again. *Rat-a-tat-tat.* "But Monroe and Reddick believed him. They also think that the drug purchase he referred to is possibly related to the death of Robert Gibbons. The tox screen done at Mr. Gibbons's autopsy showed that he had a large amount of oxycodone in his system at the time of death. It could just be a coincidence, of course. But when you investigate enough criminal cases, coincidences quickly get your attention. And then there's the additional fact that you wouldn't let the detectives interview your son."

I was finding it harder to stay calm, to think clearly now that alarm bells were clanging inside my head. I folded my hands on my lap, hoping it would disguise the fact that they were shaking.

"There's a rumor going around that Robert was addicted to oxycodone," I said.

The sheriff nodded as if this were a fair point. "There is some evidence of that. And it would certainly explain the drugs in his system."

"I also heard that Robert's drug dealer was spotted in his neighborhood on the night he died."

"Where did you hear that?" He looked annoyed. "That detail wasn't released to the public."

From your daughter, I thought but didn't say. Instead, I shrugged. "I can't remember who told me that."

"It turned out to be a false lead. It was just a man checking on his elderly parents. The neighbor who reported it saw his tattoos and drew the wrong conclusions. These things happen in the course of an investigation." The sheriff cleared his throat. "Detective Reddick has an interesting theory about the case. Do you want to hear it?"

No, I thought. But I nodded. "Okay."

"Reddick thinks that Robert Gibbons was a pedophile. That he had probably targeted God knows how many kids over the years." The sheriff shook his head, an expression of disgust flickering over his stern features. "The man was principal of an elementary and middle school, so he certainly had access. And that's the thing about serial pedophiles—they have this way of knowing just which kids to pick. The ones who won't tell, or who, if they did, wouldn't be believed. It's like a twisted sixth sense that goes along with the perversion."

Charlie, I thought. *Oh, God, Charlie.*

"But Reddick thinks that this time Gibbons picked the wrong kid. That he preyed on one who did tell, and who was believed. And that was what got him killed."

And there it was, I thought. They were building a case against me, or against Will and me. They might not have the evidence yet, but their working theory was close enough to the truth. It would be only a matter of time now.

The sheriff continued to hold my gaze for several beats too long. "I have something I want you to listen to."

The sheriff slid open the top drawer in his desk, reached into it and pulled out a small silver cassette recorder, the kind that people used to use for dictation. I hadn't seen one in years, not in these days of digital recordings. He set the recorder on his desk and pressed the play button.

A familiar voice began to speak from the small microphone.

"Michelle? It's Robert. Please call me back, either on this phone or on my regular phone. I need to talk to you. Please. It's important." There was a short pause. "I love you. I know we haven't said that to each other before, but it's true. I just wish I could tell it to you personally instead of your voice mail. So, that's it. I love you and please call me back and I love you. Again. Bye." Another pause. "I'm not sure I should have done that."

I stared at the cassette recorder in horror as I listened to Robert's voice on the night he died. It was the phone call he'd made to Michelle Cole from my burner phone. It was the one piece of evidence that could—and now probably would—link Will and me to the crime.

"Michelle grew up with my daughter, Lauren. I've known her since she was in pigtails and couldn't get through a sleepover without having to call her dad to come pick her up in the middle of the night." One corner of the sheriff's mouth twitched up. It was the closest I'd seen him come to smiling. "When Michelle heard that Robert had died on the same night he left her that message, she brought it straight to me. She had no idea about his *issue* until the investigation. She didn't want anyone to know that they were seeing one another even before the revelation, which is understandable."

Nolan looked at me then, as if expecting a response. I just looked back at him. For once, I couldn't think of anything to say.

"Michelle has three boys, all pretty close in age to my grandsons. She doesn't think he ever touched her boys, but... I think she's had some sleepless nights. The what-ifs can get to you in the dark hours," the sheriff continued. "Anyway, once I had this phone number, the one he'd called her from, I was able to look it up."

Breathe, I reminded myself. *Breathe, stay sharp and don't say a word.*

"And I found the oddest damn thing. That phone, which is registered to no one, and was activated with one of those gift cards you can buy at any grocery store, has only been used a few other times. One call out, one text out, one call in, all to the same number. All on the night of February twenty-third. Which happens to be the night Robert Gibbons died. Do you know who those calls and text were to?"

I continued to stare at him, unable to speak or move. We were finally here. He was about to read me my rights and arrest me.

"Do you have your checkbook with you?" Sheriff Nolan asked abruptly.

"My...checkbook?" It wasn't what I'd been expecting him to say.

"Yes. Your checkbook. Not everyone carries one around in these debit card days."

My hands were still shaking as I picked up my handbag and rooted around inside, trying to find the checkbook for Will's and my joint account. It was at the bottom of my bag. I pulled it out. I couldn't figure out what Sheriff Nolan was hoping to find. I hadn't paid for the phone, or anything else connected to Robert's death, by check.

"Write out a check in the amount of five hundred dollars to the Sheriff Nolan Reelection Campaign," he said.

"What?" I couldn't possibly have heard him correctly.

The sheriff looked back at me evenly. "For this campaign and all campaigns in the future. Although, between you and me, this will probably be the last one. Retirement is sounding more and more appealing, especially after cases like this one. My wife wants me to take her to Hawaii. I'll do it to make her happy, but I'll never understand paying a fortune to travel somewhere to sit on a beach, when we have perfectly nice beaches here in Shoreham."

I managed to write out the check, although if anyone looked closely at my signature, they might think it had been forged. The N was cramped, and the C swayed up at an awkward angle. I held out the check to the sheriff, who took it and put it in the top drawer of his desk without looking at it.

"I'd also suggest that you don't make any plans to move. Not anytime soon. As long as I'm in office, you should stick around in Shoreham," he said.

"Why?" The question was so much bigger than that one word. *What are you going to do with the recording of Robert's phone call? Who else knows about it? Was that check I just wrote you a bribe? If so, what was it buying me? Freedom…or just a little more time?*

The sheriff again tapped his fingers on his desk and looked steadily back at me. "One of our forensic tech guys did a thorough search of Gibbons's laptop. Do you know what he found?"

I had a feeling I knew exactly what they'd found, but waited.

"Kiddie porn. Nasty stuff, as bad as I've ever seen. That's not being made public, by the way. But I got to thinking. What would I do if someone like that perverted sack of shit—pardon my language…" The sheriff raised a hand in apology. "If a man like that targeted my grandsons? Or had targeted my daughter when she was their age? I have a feeling I would not have taken that well."

"I imagine it would be devastating," I said quietly.

"Just so. *Devastating* is the right word. When I was a kid, my dad used to tell me, 'Some people just need killing.' I always thought that he was being overly harsh. After all, my dad also made me go to Sunday school, where they talked about turning the other cheek and forgiving your neighbor. But if you live the life I've lived, seen the things I've seen…" He shrugged, as if trying to push away a whole history of bad memories. "I can't say that my father was wrong."

I stared at the sheriff, whose entire job—entire *life*—was devoted to enforcing the law, not quite sure that I was hearing him correctly. He looked right back to me, his gaze not wavering from mine.

"I'm assuming this is not the beginning of a crime spree," the sheriff stated. He didn't wait for a reply, which was good, because I wasn't about to say a word. "That this was a one-and-done sort of thing."

I exhaled, not quite believing what I was hearing.

"The way I see it, a mom or dad, or most likely both parents did the world a favor." He tapped his desk again.

I just held his gaze and my breath.

"I'm going to tell the detectives to close the case. Reddick won't like it, but Monroe will get him to go along with it. Monroe's old-school, like me. He knows that sometimes certain cases are special situations and need to be handled differently. And really, it's entirely possible that Gibbons's death was accidental. He drank too much, took too much oxycodone and passed out facedown onto a pillow." The sheriff shrugged. "Stranger things have happened."

Except for the fact that his body had been found faceup and the pillow he was smothered with had vanished, I thought.

The sheriff continued. "I had a talk with the State's Attorney on Mr. Frey's case."

"Felicia Dibble," I supplied. "She's gunning for him."

"Right." The sheriff's lips quirked up. "It didn't take much to persuade her to fast-track his prosecution on the new drug charges."

"But..." I said, another tremor of fear passing over me.

"There are steps that can be taken..." the sheriff remarked, "Ms. Dibble is going to make sure our friend Rio goes to jail for a very, very long time."

Sheriff Nolan rubbed the knuckles of one hand under his chin. "I know how to talk sense into the Rio Freys of the world."

CHAPTER 33

I sat cross-legged on our low platform bed and recounted everything that had happened that morning to Will, while he paced
around the bedroom. He had called his office to tell them he was
home sick for the day and instead waited for me to return home.
Or, I suppose, waited to see if he needed to turn himself in,
should the meeting have gone in a radically different direction.

"It's really over?" Will asked. He shook his head and looked
dazed. "Just like that?"

"That's what the sheriff said. 'Some people need killing' were
his exact words. It was like something out of the Wild West."

"But that's just it. We don't live in the Wild West. The police
aren't supposed to wink and look the other way. They have evidence connecting us to Robert's murder, and they're just going
to drop the whole investigation?"

"I guess so." I'd had longer to process what the sheriff had told
me, but it still seemed unreal. "We're going to have to be careful. I got the feeling that Detective Reddick will not be happy
the sheriff is shutting down his investigation."

"So what does that mean?"

"It means he may keep digging, in an unofficial capacity. I don't think he'll find anything, although Rio Frey's recording is still out there somewhere. It's a loose end. But evidence like that can disappear, as well, I guess. At least, we'll hope it does."

"Jesus. So it's over…but it's never really going to be over."

"Right." I looked at my husband's anxious face and wondered if he'd be able to handle the situation. Being under suspicion, being watched. At least he'd stopped drowning himself in bourbon for the past few nights.

"And the sheriff asked you for a check? Just flat-out said, 'And this will go away'?"

"He didn't put it quite like that. Anyway, if that's what it takes for this to go away, I'm more than happy to donate to his reelection campaign. And all future reelection campaigns."

I didn't tell Will my greater fear, which was that a campaign donation wouldn't be the only favor the sheriff called in. That at some point, I'd be representing a client in a case the sheriff found inconvenient and I might get another phone call from his office, requesting yet another private meeting. Only this time, he'd suggest it might be beneficial for me to lean on my client, to convince him to accept a plea deal offer he'd been reluctant to take. I didn't think the sheriff was a dishonorable man, but he clearly had a pragmatic view of the world, where the ends usually justified the means.

I wondered how I'd handle it if he did ask me. It would probably depend on the case, I thought, and on the client. But I suddenly knew with a cold certainty that I'd go along with it, if I could. I'd do anything to keep my family safe. My younger, more righteous self, the one who believed passionately in due process, would no doubt have been horrified by this. But the last traces of that idealistic girl had been forever lost the moment I decided to kill Robert.

"Maybe we should move," Will suggested. "Relocate to

Tampa or maybe Jacksonville. Sell the house, make a fresh start. Get the hell away from here."

"The sheriff told me specifically not to move as long as he's in office. It's one of the terms he set forth." It was also why I suspected that the sheriff might not be done with me just yet.

"Jesus." Will sat down heavily on the edge of the bed, causing the mattress to sag under his weight. "He can't do that, can he? He can't make us stay here."

"Yes," I said. I picked up a pillow, hugged it to my chest. "He can. He has enough evidence tying us to Robert's death that he could arrest us right now, if he wanted to."

"Why would he make our staying here a condition of this deal? That doesn't make sense."

"I don't know. Maybe he wants to keep tabs on us."

"Does he really think we're going to kill someone else?" Will asked. "That's crazy."

He seemed to have completely forgotten that he had suspected just this, when he worried that I might kill Venetia after learning that she knew what Robert was. Although I had to admit, at least to myself, it did rankle that after throwing a small—and from what I'd heard, poorly attended—memorial service for Robert, Venetia had escaped back to her pottery painting studio in Oregon without having to bear any cost for what she had kept hidden.

It bothered me quite a lot.

"No, I don't think he believes we're a danger," I said, answering Will's earlier question. "That's the whole point. He thinks we did society a favor. It's why he's willing to let us get away with it."

"With conditions."

"Right. With conditions."

"You know this is insane, right?" Will waved his hands in the air. "All of it—that we did it, that they caught us and that we're walking away with no consequences." Will shook his head. "It doesn't seem real."

"I know," I agreed.

"Does it finally end here, then? Are we safe?"

"I don't know." I hugged the pillow closer to me. "I hope so, but… I guess we'll just have to wait and see."

Detective Gavin Reddick showed up in my office two days later. Stella was at lunch, so the detective appeared at my open door and rapped lightly on the frame. I wasn't particularly surprised to see him.

"Hello, Detective," I said.

"I thought it was time the two of us talked on our own."

"I always tell my clients they should never, ever talk to the police."

"Okay, then. I'll talk." Reddick walked into my office and sat in one of the visitor's chairs without invitation. "I know what you did."

I gazed at him. He stared right back at me, his eyes dark and intense. I thought he was probably very good at conducting interrogations.

"What I don't know is how you got the sheriff to spike my investigation," Reddick continued.

"The sheriff doesn't strike me as a man who can be made to do anything."

One corner of his mouth quirked up. "True enough." The almost-smile disappeared. "I know Robert Gibbons molested your son."

I wanted to clench my hands into fists, but I stopped myself. Instead I folded them together on top of my desk.

"I get why you did what you did. I do. I don't have kids myself, but—" the detective rolled his shoulders back "—if I did, I can't say I wouldn't want to do the same thing if I were in your position. But do you know what pisses me off?"

I didn't respond, of course. But then, Reddick knew I wouldn't.

"You see, vigilantes piss me off. They keep me from doing my job." He pointed to himself. "If you'd come to us, filed a report, we could have nailed that son of a bitch. It's how it's supposed to go. We work the case, we take the bad guys down, they rot in jail for the rest of their lives. I believe in that system. I know that may sound fucking quaint and old-fashioned to you, but it means something to me. It's why I get up every morning. So when someone like you comes along and takes the law into her own hands—and I know it was you who was behind this." He shook his head. "No offense, but your husband doesn't have the stones for it. But you do, don't you?"

I swiveled my chair away from him, to look out at the river, which was a deep blue today, the sun glinting on the surface. Gulls flew around, squawking at one another, like bickering siblings. A lone boat was cruising down the river. There was a large group on board, and even from a distance, I could see that they were partying, glasses in hand, one of the women swaying in a dance to music I couldn't hear. Why was it that everyone's life looked easier from a distance?

"Whatever went down that night, you were behind it," Reddick continued. "I may not be able to prove it, but I know. And I want you to know that I know. And I hope that someday, I get the chance to nail you for it."

I was still looking away, out at the water, so I didn't see Detective Reddick stand and leave. But I sensed it. And when I finally glanced back, I was alone again.

EPILOGUE

One Year Later

Even though it was an overcast day in early March, and the fore-cast called for rain later in the day, the Clarke family went to the beach, as they always did on Sunday mornings. Will stretched out on a beach chair, hoping the sun would make an appear-ance. Natalie went for a long walk along the shoreline, her feet sinking in the wet sand with each step. Charlie threw the ball for Rocket, who chased after it, racing through the frothy waves lapping up on the shore.

Will watched his son playing catch with their dog and was glad to see Charlie smiling. The past year had changed him. He was taller, and at twelve, was starting to look more like the teenager he nearly was. His face was losing its babyish curves, slowly replaced by more angular lines. Charlie seemed happier these days, less fragile than he'd been a year earlier, although he'd never quite gone back to the silly kid with the deep belly laugh he'd been before everything happened. Maybe the abuse had changed him in some fundamental way. Or maybe it was just a normal part of his growing up and growing older.

Will then thought about the flirty text he'd received the day before from Jaime. She was divorced now. He'd heard at one point that she'd been dating someone, but maybe that hadn't lasted. He and Jaime still worked together, of course, so he saw her all the time. For awhile after he'd ended their affair, Jaime had kept her distance and had been noticeably cool anytime they were forced together by firm business. But lately, she'd been friendlier, had even laughed at a joke he'd made last week during a partners' meeting. And now the text. It was clearly an invitation to something more.

He knew he'd done the right thing staying in his marriage. Charlie had needed the security of an intact family over the past year around him while he healed. But the truth was, Will missed Jaime. He missed the excitement she'd brought to his life, missed the incredible sex they'd had on her office couch behind a locked door.

Meanwhile, he and Nat hadn't totally reverted to the relationship they'd had before everything had happened. They talked more these days, made more of an effort to spend time together, to have date nights out, although only when Lindy was available to watch Charlie. He was too old for a babysitter, but Nat didn't like leaving him alone at night. Things had been better between them. And, yet…occasionally he'd feel Nat's eyes on him. When he turned to look back at her, he would be unnerved by how cold her expression was. It was as though she were examining him for signs of weakness.

He still hadn't decided whether or not he was going to respond to Jaime's text.

It's probably a bad idea, he thought. And yet, he couldn't quite put the thought out of his mind.

Natalie walked slowly down the beach, enjoying the sensation of the cool sand beneath her feet, glad that for once the sun was not blindingly bright. She thought about her week ahead. She was in court on Monday and Tuesday, and then Wednesday she was going to have to leave work early to take Charlie for his weekly appointment with Camilla. Camilla had been cautiously optimistic about the progress Charlie was making, although she was concerned about the flashes of temper he was still showing.

"The healing will take time. Longer then you'll want it to," Camilla would say, and Nat had no choice but to believe her. The therapist had made progress with Charlie. That was the most important thing.

Thursday, Nat was going out of town. Will thought she was planning to visit her brother and sister-in-law in California. He'd actually been annoyingly enthusiastic about it, clearly overjoyed at the idea of having some time away from her.

"Of course I can handle everything here," Will had said jovially. "Charlie and I will have some guy time. It will be good for you to have some time with your brother. You haven't seen him in ages."

Will didn't know that Nat wasn't actually going to California. She was instead headed to Portland to visit her old friend, Venetia. The more she had thought about it over the past year, the more she became convinced that Venetia was nearly as culpable as Robert for all of the children he abused. All Venetia would have had to do was tell someone, and those innocent lives wouldn't have been forever changed. Her refusal to act was truly unforgiveable. Venetia didn't know Nat was coming, and certainly didn't know the careful plans Nat had made for her.

And this time, she wasn't going to make any careless mistakes.

Will also didn't know that Nat had checked their online phone records last night, as she had every day since Will first told her about his affair. She saw he'd gotten a text from Jaime. He hadn't responded. Yet. Nat hoped he thought carefully before he did.

You can't just keep making the same mistakes over and over without consequences, she thought.

Nat finally turned and walked back down the beach toward

her family. When she drew closer to them, she saw Charlie playing with Rocket. She was glad he was laughing, looking like any other twelve-year-old boy without a care in the world.

Nat sat down in her beach chair next to Will.

"He looks happy," she commented.

"He does, doesn't he," Will agreed. He turned to her and smiled, picking up her hand and holding it lightly in his. "I'm glad we came today. I wasn't sure the weather was going to co-operate."

"It worked out fine."

"I guess it usually does." Will laughed, a little self-consciously.

Nat glanced over at her husband. He'd lost more weight over the past few months. It especially showed in his face. His neck had thinned out, and his jawline was more defined. She thought back to the evening he told her about his affair, then about the text he'd received the day before from Jaime, and wondered again how many times he'd fucked his mistress, and where and how. But then she remembered how he'd shown up that night at Robert's house, even though he hadn't wanted to be there. And how he'd pressed a pillow over Robert's face, pushing it down while Robert struggled and cried out, holding it there until his body went still. She thought that sometimes she loved Will, and sometimes she hated him.

Sometimes she couldn't tell the difference between the two.

"My mom used to say, 'Everything happens for a reason,'" she remarked. "I've always thought that was such complete bullshit."

"You don't believe in fate, then?"

"No." Nat stretched out her legs, digging her toes into the cool sand. "Believing anything in life is fated is just a way to avoid taking responsibility."

"And when bad things happen?" Will asked quietly. Nat saw that he was watching Charlie carefully. They both did this. They watched and watched, looking for signs of happiness or sadness, healing or pain. Maybe all parents did. But parents of children who'd been hurt watched extra closely.

"Then you do the best you can," Nat said. "You fix it however you can."

She gazed out at the water, which was steel gray in the filtered light and dotted with whitecaps. The waves were low and rolled gently toward the shore. From her vantage point on the sand, it looked calm and soothing, hiding all the drama that lived underneath. The big fish eating the smaller fish, the even bigger fish ruthlessly taking down anything they could. Life playing out in its never ending, merciless fashion.

"Are you looking forward to your trip this week?" Will asked. He rubbed his thumb against the back of her hand.

"Yes." Nat nodded. "You know, I really am. It will be good to get away for a few days."

★ ★ ★ ★ ★